ON DANGEROUS GROUND

LAMAR UNDERWOOD

DOUBLEDAY

NEW YORK   LONDON   TORONTO   SYDNEY   AUCKLAND

ON DANGEROUS GROUND

Excerpt from "The Return" by Edna St. Vincent Millay. From *Collected Poems,* Harper & Row. Copyright 1934, 1962 by Edna St. Vincent Millay and Norma Millay Ellis. Reprinted by permission.

"The Teddy Bears' Picnic" by John W. Bratton and Jimmy Kennedy. © 1907, 1947 Warner Bros. Inc. (renewed). All rights reserved. Used by permission.

Excerpt from *The Lonely Land* by Sigund F. Olson. Copyright © 1961 by Sigund Olson. Reprinted by permission of Alfred A. Knopf, Inc.

Excerpt from *The Outermost House* by Henry Beston. Copyright © 1949 by Henry Beston. Reprinted by permission of the publisher, Henry Holt and Company, Inc.

PUBLISHED BY DOUBLEDAY
a division of Bantam Doubleday Dell Publishing Group, Inc.
666 Fifth Avenue, New York, New York 10103

DOUBLEDAY and the portrayal of an anchor with a dolphin
are trademarks of Doubleday, a division of
Bantam Doubleday Dell Publishing Group, Inc.

Library of Congress Cataloging-in-Publication Data

Underwood, Lamar.
    On dangerous ground.
    I. Title.
PS3571.N43605   1989   813'.54   88-33581
ISBN 0-385-24242-5
        Copyright © 1989 by Lamar Underwood
              All Rights Reserved
        Printed in the United States of America

        Designed by Bonni Leon
              July 1989
        FIRST EDITION
              BG

FOR MY CHILDREN
Brett, Donna, Marla, and Tracey
In the hope that they—and their children's children—
will never know a world that has no room for wild
bears

AND FOR MY WIFE
Debbie
With all my love

EARTH CAN NOT COUNT THE SONS SHE BORE:
THE WOUNDED LYNX, THE WOUNDED MAN
COME TRAILING BLOOD UNTO HER DOOR;
SHE SHELTERS BOTH AS BEST SHE CAN.
    —EDNA ST. VINCENT MILLAY,
      THE RETURN

IN WILDNESS IS THE PRESERVATION OF THE WORLD.
    —HENRY DAVID THOREAU,
      WALKING

AUTHOR'S NOTE

Since certain sequences in this novel occur simultaneously in New York and Alaska, the reader may find it helpful to be reminded that New York Standard Time is four hours ahead of Alaska Standard Time.

ALASKA

AND

NEW YORK

JUNE 20–21

ONE

The four rainbow trout finned easily to hold themselves suspended in the current, their shadows wavering over the brown pebbly streambed at a place where the Toubok River curved from the dark canyon of a spruce forest and clattered sunlit and sparkling through a field of low alder bushes. Pointed into the flow, the fish did not see or detect the enormous grizzly as it slowly emerged from the shadowed timber and walked across the sandbar to the shoals behind their position.

The great bear's muscles moved with fluid, rippling ease, so devoid of stiffness that the entire body seemed on the verge of collapse. Beneath the stumpy legs, the dry sand yielded to a depth of two inches as each footfall silently recorded the passage of the massive 1,500-pound creature. Its front feet, fifteen inches long by ten wide, bore claws that curved downward over the last half of their six-inch length. The rear feet were not as wide, their claws shorter. Tiny ears, a broad shelving forehead, and burly snout gave the bear's face a doglike appearance. The deeply dished eyes were devoid of malevolence, innocently unexpressive. Thicker and wider than the head itself, the neck led back to the prominent hump that seemed to float, unattached to the rest of the body, as the creature walked, the light upstream breeze stirring the outer frosting of silver hair and the dark brown pelt beneath.

When he reached the edge of the current, the grizzly waddled into the flow without pausing, heading directly across the rocky shoals. The trout shot upstream into a deeper pool, splinters of light as they flared through the clear water. Across the stream, the grizzly paused to shake itself. His legs and underbelly blurred with motion as luminous mist flew from the soaked fur. In a moment, he went on. Shouldering through the border of alders that grew down to the water's edge, he headed downstream.

ON DANGEROUS GROUND

As the great bear walked along the river, his presence had an immediate impact on the rhythm of the late-afternoon life sustained by the stream. On a hillside across the river, pine squirrels saw the bear and began to chirr in scolding, nervous alarm. A pair of ravens watched the beast approach, then flapped away, croaking as they flew. Peering from the uppermost snag of a lightning-killed white spruce, an osprey saw the bear wade directly through the bay-like depression where it had been fishing. The bird lifted into the air, caught a thermal, and circled away downstream. A hen mallard and a drake, floating on the current, bounced straight up and curved away over the spruce tops, their wings whispering.

All day the great bear had foraged opportunistically while wandering through the river valley. Once, when he was crossing a saddle of talus rock that bridged two ridges on the slopes above the stream, he had detected the powerful odor of prey in the mixture of scents his amazing nose sorted from the mountain air: dank rock, moss and lichen, wildflowers, rotting snow, pumice and sand.

For several yards he had coursed the trail over the stones like a bird dog, head down, wheezing as his nostrils flooded with scent. Rounding a rocky shoulder, he was enveloped by a cloud of odor the wind brought down from the ledges above. The bear looked up and instantly crouched into a stalk, as a band of Dall sheep ewes and lambs came into view, alert and tense, their superb vision focused on the menace before them. They watched, mesmerized for a moment, then bounded up the slope with a harsh rattling of hooves. The bear broke into a sprint for a few yards, then slowed and stopped as the weaving, bobbing forms disappeared over the ridge line. The grizzly watched the empty slope for a few moments, then turned and resumed his journey.

Later he spent two frustrating hours trying to dig a ground squirrel from its den. Barely larger than a mouse, the squirrel had screeched in mortal terror as the claws scratched and probed to within inches of its perch in a tunnel between two underground rocks. But the huge paws could not be forced into the tiny aperture. Finally, snorting with excitement, the grizzly began to dig for the tiny morsel. By the time he became bored with the pursuit and wandered on his way, the torn ground looked as if a bomb had struck.

Since copulating with a sow and then immediately leaving her two weeks before, the grizzly had become increasingly obsessed with feeding. He had been with the female for ten days, following her steady, aimless wanderings that are part of the great bears' courtship rituals, and the experience had burned away the last of the winter fat he had brought from his many weeks of semi-hibernation. Now his instincts had carried him down from the higher ranges to the fertile lower slopes, where he expected to find the tubers of wildflowers, seed pods, plant bulbs, and other growths that composed the greater part of his diet at this time of the year. There were pea vine roots to dig, horsetail and sourdock plants to chomp down. Also, another sense of need gripped the great bear, pulling him deeper into the river valley. Usually by this time every spring, the banks of the river had provided the special food that would satisfy the craving that gnawed at him. Carrion—a moose or caribou carcass, gift of the melting winter snows—would bring the strength and satisfaction the grizzly instinctively knew he needed. The memory of such rich feeding could not be obliterated by a diet of plants, and for days the grizzly's instincts had held him close to the river. Sometimes he wandered the nearby ridges for a while, but he always came back to the current, searching expectantly along the brushy shoreline.

The great bear continued downstream, slipping in and out of the alders like some enormous shadow. When the thicket began to thin, the grizzly stopped. Across a wide expanse of muskeg that came down to the edge of the stream, open country stretched away to a distant line of timber. Closer, on one side of the muskeg, a line of willows gave way to a belt of spruce on high ground.

The bear moved into the thicket, stopped again. In every direction, the willows had been heavily browsed, the ground scarred and trampled. The scent of the beast that had fed there permeated the air like fog. The bear stepped gingerly ahead, drinking in the smell, seeking a source for the diffused odor.

Twenty yards to one side, a thick clump of brush exploded with noise and movement. A cow moose crashed through the brush and headed across the clearing, trotting in a ragged gait.

Instantly the grizzly charged.

The moose bolted in panic, nostrils flaring, eyes bulging wildly. She looked back over her shoulder just as a paw smashed into the side of her neck, breaking it with a crack that resounded over the bear's roar and the collision of the massive bodies. The bear's bulk hurtled into the cow's shoulder, breaking bones and battering muscle and sinew into pulp. One of the cow's front legs snapped under the impact, and she was thrown forward and to one side, landing on her shoulder, her head and neck flopping limply as they thudded to the ground. The grizzly bit into the flesh, sinking his fangs deep into the blood-spurting neck, shaking his head as he tightened his grip.

Gradually, the grizzly sensed the lack of movement in his prey and relaxed his hold. He stood for a moment, watching the carcass. The cow's eyes stared ahead, wide and empty, the light inside extinguished since the initial blow to the neck.

The great bear circled, sniffing and watching. Finally, he bit into the base of the neck, braced his massive shoulders, and began to pull the cow along the ground. Despite his brute strength, the grizzly could only move the body a foot or so in one continuous pull. Stopping periodically to look around and sniff the air for intruders, then bending down to gain a new purchase on his prize, the bear worked for over an hour to move his kill twenty yards from the willows. The opening where he finally stopped was closer to the spruce trees and the river but was almost identical to the spot where the moose had been struck down.

For some strange reason, however, the grizzly's instincts were satisfied now. His paws resting on the carcass, he lifted his nose, inspecting the light currents of air.

Finally he began to feed.

A pair of magpies watched from a nearby branch, keeping their distance for now but knowing their turn would come.

"I'd feel a whole lot better about leaving you here if you'd take this." The pilot clicked back the hammer of the long-barreled .44 magnum revolver. "Hell, I'll even show you how to use it." He held the gun with a two-handed combat grip, steadied his feet on the pontoons of the floatplane, and aimed across the water.

ON DANGEROUS GROUND

To Sam Larkin, the metallic snap of the hammer falling on an empty chamber seemed a strange sound above the lapping of the gentle waves against the rocks. He glared silently at the plane as it floated over the sun-dappled shallows, some ten yards from the level slab of stone where he and his backpacks had just been put ashore. From far down the lake, the call of a loon echoed through the stillness. The cry was at once lilting and plaintive, a cry of wildness and solitude.

The pilot lowered the handgun, opened the action, and idly spun the empty cylinder. The holster belt that sagged from his waist was lined with blunt-nosed cartridges that gleamed dully. To Larkin, the idea of lugging that grim bulk and heaviness through the Alaska wilderness for the next ten days was too depressing to contemplate. He smiled at the pilot, trying to show appreciation for his offer.

"I'll be all right," Larkin said. "I've lived in New York City for seven years without a gun. That's more dangerous than being out here."

"No it ain't," the pilot answered.

Larkin studied the man's face for a sign of levity. The eyes were cold dark slits, the other features expressionless behind a heavy reddish beard and long hair that spilled from a baseball cap with a Cessna label on the front. Larkin suspected that the pilot was very young, but he could not be certain. Whatever his age, he had handled the plane well on the flight from Anchorage, setting the single-engined 182 on the small lake with a deftness and precision that Larkin had admired. Now the pilot had become an intruder. Larkin wanted him to be on his way.

"Wilderness grizzlies just want to be left alone," Larkin said. "They'll bugger off as long as you don't do something stupid, like surprise one."

"If this is your first trip to Alaska, how come you know so much about our bears?"

"I read a lot. I've been looking forward to this for a long time."

The pilot shrugged his shoulders. He unbuckled the gun, turned quickly, and eased gingerly along the pontoon to the cockpit. Larkin knelt on one knee and began checking the straps of his oversized backpack and a smaller shoulder pack.

The pilot carried a paddle as he came back to the front of

the pontoon. Kneeling, he thrust the blade down against the brown-pebbled bottom and pushed hard to shove the plane out of the shallows. "You know," he called, "a lot of those writers have never seen a bear, 'cept in a zoo. What they write about is all made-up bullshit."

"Thanks for your help," Larkin called. "I'll be careful." He could imagine what the pilot was thinking: *This tenderfoot's gonna get his smart New York ass in deep-shit trouble.* Larkin realized that almost everything about his appearance looked new and untested: his khaki trousers and long-sleeve cotton jersey, his packs, even his boyish, lightly tanned face. His blond hair was cut short and neat. The only marks of backcountry experience about him were his well-worn boots, with leather uppers, rubber bottoms, and heavy-lugged Vibram soles—a perfect combination for the springy tundra and swampy lowlands, as well as the harder ground along the slopes of the ridges.

The plane was floating in deeper water. The pilot could no longer touch the bottom with his paddle. He stood and shouted to Larkin. "Okay, so don't surprise a grizzly. But, if you should happen to, do you know what to do?"

"Shout. Sing. Whistle. Anything to make noise and scare it away."

"No, that's all wrong!" The pilot waved his hand impatiently. "If you should happen up on a grizzly, say as close as I am to you right now, there's only one thing to do."

"What's that?" Larkin called, interested.

"The only thing you can do is to relax. Otherwise, you'll die all tensed up."

Larkin chuckled at the gag before he realized the pilot was not smiling.

"Rock Lake, ten days from now," Larkin called. getting back to business. "I'll be there."

"Don't eat all your food," the pilot shouted. "If the weather socks in, you'll have to camp at the lake till we can fly. Just sit tight."

The pilot climbed into the cockpit, slammed the door, and waved at Larkin as the electrical circuits hummed and the engine sputtered to life.

Larkin stood at the edge of the water and watched the

plane taxi slowly downwind. Against the dark line of trees at the far end of the lake, the plane looked like a brightly painted toy. It made a slow U-turn and headed back toward Larkin, plowing quickly through the water. He could see white explosions of foam as the ship picked up speed. In a moment the roar of the engine was upon him and the pontoons were skimming the surface, throwing twin contrails of spray over their wakes. The plane rose slowly from the water and immediately leveled off, gathering speed. As the plane approached the shore it began to climb steeply, and was still climbing as it roared overhead and out of sight beyond the spruce hillside behind the edge of the lake.

Larkin looked at his watch. Eight P.M. here, midnight back in New York. He had left his Upper West Side apartment at six in the morning. Now, eighteen hours later, he was on a trail deep in the Alaska Range.

Larkin looked out across the water, listening for the call of the loon. Light breezes stroked the surface into wavelets that shimmered in the sunlight. Along the shoreline, the water was dark and smooth in the shadows of the low hills cupping the lake. The silence was like some strange new sound that rang in the ears. Then the loon's cry danced across the water again. Somewhere nearby, a fish swirled. Larkin felt a surge of pleasure. He was alone but not lonely.

He pulled a map from a side pocket of his backpack. The act of unfolding the map and checking his position was a formality. The curving patterns of brown, green, and blue lines had been engraved in his mind during the countless hours he had spent poring over the map in anticipation of the trip.

On the map, his landing spot was a tiny dot squeezed by flowing contour lines that marked the surrounding hills. A line indicating a trail wiggled away from where he stood and brought his finger to the serpentine course of the Toubok River, which flowed out of the Alaska Range. After hiking upstream along the river for a week, he intended to cut cross-country to Rock Lake, where the float plane would pick him up. He expected to do some superb fishing and hiking while enjoying grand views and ideal campsites all along the way. He slipped the map back into the backpack and weighed his next move. There was no need to hurry; even after the sun dipped below the horizon, it would rise again before full darkness descended. The demands that usually made him pressed for time were behind him now. Out here, he would let events flow along at their own pace. He would enjoy the view for a bit before moving toward the river to find a campsite. Despite the long hours of his journey, he felt only exhilaration.

He opened a flap of the shoulder pack and reached inside for his binoculars. He sat down on the rock shelf where the barren stone was splashed with color; lichens formed filigrees of purple, doughnuts of green, mushroom bursts of orange.

Larkin raised his knees and leaned forward to steady his elbows as he lifted the glasses. The compact but powerful 10 × 40 lenses bit into the distance and pulled startling detail into view.

Green and bright in the evening sunlight, the surrounding forest of spruce, birch, and cottonwood stretched away toward the ramparts of the Alaska Range. The spruce on the lower slopes of the mountains gave way to gulches of misty-green alder that crept up the ridges for a distance, then disappeared into the grayness of rock ledges and shale saddles. Shadowed canyons gaped alongside the slanting ridges. Above, the snow line gradually began, first in scattered pockets where the sun never reached, then in blinding white couloirs flanked by hanging curtains of glacial ice. From this jumble of stone and icy blueness, the peaks themselves erupted into the skyline, hard-etched towers looming like sentinels on the edge of the earth.

Larkin lowered the binoculars, blinking. He felt he was on the brink of some secret Eden he would be the first to enter. No glitches on the trip, perfect weather on the trail. What more could he ask?

The question produced a sudden stab of disappointment. Ted Walsh wasn't here. Sam's friend and companion of many trails and campfires had been forced to drop out of the trip, despite the fact that this trek was to have been the greatest of them all. "The finale of the carefree years," Walsh called it. Larkin was getting married later that summer.

The decision to press on alone had been an easy one for Sam. He had realized for some time that he enjoyed going solo in the wilderness.

God, he had brought a lot of stuff, Larkin thought as he

reached for his backpack. He had treated himself to a new expedition-type pack with state-of-the-art features. The freeze-dried food and gear he felt he would need brought the unit to nearly sixty pounds. He braced his legs and swung the pack up to rest on an extended knee. With a quick and practiced move, he brought the load up and onto his back, pushing his arms through the shoulder straps. He staggered slightly as he wiggled into the contours of the pack's frame and reached for his waist belt.

At that moment, Larkin could not help but think of the kidding he was being spared by Ted Walsh's absence. Walsh was the absolute master of reducing weight and bulk to gossamer. Ted's tricks—such as squeezing toothpaste from the tube and carrying it wrapped in light plastic—knew no limits. In his search for lightweight, efficient gadgets he was indefatigable.

Larkin swung the strap of the kit bag over his shoulder. The bag held his fishing gear: lures and flies, lightweight fly and spinning reels, and two pack rods that broke down into twelve-inch-long sections.

He was ready to begin his journey. He looked at the lake and wondered if he would see it again. Perhaps with Susan, his bride to be, or with their children someday.

He turned to the trail, a faint trace that led up along the slope of the hillside and out of sight through the scattered spruce trees. Leaning forward against the heft of the pack, he started up the ridge. Behind him, the loon was still calling from far out on the lake.

A sudden itching sensation on the backs of his hands interrupted the pleasure Larkin was feeling. Frowning at his oversight, he slapped at the mosquitoes and reached into the shoulder pack to get some repellent.

Even paradise had its pests.

The willow thicket was quiet in the evening shadows. The magpies had ceased their quarreling over the tidbits of flesh they could find on the ground where the grizzly had killed the moose. Smaller birds were hushed as well, leaving only the rustles of hares and ground squirrels and the swirls of rising fish. The pulse of the river world seemed to have vanished.

The carcass of the moose was almost unrecognizable now.

Except for one section where a leg and hoof angled out crazily, and another where a brown patch of head lay exposed to the sky, empty baleful eyes jutting outward, the entire body was crudely covered with an assortment of brush and clumps of mossy tundra.

The great bear sprawled belly down on top of his handi-work, his legs splayed out, his head resting on a hump pushed up by the curve of the cow's shoulder. He was asleep.

Suddenly his eyes flickered, then opened wide. Without moving his head, he flared his nostrils and lifted his ears. He detected nothing that alarmed him. Then a trace of wind stirred through the willows and died away.

The grizzly slipped down from the kill without a sound and tensed into a crouch, his head thrust forward, his legs poised like springs. The sound that had awakened him was gone again. The still air held no scents that were new or threatening.

He heard the noise again, more distinct now, getting closer. Still there was no scent to send alarm through his twenty-ounce brain. But even without the message of scent, the grizzly's instincts told him the noise represented danger. He eased toward the side of the clearing, where the willows were thicker and a stand of birch trees began.

The grizzly vanished into the cover, a shadow moving within shadows.

The magpies flew down to the abandoned kill.

Sam Larkin was frustrated. He had passed up two decent campsites when he had first hit the river. Now, nearly an hour later, he was slogging through a swamp-like area where the current was hemmed in by a thick growth of alders. Forced to wade in the shallows to make any progress at all, he was sweating heavily and achingly tired. He had broken out the repellent again, and his face, hands, and hair reeked of the clammy paste of medicine and perspiration. Clouds of mos-quitoes hovered in the still air. The sun had dipped behind the hills, and the breeze had died with it. Footing was difficult in the heavy shadows, and he had tripped twice, staggering and barely avoiding a headlong fall.

You're getting sloppy, Sam told himself. This is exactly the kind of place where you have to worry about bears.

ON DANGEROUS GROUND

Everything he had read about the grizzly had stressed the point that the animal's relatively poor eyesight was more than offset by its superb hearing and remarkable nose. He remembered an Indian proverb from an article he had been reading on the plane only a few hours before. *The pine needle fell in the forest. The eagle saw it fall; the deer heard it fall; the bear smelled it fall.*

That was irony for you, Larkin thought. A grizzly on the cover of *In Wildness* on the day I'm headed for Alaska.

In Wildness was a new national magazine Ted Walsh had edited since its inception a year ago. Difficulties at the magazine had knocked Walsh out of the trip with Sam, despite the fact that Walsh had planned the entire venture. One of the magazine's regular contributors lived on the Toubok, and Walsh had mapped out a trek that would include a surprise visit to the writer's cabin, four days' hike upstream.

Even without Ted Walsh along, Sam had decided to stick to the original plan. He had always wanted to meet the writer, Jonathan Hill, whose article and photographs on the grizzly were the most recent in a series of pieces on Alaska.

Ahead, Sam could see a bend in the alders. The current was dark and smooth where it curved into view.

Okay, it's showtime, he told himself. He raised his voice in song. Bits and pieces of "Get Me to the Church on Time" filled the air as he waded on through the dark riffles.

He broke off in mid-note, laughing. His voice sounded absurdly loud and ridiculous above the murmur of the river.

"Instead of singing, I'll settle for talking to myself," Larkin mumbled. "It'll sound a helluva lot more pleasant."

"If there're any bears around here, I hope they hear me now!" Larkin called aloud. He shuddered at the alien sound of his own voice. "This is inane," he muttered.

Larkin sloshed on around the bend. The alders seemed to be thinning out, the terrain changing. Then he saw the river pouring straight at him from a stretch of open country where the muskeg plain and stands of spruce trees formed the horizon. Beyond a point of willows on the right bank, a ramp of dry, rocky soil slanted down from the higher ground.

Larkin's spirits soared. Camp at last!

The great bear crouched in the shadows, downwind of the willow thicket. The scent of the intruder flooded his nostrils now, triggering an instinctive force that compelled him to flee. But that force was only part of the complex emotions that stirred within him. The gamy odor of the moose kill made him confused and agitated.

He watched and waited.

Within moments, the scent of the intruder became overwhelming, raging toward the grizzly like a firestorm.

The smell of the moose kill mingled with the scent of the danger. The meat provided strength, an instinctive sense of well-being.

The great bear was afraid. Yet he did not flee.

Suddenly he spotted movement. The willow branches shook, then parted.

The puny two-legged menace stood in the clearing, looking off toward the river.

Larkin had been trying to hurry. His boots made loud sucking noises as he trudged along the muddy bank where the willows grew down to the water. He paused to study the last thirty yards that separated him from the far side of the willow thicket and the beginning of the open ground. The willows seemed to be thinner up away from the bank of the river. He could see gaps in the clumps of bushes and a few scattered birches on beyond. He headed that way, expecting firmer ground.

He had to use his arms and hands to ward the thick branches from his face. The green limbs he shoved aside immediately whipped back into place, snagging on his packs. He pressed on through the tangle with dogged determination.

In a moment he broke into a clearing. To his right, away from the stream, the willows gave way to a stand of birches. Straight ahead he could see the tops of the spruces, which marked the beginning of the tundra plain. That was the spot where he wanted to make camp.

The stillness was like a kind of vapor, and his breathing was labored, as if all oxygen had been squeezed out of the air.

He stepped ahead, then stopped, listening. He had heard something.

Faint and distant, the call of a loon broke through the stillness.

Was that what he had heard? Terrific! Music for his first camp. There must be a lake somewhere over there. Loons were not river birds.

He moved along a few paces, skirting the edges of a few willow clumps that loomed in the way.

Two magpies burst into flight from off to his left, squawking as they flapped on out over the river.

Larkin gasped, startled and shaken. A feverish chill swept over him, cutting through his general discomfort of fatigue, thirst, and hunger.

Come on, for Christ's sake, his thoughts urged. Let's get to camp.

He started again, then paused in midstep, staring at the place where the magpies had jumped, his mouth wide open.

The pile of brush that held his gaze was a haphazard mound of willow and spruce branches, bulging up waist-high. In the middle of the tangle, the head of a moose stared at him with vacant unseeing eyes, like some strange mounted trophy. A leg angled out of the brush to one side.

Larkin turned and looked around. The clearing was empty. The silence made the pounding of the blood in his temples feel like physical blows. He stood frozen to the spot, his mind trying to respond to a question he could not answer. *What in the name of God was going on?*

An explanation—logical and compelling—came to him in a burst of clarity.

A hunter! A goddamn poacher! Killed the moose out of season and covered the carcass to hide it.

Adrenaline surged through his body. Random ideas shot through his mind and disappeared.

Poachers hid their kills from game wardens. . . . The wardens used airplanes and helicopters. . . . Where was the poacher? Was he hidden nearby right now, watching? Poachers had been known to commit murder!

Larkin looked around again. The silence and empty clearing mocked him in his panic. Then he heard the loon calling from the distant lake.

A lake! Was the poacher there? With an airplane?

ON DANGEROUS GROUND

Mesmerized by the vision before him, he took a tentative step toward the brush pile. Then another.

He heard a heavy nasal *woof* and in the same instant he felt his backpack explode and he was hurtling forward through the air. The breath burst from his lungs as his stomach and face hit the ground, and he was engulfed in a storm of roars and massive, twisting muscle and flesh. His mind was swept clear of thought, except for one word that flared again and again.

Grizzly!

Grizzly . . . a searing pain across his buttocks, then fangs sinking into flesh . . . *grizzly* . . . a paw crushing his shoulder, claws raking his neck . . . *grizzly* . . . a slobbering mouth biting at his head, the fangs skidding and tearing across the flesh . . . *grizzly* . . . his hands afire with pain, his hands that he flapped feebly over the back of his head for protection . . . *grizzly* . . . his face pushing down into the moss, seeking refuge and finally finding oblivion.

He was swimming up through a murky sea, unable to hold the surface, gasping and floating for a second, then going under again. Gradually this thread of consciousness strengthened, and the lucid realization that he was still alive finally came—not from growing strength but from pain.

He tried to hang on to a simple thought: *The bear is gone—but I must not move! I'll have to play dead in case the beast is still nearby.*

His thoughts touched on the sources of his agony, one by one.

His buttocks were ripped. His shoulder was smashed, and his neck felt hot and wet. His head throbbed with pain, and blood filled his right eye. He could be blind in that eye. He could not tell. His ears and hands were numb.

Despite his injuries, he was totally conscious now. He was coming back! His heart was strong and he could live with the pain. Somehow, he was going to make it! What a story he would have to tell.

He remained frozen to the ground, trying to listen, but hearing nothing except his own thoughts. The first nauseating waves of shock swept over him, eroding the little strength he had left.

Dimly, through a smear of blood over his left eye, he could see the bottom of a willow bush. Vague shapes that he knew were stuff from his backpack were strewn over the ground.

The backpack had saved him, that was for sure, he thought. Without it, the grizzly's first blow would have killed him.

He decided the bear must be gone. Perhaps he had been unconscious a long time. There was no way to tell.

He moved his arm to bring his right hand down from the back of his head.

Nothing happened.

He tried to raise his hand so that he could see it. The bloody vision of his good eye cleared.

His fingers were gone. The hand was a bloody stump of bones and torn flesh.

Larkin screamed, a shrieking, unearthly cry of terror and pain.

His howl opened the earth. He was tumbling through the core of a roaring holocaust. Fangs found his face, and suddenly he was beyond any knowing.

The great bear raked at the corpse with a final desultory swipe. He trotted to the side of the clearing and turned, crouching, watching.

The body sprawled at the edge of the stream. A dark cloud of blood settled into an eddy, then was caught by the current and swept away.

The loon was still calling from the distant lake. The sound was like the cry of something that had come from far away and was lost and afraid in the vastness.

TWO

The grizzly bear on the cover of *In Wildness* went unnoticed by New Yorkers who walked past the newsstand kiosk on the corner of Seventh Avenue and Central Park South. Even the customers who stopped to buy a morning paper barely glanced at the huge face that topped the stack of magazines alongside the piles of the *Times, Daily News,* and *Post.*

At seven-thirty, a tall, slim man wearing a dark suit of quality tailoring hurried across Seventh Avenue against the light. He was in the middle of the street when a line of cars roared out of Central Park and bore down on him as if driven by paid assassins. The man broke into a sprint, one hand bobbing heavily with an oversized briefcase, the other clutching the shoulder strap of a squash bag from which two well-worn racket handles protruded. The man bounded onto the curb beside the newsstand as the traffic swept past. He picked up a copy of *In Wildness* and held it up to the attendant.

"How's this issue doing, Tim?"

The short, graying man looked up from the *Daily News* he was reading and squinted over the top of his glasses.

"That thing? Biggest bomb since Nagasaki!"

Morgan Procter's face was expressionless as he stared down at the magazine in his hand.

"That one ain't yours, is it, Mr. Procter?" Tim asked.

Morgan smiled coyly. " 'Fraid so, Tim. But maybe not for long."

"Who thinks these things up, anyway?" Before Morgan could answer, the attendant rambled on. "Know what you need? Another winner like this." He pointed to the stack of *Charm* magazine sitting beside *Cosmopolitan* in a prominent front-row position. "I get rid of 'em fast as I put 'em out."

"I just sell the ads," Morgan said as he picked up a *Times* and *Wall Street Journal.* "Deciding what to publish is somebody else's job." He handed Tim a dollar bill.

"Well, whoever it is should come talk to me," Tim muttered as he offered Morgan his change.

Procter smiled broadly, his expression friendly and sincere. His healthy blond hair had the effect of creating a power base for his lively blue eyes and fine features, features burnished by the tans of recent sales meetings in Bermuda and the Bahamas. He waved off his change.

"Gee, thanks a lot, Mr. Procter," Tim exclaimed. For a moment, his face lost some of its pinched hardness.

"Have a good one," Morgan said as he shouldered the squash bag once again.

"And you have a good game, Mr. Procter."

"Today I'm playing a lady."

"Guess you'll let up a bit for this one."

"No way," Morgan called as he started away. "She's a hell of a player. But unfortunately for me, she's already married."

The smile on Tim's face lingered until Morgan disappeared into the crowd. He sighed wearily as he picked up the copy of *In Wildness* to place it back on the stack. Glancing at the cover, he thought, *Nobody gives a fuck about bears—unless they're from Chicago.*

He smiled at his joke and turned back to the *News.* The Yankees had been too late going to their bullpen again, had blown a four-run lead, and this morning columnist Mike Lupica was kicking ass.

When Matt Richardson walked into the main dining room of the Park-South Executive Club, he twisted the copy of *In Wildness* he was carrying into a tight roll he hoped would not be conspicuous and inappropriate in the august surroundings. The captain flashed a smile so expansive it lost all credibility as he hurried forward to greet Richardson with an energetic handshake.

"So good to have you with us this morning, Mr. Richardson. We haven't seen much of you lately."

"Don't take me off your list of regulars, Arthur," Matt said, smiling. "I haven't been getting out much."

"Ah yes. All those magazines. So many people depending

upon you. But now we have you back. This way please. Mr. Craig arrived a few moments ago."

Richardson followed the tuxedo-clad figure through the maze of tables covered with crisp white linen. Across the elegant room, beneath one of the windows that soared to the high ceiling, Anthony Craig was sipping his coffee and staring out over Central Park.

When Craig saw Matt approaching, he pushed back his chair and rose slowly, a hint of pain creasing his pleasant face. A slightly stooped man with thinning gray hair, Anthony Craig's youth was preserved in the bright eyes that seemed to dance against the scrubbed flush of his face. He was immaculately dressed in his standard uniform, a dark vested suit with watch fob and chain and crisp white shirt. His handkerchief and tie were gay islands of color within the somber sea of his business attire. He exuded money, power, influence, wisdom, and, not far below the surface, the ruthless determination of a winner.

"Matthew. Good morning." Craig clasped Matt's outstretched hand. "Sorry to get you out so early like this."

"No problem for me, sir. I'm always up early."

"A holdover from the ranch days, eh?" They settled into the chairs. Arthur motioned for a steward, who poured Matt's coffee, refilled Craig's cup, and moved away.

"Well, I'll confess, Matthew, that this dawn patrol stuff is becoming a habit with me also," Craig said. "Tell me, why is it that old men sleep less and less while becoming more and more garrulous?"

Richardson smiled.

"See." Craig shrugged his shoulders. "That's exactly what I mean. My rambling on and on at this hour of the morning."

"It's always good to be with you, Tony," Matt said warmly. He could not help wondering if the anxiety he was feeling was written all over his face. Was Tony Craig's easygoing banter a camouflage net? The seven years Matt had spent as editorial head of the magazine division of Craig Publishing had armed him with an instinctive early-warning system that forecast the arrival of big trouble. It had been set off the evening before when Craig's secretary had phoned to request the early breakfast. Despite her friendly and routine manner, Matt felt resigned to a night of worry and depression. The magazine he had given the best measures of his love and creative energy was a colossal failure. *In Wildness* and its mounting losses had produced a crisis within the company.

The fact that he had weathered many crises in his career gave Matt little solace now. When he had joined the company at age thirty-three, Craig Publishing's five magazines were reeling under the pressure of declining revenues. The tongue-wagging magazine mavens around town predicted Craig's demise and spread the word that Richardson had been brought in merely to administer last rites. They were wrong. Matt's innovative ideas forced the critics to read other signs in their swirling cocktails. Under his direction, the magazines began to pour money back into the company's multidrawered till; their clout within the business was restored.

His record in nursing Tony Craig's magazines back to health would not help him now, Matt realized. *In Wildness* was his baby, the book he had always wanted to create. He had put all of his devotion and ingenuity into it, and still it was sinking before his very eyes.

"I'm glad I could catch you this morning," Craig said. "I'm going down to Washington for a couple of days. . . . Won't be able to huddle with you before the board meeting."

"Anything special about the meeting's agenda?" Matt asked cautiously.

"You know damn well there is. I'm canceling the agenda that was circulated. I want to focus our total attention on *In Wildness.*"

Matt Richardson didn't try to hide the disappointment he was feeling. His face was open and not easily given to the mask of stoicism. Even at forty, the features were boyishly gentle and softly rounded in a way that suggested innocence and frivolity. Except for the tinges of gray in his jet-black hair and the crinkled lines that flared away from his blue eyes, Richardson's face lacked any hint of the distinction of his position or the cost of achieving and maintaining it.

"Are you going to shut me down, Tony?"

"Well . . . I'm not sure. But some of the boys are getting nervous."

"Losing their nerve is what you mean," Matt said angrily.

"I assume that the panic button is being pushed by the restless Mr. Procter."

Craig's sharp look caused a moment of silence.

Matt's bitter reference to Morgan Procter was an open indication of the adversarial relationship of the two men. As advertising director of all Craig magazines, Procter not only was Richardson's equal in Craig's power elite but wielded considerably more influence in Craig's financial affairs. Procter and his team of salesmen produced the bulk of the revenues earned by the magazines.

"Morgan has some strong opinions," Craig said sternly. "And the numbers to back them up."

"The numbers Morgan's been using to spook everybody are hardly news to the board," Matt said, trying to start a counterattack.

"I realize that. But Procter's *projections* make the situation more serious. He's convinced me that it's time to talk realistically about our game plan. We've got to give the board some glimmer of hope."

Richardson slumped back. "You mean bullshit them."

"Of course not! But you are moving on this, I assume. Other than worrying about it, what are you *doing* about it?"

"Tony, when you agreed to back *In Wildness,* I knew your heart really wasn't in it; that you did it to keep me happy because of my track record in turning the other books around. I've truly appreciated your support. But please: don't pull out on me just as we're getting started."

The redness in Craig's temples deepened. "How *getting started?* The book's been out for over a year—not that the public's noticed—and you were fiddling with it for three years before that! Research . . . dummies . . . mailings . . . meetings. You've had the shot you asked for, son."

Richardson reached down beside his chair and retrieved the copy of *In Wildness* he had brought along. He laid the magazine on the table. "This is a good book," he said. "I'm proud of it."

The rich, glossy cover of the June issue caught the light so that the colors jumped with vitality. The logo, *In Wildness,* dominated the photograph of the grizzly. The lettering was clean, yet pleasantly traditional. Beneath the main title, the words *Is the Preservation of the World,* in much smaller type, completed the quote from Thoreau and the thought of the main logo. Down the left side of the page, the cover blurbs were abundant and bold, touting great reader reward with the grizzly article and other pieces on wilderness-oriented subjects: the Outward Bound wilderness skills school, an exposé of a hit list of rivers being eyed by the Army Corps of Engineers for dam projects, a river-running adventure set in the Andes, and an interview with the Secretary of the Interior, an unpopular political appointee who had been the focus of a flood of criticism from environmentalists. The bright, cheery face of the magazine seemed to offer great appeal. But the sales figures told a different story.

On sale since late May, the June issue would probably end up selling between 20 and 25 percent of the 250,000 copies put onto the stands, compared to healthy men's-field magazines like *Popular Mechanics,* selling 40 to 60 percent of 400,000. And, Richardson was forced to remind himself, *In Wildness's* performance looked particularly bad when compared to Craig's hottest book, *Charm,* which was selling a remarkable 85 percent of 1.5 million copies in the highly competitive women's field.

"You've never killed or sold a magazine in your life," Matt said. "Look at the way we turned *Charm* around. And the others. It could happen again."

The revival of *Charm* had been Richardson's greatest triumph. Once part of a fashion-world troika with *Vogue* and *Bazaar,* the book had failed to keep pace with its rivals' creative surges during the seventies and had become, in the words of advertising agency pundits, "Tenth in a field of three." The blame, as a former *Charm* staffer enjoyed pointing out in the glow of her later success with *Bazaar,* lay squarely with Tony Craig himself, whom she characterized as, "Unwilling to pay a nickel to see an earthquake."

It had been in this climate of rumors and death knells that Richardson unleashed an entirely new concept for the magazine. He recruited a dynamic young editor—who also happened to be beautiful—named Marla Ashton, and with her assistance revamped the magazine into a bold, sexy, free-swinging product aimed at new generations of young women bent on enjoying life a hell of a lot more than their mothers had. Marla's deft editorial touch had made *Charm* part of the information network this audience wanted and needed. In many ways, the new approach was a blatant parrot of *Cosmopolitan,* but it worked. Newsstand sales soared, and the magazine became the second in history to charge a premium for the privilege of a subscription, the first having been *Cosmo* itself. Advertising dollars quickly followed the burgeoning numbers of readers.

Craig did not respond to Matt's last comment. He picked up his reading glasses and the menu. In a moment, he peered at his companion. "What about the melon, Matt? Too early in the season, or can we count on *that?*"

"I'll ask the captain," Richardson said dejectedly. The wave of a hand brought Arthur scurrying to the table.

After they had both ordered, Craig stared out the window and said without looking at Matt, "I've been more than fair about *In Wildness.* Nobody else in this town would have hung in there as long, looking like a fool. Ten million bucks down the drain!" He turned and looked directly at Richardson. "You've let me down on this one, Matt."

"Me! You're the one pulling the plug!"

"The patient is still alive . . . at least for now. Listen to me, son. I want you to get your act together for the board meeting later this week. We want to put all our cards on the table. Show them how you're going to stop the bleeding. Hopefully, we can get a general agreement to continue for a year. That'll take a lot of pressure off both of us. But you've got to play your best ball." Craig paused, looking into Matt's eyes. "Anyway, it's up to you. I can't hold the fort by myself."

The two men sat in silence as their breakfasts were delivered and fresh coffee was poured. When the steward had departed, Matt said, "We need a new editor. I should have sacked Ted Walsh months ago."

Craig's face showed no surprise. "You hired him."

"He hasn't worked out."

"Come on," Craig said as he spooned his melon. "You've been running the book yourself. It'll be the same with a new editor."

"I have somebody in mind who can help me, somebody who can make a difference."

"Don't tell me this is the game plan you're going to present to the board," Craig said in a voice of extreme disbelief. "It's not enough, son. Not nearly enough."

"That's only part of my thinking. I'm holding some other good cards. Frankly, though, this crisis atmosphere doesn't help."

"Matt, I sincerely hope you don't have to take this one on the chin. I know it means a lot to you. What I still can't figure out is *why.*"

Richardson allowed Craig's statement to hang in silence as he tried to compose himself. He was in enough trouble already without blurting out some inappropriately sentimental answer Craig would never understand. The closest the man had ever come to nature was when his limo was passing through Central Park. The wilderness magazine that bore Craig's name was Matt's inspiration, his personal dream of serving an audience with which he could identify. Once, Tony Craig himself had published magazines that came from the heart, trusting his gut feelings and building a publishing empire. Now he believed in marketing research and advertising projections—crystal balls that might reveal a hint of the numbers to come. Did the man miss the vision, the bullheadedness, that had once served him so well?

Matt decided to test that question with some gut talk of his own. There was nothing to lose now.

"The other magazines are yours. I made them profitable again, that's all. *In Wildness* is part of *me,* the best of what I know and love."

"You're being melodramatic."

"I'm not backing off," Matt said sternly. "The board will have to carry me out with the magazine."

Craig looked away, obviously embarrassed by this display of forthrightness.

"Strong words. Backed up by *my* money." Craig looked at Matt with the expression of a man who realizes that a favorite child has gone astray.

"The audience is there," Matt said. "Once we connect, the bucks will come."

"You know we're going public. Every decision we make now impacts upon our ultimate worth."

"Yes, I'm reminded of that every time I see Procter and your financial hatchet men bent over their calculators and counting paper clips," Matt said bitterly.

"Somebody has to face the numbers, Matt. You and I made a deal: you run the creative side, I handle the financial. I need Morgan—and so do you. He's done a hell of a job selling all our magazines. *He's* not the reason *In Wildness* is in trouble."

"I've never said the man couldn't sell, Tony."

Craig's face broke into a mischievous grin. "I must tell you that I've enjoyed watching you two fellows spar with each other. Creating the adversary relationship was quite a stroke, if I must say so myself, and excellent for the company in results."

"It's your privilege to run the company the way you see fit."

"I like Morgan. Maybe it's because I'm fond of over-achievers. He works hard . . . brings the corn to the mill."

"You sound like you're ready to make him president of the magazine division," Matt said dejectedly.

Craig ignored Matt's complaint. He scraped a final spoonful of fruit from the melon, gave his lips and chin soft pats with his napkin, and smiled at Richardson. "I'm on some kind of goddamn diet the-woman-who-is-my-wife has found. I said to her, 'I'll do it on one condition. No conversation about it. Not one word!'"

Richardson laughed. "Mary takes good care of you, Tony."

"Yes," Craig said. "If she didn't, I would have spent the last ten years of my life ten feet under."

Matt smiled politely, weighing his next remark as he looked around the room, now bustling with activity. He had to get the conversation back on track, back to the problem that was crucifying him. Before he could speak, Craig said, "And speaking of wives, what about Kristen? Any chance for you to get back together?"

Richardson groaned inwardly. He needed this like a migraine.

The squash ball exploded off the front wall of the enclosed court and was a dark blur as it slashed toward a rear-court corner. His racket up and cocked, Morgan Procter danced on the balls of his feet at mid-court and waited for the ball to hit the back wall and bounce back to him.

Morgan whipped his racket through the ball with a short twisting stroke. His shot hit the front wall just above the tin marker and skidded sideways in an erratic hop. Procter crouched in readiness for a return shot, even though he expected his own shot to be an outright winner.

Kristen Richardson raced toward the front wall, stretching out her racket in a desperate lunge toward the dying ball. Suddenly she pulled up, her sneakers biting into the hardwood floor in sharp squeaks. "That's too good!" she exclaimed.

Morgan leaned on a side wall, his forehead resting on his arm as he gasped, "That's game, Kris."

Kristen patted him on the rear with her racket. "I'm sorry, Morg. I played like dog meat this morning. No fun for you."

"Are you kidding?" Morgan said, looking up and laughing. "I feel like I need an ambulance."

"Come on," Kristen said. "You're really good. My God, you get everything."

"How I wish." Morgan smiled. His face glistened with perspiration, and his sweat-drenched arms and T-shirt were further evidence of the maximum effort he had displayed during the match, constantly moving, covering the court with devastating quickness.

Morgan retrieved the pair of towels he had cached in the front corner. He handed one to Kristen and buried his face in the other. Pools of bright light blazed through his closed eyes. Another reminder, he thought, of the cost of trying to play like a twenty-year-old with a thirty-seven-year-old body. What the hell! To play well—that was the thing. Dominating Kristen on the court had forced him to call on his reserve skills and energy. She was a superb player, really, tennis and squash champion of her Princeton country club. She was probably about thirty, Morgan guessed, with a sleek, athletic body and an interesting face that glowed with teenlike vibrancy. On the court, she had moved with a sense of graceful speed and control, every move precisely right for the competitive situation. Her racket work was beautiful and unintimidated, her responses to his shots immediate and decisive. In the end, when he had simply overpowered her, her cheerful, exuberant manner had not cracked, and he had wondered if what he was seeing could be for real. If her demeanor wasn't an act, staged for his benefit, then what would it be like to be with her all the time? When he had first met her, he had felt an immediate physical attraction, even though he knew she belonged to someone else. Now, the first time they had ever been alone together, she had set the lusty part of his imagination aflame once more. But during their match, he had begun to be stirred by deeper longings than those brought on by her face and body, by the shining brown legs and the magnificent breasts that thrust arrogantly against her damp cotton T-shirt.

She would be leaving now, he thought, and it would be frustrating as hell from now on to think about her belonging to another man, especially a man he despised as much as Matt Richardson. Richardson did not deserve a woman he had subjected to such chaotic behavior. And Craig Publishing did not deserve to be saddled with a box-office stiff like *In Wildness,* the magazine Richardson had conned Tony Craig into backing. That the book was still alive now in spite of its track record was due entirely to Richardson's stubbornness and personal ambition. That was fate for you, Morgan thought. He had violently opposed the creation of the new magazine, and now he was stuck with the impossible job of selling it—a job that had already marred the performance record for the hottest sales team in the business.

When Morgan pulled the towel from his face, he blinked in surprise at the sight of Kristen Richardson standing only inches away.

The sounds of the other courts—thudding balls, pounding feet, cries of exhilaration—ceased to float through the walls. Hot waves of blood throbbed in Morgan's ears and temples, throughout his body. All sense of the room itself fell away. He and Kristen were in a cocoon, scented by the spicy mixture of perspiration and the surviving touches of the jasmine she used.

Kris flicked the tip of her tongue through her lips, wetting them, and said, "Time to collect your bet."

"I didn't know we had one," Morgan answered hoarsely.

"It was a secret one. I lost."

Kristen leaned forward as Morgan's arms reached for her

shoulders. One dank tendril of blond hair curled from beneath her light blue headband. Her enormous brown eyes were locked with Morgan's. She did not smile, but rather gazed at him with a searching, almost quizzical expression.

When Morgan pulled her to him, bending his head down to the moist generous lips he had longed to taste since they had first met, Kris's face did not change. Then she closed her eyes, parted her lips, and gave herself to the fullness of his embrace.

Morgan's desire for her erupted with the feel of her exciting body sheathed by the thin smoothness of the scant skirt and T-shirt. Her breasts swelled promisingly into his chest. Her thighs and legs locked into his as he held her even closer, her mouth welcoming his, her arms snaking around his back now. He let one hand glide down over the warm roundness of her thigh. It caressed the smoothness of her bare leg, then slid on under her dress to the back of the panties that had been flashing so enticingly during their match.

Kristen pulled her lips away and looked directly into Morgan's eyes.

"I'm not going to fuck you on a squash court," she said, smiling and out of breath.

Morgan felt almost delirious. "Please," he whispered. "I need you."

Her hand played softly over the back of his neck. "Set up something nice for us," she said. "I'll come."

She kissed him lightly on the lips, wheeled suddenly, and hurried away through the low, back-wall door of the court.

Morgan Procter stared at the open door for a moment. He draped the towel over his shoulders and walked across the court to pick up his racket. His fingers played with the taut strings as he leaned back against the wall and looked around the empty court, smiling.

A new game was on!

Matt Richardson stared at the dregs of his coffee as his thoughts grappled for a way to finesse Tony Craig's question about Kristen.

Craig realized Matt was stalling. "What about Kristen?" he repeated. "What's going on?"

"As you know, we've been separated for about a year. Frankly, I don't see much hope."

"I'm truly sorry, my boy. And quite bewildered by the whole thing. You and Kris always seemed so happy. I never figured this kind of trouble would come your way."

"It's quite involved, Tony. And painful."

"Of course. Things like that take a dreadful toll. Meanwhile, you go on living in that suite at the Plaza like some salesman on the road. If you're not getting back together, why don't you make a clean break. Get a nice place for yourself. You're young, for Christ's sake!"

There it was! Matt thought. The very thing he had tried to avoid even thinking about, much less discussing with his superior. The move Craig was outlining would finalize everything: Kristen would keep the house in Princeton, he would find something new, and the attorneys would mop up. Kristen, in a recent bitter note that said no reconciliation was possible, had even suggested the same thing Craig had. The tenuous notion of rebuilding their life together was a fantasy, and Matt was almost ready to admit it.

"Right now I just try to handle one day at a time," Matt said. "What I really want on a long-term basis doesn't seem that important."

"Look, Matt. What matters is that the overall picture looks good. You've done a hell of a job on all our books. If *In Wildness*"—Craig paused, then roared ahead—"Dammit all, if *In Wildness* does go under, it won't taint your career. We gave it a good try. It just hasn't worked."

Matt shook his head. "Do you remember Jonathan Hill?"

Craig blinked, surprised at the question. "Of course. Your family is my family. Even when certain members are out of favor."

Matt stirred uneasily. "You can't blame me for feeling bitter about Jon, after the way he ran out on us."

"With your sister in tow." Craig smirked. "All that time you spent getting him ready to run *In Wildness*. Wasted."

"Perhaps not. They've had a year in Alaska now. Perhaps they're ready to get back into the traces."

"Here we go again. Your new-editor plea."

Matt ignored Craig's disdain. "After Jon and Cody left for

ON DANGEROUS GROUND

Alaska, I had to make a decision. My choice for the editorship was Ted Walsh. He seemed to have a great sense of wilderness issues, and an intense personal commitment. But his ideas haven't worked. Now I know more than ever that Jonathan is the key."

"You're trying to tell me that a kid who has never edited a magazine in his life is going to be the savior of this thing? Whatever you've been smoking, I'd sure like to have some."

"Tony, Jonathan Hill typifies the spirit of *In Wildness*. Mountains—he's been on expeditions to the highest. Rivers— he's run the ones you can't even find on the map. Wilderness— he's spent most of his life living in and around the backcountry. Yet he has a B.A. from Stanford and tremendous editorial skills. He's the son of a newspaper editor in Wyoming. All that outdoors experience combined with a background in journalism make the guy unique."

Craig shrugged his shoulders, still unconvinced.

"The hottest books are always edited by powerful personalities," Matt pressed on. "People who are, in themselves, media events. Hugh Hefner *is Playboy*. Helen Gurley Brown *is Cosmo*. Marla Ashton *is Charm.*" Matt paused in his zealous appeal.

"Go on," Craig said. He saw Matt's look of surprise. "You can't go on. You can't even name a half-dozen people who fit that mold. The personality issue is fine up to a point, but most successful magazines are edited by hardworking professionals who never get to appear on Johnny Carson or Oprah. As you well know."

"We need him—and Cody. She was an associate editor on *Country Lifestyles* for us."

"He can't have much commitment—the way he pulled out on us. I'm still surprised your sister let it happen."

"You don't understand. Cody *made* it happen. She disliked the New York lifestyle as much as Jonathan. She and I still own the ranch in Wyoming where we both grew up. After she and Jonathan were married, they couldn't wait to get out there. Later on, this Alaska thing came along. I couldn't stop 'em."

"Crazy goddamn kids," Craig said, reflecting, thinking no doubt of his daughter and her history of drug addiction, institutionalized care, and failed marriages. "They want it all their way. No responsibilities."

"Cody and Jon wanted to live the bold life. The lure of the wilderness was something they chose not to deny. They're not alone. It's just that most people don't have the means—or the guts—to go for it."

"Sure," Craig said. "He's got us backing him up. He does a piece for *In Wildness* every month, doesn't he? What's his stipend for that?"

"A thousand a month."

"A sweetheart deal. Enough for them to get by out there in the boonies, I'd bet. Nip it off, and you'll get them back here soon enough."

"His work is worth every penny we pay for it. The grizzly photograph on this cover, for instance." Matt pointed at the magazine. "That's his."

Craig shrugged, offering no satisfaction.

"Anyway, I'm going to bring them in from Alaska for a talk."

"That's fine," Craig said. "But unless you come up with something for the board meeting, we *all* might as well go off fishing."

"Trust me, Tony," Matt said as he tried to smile with confidence. "I'll be there, and I'll be ready."

Tony Craig abruptly turned to the window and stared out in silence. Sunshine flooded Central Park with brilliance. Matt knew that any appeal, any further conversation about *In Wildness* was out of the question. He signaled for the steward, gave the bill a cursory glance, and signed it.

"Strange to sit here," Craig said suddenly, "and think what a beautiful idea Central Park is but realize the number of unspeakable crimes committed down there. I'll bet that if you sat here long enough, you'd see somebody get mugged."

Richardson stared down at the park without comment.

Craig wasn't finished. "Just as in the wilds you find so interesting, there are evil forces there. The hunters and the prey, the just and the unjust. Oh well." Craig started to rise. A steward appeared from nowhere to take his chair.

As they walked slowly toward the door, Craig said, "I continue to be amazed by the performance of *Charm* and Marla

Ashton. A most unusual woman. I've never known another quite like her."

"She's unreal," Richardson said. "But even there I'm having a few problems."

Craig looked at Matt with concern. "Really? Like what?"

"She's becoming too bold, too blatant. Already some people are calling the book 'glossy trash.'"

"I wouldn't worry about labels like that. Her 'trash' is selling. That's what counts."

"Believe me, Tony, she's flirting with going over the line. Right now, I have on my desk a book excerpt she wants me to buy for a great deal of money. Some woman writing about how to be good in bed. The chapter Marla wants is the complete guide to treating your lover to a condom. This gal has sort of perfected the ultimate technique for whipping out a rubber, rolling it on, and getting you set for action—while you lie back and relax. She makes it sound so great, I feel like I've been missing something."

Craig stopped and looked at Matt, obviously surprised. "Timely," he said. "But you'd better watch her closely. We don't want to get into trouble with our distributors—or advertisers."

"I can handle her," Richardson said.

"I know you can," Craig replied, casting Matt a furtive side glance as they walked on. The gesture did not startle Richardson, who fully realized that the powerful head of Craig Publishing knew all the secrets concerning the personalities who swam in his wake. Matt and Marla—and their affair during the revamping of *Charm*—had been under his closest scrutiny. The turnaround of the magazine into a publishing gold seam had purchased Craig's silence over the other result of their liaison —the disintegration of Matt's marriage.

Now there was no need for words. Craig knew the affair was over, knew that Matt and Marla had not seen each other privately in many months. The concern Craig had voiced about Matt's marital problems during breakfast had been genuine, Matt realized. But such intimacy made him uncomfortable, exposed and vulnerable. Was the old man afraid to trust him? Was he secretly thinking that a man who could not run his personal life damn well could not run a magazine publishing division?

The two men said nothing further until they shook hands on the street and Craig climbed into his limo. The driver held the door open for a moment as Craig said, "I hope Jonathan turns out to be another Marla Ashton, Matt. For your sake."

"Let's give him the chance. For the company's sake."

"It's going to be a tough sell, considering the circumstances." Craig smiled optimistically, despite the candor and seriousness of his words. "Well, it's Washington for me now. There's new mischief afoot with postal rates. I'll see you at the meeting. Good luck, my boy."

Matt stood on the curb and watched Craig's car until it disappeared into the flow of traffic. He unrolled the copy of *In Wildness* and stared at the cover.

My little problem child, he thought. You were supposed to be my salvation.

THREE

Jonathan Hill knelt on one knee and peered through a gap in a screen of alders that lined the bank of the Toubok River. He did not feel the sharp stones his kneecap pressed against; his khaki-clad legs were numbed by the icy tug of the current, which carried snow melt, spring-fed creeks, and glacial seepage from the wildly splintered peaks towering over the treeline upstream. Jonathan ignored the fly rod in his right hand, even though its tip was a vibrating half-hoop that pointed toward a smooth glide of dark water where a trout darted and swirled, its sides flashing in lances of silver.

Jonathan held himself rigid, listening intently, his eyes searching through the tangled branches that loomed before him. Careless fool! he thought. This is how you can die! With the sun warm and the breeze soft and a trout on the line.

He watched and listened. The wind stirred the alder tops, the current murmured softly. Suddenly the reel erupted with a metallic shriek as the fish pulled out line, boring downstream. Jonathan gasped, nearly dropped the rod, then felt the line go slack as the fish broke off.

Seconds passed. Still Jonathan did not move. He fought back the desire to believe the crisis was diminishing. He could sense the danger, close and waiting. His total focus remained on the source of his alarm.

The indentations were deeply etched in the soft earth. Some of the prints looked to be well over fifteen inches long and about ten wide. Others were not quite that size. The front edges of the tracks showed where the long, down-curving claws had pointed toward the river, where Jonathan had been standing, his back to the alders as he worked his casts toward the middle of the stream. After hooking the trout, he had turned to the bank and was trying to beach the squirming, heavy-bodied fish when he spotted the tracks and froze.

The tracks of any bear were the ultimate signature of wilderness, but the size of these footprints triggered in Jonathan a mixture of awe and dread unlike any emotions he had ever felt toward a wild creature. The word *grizzly* somehow did not seem strong enough to distinguish the animal that had been here. Other words came into his thoughts: *Ursus horribilis*— the Latin name of the grizzly.

This specimen of *horribilis*, Jonathan reckoned, would have to stand over twelve feet high when erect, probably weigh over 1,500 pounds. Such a thing did not seem possible. Unlike the bears of Kodiak Island and the Alaska Peninsula, the interior Alaska grizzlies did not have access to the bountiful salmon runs that provided the easy feeding and fantastic growth rates of their coastal brethren. Still, the tracks were an undeniable reality: one of the largest flesh-eating creatures to walk the earth had stood here.

Jonathan nervously rubbed a hand through the unkempt beard that softened the sun-browned tautness of his features. His long, sandy hair cascaded down his cheeks from the wide-brimmed Stetson hat that shadowed his forehead and quick dark eyes.

The age of the tracks puzzled Jonathan. Although the indentations seemed too dry to have been made in the last few minutes, he could not be certain that the bear was not hidden nearby. He had fished this spot for breakfast fish the two previous mornings. Had the bear been here then, watching him? If so, the great beast was probably miles away by now.

But if the tracks were fresher . . .

Instinctively, Jonathan reached down to his hip. The familiar presence of the Ruger Redhawk .44 magnum and its holster was not there. He thought of the gun lying useless on his sleeping bag in camp, across the river. He had no desire to shoot a grizzly, or any other animal he did not intend to eat. He knew that the greatest danger in bear country was to surprise a grizzly, and he had hoped never to allow such an encounter to happen. Still, the powerful revolver was a comforting measure of protection, and during his first year in Alaska he had carried it with him over most of his backcountry explorations. How ironic that when he felt he needed it for the first time, the gun was not with him.

ON DANGEROUS GROUND

Once before in his thirty years, Jonathan Hill had been close to violent death, but there had been no warning of the danger. On the Khumbu Icefall on the climb to the Western cirque of Everest, he had paused beside a crevass to photograph the ant-like line of Sherpa porters working on up through the jumbled ice far above. As he peered through the lens of the 35 mm, the snow slope collapsed under his feet. In one split second, he was lining up the shot to take in the West Shoulder and the Lhotse Face looming beyond, and in the next instant he was airborne amid snow and ice clumps. Then, with the same suddenness, he was yanked to a jarring stop, swinging on the rope belay held by his two companions, staring into the blue-shadowed ice that slanted into the darkness below. That ultimate abyss could have been his tomb, but he knew he was saved even as he dangled over the gaping mouth.

Suddenly Jonathan remembered the Everest accident. A strange sense of relief swept over him. This incident was not unlike his scare in the Khumbu Icefall. The danger was past! The grizzly had not charged him at the critical moment and was probably very far away by now. A close one, possibly. But there would be no tragedy on the Toubok this day.

He stood erect. Nothing moved except the shimmering alder leaves, stirred by wraiths of air Jonathan could not feel. His eyes scouted the terrain upstream and down. Nothing. Everything looked as it had before he discovered the tracks, before he had seen himself as an intruder, trespassing on dangerous ground.

Jonathan reeled in the slack line, his movements slow and deliberate as he continued to steady himself. He could not really be certain that the bear was gone, but he had to risk a few minutes' delay before wading across the river to his camp.

There was work to be done, despite the threat of danger.

He broke down the rod and tucked the two pieces under his armpit while he pulled a camera from the light day-pack that hung from one shoulder. He eased into the alders, his fingers playing with the adjustments on the 35 mm.

Through the viewfinder, the track on the dank patch of ground seemed small and insignificant. Jonathan lifted his face from the camera and stared at the track. He could see that the shot needed some contrast of measurement.

ON DANGEROUS GROUND

Carefully, he laid the butt of the fly rod diagonally in front of the track. Now, through the viewfinder, the imprint of the great bear seemed enormous beside the silvery reel and dark wet cork of the rod handle. Jonathan began making exposures. He shot automatic exposures at first, then ran through a series of f-stops and time settings, trying to cover every subtlety of light. To Jonathan, the sheer size of the track justified the expenditure of film and effort. None of the grizzlies he had previously photographed, including the one on the current cover of *In Wildness,* could have made such a footprint.

Finally he was satisfied. He stowed the camera in the pack and waded out into the current, heading for camp.

An hour later, Jonathan had packed his gear and was ready to start the five-hour trek that would carry him back to his cabin, several miles downstream. He lingered over the dying coals of a campfire, sipping a cup of tea and enjoying the early morning view of the great peaks surrounding him.

This part of the river had been his home for four days of photography in the nearby sheep ranges, which had begun to yield their secrets to his patient and thoughtful exploration. Beyond the rim of low hills that cupped this campsite lay a wilderness land of an unimaginable immensity.

Upstream, bathed in the light of the sun's longest arc of the year, a portion of the Alaska Range soared in a jagged wall. The far edge of the range trailed off toward a distant hulking shape that rose on the horizon like some strange snow planet ascending the heavens. This was the peak Alaskans usually called "The Mountain." It was the most beloved symbol of Alaska's wildness and beauty. It had many names. The aboriginal Indian tribes called it *Denali*—"The Home of the Sun." Other Indians had referred to the mountain as *Traleika,* still others as *Doleyka,* and the Russians, when they came, called it *Bolshaya Gora.* Three names. Three tongues. It was remarkable and appropriate that these three meant the same thing: The Great One.

The textbook name, Mount McKinley, was the source of profound resentment and agitation among Alaskans, who wanted to strike down for all time the name given the mountain in 1896 by W. A. Dickey, a young Princeton University graduate, while he was leading a party of prospectors through the Susitna Valley. Dickey had originally named the mountain Denali, which he had learned from the Indians, but upon his return to civilization he was struck by a burst of political fervor following William McKinley's nomination for the presidency. The highest peak on the North American continent then came to bear the name of the twenty-fifth President.

Jonathan sided with the Alaskans and had taken their cause into print on several occasions, for he felt a deeper reverence toward Denali than for any mountain in the world, including Mount Everest. Although the summit of Everest was the highest of any mountain in the world, 29,028 feet, the actual body of the mountain rose from a base that was 18,000 feet high among the multitude of peaks in the mighty Himalayan range. Denali was a solitary gigantic universe unto itself, soaring over three and one half miles straight up from the tundra and spruce flatlands. Its two summits did not pierce the sky; the upper reaches of snow and ice were broadly massed and wide-shouldered, visible on clear days over 300,000 square miles of central Alaska.

During summer those clear days were all too rare, because the upper battlements of this frigid dome lay in the path of warm and moist winds from the south and southwest. The collisions of varying rivers of air with the mountain were weather breeders, creating winds and storms that frequently hid the mountain from view.

Even as Jonathan watched, dark streamers of cloud sailed across the face of Denali. A summer storm could be brewing up there, or a front moving in with some real weather.

No matter, he reassured himself. He could handle whatever weather the day might bring. The other pressures he had been feeling so acutely could not be easily dismissed, however.

Time and money—both running out simultaneously—were ugly realities that perched at the edge of his thoughts like vultures. No matter what happened with regard to money, in a year the wilderness adventure he and his wife Cody had enjoyed would be over. Their son Derek would be six. He would have to have schooling, playmates, sports—the activities of youth that even Jonathan's and Cody's love and attention could not replace. Where would they go? Where would the money come from? Could he count on continued sales to *In Wildness*? Although the correspondence from his editor, Ted Walsh, had given no hint of trouble, recent letters from Matt Richardson were blunt to the point of pain: the magazine was losing so much money its future was in doubt.

The cabin he now rented had originally been built as a deluxe outpost camp for a professional hunting and fishing out-fitter. When he had retired due to injuries in a floatplane accident, he had leased the property to Jonathan and Cody. The two-year price was steep, but two events had occurred that made the venture possible for them.

First, Jonathan had received an advance for a novel with a mountaineering setting; then Cody found a home for the nonfiction proposal called "Backcountry Wife." Articles and photographs for *In Wildness* had provided enough additional income to sustain them while they lived the kind of wilderness adventure they had always dreamed about: two years on the Toubok River, where their nearest neighbors, an elderly Indian couple, were three miles downstream. Access to both cabins was by floatplane to Hidden Lake, only a quarter-mile on the opposite side of the ridge behind Jonathan's cabin. Portage trails connected the cabins with each other and with the lake itself, forming a rough triangular pattern.

Mail and supplies came every three weeks by floatplane, using skis in winter. The only connection with the outside world on a daily basis was the radio program "North Winds," which carried messages to people in the remote Alaska bush. Their Indian neighbors, the Tolkats, had a shortwave radio that could be used for emergencies. The set was part of a government subsidy Tolkat received to operate as a message center for the native families scattered within fifty miles of the Toubok.

In addition to his projects for *In Wildness*, Jonathan had a firm assignment from *National Geographic* for a word-and-picture profile of the Dall sheep, tentatively titled "Sentinel of the High Wild: The Dall Sheep Through the Year." He had started the project when he and Cody had moved to Alaska the year before. Finishing the job would mean a sizable check coming his way, so he'd been anxious to complete this final trek and wrap up the project with some shots of lambs and ewes.

Jonathan watched the clouds sweep on into the mountains. Somewhere out there on the lower ridges, he thought, the great bear roamed the country. He tried to form a mental picture of the creature. How would it look while walking, hiding, hunting? How could it move so silently?

"Horribilis," Jonathan said aloud, as his gaze swept over the ranges, "I'd love to take your picture."

The wind cried down from the high passes, searching along the slopes, coming into the valley.

He heard and smelled the rain moving downriver long before the first drops pelted out of the scudding clouds. As the advance wall of the shower slid down the slopes of the mountains, the great bear Jonathan Hill called Horribilis lifted his nose to the breeze and sniffed drafts of wet forest, heavy with scent. He could detect whorls of dust the wind kicked up from the edges of the low-water channels of the streambed. He could hear the rain itself, whispering softly over the trees and tundra, then becoming a murmur of growing intensity as the stream itself was engulfed in the downpour.

The storm swirled into the willow thicket, purging the scent of death that hung in the air. The first scattered drops of rain flicked at the bear's face like bugs colliding. He shook his head, licking at the offensive drops as he had at the real flies that had begun to swarm over the remnants of the corpses. Since adding Larkin's body to the cache of moose meat covered by the brush pile, Horribilis had gorged himself repeatedly, stopping occasionally to sleep or defecate.

The shower made Horribilis uneasy. The hard gusting of the wind, the steady sighing of the rain, were forces that he instinctively knew would mask the usual stimuli of scent and sound that triggered his alertness. He trudged over toward the river, plowing directly through the glistening willows.

Lashed by the rain, the stream was a cauldron of noise and splatter. Horribilis looked up and down the river, sniffing at the gloom for clues of intruders. He turned away from the current after a while and walked back through the willows, passing the sodden mass of the brush pile as though he had no interest in it now. His route carried him into the birch trees, and he plodded steadily on through the dripping leaves that made the rain a whisper. The terrain lifted somewhat, and the white slimness of the birch trunks began to give way to the thick shapes of spruce trees, huddled against the leaden sky. Past this belt of trees, Horribilis came to open tundra that stretched toward the distant mountains. He stopped just inside the thick cover of the spruce, sniffing expectantly, gazing out into the silvery streaks of rain.

Satisfied, he turned back toward the river, heading downstream, circling back toward his kill.

During the next hour, Horribilis patrolled the perimeter of the willow thicket several times. When new breezes swept down from the mountains, shredding the overcast and heralding the return of sunshine, the great bear felt a familiar urge. He hurried back to the brush pile.

A booted foot protruded from the upper edge of the snarl of branches.

Snorting and woofing, Horribilis sank his teeth into the leg, tearing it free, scattering the cloud of flies that had started to gather.

FOUR

ed Walsh reached for the martini as soon as it was out of the waiter's grasp. He took a hurried sip from the tumbler of gin and ice, then lifted it in a toast as he said, "Here's to honest prose—and nerves of steel."

Morgan Procter was not amused. He stirred his Perrier and lime, clinked his glass against Walsh's, and took a long pull from the fizzing drink. He settled back in the banquette, his face retreating to the dimmer fringes beyond the wavering flush of candlelight.

"I'm not going to lie to you," Procter said. "The book is in a failure mode. Certain highly placed people in the company would like to see it knocked in the head."

The smile that lingered from the previous moment's toast melted instantly from Walsh's florid face. He shifted his gaze toward the red-and-white-checked tablecloth, picked up a swizzle stick, and poked at his drink. The olive beneath the ice was barely visible in this dim corner of Mario's, an obscure West Side establishment that Procter always chose when he asked Walsh to lunch, shunning his usual tables at La Côte Basque and other favorite posh watering holes of the magazine clan. Procter claimed that caution was the reason for the semi-secret choice of settings: Craig Publishing admen were forbidden from meddling in editorial affairs. Walsh saw the sham behind the excuse, however. He knew he was being put down.

"You know," Walsh said, glancing around the almost empty room, "every time we meet here, it's the same. On the way in, I feel like I need a flashlight. On the way out, I feel like I need a new résumé."

Procter shrugged. His smile held no warmth. "The book is hemorrhaging red ink."

"Book!" Walsh laughed the word. "Why do we magazine

people call our properties 'books'? This book. That book. Why don't we say 'magazine'?''

"Never thought about it. Maybe it's because 'magazine' is a word that has no pizzazz, no juice. Who cares?"

"I guess it's the editor in me. Language is my business."

"Let me tell you something, my friend," Procter said, sternness rising in his voice. "Nitpicking with words and changing commas aren't going to get *us* out of the hole we're in. You'd better come up with some real answers—starting today!"

Walsh sipped his martini. "I'm open to suggestions."

"As a matter of fact," Procter said, "I do have something in mind. It takes time to come up with a winning editorial formula. In the meantime, we have to improve the ad picture. You can help me do that with a little cooperation. Sort of an editorial-advertising crossruff. Like this Alaska junket."

Walsh grimaced and shook his head silently. Procter ignored him and continued. "Now I'm not asking you to run a piece that says the bears and caribou like the Alaska Pipeline so much that they're huddled against it to keep warm. But dammit, there must be something positive that we can stress! And you've got to go on that press junket this afternoon. Drop everything else, man! This is more important!"

"I despise junkets like that. You take all the freebies, end up feeling obligated, and produce puff articles. It sucks!"

"Let's be realistic," Procter said. "The environmental sermons you've been packing into every issue of the magazine haven't exactly been filling the stands. Maybe truth and justice don't sell tickets like they should. I don't know. Ad-wise, I can tell you that kind of integrity may be great for selling Bibles, but it isn't going to put any linage into our book."

"The magazine is devoted to wilderness, Morgan. The Alaska Pipeline hits the very heart of the idea. If we try to sidestep it—finesse it!—the readers will know that everything we pretend to stand for is bullshit. We'll be dead then for sure."

"The Pipeline is there! They're pumping oil through the goddamn thing! Be reasonable! The world's not going back to Walden Pond, for Christ's sake!"

Ted Walsh smiled, trying to break the tension. "What the hell do you know about Walden Pond? I'm amazed you ever heard of it."

Procter could not help laughing. "Mike Williams refers to Walden Pond all the time. He has the T.A.P. account at Kline-Wolfe. He's giving me a hard time because you're not on board that press trip yet." T.A.P. were the initials of Trans-Arctic Petroleum. Kline-Wolfe was the company's advertising and public relations agency.

"The Pipeline is pumping two million barrels of oil a day," Walsh said, his voice ringing with disgust. "But that's not enough for the oil barons involved. What they want now is to open up the Arctic National Wildlife Refuge to explore for oil *and* gas."

"They say the original Prudhoe Bay field will run out," Morgan countered. "This new place isn't far away. They can use the facilities they've already built."

"After they've put in a *new pipeline* to pump the gas."

"They haven't hurt anything so far," Morgan said meekly.

"They haven't?" Walsh was incredulous. "I was up there while the construction was going on. I know what this junket is *really* all about. To tell the world what a great job the oil companies did—how well the environmental safeguards are supposed to be working. What rot!"

"There's too much at stake here," Procter said, his voice rising in anger. "I'm not going to lose forty-eight pages of new business and a million bucks of revenue!"

Procter and his *In Wildness* ad director, Vince Cummings, had been working for weeks to be included in the magazine schedule for a new series of environmentally oriented advertisements being launched by T.A.P., one of the companies associated with the Alaska Pipeline consortium. Despite the fledgling magazine's weak numbers, the admen's barrage of presentations, luncheons, dinners, and theater dates had finally resulted in the plum of an account being scheduled. Suddenly, the day before, a telephone call and hand-delivered letter had killed the insertion order. And Procter knew that the *reason* was seated right across the table.

Ted Walsh had abruptly canceled the magazine's participation in an elaborate public relations junket T.A.P. had set up to take place on the Pipeline. Morgan recognized the carrot-and-stick routine of the agency, with the forty-eight-page schedule being dangled as bait.

"I'll go to Tony Craig about this if I have to," Morgan said, continuing his attack. "He'll be pissed! Dick Kline, the head of the agency, is one of his oldest and dearest friends. In addition to being one of the major sources of revenue for *all* our books."

"Your threat is duly noted," Walsh said grimly. "I'm not worried. Matt Richardson will back me up on this."

Procter's voice was low and stern as he said, "I'm talking about survival here."

"Not necessarily of the fittest," Walsh quipped, sipping his martini. He looked around the room. The tables were filling now with a mixed crowd of noisy and enthusiastic young executives and secretaries; none were Craig people of his acquaintance. Suddenly, feeling his gut tighten with tension, he found himself wishing he had not ordered a real drink. How many meetings in your life have you endured like this, he thought, with the food and drink sour on the tongue and wretched in the stomach? How many toasts lifted in fellowship when no fellowship at all was present, only fear and greed? Still, the luncheon was necessary. As much as he despised Procter's bullying, he had to endure it.

"Specifically, Morgan, what has you going to the whip on this? You have other magazines. You've opposed this one from Day One."

Procter laid his hands on the table and leaned forward slowly. In the soft half-light he looked like a man who had wandered into the wrong restaurant. His pin-striped suit—a navy blue tropical worsted—was designed by Giorgio Armani. Against the crisp whiteness of the Sea Island cotton shirt, the muted stripes of his silk tie narrowed to a precise knot over the gold-clipped collar. A sliver of a Girard Perregaux showed beneath the crisp barrel cuff of one wrist as it elegantly crossed the other and helped to highlight the long brown hands that fidgeted nervously. To Walsh, Procter looked like a professional golfer who had just spent a large chunk of his winnings in expensive midtown shops.

"I'm sure you saw the preliminary sales figures this morning," Procter said. "This issue is going to be the biggest stiff to ever hit the streets. Thank God, I just sell the ads."

Walsh winced, reliving the stinging disappointment of the sales report that had descended upon him that morning. The low numbers were like a physical blow. He had been convinced that with this issue he could make the magazine a bestseller—finally.

Ted Walsh looked at Procter and tried feebly to compose himself. He knocked back the dregs of his martini and continued to see Procter staring at him in silence. "No matter what we try," Walsh said, "we can't seem to get hot."

"We can't keep selling this thing with mirrors," Procter replied. "Which is what we've been doing. The numbers stink! We could be down 30 percent in the last half of the year."

Walsh gazed at his empty glass. Morgan Procter diverted one of the scurrying waiters with an authoritative wave and ordered a second round. The two men stared at their menus until the drinks arrived. Ted took a sip and stared vacantly across the room as he said, "Do you think they'll kill the book if things don't turn around? Or just fire me?"

"I don't think they'll kill it or sell it—yet," Morgan said. "But you know the Craig philosophy: the editor is responsible."

"I take the drop, then. That it?"

Procter shrugged, obviously feigning naiveté. "Richardson doesn't tell me what editorial moves he's planning. And I haven't heard anything on the street. But things are going to hell so fast you'd better get moving, man. Richardson and Tony Craig aren't exactly famous for doing social work among editors who can't give 'em what they want."

Walsh stared at his martini, his face tight with concern.

Procter turned his hands palms up and sighed. "What the hell. Why should you listen to me? Richardson runs the editorial show. He's your boss. Anyway, it's only a job, right? You've got money in the bank. Why should you worry?"

The remark was not without its effect upon Walsh. Its absurdity was no joke. His salary as editor of *In Wildness* was tied to the magazine's newsstand and subscription performances, and both areas were disasters. His basic $70,000 stipend took a severe battering from child support payments, a divorce settlement, and other debts accumulated during a three-year period of personal ruin when he had tried to make it as a writer. A gamble on a book project had consumed two years of time and work and left his life in chaos. The book—a crusade against the damming of wild rivers called *Rivers in*

Crisis—had been remaindered six months after publication, selling fewer than 2,000 copies. By then the magazine and advertising contacts that had nourished his career as a writer/editor on environmental subjects had undergone so many upheavals that another year passed during which he was forced to live on marginal free-lance projects, with no solid sources of income. During all this, his admittedly excessive behavior—drinking, irritability, and a cavalier attitude toward earning a living—had driven his wife into the arms of a widower friend with a successful real estate business in Florida. She was there now, remarried, with Walsh's six-year-old daughter, whom he realized he hardly knew.

His eventual salvation came from a headhunter friend who persuaded Matt Richardson to consider Walsh for the top slot on his new magazine, *In Wildness*. With his act considerably cleaned and polished, Walsh impressed Richardson sufficiently to get the job. As Matt told a friend, he saw in Walsh and *Rivers in Crisis* the kind of courage and sensitivity he wanted in the pages of his fledgling magazine. For Walsh, getting the nod meant a new lease on life, a steady income, and a chance to rent a decent apartment on East Twenty-first Street.

The flush of success that came with the appointment—the parties and promotional appearances kicking off the first issue—seemed never to have happened now. More than anything, Walsh missed the clarity of that time—the sense that he knew exactly what he wanted to accomplish and how to accomplish it.

"Look, Morgan." Walsh's voice was warm and appealing. "I apologize if being a smart-ass makes me seem rude sometimes. It's just that these setbacks have made me uptight, and I may overcompensate."

Time to close, Morgan Procter told himself. "There's a special incentive involved with the Pipeline trip. T.A.P.'s field PR man, Jack Burke, is in town. I believe you know him. He wants you to fly to Fairbanks with him today. He's got a chopper up there waiting to take the two of you out on a wilderness fishing trip for three days. Anywhere you want to go. Just the two of you before the regular Pipeline junket begins."

"Yes, I know Burke," Walsh said. "But I can't up and leave for Alaska without making preparations."

"Burke's handling everything. All you have to do is to be at JFK by seven o'clock. Your staff can handle things here. Your next issue doesn't close for three weeks anyway."

Walsh reflected on the new offer. As ashamed as he was to admit it, the prospect was tempting. He had always gotten along rather well with Burke, a former journalist himself who had jumped ship to public relations and a life of high salaries and expense accounts. They had spent a lot of time together during the Pipeline construction, including some first-class fishing trips.

Walsh picked up his menu from the corner of the table. "We should eat something," he said slowly. Then, almost as an afterthought, he lifted his glass in gesture, and added, "And I'll do this once more."

Morgan Procter took a desultory look at the menu and signaled their waiter.

After Procter had ordered—another martini and shrimp scampi for Walsh, and a glass of white wine, salad, and filet of sole for himself—he looked across the table to see Walsh's face locked into a sort of grimace, a strange sense of resolve in his features.

Walsh's eyes glistened as he said, "You realize, don't you, that it's all we've got left?"

Morgan stared at Walsh with a vacant, bored expression.

"The Alaska wilderness," Walsh continued. "It's all we've got left. The map ends right there. When it's been draglined, condoed, and shopping-malled like the rest of the country, the lessons we've learned will be useless—except maybe in outer space."

Morgan allowed this diatribe to float away, like smoke dissolving.

"We need those pages, Ted. Are you going to meet Burke at the airport, or do I have to get Tony Craig to send somebody else?"

Walsh stared down at his martini, trying to sort out the confused mixture of emotions he was feeling beneath the shadow of the gin. Fucking space-peddlers! Were they all the same in their disdain for editorial integrity? Taking the trip under these circumstances would mark him as a coward. Yet, if he did not go and the magazine lost the sale, he would be blamed and most likely sacked.

Perhaps that would be better for *In Wildness*, Walsh reflected. Obviously, his own editorship had been a disaster. With a new editor, the magazine might yet have a chance.

You're talking nonsense! he told himself. As tenuous as his grip on the editor's chair was, he had to hang on. Survive, work hard, and wait for things to get better. That was the game plan now.

Walsh finished his drink, glanced around the room that was now humming with animated talk and laughter, and looked down at his shrimp scampi.

"Okay," he said suddenly, without looking up. "Okay. Okay."

"Okay what?" Procter asked.

"Okay I'll go."

Morgan smiled broadly. "You'll do it?"

"Why not? Why not, anyway? Haven't been in the field for quite a while. Do me good. Sharpen up my thinking about the book."

"Super!" Morgan said with genuine enthusiasm. "They'll love it—the editor himself coming up. I'll let 'em know immediately."

Procter fell to his sole with zest now. "What about the side trip?" he asked as he sipped his wine. "The fishing?"

"Know a guy named Jonathan Hill?"

"He used to work here with Richardson and now does free-lance for us. He was supposed to be the first editor of *In Wildness*, but he ran off to play Huck Finn or Tom Sawyer or whatever the hell it is you do out there. Am I right?"

"Right. He's in Alaska," Walsh said. "Jonathan lives in a cabin on a river called the Toubok. Supposed to be good fishing there."

"Then pay him a visit," Morgan said cheerfully. "T.A.P. will arrange it. They can arrange anything, anything you want."

"It's ironic," Walsh said. "I was scheduled to be up there all this week, hiking and camping with a friend. I begged off because of the shitty way things were going here. He went on without me." Walsh felt a new wave of tension as he remembered the guilt he had felt because of letting Sam Larkin down.

"Another good reason for going on up," Procter said. "You can catch up with your friend and see Jonathan Hill at the same time."

"I'll have to go in by floatplane or chopper. No need to alert Jonathan and make a big deal out of this. I'll surprise him."

With his immediate problem solved, Morgan bubbled on about the advertising. "If Tony Craig would let us take cigarette ads . . . but Richardson has poisoned his mind on that issue. He has the old man believing it would hurt our so-called 'pure' outdoor image. What bullshit! It's just a sample of what I've had to put up with while trying to sell this thing. But we'll do better if you'll just work with me on some things I've been thinking about. . . ."

Feeling sluggish with food and drink and the wash of the warm June sunlight, Ted Walsh ambled back to his office in the seedy West Side building where *In Wildness* had been renting space since its inception. The small Craig Publishing Building on Fifty-seventh Street could no longer house all of the company's magazines, and some of the publications had been assigned quarters of varying opulence, ranked by profitability, throughout the neighborhood. *Charm's* luxurious digs in the Solo Building on Fifty-seventh Street were the finest. The *In Wildness* offices were downright shabby and would remain that way, Tony Craig had insisted, until the magazine started turning a profit.

What the hell, Walsh thought, the side trip to the Toubok will make the junket justifiable. A meeting with Jonathan Hill could be valuable. While contributing to the magazine, Jonathan had never shared his thoughts on the book's overall direction. Walsh wondered if he even knew about the mess the magazine was in.

He turned onto Eighth Avenue, lingering before the shop windows he passed. His image reflected in the plate glass was as disturbing as his mental turmoil. Always stocky, he had now become flabby, a condition he attributed to the problems that had kept him desk-bound and sedentary for so long. Where was the young man, he wondered, who could carry a canoe and a fifty-pound pack over ten miles of portage trail without stopping? What would that young man say now if he were here to interview this pathetic figure?

He tried to dismiss the thought as he glanced at his watch. Two-twenty. He barely had time to clean up a couple of things at the office, taxi to his apartment, and get on out to JFK. This time tomorrow, he would be on the Toubok River in Alaska. Sam Larkin was somewhere out there, somewhere on the trail to Jonathan's cabin. Surprising him and Jonathan was going to be a real hoot.

Walsh thought about the river itself, anticipating the pleasures to come, the pleasures he had been denied when he had dropped out of the trip. Now the images of the river swept through his thoughts once again, just as real as they had been during the many weeks of planning the trip with Larkin.

God, that was country up there, with a sense of isolation both satisfying and scary. For a while a man could feel it was all his to enjoy, with not a care on earth to spoil it. Then, perhaps, you'd hear the distant sound of white water, and a knot of uneasiness would tighten inside you, making you wonder if you could hack it, wonder if you shouldn't be safe at home somewhere. You couldn't get along in the deep wilderness without being tested a bit, reaching down deep inside yourself to revive skills and feelings gone rusty. Living where you had to live to earn a living cut you off from the things that brought out the best of you. You had to go farther and farther away to find the good country now, and that meant you went less and less. Sometimes it seemed like an incurable illness, this love of wild places.

Walsh stepped around a sleeping derelict, a filthy, scab-ridden torso naked from the waist down.

Never mind that you've been coerced, Ted Walsh decided. Get what you can out of the trip. Detox, give your spirits a lift! Of course, there was a price. There always was.

Morgan Procter was enjoying the walk back to his office. His custom sunglasses masked his expression, but the sense of confidence he was feeling was evident in his long purposeful strides. He tried to focus his thoughts on his agenda for the afternoon, but his head was still buzzing with the satisfaction of his successful coup.

He had proven that he could sell, and that he could manage people on every magazine in the company. Despite the odds, he was going to prove it all again with *In Wildness*. His prospects of ultimately being made head of the entire magazine division were not going to be spoiled by his rival's ambitions with this new book. If Craig pulled the plug on *In Wildness*, his own skirts would be clean. Let Richardson take the rap he deserved for this turkey.

Richardson! The thought of the man's name instantly swept Morgan back to the morning's strange encounter on the squash court. He had never really expected to have an affair with Kristen Richardson. Despite the fact that his desire for her had haunted him for years and had been rekindled at every Craig social function where they had met, he had been resigned to his fate: she belonged to another man.

Now out of a casual game of squash had come a covenant that seemed almost unbelievable in the richness of its promise.

Morgan searched his memory for those occasions when he and Kristen had been surrounded by other people. Had there been signals he had missed? Subtle gestures that she was interested? He could not recall any such indications. All he could remember was the moment he first saw her, on the clay tennis court at Tony Craig's estate in Connecticut. Dressed in a short white skirt, brown legs flashing in the sun, her beautiful strokes winning point after point, she was a captivating figure, and later he could not get her out of his mind. When he had joined her and Richardson for a drink on the shaded terrace beside the court, he had begun to ache with longing. Her smile, her girlish zest, seemed so fresh and appealing that for weeks afterward he found he was comparing other women who interested him to Kristen. He had been surprised when this happened, because until then he had always compared his favorite dates and bedmates to his wife, who had died at the age of twenty. He had loved her with unbridled enthusiasm and devotion during the year they were married, but that had not prevented her death in an accident so freakish and bizarre in its injustice that he had never completely recovered. A lightning bolt or surge of electricity—nobody was ever sure exactly which—had killed her with the suddenness of a gunshot while she was talking on the phone during a violent electrical storm.

The tragedy that had shattered Morgan's life was not the first to strike him, despite his young age at the time. His parents had died in an automobile accident when he was eighteen. Booze had already reduced his father to a weak, ineffectual shell of a man, mowing grass and doing odd jobs at a goat farm of a country club, when the first disaster came. With a fifth of vodka under his belt, the elder Procter had tried to pass one eighteen-wheeler on a two-lane highway only to meet another head on, at one in the morning. The vintage VW bug was no match for a Diamond Reo.

Bitter over his loss, with no close family to turn to, Morgan had enlisted in the army and volunteered for Vietnam. His war experiences ended quickly and disastrously. At a bend in a dirt road leading into a sweltering group of huts and outhouses called Ben Cat, his armored cavalry column of jeeps and armored personnel carriers was hit by a precise barrage of rocket fire. As Morgan and the other troops scrambled for the cover of the jungle, amid exploding shells and burning vehicles, the VC regulars tightened the knot of the ambush. A wall of fire, unleashed by Russian-made Kalashnikov automatic rifles, erupted from the trees. Something slammed into Morgan's upper thigh, and he crumpled into a ditch, crying, "I'm hit!" His shout was lost in the confusion of the small-arms fire and the other cries of hurt and dying men, the expletives of officers and noncoms trying to rally the beleaguered unit. The last thing Morgan heard before unconsciousness took him out of the war was the thud of choppers bringing in a relief force of firepower and men.

He returned to his native state to enter the University of Maryland on GI Bill financial assistance and an athletic scholarship earned as a walk-on candidate for the golf team. He had just begun his junior year when he started dating an irresistible journalism major named Patty Gentry, the daughter of a publisher specializing in regional magazines. During six months of dating and just over a year of marriage, Morgan not only discovered happiness beyond his most fanciful dreams, but found his life finally taking real shape in the form of a planned magazine career. Then tragedy stalked him once again, just at graduation time.

His golf coach and closest friend had brought the news to the tiny hut where Morgan and three of his teammates had taken shelter from a thunderstorm that had drenched the golf course for over an hour. Later, nobody ever admitted that the telephone lines into the tiny over-garage apartment he and Patty rented were improperly grounded. A window had been found to be open. Perhaps the lightning had shot through it, igniting the telephone Patty held as she talked to her mother. She had died instantly, Morgan was told. Heavily sedated, he stayed at a friend's house for several weeks after the funeral. Finally, he took a bus to Pinehurst, North Carolina, to attend a qualifying school for the PGA tour. When he failed to gain tournament status, he rode a bus to New York and lived in another friend's apartment while he began making the rounds of the magazines.

Now, after fifteen years, the scars really had begun to heal. Sometimes, entire weeks would pass without his thoughts dwelling on his loss. Suddenly, at odd moments, the memories would come flooding back. When that happened, it always seemed that he was another person entirely than the young man who had lived that earlier life, the young man who had been to war, then had come to know the joy of love. When that joy had been snatched away, he had felt only guilt and unworthiness in its place. Eventually his guilt over surviving had begun to fade, and he had lived for a time under the shadows of bitterness and anger. Today, even those senses of outrage were gone, dimmed by the passing years in the same way the very best of himself seemed lost, held captive by the distant past. His ability to love. Would it ever return? he sometimes wondered. Would he always feel restless? Why did he never truly long for peace, only for fulfillment? His questions went unanswered with each passing day, just as they had years ago when he had asked why his wife had died.

He had not lacked for female companionship. Many women found him attractive, and he attributed this to fitness and his persistence in looking his best, not to God-given physical features. He appreciated the number of lusty encounters that came his way, but nothing permanent had ever come of them.

The tryst with Kristen could change his life, Morgan decided, dreamingly, as he walked. What did she want from him anyway? A good healthy romp in the hay? Then he would be happy to oblige. And if that's all there was to it, well . . .

Morgan thought about the arrangements he needed to make. Better get moving right away, he decided. Today even. Call her and invite her to his apartment at the Pierre Hotel for a few days. He loved living at the Pierre. The rooms were luxurious, the room service efficient, and the kitchen and cellar excellent.

Besides all that, he liked the soap.

FIVE

The shower that had swept along the Toubok early in the morning had passed quickly, as such storms often did in the Alaska high country, replaced by vaultless blue skies and warm sunshine. Shirtless, wearing khaki shorts and an old pair of sneakers, Jonathan Hill flicked the sharp blade of a hoe at some of the first weeds to invade his garden, a half-acre plot of plowed ground that was beginning to show promise of the bounty to come. He paused at the end of a long row of tomato plants to watch his son stalk a bear in his Davy Crockett getup.

The bear was their yellow Labrador retriever, Buck, curled half-asleep in the shadow of a vine-covered pea fence. Wearing his coonskin hat, Derek Hill edged up behind the dog in a low half-crouch, every step carefully placed. He carried a small replica Kentucky rifle at the ready.

Jonathan wished he had a camera, and he looked up the grassy slope toward the cabin with the thought of yelling for Cody. He could hear the battery-powered radio playing softly and the occasional clatter of pots and pans being put away after the noon meal. He dismissed the idea as Davy Crockett broke off his stalk two feet from the dog, raised the rifle to aim, and shouted a high-pitched "Bang!" Achieving no results except to thoroughly wake the animal, the youngster charged quickly and poked Buck solidly in the ribs, continuing to yell "Bang! Bang!"

The patient Lab jumped to his feet and trotted toward Jonathan with Derek in pursuit. "Bang!" shouted the child.

"Easy, son," Jonathan said gently. "We like having old Buck around. You'll chase him back to Anchorage."

"Grizz!" Derek yelled. "Bang! Bang!"

"Come here, lad." Jonathan dropped the hoe and reached out to take the youngster in his arms. Derek raced up eagerly, and Jonathan scooped him up and lifted him high over his head. He was a slim-waisted man of medium height, but his sun-browned arms and shoulders were thickly muscled, and the hands that held the child were massive in size and showed their exposure to country living: browned-over calluses, gnarled and wrinkled knuckles, battered nails, thin scratches and cuts. Looking at the face that giggled down at him from against the sky, Jonathan Hill could see himself in Derek: curly-haired and round-faced, with sparkling dark eyes. Plain as all get-out, but cheerful in a most pleasing way.

Jonathan eased the youngster down. Derek wore overalls and no shirt, the long tail of the coonskin hat flopped down over his bony shoulder. "Let's go fishing, Daddy."

Jonathan looked longingly at the river. Down the hill, beyond the breeze-stirred birches, a sheet of hammered silver reflected the keen slant of the strong sunlight. He shook his head. "Too much work, son. Maybe tomorrow. Anyway, it's about time for your nap."

"Story! Story!" Derek ran up the slope toward the cabin. Buck followed without a command. Jonathan picked up the hoe and watched them go. Cody would read to the child for a while before putting him down for his nap. Today's story, Jonathan reflected, would no doubt include a lot of material inspired by Davy Crockett. Derek had nearly fifty hats in the footlocker beside his bed, and he wore a different one every day. Tomorrow Davy Crockett would be replaced by a soldier, or a hockey player, or a cowboy. Since the interest in hats had started two years before, it had mushroomed because friends—and even Jonathan and Cody themselves—could not resist contributing interesting items to the collection.

Jonathan turned back to his hoeing and started on a row of cauliflower. The garden, which would grow prodigious vegetables in the constant sun of summer, was too important for desultory maintenance. Cody's patient skills at canning would turn the yield into a fantastic larder for the months ahead. Jonathan's photography trip in the sheep ranges had caused his work in the garden to get backed up, and a number of other chores needed his immediate attention: replacing the galvanized tin on the legs of the cache so that even a creature with the cunning ferocity of a wolverine could not climb up the twenty feet to the platform that would hold their meat supply in winter; widening the pool of the spring that trickled alongside the cabin and down into the river—he wanted to make its cool, shadowed area wide enough and deep enough to stock it with trout from the river to keep it bug-free; repairing the rotting front steps of the cabin; shoring up one wall of the root cellar, where blocks of ice cut from Hidden Lake, sledded overland and packed in moss in midwinter, provided what summer refrigeration they had. And, like any suburban homeowner, he faced a session of lawn-mowing, shortening the grass of the clearing with a hand sickle sharpened to machete keenness.

These tasks, while important, would produce no income at all. Jonathan realized that he had to spend more time at the typewriter, either working on magazine pieces or breaking through the block he had encountered on his novel. Unlike Cody, who was steamrolling through the pages of her book, Jonathan was so bogged down in his that he'd started to believe he might not be able to write it, despite the encouraging advance he had received the year before. He had already begun to think about the prospect of having to give the advance back to the publisher, since it did not seem likely he was going to deliver an acceptable manuscript. Of course, he did not have the money to pay back, and every hour he slugged away on his problem-ridden novel, he was losing magazine projects that could earn checks. Meanwhile, he thought, bending down to pull up a stubborn clump of grass, goddamn weeds are growing in my garden.

As he worked, a breeze played across the garden, down the clearing past the trees and the river, toward the mountains beyond the flat open country of tundra and spruce. The cabin sat near the southwestern slope of the Alaska Range; the familiar peaks of Mount Foraker and Mount Russell loomed steeply, shouldered by the smaller ridges and shadowed valleys that hid many of the sheep ranges, one of Jonathan's favorite backcountry destinations. From the Toubok Valley, the white hulking shapes of the nearby mountains were a buttress that hid from view the greatest summit of them all.

Even though they could not see Denali from the cabin, Jonathan and Cody could feel its presence. The knowledge that on any given day they could hike a mile or so up the nearby ridges and have a chance to see the mountain gave them a tremendous sense of well-being.

Jonathan felt the same way about all the Alaskan wilderness. Here in the Toubok Valley, and on up through the Alaska Range and Denali National Park, were some of the finest pieces of wild country in the world. But there was vastly more of Alaska out there than he had touched in his travels for magazine assignments, and he could feel its pull, the wilderness lure he could never deny. All he needed was time, time to come to know it all, piece by piece. For now, just knowing the wild country was there, waiting, was reward in itself.

The native Aleut Islanders called the mainland *Al-ay-ek-sha,* the Great Land. To the first Russians, it was *Alashka.* The beauty of both words was embodied in *Alaska.*

Al-ay-ek-sha. Its wildness and beauty called to the bold and strong. You could starve in the midst of plenty if you did not have the skills to take what you needed from the land. The deep-winter cold was a relentless foe, if you were unprepared for it. In the wilderness isolation, silence could become a shriek in your ears and make your brain feel ready to explode with longing for human contact. The physical toil of walking across the springy tundra or through the mountains could quickly reduce your body to extremes of exhaustion, if you were not fit. The mosquitoes and black flies and no-see-ums could drive you insane. You could drown in fresh or salt water, or under the ice, in thousands of situations where your cries would be heard only by wild creatures, whose normal activities would quickly resume once your screams were silent.

But if you could meet these hardships, and still find your heart lifted by the Great Land, then you were an Alaskan. And the rest of the world was called *Outside.*

Jonathan reached the end of the row of tomato plants and turned his attention to the bush beans. He was anxious to clean up the remaining rows and knock off for a quick swim. The blade of the weeding hoe slashed into the trespassing greenery with a renewed burst of energy. Occasionally Jonathan looked up at the river and the mountains beyond, thinking about his sheep article and his novel and then about the money and time that were running out. Why was there always pressure? he wondered. Even here. And time had a way of slipping

away from you out here on the river. What was that line from
Marcus Aurelius that he'd always liked? "Time is a sort of river
of passing events. . . ." That was it. Out here, time seemed to
have become something that had no meaning, except for events
that actually affected your life. Time was ice-out on Hidden
Lake, or a three-day blizzard that was actually enjoyable from
the snugness of the cabin. Time was a moose hunt for winter
meat, or seeing the first geese and ducks headed for the Arctic
prairies in the spring. Time was when you planted your garden,
or cut and stacked your thirty cords of firewood. The events
flowed on, changing with the seasons, each special in its own
way.

The Tlingit Indians named the twelve moons of the year to
reflect the flow of the wilderness seasons, and Jonathan enjoyed the truth and beauty of their simple calendar.

Now, in June, the Salmon Moon rode the pale evening
skies, pulling the tides that carried multitudinous shoals of
salmon back to their native rivers after two or more years of
wandering the ocean depths. The great fish could sort out the
complex subtleties that made each current different and find
the streams of their birth. Clearing the rapids with spectacular
leaps, they would make their way to the smaller tributaries
where the shallow waters were favorable for spawning. Then,
their mission completed, they would perish. Their rotting bodies would be their final gift to a cycle of renewal that held
together a very complex food chain for a diverse web of creatures.

Although a steep falls far downstream barred the salmon
run from this part of the Toubok, Jonathan and Cody enjoyed
the yearly saga of the returning fish by flying out to other rivers
from time to time, both for sport and to replenish their supply
of the succulent table fare.

Jonathan's interest in the Tlingit calendar was a reflection
of his fondness for all four basic strains of the native Alaska
peoples: the Eskimos, the Aleuts, the Athapascan Indians of
the interior, and the coastal Indians of the southeast.

Of all the coastal tribes, the Tlingits were Jonathan's favorites. They were fabulous fishermen, and they were warriors
when they had to be. When the Russian fur-seekers entered
their lands after virtually enslaving the isolated Aleutian Is-

landers, the Tlingits extracted an awesome price in spilled blood and smashed heads. They were a people dedicated to their tribal customs, and they held nature in reverence.

When nature turned on them with some sudden display of fury, the Tlingits stoically attributed the misfortune to a mysterious power they called *Yek.* At times, *Yek* could be summoned or banished by the shaman, or medicine man, with his chants and prayers. Most forms of *Yek,* however, were totally unpredictable and devastating.

Yek was a pod of killer whales following a run of salmon up a quiet fjord-like bay into the midst of your small fishing boats. *Yek* was a grizzly you thought was dead taking off half your face with a single swipe of a paw.

Like most primitives, the Tlingits believed the earth was flat and the sky a solid vault. The stars were community-house fires. The earth rested on a post supported by "the Old Woman Underneath." She was not beyond the reach of *Yek.*

When the *Yek* was running well, you could expect earthquakes spectacular enough to move mountains; volcanoes whose ash-spewing maws turned daylight to darkness for days and affected the planet's weather; tidal waves that sometimes reached over two hundred feet in height and raced across the ocean to Japan and even Antarctica; avalanches that cut through valleys like scythes.

"Jon!"

The sudden sound of Cody's voice startled Jonathan. He looked up to see her headed down the slope toward him, striding purposefully, her hands jabbed into the pockets of her shorts. Her mouth seemed strangely pursed as she walked, staring at the ground in thought. Her long red hair was tied back with a piece of ribbon, but she ignored the curly pieces that had broken free to fall down over her forehead. She looked up at him as she drew near, wiping back the loose hair with one hand. Her green eyes were angry against her fair, lightly tanned complexion. Without makeup, her strong but pretty features seemed as natural as the outdoors, exuding the sense of health and vitality shaped by the active life she led. Lovely as she was, the problem that now burdened her was obvious in her strained expression, almost as if she were fighting an injury. Jonathan got ready for bad news.

ON DANGEROUS GROUND

"Jon, there was a message for you on the 'North Winds' broadcast. They've sent for us from New York. It's Matt. He's in trouble."

Jonathan Hill slashed the blade of the hoe into the ground and leaned on the handle, grimacing at the sky.

What had just descended upon him was not *Yek*. But in terms of shaking up his life, it would do!

SIX

The newsletter Matt Richardson's secretary, Helen Sullivan, had just put on his desk was like the face of a familiar enemy. He smiled bravely at her, unwilling to show immediate concern even though he could not have been more frightened had he just stepped on a rattlesnake. The folded pages of the imitation typewriter format of *Inside Korner,* the media gossip sheet, unfolded in Matt's hands, ready to strike.

Richardson glanced up at the attractive, silver-haired woman who had been with him throughout his career. He found no reassuring smile, no hint of the cheerful attitude that had bolstered his own sagging spirits so many times in the past. Helen's face was full of concern, just as it had been when she walked through the door. Her fingers fidgeted nervously.

"Helen, I know we have problems," Matt said. "But why the sackcloth and ashes?"

"Don't joke! Read! That just arrived by special messenger."

Richardson shrugged dejectedly, his phony smile melting as he saw that the lead item on the first page appeared under the heading MagWorld.

IT'S POST TIME AT CRAIG!
Matt Richardson faces an uphill battle to gain the coveted chairmanship of Craig Publishing, which is being relinquished by aging czar Anthony Craig, whose surprising plans to retire by year's end were revealed by a Craig source close to *Inside Korner.* Meanwhile, *Matt Richardson's Power Erodes:* Magazine div editorial honcho Richardson, considered a shoo-in for the top spot as early as two years ago after reviving five ailing Craig magazines and turning one *(Charm)* into a hot book, is rumored to have lost his good early speed. Disenchanted Tony Craig covers his earlier bets on Richardson by denying him full

control of the magazine division. Responsibility is split between Richardson and adman Morgan Procter. Full control of the magazine division is the likely stepping stone to Craig's chair. Craig and his twelve-member board may not give their nod to either man.

"Bastard!" Matt shouted without looking up.
"Go on," Helen urged. "It only gets worse."

Weak Stretch Runner: According to some sources, print-oriented Richardson lacks the depth necessary for piloting a company that could become a multimedia giant. Matt built his early reputation by providing the editorial vitality needed by Craig's sagging books. *What Have You Done for Us Lately, Matt?:* Richardson's gamble (with *Charm* charming 'em, why not?) on the first *new* magazine of his career has had disastrous results. *In Wildness* has an elite "wilderness" outdoor slant, unlike hook-and-bullet traditionalists. Critics say the book lacks focus, that the approach is a mishmash that swings from kayaking to environmental sermons. The book lost $7 million the first year out of the gate. . . .

Matt looked at Helen in surprise. "Seven million! It's more like ten."
"Korner was never famous for accuracy," Helen answered.
"When does this hit the street?" Matt asked.
"Tomorrow. That's an advance copy."
Matt could imagine the effect the item would have around town as its fallout spread. Korner was obviously being fed by someone inside Craig Publishing, and Matt's neck was the target.
The item went on:

New Blood Needed: With plans announced for Craig to go public, the withering profits and low-key expansion the company is experiencing under Richardson's influence become critical. The talent-laden Craig Publishing board is loaded with alternatives. Newspaper division chief Jim Vance (axed two dailies, nursed two to health) has poten-

tial. Ditto, in spades, TV-radio's Ben McGraw. With two
VHF and five UHF TV outlets and five radio stations,
McGraw is a strong part of the revenue picture. *Dark
Horse (for Now!): Charm*'s dynamic, beautiful editor/per-
sonality Marla Ashton is someone to watch. The clout that
produced her latest megabucks contract (she almost
changed horses) also landed her a spot on the firm's board.
Inside Korner Predicts: Richardson skid accelerates at key
board meeting this week. Craig dumps *In Wildness*, cuts
losses now! As the broadcasting division's expansion-
minded Ben McGraw might say: the $7 million should have
gone to the tube, not down it.

"Goddammit!" Matt shouted, shredding the newsletter.
"This has Morgan Procter written all over it!"

"But the item took a shot at him, just like it did you. Perhaps one of the other board members—"

Matt dismissed the comment with a wave of his hand.
"That was just to throw everybody off the scent. He's one slick
son-of-a-bitch, that guy. Unless . . ." Matt paused and stood
up. He moved to the edge of the window and stood looking out,
his back to Helen. "Unless it's Tony Craig," he said softly.

"Craig?"

Richardson turned around, his face mirroring sudden new
torment. "If it is Craig, I don't have a chance. Anything I do will
be like committing suicide to keep from getting killed."

"But why? This morning—"

"This morning, he did not exactly throw flowers in my
path," Matt interrupted.

"What will you do? Mr. Craig's out of town."

"I know," Matt said, grimacing. He glanced at his watch.
"Is the board meeting set? Friday?"

"Locked. Ten-thirty."

"Only three days away," Matt sighed. "I feel like I'm heading for the gunfight at the O.K. Corral. Morgan Procter's coming
in with a whole posse totin' shotguns. I've got a single six-
shooter—and I'm not even sure it's loaded."

"Jonathan and Cody should have the message by now.
They could be here tomorrow, if they leave right away. They
won't let you down."

"I hope not. I can't win this one without them."

"You've beaten Procter before; banning the cigarette ads from *In Wildness,* for instance."

"The man is stronger than ever, Helen. This magazine is number one on his hit list."

"Somehow . . . you must stop him."

Matt looked directly into Helen's eyes. He spoke very slowly. "I'll destroy him if I have to."

Helen nodded. In her expression, Richardson perceived something beyond agreement. He knew Helen understood the way he used power, his capacity to be relentless when necessary.

What he saw in her face now was forgiveness.

SEVEN

Horribilis crouched in the shadows of the birch trees, his senses keyed on a shattering sound that moved steadily toward the willow thicket from downriver.

The great bear had heard this noise many times in his life and knew it belonged to a strange thing that lived and hunted in the skies, higher and swifter than any bird, its cries unlike any creature of the forest.

The grizzly sniffed the air in vain as the noise rose to a crescendo. Never had this menace been so close. He was on the brink of fleeing when the floatplane roared over the birches, following the river, in a violent explosion of sound.

Horribilis caught a fleeting glimpse of the sky-thing through the tops of the birches. The sound immediately diminished and steadily grew more faint. The bear remained hidden, expecting the invader to return. Soon the sound was gone. The willow thicket was once again an island of quiet.

The great bear plodded out of the birches and circled the willows, snorting and woofing in agitation. The air was still heavy with the scent of his kill. The new intruder had not tried to feed. Horribilis turned his face toward the sky and roared.

The floatplane looked like a small bird as it passed the far end of Hidden Lake and turned into the wind, dropping steeply toward the open water. Jonathan Hill watched the plane level off just above the surface, the floats appearing animated as they reached down cautiously for the first skimming kiss of the waves.

A wilderness taxi, Jonathan reflected. A limo. You are linked to the outside world, even here. The shore of Hidden Lake was no different than any other commuter platform or airline ramp.

He turned to Cody and Derek, forcing a smile, trying to

hide the sense of loss he was feeling. The few times they had separated like this were during magazine assignments that took him to other parts of Alaska. Sometimes Cody and Derek stayed in Anchorage, visiting friends. Trips to the lower forty-eight were usually taken together.

"I'll check with Matt from Anchorage," Jonathan said. "I may be right back."

"Just do what you think is best," Cody said, smiling.

Jonathan frowned. "If I do have to go to New York, I'll be back in a couple of days. They'll let you know on the radio."

"Don't worry about us." Cody threw an arm around Derek, hugging him close.

Jonathan could not deny the sense of guilt he was feeling, guilt made more intense by Cody's unselfish display of understanding. Earlier, when the radio message summoning them had first arrived, Cody's usually unflagging support had been shaken by anger.

"Just who the hell does he think he is?" Cody had shouted, waving her arms. Her face was livid. "Snaps his fingers, and just like that we're supposed to come running like a couple of lapdogs!"

Jonathan had poked his hoe into the soft soil of the garden in frustration. "I'll just go to Anchorage when the floatplane gets here. One of us has to talk to him on the phone. You know that."

"No! Once he gets you on the phone, he'll have you on a jet to New York so fast you'll think he still owns you."

"Cody, for God's sake. He's your brother."

"That doesn't give him any right to push us like this."

Jonathan could feel his own anger rising then. He felt he could deal with Richardson, and he did not like being hassled, not even by Cody.

"Why don't you come along?" he snapped, bitterly. "You obviously don't trust me to handle this."

"We already know what he wants. He's going to make his ultimate plea."

"I'm not going to take over *In Wildness*. He should know that by now."

"He's got your office ready and your name on the door."

Jonathan chuckled, trying to soften the moment.

Cody grimaced, her eyes blinking. "What's so goddamn funny?"

"It's just ironic. We're talking about one of the most desirable jobs in publishing like it's a prison sentence."

"Go ahead and make jokes about it. But you won't be laughing when you're behind that desk. You've already been there. We both have."

"Matt and I did some nice things together."

"Bullshit! He'd publish *Screw* if he had thought of it first and wouldn't get arrested. You've seen what he did with *Charm.*"

"He had to put some points on the board to earn his shot with *In Wildness.* You know what trying the magazine means to him. Nobody else in town would touch it with a barge pole."

Cody shook her head in blatant rejection. "If he had worked just as hard at launching *In Wildness* as he has at being the Mr. Big of magazine publishing, he would have been successful with the book long ago. But he didn't. So now he's let the whole idea land in the laps of a bunch of pirates who just can't wait to scuttle the ship."

"What else could he do? He needed power to get the backing for the book."

"We could have started small, built slowly," Cody said, pleadingly, as though her idea might yet be tried. "That way we could have stayed in control, made it a family business. But no, his ambition came first."

"You're not being fair. Matt's heart is in the book. I know it is."

"So what are you proposing that we do? Give up the lifestyle we decided on? Go back there and take part in the massacre that's coming? For what? The greater glory of Craig Publishing and Matt Richardson? Thanks, but no thanks. I like what we're doing out here."

"I'm not going back, goddammit!" Jonathan said abruptly. He dropped the hoe and started down the slope toward the river. "But I *am* going for a swim."

The path to the river curved down through the birches, gentling the grade of the hill, the narrow, brush-lined trail laced with exposed roots. At the bottom of the slope, the walking was easier. The trail paralleled the stream through a sunny field of birch brush and willows and then plunged into the shadow of the downstream shoulder of the mountain. The current here was smooth and deceptively slow, as the streambed deepened into a wide pool where the water eddied and swirled below the bluff before curving sharply out of sight downstream. Dry in this season, a ramp of soft sand and small, current-smoothed stones ran out to the edge of the water. Jonathan kicked off his sneakers and unbuckled his shorts. The weight of the heavy belt dropped the khakis to his ankles, and he dove into the river.

The cold was a searing shock and the pressure of the current relentless as he angled upstream and across. When he touched the gravel on the far side, he knifed around quickly and started back, feeling the exertion in his muscles but breathing easily and moving strongly and noisily across the flow. He hit the rocky spit dead on and immediately started another lap across the stream. When he returned this time, he was really aching and breathing harder. He sloshed out onto the bank and sat down at the edge of the current, leaning forward to rest his arms and head against his upraised knees.

Cody was a marvelous woman, and he had been damn lucky to find her. A man like himself could travel a lot of trails, pitch a lot of camps, live and work in a hundred different towns, and never meet anyone like her. The uncertainties of free-lancing, their adventure in wilderness living—she had met these challenges with enthusiasm equal to his own.

But what about Matt? Jonathan wondered. He had already turned his back on his friend and mentor once by giving up the *In Wildness* editorship. Another rejection would wipe out whatever kinship had survived from the good times they had shared. It had been Richardson who had taught him the craft, not only editing and publishing but writing as well. Because of Matt, he had found Cody and started building the life both he and she truly wanted.

"And I left Matt hanging as his reward," he said softly, talking to himself. "Just when he needed me the most."

He heard a sudden noise and looked back toward the path to see Cody. She seemed amazingly changed, smiling and whistling some scrap of a tune as she walked toward him. She was carrying the rolled-up tube of a foam backpacking sleeping pad.

Jonathan's heart leaped. Everything was going to be all right.

Still whistling, Cody smiled at him mischievously, untied the cords on the ends of the pad, and let it unroll across the ground.

"Tell me something," Jonathan said, smiling. "How come they call you 'Cody'?"

She laughed aloud. The question was their favorite private joke. " 'Cause I was born here, dummy . . . in Cody, Wyoming," she chuckled.

Whistling again, Cody kicked off her moccasins, then pulled her shorts and panties down over her thighs in one quick motion. She unbuttoned her shirt, revealing bra-less, appealing breasts, tossed the garment aside, and eased down onto the pad. Her arms went out to pull Jonathan to her, and as his lips pressed against hers, she whispered, "Welcome to Cody, cowboy."

Later, dried and clothed after a romp in the river, they lay on their backs on the foam, looking up at the high arch of the sky and listening to the murmur of the current. The light, pleasant breeze that had blown in since the storm that morning provided a respite from mosquitoes and played tricks with the long set of rapids five twisting miles of river upstream, a tumbling, seething torrent of white water. Once in a while, a trace of the booming sound would descend, borne cross-country by the wind, then disappear, carried away to some other part of the river.

"That was a lovely surprise," Jonathan said.

"Just a little something to remember me by when you're in New York."

"I'm not going to New York, woman."

"You'll go. And you were right—you have to. Just promise me one thing." She curled against him and put her head on his chest. "Don't agree to anything that we don't talk over."

"If I go, why don't you come too?"

"I want to stay here. The garden needs tending, it's a nice time, and my writing is going okay. We'll be all right."

"Come with me—to Anchorage anyway."

ON DANGEROUS GROUND

"We were just there, two weeks ago. I'll hang on here. Don't worry about us."

"If you go to the Tolkats', take the .375 magnum."

John Tolkat and his wife, Kichna, both Talkeetna Indians, were their downstream neighbors, homesteading a piece of land they had occupied since John had worked as a guide for the outfitter whose cabin Jonathan and Cody had rented. Over sixty now, his children moved to the cities, Tolkat devoted his time to trapping, fishing, and occasionally guiding hunters and fishermen. Cody loved to visit Kichna and share her amazing fund of lore and skills, and Jonathan frequently ran the trapline with the older woodsman during the winter.

"I promise I'll take the gun. Actually, I don't think there are many bears on this river. No salmon. Besides, they're so shy and wary that you never see them . . . like your special friend. What'd you call him?"

"Horribilis."

"Ursus horribilis," Cody said. "How marvelously expressive the Latin names of some creatures are. But you didn't actually see him."

"No," Jonathan answered. "But wait until you see the photographs I made. With a track that clear, it doesn't take much imagination to form a mental picture of the guy. He has to be monstrous in size."

"Sexist," Cody teased. "How do you know it wasn't a female?"

"Too big. Male grizzlies are larger." Jonathan looked upstream, reliving the chilling sense of fear that had swept over him the moment he first spotted the tracks.

"Are you going back to look for him?" Cody asked.

"Maybe. I have a curious feeling about doing it, though, like perhaps I should leave him alone. If I did get some shots and publish something, some cretinous bastard would try to find him and kill him." Jonathan turned back to Cody, his gaze resting again on her face. "Anyway, I don't think we'll see old Horribilis down here. We're well out of his probable range."

"I'm more worried about Matt's probable range," Cody answered.

"I can handle Matt."

"He has plans for you. I just know it."

"I'll take the money and run."

Cody was quiet for a moment. Jonathan languished in the softness of her tightening embrace. Her lips touched his neck, flickered softly, then pulled away.

"Jon . . ."

"Ummm?"

"Do you feel guilty about Matt and *In Wildness*?"

"Why should I?"

"But do you think you made a mistake . . . pulling out?"

"I couldn't help it. When we started tooling up the book, I began to realize what a chore administering a big-time magazine would be for me. The details, the corporate bullshit, the cover-your-ass memos, the hand-holding the staff needs, the hassles with advertisers, the endless production harangues! I wouldn't have been any good to Matt or the book. I'm a photographer and writer. I belong in the field."

Cody's eyes searched his, questioning. "It's just that if going back is what you really want, I don't want to hold you here."

"Nothing's changed," Jonathan said quickly. "I just want to see what Matt has to say. I'm nervous about the way I'm floundering around with my book. And our money is running out."

"We have another year here, regardless of the money. After that . . ."

"After that," Jonathan interrupted, "at least one of our book projects has to work out, or we're in trouble. When Derek starts school, I'm not going to open the mailbox with a prayer every day, hoping for free-lance checks to keep us alive. I guess I'll have to go back to my dad's newspaper."

"Jon, try not to worry about the money. We'll always have the home ranch, with Matt."

"It's too expensive to operate such a small spread. You know we can't make it pay out a decent income."

"Yeah, but it's a great place to live and work. We wouldn't need much income to get by." Cody's face seemed to shine with sincerity and enthusiasm over the idea.

"We have to have some kind of base—something we can count on. I've thought about guiding and outfitting in Wyoming. Maybe some kind of wilderness skills school for young people. Backcountry living . . . mountaineering . . . camping in summer . . . cross-country skiing in winter. I could always go on the chicken-and-peas circuit, lecturing and showing my slides. I don't know."

"What about right here?"

"We can't buy this place. There's just no way."

"I mean Alaska."

Jonathan stared at her, raising himself on an elbow. "You feel it too," he said, smiling. "You would hate to give it up."

"I think we should talk about it, see if there's a way to make it happen."

"The land withdrawals have knocked out homesteading. Anything worth buying is going to come at a dear price."

"As you said, one of our books might make it. And you have a lot of magazine contacts."

"Only for eating money," Jonathan sighed.

"Money's not everything. It's really not."

"No, but feeding my family and providing a place to live are pretty high on my list."

"Hey," Cody teased. "Where's my Earth Day radical? The fellow out to slay the corporate dragons who are spewing poison into the air and water and driving off the buffalo?"

Jonathan laughed. "He ran into a windmill. Got some sense knocked into him."

"And what does he believe in now?"

"Oh, he's still armed and dangerous. It's just that he doesn't march. He believes in Kodachrome 64 and High-Speed Ektachrome. Also double-spacing and typing on one side of the paper only."

"And avoiding clichés like the plague," Cody whispered. Her lips touched Jonathan's softly. Their tears mingled in the fullness of their embrace.

Cody watched as the floatplane taxied in slowly. Close to the shore, the engine was cut. The prop windmilled for a moment, then was still as the plane drifted into the shallows.

Jonathan reached down and picked up Derek. "What should I bring you, lad?"

"A Yankee cap," Derek squealed, touching the Stetson cowboy hat he was wearing.

Jonathan smiled and put Derek down. Cody opened her

arms as Jon reached for her. She could feel the strength of his shoulders through the suede-leather jacket he wore. She played a hand over his chest, straightening the collar of his turtleneck, then moved her fingers through his long hair. "Better do something about this hair, if you have time," she chided. "Needs a professional job."

Jonathan's lips answered with a lingering kiss. He pulled away. "I can handle New York—Matt and the whole crowd. If I go, I'll be back soon." He reached down for his briefcase and a compact carry-on suitcase. Toiletries and his single good suit were inside.

A shout echoed from the floatplane. "Hey, hoss, them New York people coulda saved me a trip if they had called yesterday." Red Mullins was standing on a float of the Cessna, coaxing the ship toward the shore with a paddle.

"I thought you were flying up north," Jonathan called. "Trying to get what's left of the Pipeline money."

"Naw, man," Mullins answered. "Company's still got me playing taxi out of Anchorage, hauling everything from drunk Indians to fellers like that damn fool pilgrim I brought out here yesterday."

"Who was that?" Jonathan queried.

"A backpacker. Sierra Club type. Dropped him off down at Loon Lake. Supposed to pick him up at Rock Lake next week."

"What's wrong with that?" Cody asked. "That's a nice trek."

"Damn fool didn't have a gun," Red shouted, his voice loud and angry as the plane coasted through the shallows and slid to a stop beside the shore. "I offered him mine, but he wouldn't take it."

"That's not smart," Jonathan said. He turned to Cody and pointed at the .375 Winchester magnum rifle they had carried over the quarter-mile portage trail from the cabin. The gun rested against a rock beside the trail. "That reminds me, Cody. Don't go anywhere without that!"

Cody snapped off a smart military salute without speaking.

"You folks haven't seen anything of that guy, have you?" Mullins asked.

Jonathan and Cody shook their heads. Red looked toward the horizon that hid the downriver part of the Toubok. "He ain't hardly had time to get this far," he said. "I flew kinda low along the river on the way in here, thinking I might see him. But I didn't."

"I'll probably run into him," Cody said. "He has to pass the cabin to get to Rock Lake."

"I just hope that cheechako knows what he's doing," Red said. He shrugged his shoulders. "It's a free country—even for idiots."

Mullins handed Cody a foot-thick package of mail, including magazines and newspapers. "That's all there is since you were in last."

Cody took the bundle eagerly, already anticipating the pleasure of poring over the letters and reading material. Jonathan bent his face to hers and pecked her on the lips. "See you later," he said. He patted Derek on the shoulder. "Take care of Mommie, squirt." Cody felt the child hold her leg tightly. "Bye-bye, Daddy," Derek chirped.

Buck scrambled along the shore, his patrol of the surroundings completed. Jonathan rubbed his wet hassling muzzle and turned to leave.

Cody watched Jonathan ease carefully along the float on the passenger side of the aircraft and lift his baggage into the hold area behind the back seat. The plane turned sideways as Mullins pushed the craft toward deeper water. Cody could not see Jonathan as he climbed into the plane on the opposite side. Mullins got behind the controls and closed the door. He started the engine and turned the ship toward open water. The prop wash and the sound of the engine created a maelstrom that engulfed the shoreline. Cody held Derek's hand and her hair as she squinted toward the plane. She could barely see Jonathan as he twisted to look back and wave.

The engine revved up and the plane splashed ahead with the wind, slowly at first, then with the floats skipping over the waves at speed. The plane taxied for what seemed to be a long time, then turned into the wind for takeoff. The sound of the engine grew steadily as the plane picked up speed and lifted from the surface. Climbing over the lake, the Cessna banked and soared on out of sight over the spruce hills.

"Daddy, bye-bye," Derek yelled, waving his little hand.

Cody felt a tightening in her throat and the beginning of tears. Okay, admit it, she said to herself. The show of strength she had maintained for Jonathan was over. Saying goodbye out here was not the same as in other places. The loneliness, the sense of loss, were profound.

Derek was tugging at Cody's hand, pulling her toward the trail to the cabin. This will pass, she told herself. If Jon had not been camping in the sheep ranges for the past four days, this dark mood would not have struck. Their lovemaking under the open sky had been intensely moving and erotic. The satisfaction still lingered, a mental imprint of Jonathan's urgent thrusts, her own loins melting into his, her legs holding him, pulling him, urging him toward possessing and being possessed.

Now she had lost him for a while. Matt had taken him away, and there was not a damn thing she could do about it. Poor Jon. He was going to be under a lot of pressure back there in New York. Matt wasn't going to give up without a fight. Over the years, she had watched her brother overcome every obstacle in his path, from breaking broncs, to working his way through college, to rising to superstar status in the magazine publishing business. He did these things with a combination of talent and sheer brute effort, the same kind of brute effort that had served their late parents in wresting a living from the harsh high-country ranchlands.

When she and Jonathan had last seen Matt, while skiing over the Christmas holidays, he had already begun to fear for the future of *In Wildness.* The luxurious chalet Matt rented for them at Vail was the setting of furious arguments as he tried to talk them into returning to New York. Cody had been shocked over the obvious stress Matt was feeling: his marriage a mess, the new magazine in trouble, enough problems with all the other Craig magazines to occupy any normal executive. At times while they were together, Cody had to fight very hard to quell a basic desire to please her big brother, to see him happy again. Nevertheless, she and Jonathan had stood firm: Matt was asking too much. Had the magazine truly been *theirs*—a family business, the way she wanted it to be—things might have been different. But Matt had blown that opportunity seven years before when he became Tony Craig's hired gun.

ON DANGEROUS GROUND

The only thing positive about those seven years, as far as she
was concerned, had been the opportunity to meet Jonathan.
After they had met and fallen in love, everything seemed simple. If Matt wanted to lift that bar and tote that bale for Craig
Publishing, fine. The life she and Jonathan wanted was out
here, and they damned well weren't going to give it up.

"Let's go home, partner," Cody told Derek. She lifted the
mail by the cord that wrapped the pile and picked up the rifle.
Buck raced up the trail, ranging ahead. Derek skipped alongside as she started up the path, climbing through a stand of
birches.

She missed seeing Matt, Cody thought, but not in New
York. Why hadn't he come out for some fishing, or hiking?
Couldn't the man relax—ever? Perhaps Jonathan could cheer
him up. Perhaps there would be a way, after all, for Jonathan to
help with the magazine without actually working in New York.
The next few days would tell. They would be lonely days, filled
with anxiety over what was happening in New York.

She wasn't worried about herself and Derek, really. She
knew how to live in the wilderness. If an emergency did occur,
their Indian neighbors' shortwave radio was always available.
The Tolkats' doors were never locked, and Cody knew how to
operate the set.

Tomorrow she might pay the Tolkats a visit, Cody reflected. She could call Anchorage and check on Jonathan. A
day with their Indian neighbors would be a perfect way to pass
some time during Jonathan's absence. The tall tales and animal
legends the Tolkats told so convincingly were filled with lore
and natural wisdom few books could equal. Their skin as
brown as pine spills, their faces creased by the lash of weather
during untold years in the wilderness, the Tolkats were part of
a disappearing Alaska, lost to the white man's ways and his
money.

She thought ahead to the work waiting for her in the cabin.
She expected to be finished with her book in a few weeks. The
godsend of an acceptance check had been in her thoughts often
lately. She had been hoping to finish a chapter on sourdough
bread today.

Suddenly, an inspiration struck her. She thought of the

backpacker Red Mullins had mentioned. When the guy showed up at the cabin, she would treat him to some of her sourdough pancakes.

His reaction might be useful for the book.

EIGHT

By now he should have been over the Haul Road.

Sonny Youngblood laid aside the map he had been scanning and leaned forward expectantly, squinting against the glare that slanted through the cockpit of the Jet-Ranger helicopter. Tiers of low hills stretched toward the horizon, their flanks dark in the face of the late-evening sun. He lifted his sunglasses and rested them on his forehead, rubbing the callused indentations that years of constant use had left on the bridge of his nose.

Can't see with 'em on, can't see with 'em off, he thought.

Blinking painfully, he continued to search the strange pattern of light and shadow that was the vastness ahead. It'll be pretty hard to miss something that cuts the whole damn state of Alaska in half, he laughed to himself, and just then he spotted the truck.

It was weird, he thought, how one of those big old Macks looked like a tiny bug when you saw it from so far away, barely moving through the stark hills that seemed to belong on the moon. A rooster-tail of dust arched steeply in the truck's wake and hung over the road for hundreds of yards in a stubborn contrail. The real moon rode full and bright on the desolate horizon, as if its presence were a reminder that this land was indeed a part of the real world, and a man had better get used to it.

Deftly maneuvering the pitch control, he sent the Jet-Ranger chopper into a steep descent without reducing power. He watched the altimeter needles sweep downward through the numbers. Out of two thousand. Out of one thousand. Finally he leveled off, skimming the sparse tundra, the crest of a ridge looming ahead. He held the machine just above the ground as he followed the gentle incline of the slope; the sense of speed was exhilarating at 120 miles an hour. The summit of the ridge grew into a dark wall that filled the horizon, then flashed past in an instant blur. The broad valley stretched away to form the pass through the distant ridges. He kicked in some left rudder and turned slightly toward the valley's open, undulating reach.

This low, he could no longer see the road, but he kept the truck's rising plume in sight as he thundered ahead. Suddenly, from a slight depression, three caribou clambered onto a knob of higher ground, then paused to look back toward the strange sound that had startled them. The chopper whipped directly over the frightened beasts as they broke into a run, their antlerless heads almost colliding with the aircraft's skids. In autumn, when their antlers towered three feet over their heads, they would have been hit.

"Run, you bastards!" the pilot yelled, beginning a banking climb. Then, thinking of the late hour, he sent the ship back toward the ground and once again was beating along in a straight line to intercept the distant truck.

Hell, he'd done so much of that stuff anyway that it was getting old—hassling caribou and moose, wolves in winter. Some of the boys flying choppers up here had been caught doing it, but that was because they were fools, not picking the right time and place. A little proficiency run—that's the way he looked at it. Target of opportunity. He'd never hurt any of the animals, either, just chased 'em a bit, trying to get back the old feeling but knowing all along that nothing would ever be like Nam. Even now he could feel the Huey Cobra's swift attack approach, shuddering as the rockets and guns clattered and exploded, the air filled with the smell of cordite, the taste of fear like copper in his mouth. Two tours of it, that was enough. When he'd left, he was as tired of the place itself as he was of the combat.

Soon he was close enough to make out the green cab of the truck and the dark, dust-covered tarp that covered the load of the flatbed trailer. Beyond was the Pipeline itself, twelve feet above the ground, resting on vertical support mounts. The 48-inch-diameter pipe sliced directly south through the hills, a long glowing thread, passing to infinity.

The pilot began a hard, steep bank, gaining altitude. At

2,000 feet he leveled off, parallel to the Pipeline and the Haul Road, where the truck bored ahead on its dusty journey.

He glanced at his compass, easing in a touch of left rudder to center the needle, then quickly scanned the instrument panel. The dials, gauges, and amber lights showed no anomalies in the pattern he expected. Satisfied, he reached for a cigarette, lit it, and turned back to the window. His face glowed in the late-evening sun that was splashing its light from a low cloud bank as it dipped toward the horizon.

Despite the late hour and his aching back, Sonny Youngblood was as happy as he had ever been in his tumultuous thirty-five years. Beyond the steeper, shadowed hills ahead was Fairbanks, where he would be taking on a plum of a mission. For the next four days he was assigned to haul some big wheel from the public relations office of T.A.P. and a magazine editor from New York on a wilderness fishing expedition to the Toubok River. Youngblood had been to the Toubok before and had enjoyed fantastic fishing. The stream flowed through a remote valley near the Alaska Range, and its lack of easy access protected it from the overfishing that had occurred on many rivers in Alaska.

Since Youngblood only read *Playboy* and *Penthouse,* he had never heard of the magazine—something called *In Wildness*—but it was obvious to him that the guy had clout. If this fellow could get the company to deal over a Jet-Ranger for a sideshow like fishing, more power to him. He hoped they would all get along and that he wouldn't be treated like a hired hand while they were in the field. He was really looking forward to getting into the timbered valleys around the Alaska Range, with snow-capped mountains looming all around. He was tired of the stark mountains of the Brooks Range and the Arctic barrens: the constant searching winds, the dullness of the land, the bugs. He had been flying up there for several weeks, in and out of Prudhoe Bay, where the crude oil pumped into the Pipeline began its eight-hundred-mile journey across the northern slope of the Brooks Range and straight on down through the center of Alaska to the port of Valdez.

The fishing trip assignment was indicative of the edge he had gained on his fellow chopper pilots during the ten years he had been flying for Nor-Air in support of T.A.P. and other contractors affiliated with Alyeska, the Alaska Pipeline consortium. Early on, he had built a reputation for being able to handle the most difficult missions. "He'll fly when the birds are walking," his dispatcher was fond of saying, and it was true. During a blinding snowstorm he had airlifted a trucker whose appendix had ruptured at a Haul Road camp deep in the Brooks Range. He had brought the guy to the Prudhoe Bay airfield, where an airplane evacuated him to the hospital in Fairbanks. That one had made the newspapers, and he still treasured the clippings.

His proficiency and good fortune in Alaska had enabled him to sock away $150,000.

As far as Sonny Youngblood could see, this whole Pipeline deal was a bonanza for anybody lucky enough to get on board. But most of the early Pipeliners had pissed it away on whores and whiskey, looking for a good time after working twelve hours a day, seven days a week, for six-week stretches. Then, too, there had been the dumb shits who came with their wives and kids to live in trailers and motor homes and have everything they made be burned up by inflation. For Sonny, the pleasure came in watching his bank account grow, bullshitting with his aviator buddies, and occasionally visiting a discreet social club in Fairbanks that catered to a select clientele with a bevy of decent-looking ladies, all good sports.

Youngblood had never expected to stay in Alaska this long. When the Pipeline was completed in '77, he'd thought he would go back to Texas and hire on in crop-dusting again. But the flying opportunities and the money were too good for him to turn away, despite the fact that he was sick of the place: daylight all summer; near-darkness all winter; 65-below temperatures that could make metal bars snap like pieces of wood and sear the skin off a bare hand unlucky enough to touch metal; clouds of mosquitoes; endless wilderness waiting to swallow you if you screw up just a little bit; nothing to do but to work and drink and bullshit; worthless goddamn Eskimos and Indians.

When he got around to leaving, he wouldn't miss the white people up here, either, that was for damn sure. The white Alaskans resented the Pipeliners like all get-out, even though some of the two-faced bastards had raked in a lot of Pipeline money.

Hell, he was just trying to do a job. He couldn't see any call for the kinds of signs many people in Fairbanks and Anchorage had stuck on the bumpers of their vehicles during the height of the Pipeline construction. Like: HAPPINESS IS 10,000 TEXANS HEADED SOUTH CARRYING AN OKIE UNDER EACH ARM.

Fuck 'em!

Time to alert Nor-Air's Fairbanks base of his approach. When his passengers arrived, he intended to fly them straight down to the company's Fox River camp near the Alaska Range, despite the late hour. While the good weather held, he wanted to make the most of it. At Fox River, they could get a steak and a drink and some sleep and only be an hour away from the Toubok. A short hop tomorrow would put them on the river.

Adjusting the radio and looking out the side window, he saw the Haul Road and the Pipeline stretching into the dusky distance.

Curiously, in that slant of evening light the metal cylinder seemed to possess the soft luminance of pure gold, freshly panned.

2

ALASKA
AND
NEW YORK
JUNE 22–24

NINE

The engines revved higher in a final surge of power as the arc of the sinking jet flattened. Jonathan Hill saw the water the plane was skimming suddenly become a blur of concrete, and instantly he felt the jolt of the tires. The nose of the jet floated at a cocked angle for a moment, then it too thudded down, and the snarl of reversed engines thrust Jonathan against his seatbelt. The plane lurched to a near-stop, then eased into a left turn alongside the Grand Central Parkway. From his window, Jonathan watched the color and glint of rush-hour traffic. He was back.

As the plane taxied toward the gate, Jonathan flipped through the pages of the copy of *In Wildness* he had been studying. He stared at the grizzly on the cover, the sense of exhilaration he usually felt from seeing his own work in print dulled by the anxiety he was feeling about the magazine.

So he had been summoned to take over the book. Well, he damn well would not do it! Despite their friendship and family ties, he would urge Matt to find someone more suitable to clean up the mess. He planned to offer whatever advice he could, try to peddle some of his own editorial wares around town, then shove off for home. He had already lost the first round of the confrontation; he should not be here at all. Why had he been so weak when he had talked to Richardson on the phone from Anchorage the previous evening? As Cody had predicted it would, his resistance had crumbled and he had been pulled meekly along by Matt's appeal.

Jonathan stirred uneasily in his seat as he thought about the next two days. Turning Matt down wasn't going to be easy, but it had to be done. Coming back to a structured life in New York would seem devastating after the freedom of living so close to nature. Surely Matt could see that. Surely he possessed the power and skill to save *In Wildness* without demanding such a sacrifice.

A few minutes later, his briefcase and bag in hand, Jonathan ambled down the concourse toward the LaGuardia taxi stand. He felt acutely conscious of the fellow passengers who crowded the corridor with him, and he could sense the tension of the business people who scurried ahead, eager to do their thing in Manhattan. He eyed a bank of telephones and thought of calling Richardson, when he suddenly saw Matt striding toward him.

Matt's face glowed with pleasure as he grasped Jonathan's hand. "I was about to walk right past you, kid. You look different—sort of like an old bear."

Jonathan laughed. "You wouldn't say that if you had ever seen one of the real bears, up on the river in Alaska."

"They're easy," Matt joked. "Wait until you see the kind of predators we've got around here. Ours wear disguises."

"How are you, Matt?" Jonathan asked warmly.

Richardson shrugged. "You know me. I'm nothing if not a survivor."

"You didn't sound too good on the phone."

"I feel better now that you're here." He picked up Jonathan's bag. "Let's race on, kid. Things are happening."

As they walked toward the exit, Jonathan brought Matt up to date on Cody and Derek and life on the river. Richardson listened politely, but seemed preoccupied, even when Jonathan told him about the grizzly track he had recently photographed.

"I'll get the shots developed today," Jonathan said. "Might even make a cover."

"Hope it works better than the shot we've got on the cover now," Matt replied dejectedly.

"Newsstand sales still lousy?" Jonathan said.

Matt stopped and turned to Jonathan, his expression revealing great weariness and inner torment. "It's more serious than that, kid. They're trying to put me out of business."

"What do you mean?"

"Come on," Matt said, walking ahead. "Let's talk in the car."

At curbside, a uniformed driver took Jonathan's bags and placed them in the back of a long black limousine.

"VIP treatment today," Matt said.

"A pickup truck would have seemed a luxury to me," Jonathan joked.

When they had settled into the rich plushness of the car, Matt reached into his breast pocket for a folded sheet of paper. He tapped the document nervously as he said, "Here's the game plan. We'll go straight to the Plaza and check you in. You can catch a nap if you want, but as soon as you feel up to it, I'd like you to get over to the *In Wildness* offices."

"Walsh will pass out," Jonathan interrupted. "Or maybe jump out the window."

Matt shook his head. "He's not there. He's in Alaska, of all places. Some kind of oil company junket to the Pipeline."

"That's amazing," Jonathan said.

"The way my luck has been running, I'm happy your planes didn't run into each other. Never mind him. Maybe he'll go native on us. Save me from firing him."

"What do you want me to do?"

"Talk to the staff. Look over the inventory and whatever layouts they've got. Stay at it as long as it takes. I can't be with you this evening or tomorrow morning. I thought we'd meet at '21' tomorrow for lunch. You can give me your report then."

"I still don't know what I'm looking for?"

"I'll take any opinions you can give me on the reasons this magazine is about to go under," Matt said sternly.

Jonathan slumped back in his seat. So it *was* bad. Far worse, really, than he had expected.

"You'd better read this right away," Matt said, handing him the folded paper. Jonathan immediately noticed that the format of *Inside Korner* had not changed while he had been in Alaska. He looked at Matt questioningly. Richardson nodded toward the paper and turned to gaze out the window.

Jonathan started to read as Matt fidgeted nervously.

"Seven million!" Jonathan exclaimed, as he looked up from the paper. "Matt, I had no idea."

"It's more like ten," Richardson said. "Now you know why I was so desperate to see you."

"You think that by telling the board meeting you have a new editor, they're going to say, 'Oh, then everything's fine'? Come on, Matt. These people want blood!"

"I just may be able to hold 'em off," Matt said, "unless Tony Craig has been lying to me. But *you've* got to be on board. My entire program for saving the book is based upon you . . . and the film."

"What film?"

"It's the pilot for the *In Wildness* television show. You'll see it tomorrow. I'm convinced that if we can get that show on the air nationwide, and have you at the helm of the book, we'll turn this thing around. Anyway, that's what I'm going to tell them at the board meeting—once I finish begging for mercy."

"How far along is this TV thing?"

"Everything's set to go: the pilot's made, the stations are lined up but not signed, the prospects are good for selling time. But the company has to put up $500,000 to get it off the ground."

"No way will they do it," Jonathan said, shaking his head.

"They might feel they have to. We're in pretty deep already. Anyway, the film will sell itself."

"I don't see how it will make all that much difference."

"We need exposure. I'm convinced that we've done a lousy PR job. People just don't know we're out there! Once we're on that goddamned tube, they'll come running."

"Well, you don't need me for that," Jonathan said.

"Oh, but I do," Matt replied. "We're going to build the thing around *you.*"

Jonathan looked at Matt in surprise and exasperation. "You've been in the city too long, Matt. Why don't we turn this car around and head for the mountains together so you can clear your head?"

Richardson leaned forward, his face hard and stern. "I couldn't be more serious. The book needs a personality people can identify with: a Hugh Hefner, a Helen Gurley Brown, a Marla Ashton. And you're elected! Other than John McPhee, there isn't a person alive who can match the combination of your wilderness experience and writing skills."

"The role you're describing has no appeal to me whatsoever. I say what I have to say with a camera and a typewriter."

Matt shrugged, leaning back, easing the tension. "From what you told me on the phone, your muse has gone a-courting elsewhere. Are you hopelessly blocked in your novel?"

"The story line I was developing has taken me into the Black Hole. It's 100 to 1 that I'll have to pay back the advance."

"You're too close to it out there in the mountains. You'd be better off letting the story cool awhile, then working on it back here."

"That's too high a price," Jonathan laughed.

"How about a great big sack of money?" Matt asked in seriousness. "Aren't you and Cody tired of living like gypsies?"

"If you could live the life we lead for one month, you'd know the answer to that question," Jonathan replied.

Matt sighed wearily. "My appeals do not end here. A lot can happen in the next few days—things that may make you change your mind."

"No way," Jonathan said quickly, but congenially.

They sat quietly for a moment, staring out the windows. The car was halted in traffic on the Queensboro. Past the stanchions of the bridge, upstream toward Hellgate, the wake of a tugboat cut the gunmetal gleam of the East River.

Jonathan wondered about Kristen and Marla Ashton. He started to ask Matt about them, then paused. He was beginning to feel the effects of his long journey, made longer by two plane changes to get the only seats available. Suddenly he wanted to sleep, and he did not wish to squander his reserve energies. There was work to be done. Perhaps he *could* contribute some fresh thinking to the magazine, help Matt in that way at least.

Ted Walsh's absence was actually a stroke of good fortune, Jonathan reflected. The man's head was as good as on the block, and a direct confrontation would have been unpleasant.

Poor Ted, thought Jonathan. He was a nice enough guy, really. And his book on dams had been an honest and distinguished piece of journalism. Even so, he did not possess the credentials for piloting a big-league magazine. And what, in the name of God, was he up to in Alaska?

TEN

Ted Walsh slumped across the bench-type rear seat of the Jet-Ranger helicopter, his head resting on a rolled-up down jacket as he tried to will away the tide of nausea that had been rising in this throat all morning. The two long pulls he had secretly taken from a bottle of vodka before taking off from the base at Fox River had not offset the hangover produced by steady drinking during the long flight from New York the previous evening.

Walsh's host seemed to be faring much better. Jack Burke of T.A.P. sat beside the pilot, gesturing and talking excitedly while Sonny Youngblood put the Jet-Ranger through demonstrations of steep, sharp turns and ground-skimming maneuvers. The aviator had met the two men at Fairbanks in what should have been the middle of the night. The constant light was so disconcerting to Walsh that he had slept very little before their early morning departure for the Toubok.

Despite his abject misery, Walsh suffered his condition silently. He cupped a hand over his upturned eyes, the dimness soothing for a moment. The stabbing pain behind his temples continued, however, seemingly synchronized with the thud of the rotor.

Walsh's rest was interrupted by a sudden darkening within the ship, as though a curtain had been pulled. He took his hand from his eyes in time to see the blue sweep of the sky disappear from the window, to be replaced instantly by the immense wall of a mountain sweeping past, distressingly close. They had penetrated the pass.

"Hey, Ted. You've got to see this!" Burke shouted over his shoulder.

Wearily but dutifully, Walsh rose and leaned to the front between his companions. The glare from towering, snow-covered peaks seared painfully across his vision. He blinked, rubbing his eyes, then gasped as he focused on the view ahead.

A mere hundred yards away on both flanks, the sides of the mountains fell away from the high snowfields into jumbled masses of ice-rimmed boulders and sheer rock ledges that hung over glacier canyons. Blue in the shadows, the rivers of glacier ice pitched steeply toward jagged walls of brush that seemed to be creeping up the slopes, feeding on the moisture from above, spreading patches of alder, willow, and birch brush across the faces of the mountains. The deeply cut gorges of ice disappeared into the bands of brush for a distance, then emerged as braided rivulets that splashed down the lower slopes. On the floor of the valley, a milky, silty river twisted through barren banks of sand and gravel, veined by the tumbling cataracts from above.

"This here's called 'Misty Pass,' " Youngblood shouted as he pointed to the almost imperceptible break in the ridges ahead. "Takes us right through the range out onto the Toubok River valley on the other side."

"She's a narrow fucker!" Burke exclaimed. "You sure we can make it?"

"Don't worry. I've made this run before."

Walsh eased back to once more lie across the seat. Burke turned to him. "Still feeling lousy?"

"I've had better days."

"You'll perk up once we get on the river," Burke said. "Wait until one of those big rainbows runs the line right off your reel. *Zrrrrrr.*" Burke's hand turned in a gesture of reeling in a fish.

Although there was plenty of room for the chopper to negotiate the pass, Youngblood took the first two turns by banking the aircraft on its side, to his and Burke's delight. Walsh continued to suffer silently. Back in level flight, the pilot pointed out a smaller canyon, spurring off to the right.

"Dead end up there," Youngblood shouted. "That's how you can buy the farm in these passes. Sometimes, too, the wind comes shooting out of these side-draws like a bat out of hell. Flipped one old boy right over on his back. Didn't get the bodies out for days."

"Just forget the stunts and get us out on the other side!"

Walsh's irritation had grown into anger. He bolted into an up-right position. "How much longer in this crap?"

" 'Bout ten minutes," the pilot said, coolly.

"Hell, Ted," Burke called over his shoulder. "This is enough fun to sell tickets."

"Not to me," Walsh said, slumping back on the seat again.

They thudded deeper into the pass without conversation. Burke raised a 35 mm camera and started shooting, the motor-drive attachment whirring in the cockpit like some insect.

Midway into Misty Pass, the Jet-Ranger encountered pock-ets of unstable mountain air that alternately caused the craft to sink or rise several feet with dramatic suddenness. To Ted Walsh, still slumped across the rear seat, each tremor that shook the chopper was the signal for a new wave of nausea.

Goddamn Burke. The endless succession of brandies the T.A.P. public relations man had shoved in front of Walsh dur-ing the flight from New York was now having its inevitable kickback. Ted's head throbbed. His mouth was tainted with a sour reek.

Walsh cursed his weakness. Why couldn't he have resisted and let the steady whisper of the jet's engines lull him to sleep? When he had finally closed his eyes, trying to escape Burke's views on the Pipeline and the environment in general, Jack had responded with a fresh round of drinks, saying, "Come on, Ted. Just one more. Hell, we've hit Dodge City . . . end of the cattle drive. Time to shake off the dust and relax." He had taken a sip of his cognac and added, "Guess I'm used to it—seeing that corrupt politicians or boozing writers have a good time. If I do my job right, I'll end up needing a new liver." He had laughed heartily at his own gag.

Burke's Pipeline spiel ran through the standard catalog of pap Walsh had been hearing for fifteen years: the country des-perately needed oil, the Pipeline was providing it. Alaskans needed jobs, new Pipeline activity would be a boon for the economy. The environmental safeguards that had gone into the construction were disaster-proof; only a couple minor incidents of spillage had occurred. Under the weight of the brandy and Burke's droning monologue, Ted had sunk deeper into worry and depression. He was feeling anxious about accepting the favor of this fishing trip as part of the Pipeline junket, for he truly despised the idea of running the kind of milksop piece such a gift was supposed to buy. Walsh felt that regardless of how carefully the Pipeline had been built—whether or not it spilled a drop of oil in a hundred years—the Haul Road along-side it was a dagger through the finest wilderness in the world. From the base established by the road, the tentacles of civiliza-tion would ultimately spread in every direction, feeding on and ruining a land of unequaled beauty.

Walsh knew his opinions about the Pipeline and the new threat of further exploration weren't going to be changed by this junket. The piece he should be running in *In Wildness* would speak against the devastation still to come in the great wild lands. For some time he had been outlining such an article in his thoughts and had even hit upon a title: *The Devil Finds Work: A Pipeline Perspective.* He knew he should assign the piece to one of the magazine's regular contributors, but lately he had begun to toy with the notion of tackling the project himself. The possibility of the article forming the basis of a new book excited his imagination.

Now he was trapped. He could neither assign the story nor develop it himself. The reason was simple, he admitted: he was afraid of the consequences. As much as he wanted to tell Mor-gan Procter to take his ad schedule and shove it, he would have to play ball. Or lose his job.

Walsh thought of the river waiting somewhere just ahead. Immediately he began to feel better. Everything was set up just the way he wanted, thanks to his long-standing relationship with Burke and the fact that the man was a mover and a shaker.

During the cab ride to JFK, Ted had thought of a way to make the trip to the Toubok more interesting. Within minutes after meeting Burke, one phone call from the PR man to Alaska had set the preparation for the plan in motion.

Burke had resisted the kayaking idea for a few minutes, even though it would not involve getting on the river himself, but Walsh's insistence that it was a good plan had prevailed. Ted was an old hand at white-water kayaking—a bit rusty, he ruefully admitted—with several tough rivers to his credit. And, as he had confidently pointed out to Burke, the detailed topographic maps he had seen of the Toubok showed it to be a relatively easy run, with only one set of rapids of Class IV difficulty—the white-water stretch near Jonathan's cabin.

The projected visit to Jonathan's place had now been expanded into an elaborate combination of fishing, camping, and river-running. Today, after being dropped off at the river, Ted would kayak solo downstream while Burke and the chopper pilot flew on ahead to scout campsites and good fishing areas. Ted expected to reach Jonathan Hill's cabin by late afternoon and planned to spend the night there. When the Jet-Ranger picked him up the next morning, he would go on to explore the lower river with Burke and the pilot. Hopefully, they would run across Sam Larkin somewhere downstream. God, he was going to be surprised.

Walsh had insisted on an early start this morning. A sleek fifteen-foot kayak designed for quick turns and maneuverability was lashed to one of the skids of the Jet-Ranger. The baggage hold was crammed with top-line gear: double paddles, flotation vests, helmet, waterproof bags and packs, tents, fishing equipment, and enough food and liquor for a small army. The remote waters of the Toubok would yield battling rainbow trout and grayling. In the evenings, they would be cooking fish or steaks over a campfire while they enjoyed a few belts. They would fall asleep in their sleeping bags to the sounds of the restless current.

Suddenly, a new sense of dread crowded into Walsh's thoughts. Were the good moves gone? Could he still read the water, become one with the flow as he encountered the cascades, chops, eddies, and rips that had to be negotiated with split-second timing? Today's run would include the most difficult rapids on the river. Could he handle it?

You can always portage, he told himself. If you don't feel up to a piece of water, you can pull out and carry around it.

Ted Walsh pulled himself upright on the copter seat and leaned against a side window, pressing his face against the coolness of the glass, trembling slightly under the feverish chill that swept over him. He squinted into the sun glare that came off towering peaks and snowfields.

Beyond those spires, Walsh thought, he would find his river of temporary peace and contentment. As the presence of the mountains swept over him, a familiar verse came to mind: "I will lift up mine eyes unto the hills, from whence cometh my help."

That was ungrammatical, he realized. The 121st Psalm needed editing! Make it: ". . . unto the hills, *whence* cometh my help." The *from* was redundant and wrong.

You're crazy, he told himself. No, you're drunk, he corrected.

Walsh's late father had hammered the Bible into him with an exactitude consistent with the hard-line Baptist life he lived. He was a successful hardware store owner in a small farming community, and even when he saw crops fail and hard times descend he never wavered in his trust of what he called "the Will of the Lord."

What was God's will now? Ted wondered. Had he failed God and mankind with his floundering career, or only himself? He had been given a great opportunity to serve the wilderness cause with *In Wildness*. Had God sent him?

In Wildness should have captured the magazine audience he was devoted to serving with all his skills and training. Yet his best efforts had failed.

He had to face the fact that he might be fired soon. If the worst happened, Ted knew he would be devastated. Still, he would have to go on—writing, editing, whatever he could do to get by. The Alaska Pipeline book he was projecting in his mind would become a feasible project after all, if the ax fell at *In Wildness*. The advance wouldn't be enough to live on, but he assumed he'd get some kind of severance if they let him go or killed the magazine.

Free-lancing again. In this business, you were never fired, never out of work. You were free-lancing.

"How's Ted Walsh?" someone would ask. "Oh, he's free-lancing and working on a book."

Why didn't they just say it? Walsh wondered. "How's Ted Walsh?" The answer should be, "The poor son-of-a-bitch fucked up and is starving to death."

Surely it won't come down to that again, Ted thought, trying to convince himself. Looking at the mountains, he heard the words come back to mind:

I will lift up mine eyes unto the hills, from whence cometh my help.

My help cometh from the Lord, which made heaven and earth.

Suddenly then Ted Walsh could no longer see the mountains. He buried his face in his hands, trying to rub away the burning flush of tears.

"Please," he whispered. "Please help me."

Jack Burke's voice rang out above the loud thuds of the Jet-Ranger's rotors. "There she is!" Burke shouted. "We made it, Ted!"

Walsh looked ahead as the chopper rounded a final shoulder of gray talus, and the Toubok valley stretched away before them. Small lakes shone here and there, and the gleam of the Toubok itself danced through a gap in the forest. Miles away, across the flat reaches and gentle hills of the valley, the profile of Mount McKinley soared from the spruce plain.

"The mountain's out today, Ted," Burke exclaimed, pointing. "Denali . . . the Great One."

To Walsh, the immensity of the scene, the sweep of the country after the harrowing confinement of the pass, was overwhelming and comforting. Without shifting his gaze, he felt for the latch of the ice chest that rested on the floor beside his feet, flipped it open, and plunged his hand into the ice cubes. He extracted a beer, held it forward for Burke. The PR man accepted the offering with a broad smile and gave a hearty thumbs-up sign in return. Ted fetched a brew of his own and popped it open. The chopper was banking over the river now, headed downstream. From this height the movement of the inky-black flow seemed imperceptible, except where the face of the current was slashed by rocks and fallen trees.

"I guess the crowds don't get in here to ruin this," Burke said.

"It's fished some," Youngblood called. "Floatplanes land on Hidden Lake and fish there or on the river." Youngblood gestured toward the sweep of the country ahead, but Burke could not spot the lake.

"There's two or three cabins on the river, too," Youngblood added in afterthought.

"Way in here?" Burke was surprised.

"Yeah," Youngblood chirped. "Indians . . . and hippies. You know, long-haired crazies growing marijuana and fucking around trying to make like they're pioneers or something."

"Seems strange for anybody to live so far out," Burke said.

"I saw two of 'em once on Hidden Lake," Youngblood continued. "Guy looked like your standard-issue bearded hippie. But the girl was really something."

Walsh smiled secretly at this obvious reference to Jonathan and Cody. He took a long sip from the beer, the coolness tart and soothing over his sour stomach. Sunshine burned on his face through the side window. Be funny to get back to New York with something of a tan, he thought. No one would ever expect that from a trip to Alaska.

Youngblood gestured toward a stretch of river directly ahead of the ship. "That's the place," he shouted, turning toward Walsh. "That's the place on your map where you said you wanted us to drop you."

Ted's finger traced over the maze of curving lines on the topographic map. The blue line of the river twisted and turned through the browns and greens that symbolized the shape of the land. Looking ahead, Walsh could see that the pilot was correct. This was the place where the river curved across the open tundra in a wide sweeping bend. A long sandbar, conveniently dry, stretched from the treeless, low-brushed bank on out to the edge of the current.

Youngblood pointed the nose of the ship toward the beckoning strip of land. Walsh could feel the g-forces tearing at his stomach as the descent steepened.

The problems that had been haunting him for so long were behind him now. He had found his river. He was alive again!

ELEVEN

Morgan Procter awoke late, something unusual for him. A dinner and theater date with Mike Williams of Kline-Wolfe was responsible. After the show, the T.A.P. account executive had insisted on another round of drinks at "21," and it had taken Morgan until 1 A.M. to finally pack the boozy, wobbling media buyer and his wife into a cab and say goodnight. The results of the evening had capped off a productive day—a perfect right and left, Morgan reflected as he lay in bed, staring at the ceiling of his hotel apartment. An insertion order for forty-eight pages of T.A.P. advertising would arrive at *In Wildness* today. In the evening, Kristen Richardson would be meeting him here in his apartment.

Morgan tossed aside the sheets, swung himself stiffly out of bed, and padded barefoot and nude across the deeply piled carpet. He gave the drapes cord a long, strong pull and stepped up to the bank of windows to see what kind of day this was going to be.

Framed in a wide shaft of pewter light, he gazed north from the tenth floor at the gray-green expanse of Central Park. To the east a low bank of clouds reduced the morning sun to an orange wafer. The few joggers moving along Fifth Avenue and into the Park melted quickly from view into the hazy, colorless background. Suddenly, as he watched, the sun slipped free of the clouds that had brought showers during the night, and a wave of color and light swept across the park, illuminating the deep-green landscape that stretched away between the flanking borders of the Upper East and West Sides.

Morgan Procter watched the Park with longing. He could imagine how it would be down there right now: the smells of wet pavement and early-summer lushness, the morning air stabbing into his burning lungs, his muscles excited in the labor of the run.

Normally, he would have been pulling on his togs to join the runners in the Park, favoring a four-mile route along the transverse road and around the reservoir. He considered his usual thirty to thirty-five minutes—varying only with the lateness of the hour he had gone to bed and the amount of alcohol he had consumed—to be an acceptable mark. His exercise was a daily ritual, as evidenced by his lean, almost spare figure and smooth, easy way of moving. Today, however, would allow no room for such diversion. Over the next few days, his total energy would be needed if he was to focus on tasks that would bring to fruition years of hard work. Only one result would be satisfactory: his being named President of the Craig Magazine Division. Ultimately, he would try for Tony Craig's chair as head of the entire company.

You must keep moving ahead, Morgan reminded himself, otherwise you go under. The company needed leadership, direction, a strong commander. Tony Craig was sliding into semi-retirement. Richardson had proven himself a feckless candidate for the top slot since he had stumbled over *In Wildness.* Now he was vulnerable, and Morgan knew exactly what to do to put him away. He had nothing against Richardson personally; their duel was strictly business. And it was entirely a quirk of fate that he was about to become involved with Matt's estranged wife.

Reluctantly, Morgan left his vantage point and turned toward the bathroom. As he passed his spacious bed, he paused a moment and looked down at the barely ruffled sheets. Unless something went terribly wrong, he would not be alone here the next two nights.

Touching the sheets, Morgan remembered the warmth of Kristen's skin, the lushness of the body that had pressed into his on the squash court. A pleasant glow spread through his loins in the beginning of an erection.

Not yet! he laughed to himself, and hurried toward the shower.

Kristen Richardson turned slowly into the Princeton Junction parking lot and cruised up the first corridor that led through the parked cars. Unable to find an empty slot, she swung into a second aisle. Finally she steered her 300E Mercedes into a beckoning hole between a Volvo and a BMW. The cheeky rattle of the diesel died stubbornly, to be replaced by the *tick, tick* of cooling metal that was the only sound to break the stillness.

She sat quite still for a time, staring past the parked cars to the distant line of trees where the tracks of the trunk line to Princeton glinted in the morning sun. The two buildings of the station seemed far away across the lot, crouched beneath the high-tension lines that powered trains between Philadelphia and New York. She was thinking about the time it would take her to walk across the lot, through the tunnel beneath the tracks, and up onto the platform to catch the next train to New York. She did not wish to linger overly long on the platform, waiting.

Idly, she ran her hand across the squash bag that rested on the seat beside her and let her fingers come to rest on a larger overnight bag. Packing it that morning had seemed an act of finality, like signing a contract.

Showered and feeling tense but pampered in the softness of her velour robe, she had poked about the bedroom, choosing her attire for the trip.

Your basic tryst wardrobe, she reflected. Now what should it include?

She opened a drawer of lingerie and stirred through the fine contents. Sorry, Morgan, she thought, I've got no garter belts, no fishnet stockings, no peekaboo bras, no Frederick's of Hollywood toys.

What did she have? She paused before a full-length mirror to take inventory.

Her blond hair curved toward enormous brown eyes that dominated the pleasant features whose softness was veiled by the beginning of a deep summer tan. "Bright eyes," Matt had called her at times, and indeed they were a conspicuous feature, as was her generous smile. My face is not a liability, she thought, as she tilted her head slightly to catch another angle of the light.

She opened the sash of her robe and slid the luxurious garment from her shoulders. Her five-ten body was far from sparse, but the brown tan and bikini whiteness glistened with tautness. Her upper thighs and hips curved strongly toward her slim hard waist. Could become a liability here, she thought, rubbing her hands over her thighs, but I won't let it.

Her legs were brown, sleek, and long. They tapered nicely beyond the golden triangle of soft down, which failed to conceal the shadowy line of the cleft and the prominent lips alongside. No problem there.

She looked at her breasts, which she knew were magnificent, full and firm, with wide brown aureoles. Pay dirt! she thought, lifting her fingers to the nipples. She sighed and closed her eyes, remembering the moment when Morgan Procter had taken her into his arms on the squash court. Her nipples hardened under her fingertips as she recalled the excitement created by Morgan's eager, hard thighs pressing into hers. Soon she would experience that again—and more. Today would be very special. She wasn't going to back out now, no matter what happened.

After she had dressed in a short, straight skirt, a wide-collared J. G. Hook blouse festooned with a string tie, and a bright linen blazer, she packed the toiletries she would need. Suddenly, remembering her earlier search for lingerie, she poked through another drawer, her hands feeling into a forgotten corner. The neatly folded silk peignoir was so light in weight it almost seemed to float, so diaphanous that it was a mere wisp of translucence over her fingers. She added it to the bag.

Her choice of Morgan Procter to break her sexual drought represented an amusing twist of irony, Kristen thought now in the parked car as she glanced nervously at her watch. Not because she knew Morgan was her husband's business rival—she didn't give a damn about that!—but because he had never hit on her. The half-dozen guys who had made advances had been summarily rejected; they did not appeal to her physically and, just as important, she had ruled out any possibility of becoming involved with old friends, either single ones or husbands. Her home turf, she decided, would remain a friendly and comfortable place where she could be liked and appreciated by everyone without the tension of romantic involvement.

Kristen's heavy sports commitments spilled over into an active social life she had continued to enjoy since the separation. Hell, she thought, Matt had never been involved anyway.

Their social credibility in the area had been salvaged only as a spin-off of the popularity that stemmed from her prowess at tennis and squash, her involvement in exercise classes and running clubs. At Stony Brook, the country club where the area's finest standard-bearers of money and power mingled and relaxed, Kristen managed the difficult feat of not only reigning as the club's best female player, but doing so with a vivacious flair that made her well liked. Male members who found her appealing were resigned to accepting her as a buddy, both on- and off-court. Wary at first of this casual, open relationship with their husbands, the females were eventually swept into the net of her friendship by her charm, their admiration of her athletic skills, and the certainty that, although childless and attractive, she was not a threat. She was intelligent—she read voraciously—and sensitive to the problems of child-rearing that dominated the conversations of her friends. So established and well nurtured were her country club relationships that they could not be seriously damaged by Matt's constant absences, his aloofness from the atmosphere he knew she enjoyed.

Kristen stepped into the sunshine, slung the bags over her shoulder, and headed across the parking lot.

Another step closer to adultery, she thought nervously.

Adultery! The word was a joke. It had never bothered Matt at all.

She could not understand what had driven Matt into the bed of Marla Ashton. Had he always been a liar and a cheat? She didn't think so. But then what *had* he found in Marla's arms that made him happy? Was it a mid-life crisis, their eleven-year difference in ages, his agony over being childless? Often during their separation, she had found herself looking inward, aching to know if she had failed him in some way. Whatever had possessed him, whatever pleasure he had sought, would remain a secret now. She had no interest in poking through the ashes of the whole mess. Matt *had* lied, *had* cheated. He had made a mockery of her trust and faith, and she could not forgive him. You played by the rules. Everything depended on that. When you broke them, you were not only a loser but a coward as well.

As she climbed the steps leading into the station, Kristen tried to force herself to relax. She had been waiting too long for something exciting to happen. Rebuilding her life wouldn't be possible without some bold moves, and now she was making one.

Morgan Procter. He was incredibly good-looking, a superb athlete, and a nice guy, despite the business clashes Matt had described. She liked Morgan's sense of purpose, as evidenced by the way he had destroyed her on the squash court, playing for every point without letup. He was a man of considerable mystery, too. She knew very little about him, except that he headed one of the hottest sales forces in town, and had been in Vietnam, and had been a jock in college. She smiled at the memory of rumors that Procter had turned down an invitation to be *Cosmopolitan*'s Bachelor of the Month a few years back. Why wasn't the man married? He obviously was not gay.

Tonight she was going to turn Morgan every way but loose while she treated herself to a much needed shot of pure lust— and romance too, if she got lucky. This afternoon she had a squash and lunch date with Brian Scott, a friend from Princeton who worked in New York. Later, she would help a squash pro, Khalid Usman, conduct a clinic at the small uptown racket club he had started. She was not only looking forward to the session, but had actually begun to think about the possibility of teaching squash and tennis full-time. Her Pakistani friend was well connected and eager to help her turn her abilities into a profession.

Fifteen minutes later, the train still had not arrived. Kristen got up from the bench in the corner of the waiting room, hefted the bags once more, and walked toward the door, her low heels clicking noisily in the empty silence. The dozen or so people waiting along the platform were pacing restlessly and peering down the tracks for a sign of the train. Kristen recognized no one, although two of the younger executive types smiled as their glances fell on her squash bag and the protruding racket handles, wrapped in terry cloth and discolored from heavy use. She smiled back at the fellow addicts and drifted on down the platform, lifting her face to the sunshine as she left the shadows of the awning. Far down the tracks, a single light winked into view, then came on steadily as the train approached.

Kristen's thoughts stirred with a disquieting sense of fear that had started to grow once she left the car. You can still go back, a voice said. Walk away now! The voice in her head had become commanding.

The rapidly growing train seemed to steady her nerves. A few more seconds and she would be on her way. Action would smother her anxiety.

Suddenly she heard murmurs of disgust from some of the men. She saw them shaking their heads and moving back from the edge of the platform as they watched the oncoming train. Something was wrong. The train was moving much too fast.

The shriek of a horn punched out ahead of the gleaming silver locomotive as it ate up the last few hundred yards of track, its speed in frightening contrast to the subdued hum of the electric engines. Kristen realized suddenly that she was seeing the Washington–New York Metroliner. The train whipped past the platform in a 130-mile-per-hour blur of hurtling metal and noise, leaving the station area a vortex of swirling trash, dust, and hot gaseous odors.

Kristen turned aside, shielding her eyes, trying to hold her hair in place with one hand, the calmness she longed to feel shattered by this new intrusion of power and speed, overwhelming in its purpose.

TWELVE

The willow thicket beside the Toubok had become a shambles. Beneath the tree branches and dead bushes—remnants of the brush pile Horribilis had pulled together to cover his kill two days earlier—white bones, rotting flesh, and patches of faded moose hide were scattered in disarray. The open ground between the clumps of willows had been trampled into a muddy morass by the grizzly's restless patrols of the area. The scent of death was a burden the light morning breeze could not disperse.

Glutted by feeding upon flesh, the great bear felt the urge for the elixir of plants, bulbs, and roots found on the ridges above the river. He waded out into the stream and headed across some thirty yards of shallows, where the smooth dark flow was ripped by protruding rocks. The current broke noisily over the boulders, the choppy rips sweeping on past the huge beast as he pushed along, his feet digging into the pebbly bottom.

Horribilis could sense the smell of his kill falling away behind him. He could hear little above the sound of the current.

A clump of alder bushes loomed on the far bank, and the grizzly was making for these when a rhythmic booming sound exploded into his consciousness. He stopped and looked around, a mixture of surprise and fright surging through him. He got a fix on the noise, as he looked up and to one side.

A vague speck to the bear's limited vision, another sky-thing was sliding across the horizon.

Before Horribilis could react, the sound of the intruder changed pitch. The object wavered and started to turn.

"I hope your friend's enjoying his boat ride," Sonny Youngblood said to Jack Burke. "The area we're headed for downriver is a lot better fishing than up there where we left him."

ON DANGEROUS GROUND

Youngblood and Burke were alone in the Jet-Ranger, headed on their exploration of the river valley while Ted Walsh made his kayak run.

"Yeah, I hope so, too. Ted really wanted to do the solo kayaking bit. I just hope he doesn't break his neck before he gets to his friend's cabin. It'll be my ass if anything happens."

Burke lifted his face to the sunshine, trying to relax. Despite his pleasure over their lucky break with the weather, he felt a nagging sense of foreboding, of having made an error in judgment. He should not have let Walsh loose on the river alone, despite the editor's solemn promise to portage the one set of difficult rapids. Several times before in Burke's career, this exact feeling had foreshadowed blunders of serious consequence.

Naw, he told himself. Walsh was a woodsman of great experience, a hell of a lot more proficient in the backcountry than he was while sitting in the uneasy chair of magazine editorship. He would have a simple run down to Jonathan Hill's cabin, no different than any number of trips weekend paddlers enjoyed on rivers like the Delaware or the Potomac.

But this was Alaska.

The worry came flooding back again, stronger than ever, as Burke looked down at the twisting sheen of the river, surrounded by undiminished wilderness.

Shake it off! he commanded himself. It's too late now to worry about it anyway.

Burke leaned forward in his seat and raised his camera toward the sweep of the valley ahead. His eye was pressed against the viewfinder, lining up the shot, when he suddenly felt the chopper bank steeply to the right and heard Youngblood shout, "Jesus Fuckin' H. Christ! Look at that!"

Horribilis crouched as low to the ground as he could and tunneled into the alder thicket. The heavy brush swallowed the massive bear like ocean waves as he burrowed deeper and deeper beneath the canopy of greenery. In the shadowed heart of the thicket, he froze rock-still, his eyes flickering and nostrils quivering.

The sky-thing was coming! The thudding noise of its roar invaded the alders in growing explosions of sound.

Horribilis looked toward the sky and waited.

"He was there a minute ago. Right there by the edge of the river." Youngblood held the chopper in a steep bank, circling the spot where he had glimpsed the bear as the Jet-Ranger flew along the river.

"Maybe he spooked into that brush," Burke said, leaning over to peer past Youngblood.

"I've seen lots of bears from the air since coming up here," Youngblood said. "But nothin' nowhere near the size of that son-of-a-bitch!"

Youngblood straightened the chopper and brought it thudding directly over the alder thicket. He hovered the machine and lowered it gently down toward the tops of the brush, which were heaving and tossing under the torrents of air that slammed down from the whirling rotors.

"This'll get the bastard out," Youngblood called. "Even if he's got a den or a cub in there!"

Horribilis had never known the kind of trauma and shock that engulfed him as the sky-thing loomed over his hiding place, dropping lower and lower, its dark twisting body blocking out the sun, its roar a shattering painful assault on his hearing, its cold breath beating down through the brush against his body.

The grizzly could endure the torment no longer. He bolted through the alders, his great hulk plowing through the thick branches and leaves. He hit the river running at full gait, the water exploding in a gigantic eruption as he headed toward the far bank and the mountains looming beyond.

"Fuck! He's gettin' away!" Youngblood saw the bear over his shoulder as he hovered the Jet-Ranger over the alders. He poured on the power and literally stood the chopper on its side in a tight turn.

"Aw, let's go on and find some good fishing water," Burke said. He groped for his seatbelt. That *feeling* had returned! He was making a mistake here!

"Shit, we didn't get a shot of him yet," Youngblood countered. "You still got some film don't you?"

Before Burke could answer, the pilot had the craft thudding along the river, the turboshaft Allison engine screaming under a new surge of power.

"Get ready!" Youngblood yelled. "This'll be a good one!"

The great bear stormed on through the shallows of the river, sheets of spray ripping across the water with every stride. He was angling upstream toward the high wall of the dark spruce forest that rose just ahead. He no longer saw or was conscious of even hearing the chopper as he loped along, every ounce of strength and will bent on gaining the refuge of the thick timberline.

Suddenly, the sky-thing whipped around a bend in the stream, barely skimming the water, and came straight at the bear.

The grizzly veered to one side, toward the willow-covered bank. He sensed he could not make the sanctuary of the timber or the dense bushes. The sky-thing was bearing down, charging him!

Horribilis stopped as he gained the bank and turned to face the danger, sniffing the air and trying to see better.

With the thundering devil only yards away, he stood up on his rear feet.

Closing on the target at 120 miles per hour, his hand poised on the pitch control to lift the Jet-Ranger at the last instant, Sonny Youngblood felt all the old exhilaration of combat flying. But the reflexes that had brought him through the jungles and deltas of Vietnam were not as keen now, and when he saw the grizzly stand erect, Youngblood's surprise slowed his reaction by a micro-second.

The aircraft bounced aside to clear the bear's head. In that instant, answering an instinct as old as the species itself, the great bear thrust out one paw to strike at the demon intruder.

The right skid of the Jet-Ranger collided solidly with the grizzly's paw. Horribilis was hurtled back and to one side.

The chopper tilted sharply for an instant. There was no margin for error! The tip of a rotor blade clipped a car-sized boulder at the edge of the stream, and a jagged fragment became a deadly missile. It slashed into the small tail rotor, severing the directional controls.

The Jet-Ranger wrenched sideways, shuddered, and plummeted out of control into a sweeping turn. The damaged rotor blade flailed the air as the engine and twisted rotor shaft screamed with the sounds of tortured metal.

"I fucked up!" Youngblood yelled. The instrument panel was alive with a harsh fire-warning bell and so many flashing lights that he knew the ship was doomed. Still, he worked desperately on the pedals and control stick, trying to right the craft, screaming, "I don't have anything!"

Burke was screaming also. *"Naw* . . . Don't let it! . . . Get it up, boy!"

Slamming into the shoreline, the chopper exploded. Great chunks of metal shot out in a fan-shaped spread. The core of the machine became an orange-and-black fireball that bounced along the shore, twisting and turning, finally ending its journey well back in the trees, hissing and smoldering, a few flames licking up from the battered junk that remained intact.

Horribilis stopped at the edge of the spruce forest. Whiffs of smoke brought him the stench of smoldering metal, jet fuel, and burning flesh. The river was quiet again, his pursuer was gone.

The great bear turned and moved away through the trees, ignoring the severe gash in his paw, the beginning of pain in his smashed shoulder. He moved quietly through the forest, trailing blood that was instantly absorbed by the spongy tundra.

THIRTEEN

he act of watching a film during the afternoon was so strange to Matt Richardson that he felt ill-at-ease and vaguely guilty of sloth as he settled into a posh chair in the center of the private screening room.

Matt fidgeted nervously, wishing now that he had accepted the coffee offered as he entered the studio. The generous expanse of the chair's armrests contained a telephone, various call buttons, an ashtray, and a beverage holder. Alone in this unfamiliar setting, Richardson felt conspicuously out of place.

He tried to focus on the film as images of wilderness brought the screen to living brilliance, with the accompaniment of a haunting melody pumped into the room by a sound system that was obviously state-of-the-art. Matt had seen various pieces of the film during its production, but this was to be his first look at the finished product, with full sound and music. It was the pilot film of what he hoped would become the nationally syndicated *In Wildness* television show. When he unveiled the film at the board meeting, he would be playing his trump card.

Dammit, you've got to concentrate! Matt prodded himself, as the film started with a segment on grizzly bears in Yellowstone Park. When the half-hour film ended, he would go outside to producer Stanley Solokin's office for a meeting on the syndication and selling of the show. He already knew the numbers: Solokin needed $500,000 to get the program launched as a weekly show over 350 stations nationwide. Craig Publishing would have to put up the money. Since the project had gone forward in secret, Solokin had financed the pilot film on his own but would need a budget for future shows bearing the *In Wildness* name. If the backing failed to materialize, he would try to sell the show elsewhere. He had already intimated he had other interested sponsors.

Could he sell the show to Tony Craig and the board? Matt wondered. He had to! Just as he had to sell Jonathan on the editorship. The television show would give *In Wildness* the boost it needed for national recognition. With Jonathan in the editor's chair, the editorial product would have a rebirth.

As he watched the film, Matt began to feel a deep, familiar sense of satisfaction, the same flush that had swept over him during the turnaround of *Charm*.

The film seemed to grow stronger as it went along. The photography and editing were superbly crafted, the music warm and memorable, and the voice of the narrator strong yet friendly and convincing.

After a while, Matt could sense the film nearing its climax. There was a shot of a grizzly standing on a promontory overlooking a valley. The camera began to pull back and up, revealing the great domain of the high country that was the bear's home. The music swelled from plaintive rising cadenzas as the narration quoted from Henry Beston's *The Outermost House*.

". . . Do not dishonor the earth lest you dishonor the spirit of man. Hold your hands over the earth as over a flame. To all who love her, who open to her the doors of their veins, she gives of her strength, sustaining them with her own measureless tremor of dark life. Touch the earth, love the earth, honor the earth, her plains, her valleys, her hills, and her seasons; rest your spirit in her solitary places. For the gifts of life are the earth's and they are given to all, and they are the songs of birds at daybreak, Orion and the Bear, and dawn seen over the ocean from the beach."

The music soared to a driving, uplifting peak of sound as the words *In Wildness Is the Preservation of the World* appeared on the screen.

The house lights came on. Matt cupped a hand over his eyes and sat very still. He looked like a man at prayer.

The music and the images that had been on the screen still stirred inside him. He felt lifted, strong and undaunted, from the mistakes he had made, over and through the obstacles and dangers that threatened his dream.

This magazine could not die! Not because it was *his,* but because it was needed. By being the instrument to bring about its birth, he had given his own soul a rebirth. If his life had been devoted to magazine profits, it had been given to ideas and communication as well.

Cody was wrong, dammit, dead wrong and unfair, to accuse him of mishandling the magazine. Family business, my ass! Good magazines couldn't be cultivated with the simplicity of beans or wheat. Money was the fertilizer magazine concepts needed, gobs of it. He wasn't a banker or venture capitalist. He was a publisher, and he had needed to build power and stature before *anybody* would listen to him about *In Wildness.* Had he been a wild-eyed kid, like Cody, when he first thought of doing the magazine, starting on a shoestring might have seemed feasible. For years the idea of doing the magazine had been but the slimmest of notions in the back of his mind. The concept really began to gather momentum in his thoughts, bursting into full life like a flame that would not go out, just at the time he was settling into the biggest challenge of his career, his appointment as editorial director. Getting there had taken a lot of tough years and hard work. From the moment he had received his first thrashing as a reporter for the Montana State University campus newspaper ("Richardson, I won't tolerate writers who can't get their facts straight!" the editor had screamed), to the time of elation when he joined Craig, he had waged an unrelenting war against reader indifference. And he had found more personal delight from touching the minds and hearts of newspaper and magazine audiences than he ever had from his paychecks or the power wielded in corporate boardrooms. He —Matt Richardson from Cody, Wyoming—had entered millions of homes, talked to people, told them things that actually affected the ways they led their lives. He had not chosen a career; it had chosen him and had led him here, to this place and this moment. He could still cut it as a rancher, anytime he felt like it. He was not callused and leathery-tough, but he could still rig up a pack train of horses and ride into the high country for weeks, alone. He knew how to fence off a pasture or drive cattle. But these things were not his work. *This* was! And he damned well wasn't going to give it less than his best.

Cody and Jon—a family business. Well, *In Wildness* would

be a family business once the Craig stock issue began. As insiders, they could receive some of the initial shares the top executives would be dividing. All they had to do was to get on board, get with the program right now. Their future, and Derek's, would be assured.

Matt picked up his briefcase and rose slowly, looking at the blank screen. The film would make the difference. Its power and potential would be obvious to Craig and the board. All he needed to do now was to make sure that Jon and Cody saw the light. After that, he could relax a little. After all, he still had a lot of other magazines to worry about besides *In Wildness*. And he had to face the wreck of his marriage.

As he eased along the aisle to leave the room, the thought occurred to Matt that he was practicing triage. Save the magazine, establish Cody and Jon's future, let his own marriage die. That was triage, all right. But he knew he couldn't win 'em all anymore. He didn't even have the strength to try.

FOURTEEN

He was a water-dancer now.

Weightless, he glided over the brown-humped boulders of the streambed, startlingly clear beneath the glassy slide of current that bore the kayak. In riffles, he bobbed jauntily on the quick water, weaving through patches of boulders, his arms rocking from side to side as he flicked the twin blades of the paddle.

Then he hit the rapids.

The water-dancer was lifted on the backs of spouts of white water, cauldron chutes roaring surf-like over and through the rocks, alternately flinging the nose of the kayak skyward or sucking it down into the torrents. The dancer's body twisted and shifted in the narrow cockpit, urging the craft to respond. But here the current ruled the stage, and the dancer was shoved sideways, pirouetting for several turns, then hurtled against a blunt shelf of stone. The craft smacked the ledge, recoiled into the foam of the current. Whiplashed, the dancer lost the final thread of balance and floundered sideways, disappearing into the waves. The yellow keel of the kayak bobbed downstream in the sunlight.

In the first seconds he was in the water, Ted Walsh felt a simultaneous surge of both disgust and panic—disgust at dumping in his first test of white water, panic from the sense of being trapped. Upside down in the tunnel-like torrent, his legs and waist pinned in the kayak, his hands seemingly useless on the shaft of the paddle, he desperately tried to roll his craft upright. The Eskimo Roll maneuver he once could perform with ease eluded him now, and he panicked. Gasping, he felt burning stabs of pain in his nostrils. The helmet he wore felt like a snare, squeezing the last trace of controlled thought from his confused brain, which now screamed "Bail out!"

He did not remember dropping the paddle, but his hands were suddenly grasping the edges of the spray curtain snapped to the cockpit and tied snugly around his waist. The snaps were tearing loose, the curtain was free in his hands! He let the plastic cloth go and shoved hard on the sides of the cockpit, twisting his body downward. The raised edges of the deck scraped his ankles painfully, then he was wallowing upright through the surface, arms flailing into the brightness and sweet air. He choked and spat water, his eyes burned, his ears were muffled explosions of cascades. The current circled his flotation vest like a rope and pulled him along the surface as he groped for balance and composure.

Walsh looked around for the kayak, his mind screaming with dread: the craft might float away if it had drifted downstream, or pin him against a boulder if it was still on the upstream side. And the paddle! Where the fuck was the paddle? He was up Shit Creek without a paddle! Then, thinking clearly for the first time since he'd turned over, he remembered the spare paddle lashed inside the cockpit, and suddenly he saw the kayak itself, spinning lazily in a back eddy off to the side of the current. The river had lost its fangs along here and stretched away like a wide still bay into the tundra plain.

Ted Walsh felt his sneakers jolt onto shallow rocky bottom. He staggered, falling to his numbed knees. He got up weakly and sloshed toward the kayak. Hurrying to the downstream side of the eddy, he waded in to his waist, got one hand on the slippery keel, and raked the kayak toward the shallows. He lifted the craft from the water and lugged it, upside down and dripping, well up onto the dry sandy shore and eased it down among the scattered skeletons of sun-bleached driftwood branches. Walsh slumped to the ground, breathing hard and shivering. He looked back upriver at the tail of the rapids he had come through. The last of the white water was bright in the sun, and foamy streaks slid into the smoothly surfaced pool that led down to the shallows. He unsnapped his helmet and pulled it off. His hair was warm and dry as he peered toward the sun, smiling.

He had done it! As rusty and out of shape as he was, he had taken the river's best shot and come through—respectably if not skillfully. He should be about five miles from Jonathan Hill's cabin now, well ahead of schedule. He could linger here for as long as he wished, still enjoying the pleasure of being alone on the river. He would build a fire, change clothes, and dry out. The watertight plastic bags of gear stowed in the cockpit seemed to have taken the spill without a problem. He could see the blades of the breakdown paddle tied securely alongside the bulging sacks of equipment. He had everything he needed to be comfortable.

This looked like a good spot to break out the pack rod and do a little fishing, maybe even cook up a few grayling or trout for lunch. After that, he figured he would work on his Alaska notes and just sit and relax until pushing on down to Jonathan's place in a few hours. No need to rush things now. He was sick of deadlines and being crowded and pushed and cut off from his rivers and other things he loved. In the rapids just now, he had regained some of the precious sense of self-reliance that had been ebbing away for months, leaving him tied to peripheral satisfactions and values.

Before the rapids, the paddling had been easy enough for him to work the stiffness from his body, find the keen sense of muscle-memory that went into every smooth stroke of the paddle. This is how a fighter must feel, he had thought, when he goes into training to pump the sludge from his system. And that was only the physical side! You did not have to be a Buddhist monk or a practitioner of Zen to realize that being out here did something to make you whole again. Already the river had served up a banquet of simple pleasures that had touched his throbbing nerves like some sort of tranquilizer: a wolf surprised on a sandbar, then disappearing in the blink of an eye, so quickly that it seemed hard to believe the animal had ever been there at all; six recently hatched mallard ducklings paddling awkwardly downstream in their mother's wake, teasingly close to the kayak for a distance, then finally vanishing into a weedy bay; red squirrels chirring and frolicking in the pine tops; a spruce grouse hurtling across the stream, followed immediately by a large dusky projectile—a goshawk whose rapier wings rent the air with a tearing sound. And in one place where the river flowed through a low swamp-like basin, he had surprised a beaver as it swam across a backwater pool, its tail slapping the dark surface as it dove in alarm.

It had been a great morning to be alive and on the river.

Walsh dug into a clammy pocket of his trousers for one of

the waterproof containers of matches he had brought along. He heaped some driftwood twigs into a small mound, got a blaze going, and started adding on larger branches. In a few minutes, a comfortable fire was glowing against his backside as he gazed off downriver. His friend Sam Larkin was somewhere out there, perhaps at Jonathan's cabin, perhaps around the next bend. What a reunion they were going to have!

The pain flowed like liquid fire through Horribilis's shoulder and leg and erupted in the bloody mass of his right paw. He lunged ahead, oblivious of his surroundings now, his total senses of awareness and energy focused on attaining the distant mountain region that was his home. His general direction was upstream, but he did not follow the exact flow of the serpentine course of the river. Instead, he crossed and recrossed the stream several times, cutting over the bends, traversing the ridges that the stream curved around.

Twice, when he felt the light breeze wafting upriver from behind him, the great bear paused and studied his back trail. Standing rock-still and almost invisible in the spruce shadows, reading the wind with his great nose, his ears a sensitive antenna that sorted out the chirring alarm of a red squirrel from the sighing spruce tops, the grizzly waited for the dangerous sky-thing to pursue. Waited for the putrid smell. Listened for the roaring thunder that he instinctively knew was death. Watched for the creature itself to swoop toward him as it had done before.

Moving on after a second futile stop to ambush his attacker, Horribilis felt the stiffening of his injured muscles, and the pain of walking now swelled into a dangerous living force. He walked with difficulty, favoring his right paw, his massive body jerking and heaving in an exaggerated limp.

The stream was close once again. He heard the sweep of the current past snags and rocks, smelled the water itself, along with the moss and dankness of the low terrain that lined the course of the current. He pushed through a dense patch of willows and emerged in a sunlit expanse of open tundra. Shallow here, the stream riffled in a dancing sparkle between the naked backs of sandbars and on out across a long unbroken stretch of open tundra country, framed by the peaks beyond. A small island of spruce stood at the edge of the stream before the current curved away across the open ground.

The great bear headed for the spruce trees without pausing. When he was safely inside the dense growth of black trunks and green branches, he turned to face the way he had come and lay down at the edge of the trees, his head resting beside a copse of blueberry bushes. Pressing down into the foliage as deeply as he could, he brought his face to his injured paw and licked it, tentatively at first, then in great sweeps of his hot wet tongue. His own saliva mingled with the taste and scent of his blood, wet earth, and moss.

Slowly, almost imperceptibly, the level of the pain-danger in Horribilis's shoulder and leg blossomed into a throbbing crescendo. All of the great bear's senses were focused on his misery. The flames that swept through his blood, into his muscles and nerve endings, were drowning out his instinctive remembrance of fear and creating some new sense within him.

The force that began to flow through him now was something he had never felt before.

That feeling was rage.

Derek Hill was a happy little cowboy. The Stetson hat he wore bobbed jauntily up the trail ahead of Cody as she hurried to match the youngster's enthusiastic strides toward their favorite fishing spot, a short hike from the cabin. Impatient, Buck raced ahead out of sight, despite Cody's shouts to turn him.

"Deserter!" Cody playfully cursed the yellow Lab under her breath. Jonathan's powerful commands would have turned the dog like a check cord.

At a rivulet that trickled across the trail, Derek's leap fell short, one boot skidding off a rock into the icy water. His pant leg wet to the knee, he trudged stoically ahead, as though nothing had happened.

Cody looked at the trail ahead. The open stretch of tundra country they had just come through was giving way to thicker forest where the trail plunged back down to the river, passing stands of spruce and bending on out of sight into the heavy forest of birch and cottonwood.

As she walked, Cody was barely conscious of the small day-pack on her back. But the heavy .375 magnum kept biting into the top of her shoulder. She moved the rifle constantly, seeking a comfortable position, and, finding none, cursed its burdensome weight. She had brought the gun along reluctantly. If there was serious danger here, she reasoned, why be here at all? The thought was foolish, she admitted. Of course, there was danger; and without the gun she and Derek would be vulnerable, alone on the trail. Besides: she had promised Jonathan.

The trail slanted into the shadows of the birches along the stream, and a catchy tune came to Cody's mind as she remembered Jonathan's warning: "Make noise!" Glancing down at Derek to see if he was going to start laughing at her, she began singing.

> "If you go down in the woods today,
> You're sure of a big sur-prise."

She saw Derek looking at her quizzically. She paused, smiling at him, then went on singing as they walked.

> "If you go down in the woods today,
> You'd better go in dis-guise.
> Because today's the day the teddy bears have their
> pic-nic."

Cody stopped again, laughing to herself. The sound of her voice did not mix well with the environment of the trail. A klaxon horn would be more effective and just about as charming, she decided.

The walking was easy on the well-defined trail, despite the thickness of the surrounding foliage. Occasionally, Cody could hear the murmur of the river as the nearby current swept over snags and rocks. She heard the lilt of birdsong back in the trees and was trying to identify the call when a red squirrel suddenly began to chirr excitedly. Cody stopped and stared through the trees. The quick nervous sound continued, but the squirrel was hidden by the green wall of the forest.

Cody moved on ahead, conscious that the chirring had not stopped.

The dry snap of a limb breaking was as startling as a sudden gunshot. She whirled toward the sound, sweeping the rifle from her shoulder, reaching for Derek with her free hand. She clutched his shoulder, pulling him against her leg.

Cody saw nothing, heard nothing, except the familiar cries of the squirrel, still sounding from the distance. Whatever the squirrel could see, whatever had broken the limb, was somewhere beyond the shadows and the trees.

The sound could have been made by anything, Cody reasoned. Probably just a rotted limb falling.

The frantic chirrs of the squirrel continued without pause, mocking the peaceful silence. Cody waited, hoping the sound would stop. She could feel Derek's small arms clutching her legs. She patted him on the shoulder with one hand.

She thought of firing the rifle into the air, trying to spook whatever critter the squirrel was so agitated about. She had four cartridges in the gun, certainly enough to spare one shot. That would be silly, she suddenly decided. The recoil would be unpleasant, the sound of the blast would be frightening to Derek.

She lowered the rifle, thinking, There's probably nothing out there at all. The squirrel probably heard us coming up the trail and can see us from the top of a tree.

This idea was instantly snatched from her mind by the unmistakable noise of crashing brush.

Cody jerked the stock to her shoulder and tried to align the iron sights on the trees in the direction of the squirrel's hidden perch. The birches were shapeless and dark, the noise was gone. But she had no illusions now. She knew something had lurched through the brush, then stopped again. She fought back the electric sense of fright that gripped her painfully.

Stay calm! her mind screamed. You can shoot this thing! *Safety off*— she checked the button with her thumb. *Stock snug against your face*—she could feel her hot pulse pounding against the wood.

Agonizing moments passed. The rifle was becoming an unbearable heaviness. Suddenly there it was again—the dry rustle of brush being shoved aside, the crackle of twigs and sticks crushed by some heavy weight. The sound was on the move again, slanting off to the left. Her rifle barrel tracked the noisy path. She thought of shooting blindly into the cover, instantly rejected the notion as she strained to see. Any clue would help —a patch of fur, a piece of leg, a rump or tail. The thought crossed her mind that in the next few seconds she and her son could cease to exist. Their bones and flesh could be scattered about this lonely glade. The squirrel would still be alive, chirring. The whole world would just go on as though nothing had happened.

She lowered the rifle, screaming as loudly as she could, "I'll shoot, you bastard!"

"Mommy!" Derek shrieked, tugging at her, crying in a sudden burst of agony.

The brush erupted with heavy movement. She could hear the quick thud of heavy feet, a guttural animal grunt. The rifle came back smoothly to her cheek. Her finger was on the trigger as she leaned forward, amazed at her calm now. A hump of brown tore out of the trees, into the rifle's sight picture. Instantly, she fired, felt the stabbing jolt of the recoil, then saw nothing but the blurred movement of the rifle, bucking skyward. Her ears rang, the stinging in her cheek seemed to burn right into her eyes. She blinked, and there, crashing hugely away through the trees, smashing down everything in its path, was a cow moose.

The beast was gone in an instant. Cody could hear the crashing sounds fading away through the forest. Derek was crying in terror.

Cody tossed the rifle aside and dropped to her knees beside Derek, holding his trembling body close, still shaking herself as she gasped, "It's all right. It's all gone now!"

FIFTEEN

"This will be a memo to Tony Craig. Subject: *In Wildness*. Copies to Richardson, Cummings, and . . ."

Morgan Procter flicked the OFF switch of the compact recorder he held in one hand and lowered the unit from his lips, speculating. In addition to Richardson and his own advertising deputy, Vince Cummings, Procter wanted to get a copy of his upcoming message into the hands of Sam Zeigler, Craig's chief financial officer. Should he send it in the blind, as he sometimes did, or go ahead and acknowledge to all concerned that Zeigler was included in the memo's distribution? He looked at the folded copy of *Inside Korner* lying on his desk. He gave the switch a decisive click and said, "Copy Sam Zeigler as well."

Morgan continued then, his voice strong and unfaltering.

"Dear Tony. It is always a great pleasure to report to you on special instances where hard work has caused large numbers of dollars to flock together within our walls. In the case of *In Wildness,* these occasions have been all too rare. Still, my boys have carried the flag held high, and in the instance of Trans-Arctic Petroleum the effort has paid off in the landing of a forty-eight-page schedule, over a cool million in new business. The insertion order is in the house, much to the credit of Vince Cummings, who personally led the charge on this one.

"That's the good news. The bad news is that I feel compelled to once again call your attention to our overall precarious position with this book and plead with you—consider me on my knees here, Tony—to please lift the moratorium we have on cigarette advertising. We're talking about three million bucks' worth of business just sitting out there waiting for someone to make the calls and pick up the orders. I want that money! How else is *In Wildness* going to survive?

"To say that cigarette advertising is harmful to our wilderness and outdoor image is the height of the kind of fuzzy thinking that has dominated all decision-making on this book. The current trend in cigarette ads is to use the imagery of the outdoors. In today's ads, I see such things as backpacking, camping, river-rafting, fishing, and cross-country skiing. I haven't heard of readers of our other magazines sending hate mail and subscription cancellations because of the cigarette ads they see. Let's be realistic. The windfall enjoyed by magazines since cigarette commercials were banned from TV is too good to miss. *In Wildness* should be cashing in, just as our other books have already been doing."

Morgan paused, thinking about that last section. Was it grossly overdone? He switched off the advancing tape, laid the recorder on his desk, and stretched his long, white-shirted arms toward the ceiling. He rolled his head in a circle, feeling the stiffness drain from his neck and shoulders. He stood up slowly, his arms outstretched as he twisted his torso from side to side. The tautness of his midriff brought a flush of satisfaction as his stomach muscles tightened with the movement. Let the memo rest a few moments, he thought.

He glanced at his watch, realizing as he did so that he was as nervous as a teenager on his first date. Two hours to go. Unless Kristen backed out, she would be walking into his apartment somewhere around seven o'clock. Before he left the office, it was imperative that he speak to Marla Ashton on the phone. Why hadn't she returned his calls? Where the hell was she?

Morgan stepped from the pool of light cast by his single desk lamp and crossed the sallow dimness to the windows. The cord pulled easily, and the heavy drapes swung aside.

The sudden light was an uncomfortable flash across his eyes, and Morgan Procter turned from the window and stood looking over the room that was one of his favorite places on earth.

The main room was in itself spacious, but two alcoves that flared from side walls gave the office an apartment-like potential for livability. One alcove was a conference area, the polished sleekness of the long table and chairs stretching toward a panel wall that hid a rear-projection screen and film system. A swath of corkboard cut across the side walls. The other alcove was a wood-paneled, den-like nest of dark leather chairs and a couch; heavy wooden coffee and end tables; a large-screen television; and on one wall a component stereo system and VCR alongside a hutch-type cabinet that served as a bar.

The main office was dominated by Procter's massive oaken desk, which jutted into the room like the bow of a clipper ship. It was flanked by two high-backed chairs. At the end of the room was a long low coffee table that this afternoon was bedecked with a white burst of fresh carnations. The paintings on the walls were mostly beautifully framed originals of sporting scenes by LeRoy Neiman. Among them were sprinkled other artists' renderings of famous golf holes: the sixteenth at Cypress Point, the twelfth at Augusta, the eighteenth at St. Andrews.

Procter headed toward the far corner where an assortment of golf clubs stood uncased. His route carried him past a wall of high dark bookcases where the richly bound volumes were interspersed with pictures and memorabilia. The books were bound volumes of Craig magazines and published books by regular contributors to the company's properties. The knick-knacks and photos were physical reminders of one man's journey up the road to power and success.

In one photo, Procter was lining up a putt while Bob Hope kibitzed and Arnold Palmer leaned on his putter against a background that included a sun-splashed expanse of Carmel Bay and the eighteenth fairway at Pebble Beach, California.

"Morg," Bob Hope had scrawled on the bottom of the picture, "aren't you glad Arnie and I invented this game?"

The photographs continued along the length of the bookcases. Sports figures, magazine industry figures, personalities, like Cheryl Tiegs and Helen Gurley Brown. Procter's winning smile beamed out from these moments captured with the famous and the beautiful. There was a shot of the University of Maryland golf team with a very young Procter acting as its captain, along with a plethora of awards and citations from magazine industry groups.

Morgan retrieved a putter from the loose batch of clubs and gripped it smartly. His hands slid into a precise and comfortable position on the rich dark leather of the handle.

The shaft was light brown wood, the head a blade of bronze. The club had been handmade by the master Scottish craftsman Laurie Auchterlonie and presented to Procter by Tony Craig.

Morgan raked a ball from the corner and took his stance. His target, thirty feet away across the smooth carpet, was a circular plastic device that simulated a golf hole. Procter aligned his feet, glancing back and forth from the cup to the putter blade to the black shoes that emerged from the cuffs of his dark blue trousers. He shuffled his feet slightly, moving the right foot ahead an inch. His hands felt the precise muscle memory of the good stroke. *Tap.* As the ball neared the hole, Procter saw it veer slightly to the right. He twisted his upper body to the left, trying to will the ball into the cup. It missed on the right by less than an inch.

Morgan raked out another ball. You were doing that in Bermuda, he told himself. Get the right hand farther over, the palm dead square to the hole.

He resumed his stance and grip, feeling for the right-hand position he wanted. God, he loved the precision and physical excitement that produced excellence in sports.

This time he stroked the ball dead into the middle of the cup. Another ball followed as though it were on rails. Make it three in a row, Morgan told himself. It'll be a good omen.

The final ball neared the cup, heading in, then failed to get over the lip by some infinitesimal amount of roll. Morgan groaned. Then, smiling to himself, he put the little fantasy play into its proper perspective by dismissing it and walked back to his desk. He picked up the recorder, pressed the rewind button, and rolled back the tape. He found his beginning and listened intently to the strange crackle of his own voice emerging from the tiny speaker. He was satisfied with what he heard. He would let the bitter words stand. He spoke once again into the machine.

"It is clear to me that people who want to smoke will do so; those who don't, won't. I've never had one of the damn things in my mouth, and I suppose I've seen every cigarette print ad produced in the last twenty years.

"May we meet with all concerned on this at an early date, Tony? I'm just trying to keep the ship afloat, and I can't do it without some bending and stretching on the other side of the hall."

Morgan Procter popped the tiny cassette from its compartment and pressed a buzzer on his multi circuited phone unit. In a moment, the door opened and Alice Garland, his secretary, came toward his desk, the ever-present note pad and pen at the ready. She was an attractive woman in her mid-thirties, coiffed and dressed in a superb balance of femininity and business formality. She was precisely right for the Procter style and surroundings. Morgan was very fond of her, but even though she had been with him for ten years and knew more of his secrets than anyone, they maintained a relationship that was never completely casual, even when they were alone together.

Procter swept a hand at a stack of sales-call reports he had gone through earlier and placed the cassette on top of them. "I'll be shoving off soon," Morgan said. "And I'll probably be late tomorrow."

"You have several appointments," Alice said. "Just when will you be in?"

"I don't know exactly. I'll call. Frankly, I want to make myself scarce while that nonsense boils up." He pointed to *Inside Korner* lying on his desk. "And I have some personal odds and ends I want to take care of."

Alice nodded at the newsletter. "It's already started, and it's spreading fast. Vince Cummings called from Chicago. Said they'd heard about it out there and that he's dying to talk with you. Shall I get him?"

"No. I only want to talk to Marla Ashton."

"Her office promised they would have her call the moment she arrived or phoned in."

"Good. I'm going to whip through this pile of expense account reports, then be on my way."

Fifteen minutes later, Morgan had reduced the pile of vouchers to a single submission that he stared at for several moments, shaking his head. He popped a new cassette into the recorder and dictated.

"Alice, this is a Blue Darter to Jerry Shea."

A Blue Darter was a small, single-page note of blue paper with the initials *M.P.* on top. They were hand-delivered in envelopes marked PERSONAL AND EXTREMELY CONFIDENTIAL after being signed in Procter's name by Alice. To the advertising staffs of Craig magazines, the appearance of a Blue Darter was like the point of a stake about to be driven into the heart. This one was to read:

"Jerry, I have reviewed, signed, and sent forward for payment your latest batch of expense reports. I am, however, compelled to ask you: Does your wife ever cook you a meal?"

Morgan saw the door open and Alice looking in. "Miss Ashton is on the phone."

"Good," Morgan responded and eagerly picked up his own phone. "Marla, is that really you?"

"What's up?" Marla answered. "Your secretary's message sounded somewhere between panic and berserk."

"Not at all, but thanks for getting back to me. I know you're busy. Now, darling, I know I've used up my quota of lunches, but a true emergency has arisen. I must see you tomorrow. Alone."

Every month Marla gave Procter three luncheons at which she would meet with important advertising clients and wow them. Her condition for window-dressing Procter's sales maneuvers was that there be no hard sales talk in their presence. These sessions were friendly enough, sometimes quite charming, and her easy manner and dynamic personality did indeed make it easier for Procter to set up deals.

"That *Korner* newsletter got you all hot and bothered, Morgan?"

"I need to discuss some things."

"I'm not a political person, Morg."

"Lady, you're as much of a hustler as everybody else at your level or you'd still be somewhere out there in Yumpsville, covering the P.T.A. or something equally exciting for the local weekly."

"Morg, I'm truly shocked. You mean to tell me talent and hard work aren't enough?"

"I'm talking about something more important here."

"Like survival."

"You know me too well. Now, what about lunch? I'll even promise to order an obscenely expensive bottle of wine in your honor."

She hesitated, leaving him mentally wringing his hands as he waited. Arrogant bitch!

"All right, Morgan."

ON DANGEROUS GROUND

Procter smiled. This was more like it. "One o'clock then . . . at Lutèce. You won't be bored."

When he hung up the phone, Morgan leaned back in his chair, his hands behind his head, his eyes closed.

Survival! he smirked. Yes, Marla Ashton would know a thing or two about survival. She had worked and screwed her way into a very strong position in the company, right into the boardroom itself. Would she back Richardson one hundred percent? Or would she start exercising the "dark horse" possibilities *Inside Korner* had mentioned? The luncheon tomorrow would clarify her true colors, eliminate any chance of a surprise at the board meeting.

Morgan Procter hated surprises.

SIXTEEN

Horribilis was on the move again.

Lurching slowly, awkwardly—his right leg and shoulder unable to support his usual rhythmic gait—the great bear was far out on the spruce and tundra plain, heading cross-country over a wide bend in the Toubok. Only one instinct mattered now, and it possessed his tormented being with a force as strong as intelligent reasoning: the pain that racked his body was a danger and must be escaped. Behind him now, the river was part of the danger. The forest beside the stream was no longer a place where his powerful senses could tell him what to do. Every scent and sound was a threat; the sky-thing waited in every shadow. Moving stiffly from the spruce thicket where he had rested while waiting in ambush, he instinctively continued fleeing toward the refuge his mother had taught him ten thousand days and a million dangers before: the high, brush-choked passes just on the snow line of the great ranges. There, where he spent his winters, sheltered and serene, he would be beyond the pain-danger.

Crossing a boggy section of tundra carpeted with muskeg tussocks, Horribilis sensed new waves of the pain-danger as the injured paw skidded weakly over the grassy clumps, jolting down into the watery seams, twisting his leg and shoulder. He could not know that bones, ligaments, and tendons had been smashed, but the overwhelming senses of danger and vulnerability were deep torments raging within the beast.

He paused and gazed vacantly at the distant mountains, his face totally without expression, his eyes fighting to see what lay ahead. His nostrils flared as a wisp of breeze crossed his face, gently ruffling the fur behind his pricked ears and on along his stump-like neck. Among the scents of sphagnum and dank grasses, he could detect the odor of his own blood spreading darkly through the scummy water around his paw.

Overhead, a golden eagle circled in the brightness, its shadow floating over the tundra. Horribilis glimpsed the fleeting outline of the bird on the muskeg and instantly tensed, his mouth shaping into the beginning of a snarl. But now the tundra was empty again; the intruder had vanished as quickly as it had come.

The great bear could sense the danger of being in the open. Usually he avoided such areas, aware that the sky-thing hunted there. Only in cover did he feel a sense of security: copses of spruce, river bottoms, the willowy banks of creeks, birch brush tangles on hillsides, the deep hidden gulches of the higher slopes, and places where forest fires had ravaged the timber, leaving acres of blackened logs strewn at every angle, entwined and brush-choked in a veritable fortress.

Moving on ahead, the grizzly resumed the awkward, difficult pace toward his sanctuary. When the tundra plain began to give way to scattered stands of spruce, with heavier birches looming just beyond, the great bear stopped once again. He could smell the river, its scent of danger—directly in his path.

With every breath, the trauma of the morning came flooding back into his senses. Still he did not turn. The pain-danger was a burning, uncontrollable menace that compelled him to keep the mountains in front of him, even though he would have to cross the river.

He watched and listened for a long while. Finally, satisfied there was no immediate threat, he moved slowly toward the river, a hunter again—alert, cautious, deadly.

Ted Walsh took a final walk around his temporary campsite. The rocky ground bore no trace of the hours he had passed here, except the smudge of water-soaked ash and black embers where his fire had been. At the edge of the river, the bow of the yellow kayak pointed downstream, packed and ready to go.

A familiar, disquieting sense of pressure began to build in Walsh's chest as he glanced at his waterproof Rolex, acquired during the palmy days when he had first gained the editorship of *In Wildness.* Two o'clock already. Time to get on down to Jonathan's cabin and see what the rest of the day would hold. There would be a lot of talk about the magazine, and he had made up his mind to graciously accept whatever criticisms Jonathan felt like making. That's what you're here for, he reminded himself—to help *In Wildness*. If Jonathan told him bluntly that his editorial direction—or lack of it!—had wrecked the magazine, he would have to endure the comments. Just as he would have to endure the rest of the trip with Burke, including the Pipeline junket itself.

Walsh picked up the paddle, testing the metal ferrule where the takedown shafts were joined. He looked down at the narrow cockpit, then back upstream at the tail of the rapids and the pool below. Something swirled on the surface; a grayling probably. He could have caught dozens here but he'd stopped after taking four with his fly rod. They had leaped and pulled beautifully in the current, their high dorsal fins arching sail-like from their sleek, hard bodies. In his hands as he prepared them for the frying pan the fish smelled of green ferns, and their sides shimmered with subtle colors beneath the dominant gray. After lunch, he had rested with his back against a driftwood tree trunk and scribbled notes for a while. Lulled by the warm sun and the incessant murmur of the rapids upstream, he had quickly fallen asleep.

Lingering still, savoring the last moments of what he knew was a very special place, Ted Walsh realized he would come back here someday—with a lot of food and good books, some whiskey. He would stay as long as he wanted the next time.

Now—on down.

He lifted the kayak toward the current, grimacing at the task he would have lowering his considerable bulk into the cockpit.

A good diet would be a necessary part of his self-improvement program, he laughed to himself.

Horribilis crouched in the tangle of an alder thicket, his great body invisible in the shadows, his face a brown anomaly filling a crease in the green screen of bushes. The Toubok current was swift here, the river curving quickly into view from a sharp bend in the birch forest along the opposite bank and sweeping past the great bear in a sunlit expanse of open water that stretched away downstream as far as he could see. The glade-like scent of the birch forest blended with the smell of the river in the grizzly's questing nostrils. He could hear the rush of the current and sometimes a trace of wind in the quivering leaves of the birches. He watched and waited for several minutes, poised to cross the twenty yards of river but held motionless by his fear.

Then, so suddenly that he seemed to have left all caution behind, he slid from the brush in a catlike motion and pushed out into the current. Barely touching his belly, the quick flow swirled past the bear's stumpy legs as they dug into the pebbly streambed. He was aware of the sunshine on his back and the cool scent of the birch shadows just ahead. The current filled his ears with its steady licking rush, unvarying until a single note of sound, wooden and heavy, popped through the clatter of the water.

Horribilis wheeled upstream toward the source of the disturbing noise. The water slid empty and quiet around the tight bend in the birches. There was no scent of danger.

Still the grizzly was not satisfied. He stood on his rear feet, a towering, dripping figure, one paw bloody and meat-red in the sun.

If only I could go on like this forever, Ted Walsh was fantasizing, letting the current do the work, dipping the paddle occasionally to keep the bow straight, penetrating deeper and deeper into the Toubok Valley without making a sound. Of course, that was not possible. Unless his map was wacko, he would come upon Jonathan Hill's cabin in ten or fifteen minutes.

The sun was warm on his face, and he found himself regretting that he had worn his helmet and flotation vest. There was no white water ahead, and he should have stowed the protective gear with his other packs and taken this part of the ride in comfort.

He felt the current quickening as the river pinched into a shadowy canyon of spruce and birch forest. A wall of trees rose straight ahead, and the current swung sharply to the left, fast but smooth and silent. He back-paddled on his left, to swing the bow over slightly to take the curve. Then, seeing he had overcompensated and that the bow was getting around to the left much too far, he stabbed at the water with the right-

ON DANGEROUS GROUND

hand blade of the paddle. The wooden shaft thumped against the side of the kayak with a loud hollow sound.

Sloppy! Walsh thought in silent criticism. He got the bow back around and stared eagerly ahead, fascinated as always with the way a new vista came into view at every bend of the river. At this sharp curve, the tree line on the right bank had become a screen of alders, rushing past like a piece of film. He felt a sliding skidding sensation as the kayak took the bend, knifing into an open stretch of water. The sun flashed across his eyes in a sudden, painful flare. He blinked into the brightness.

The tall, shadowy form hulking in the middle of the stream was a grizzly. Walsh knew that instantly. But in that same micro-second, shock numbed his ability to think and act clearly. A worthless thought about this being some kind of mistake occupied his confused brain. He sat motionless, holding the paddle, the yards closing rapidly.

Twenty yards from the towering figure of Horribilis, Walsh exploded into action. He lunged at the water with his paddle . . . then again . . . and again. The bow swung to the left. The bank was ahead! He continued to flail at the water, a small cry of desperation emerging from his lips.

Suddenly he was aware that the bow had come around too far. He was floating downstream again. Backwards!

A shadow fell over the kayak.

Ted Walsh started to scream.

SEVENTEEN

Morgan Procter lifted a beadily cold bottle of Montrachet from its nest in the silver ice bucket. He snuggled a linen towel around the neck of the bottle and poured generous portions of the white Burgundy into a pair of Waterford's finest. Across the expansive living room, Kristen Richardson had just completed a tour of the suite and stood by the window, gazing out into the burnished light and dusky shadows of the long June evening.

Morgan picked up the wine glasses and paused, staring at Kristen. Profiled against the window, she presented the living image of his fantasies and innermost physical longings, the one woman he ached to possess. Smoky in that light, her heavy blond hair fell over the gentle slope of her erect shoulders. The appealing image was countered in the front by the shadowy outline of her breasts, molded against the simple blouse. Her back was straight and delicately narrow, continuing sensuously beyond the firm midriff to where her skirt pressed down over a never-ending sleekness of thigh and leg.

Morgan could not believe the tide of good fortune he was riding. And he had no intention of spooking it by questioning its presence.

Kristen smiled as Morgan approached. She uttered an almost inaudible "thank you" as she accepted the wine. She held the glass nervously in both hands as her eyes swept from the carpet to Morgan's soft smile.

"Well," Morgan said. "What shall we drink to?"

"To better backhands," Kristen said, raising her glass.

"Perfect!" Morgan laughed, as he clinked his glass lightly against hers. He took a sip of wine and said, obviously pleased with his choice, "That's not a bad way to start the evening."

Kristen smiled warmly in agreement.

"How did the squash clinic go?" Morgan asked. "Test of patience, I suppose."

"It really was a lot of fun. Fortunately, I only had to demonstrate the strokes. Khalid handled the lecture."

"He's a terrific player," Morgan said. "He's put me through the wringer more than a few times during playing lessons."

"Judging by the way you play, I would say your money was well spent," Kristen chuckled. "Like this apartment," she added, looking around the room. "It's very nice."

The suite that had earned this praise was decorated in the French manner with a superb combination of simplicity and elegance.

Morgan grinned. "I'm glad you like it. Actually, though, it's not mine. It's all compliments of Craig Publishing. Tony indulges my little passion for hotel living. I'm afraid I like the fantasy of picking up the phone and pretending I have servants."

"I see," Kristen said. "Damn nice of Craig, don't you think?"

"As a matter of fact, I do. I have a couple of pieces of property of my own outside the city. Condos."

"Really? Where are they?"

"Shinnecock Hills, out in the Hamptons on Long Island. I'm a member there."

"Famous course," Kristen said. "I've heard a lot about it. What about your other place?"

"Stratton Mountain, Vermont. For skiing."

Kristen smiled. "How'd you manage to stay single so long?"

The moment was inevitable, Morgan thought, tensing, feeling the shadowy sense of pain and loss clutching at him from the past. "I *was* married once," Morgan said, his voice mellow. "Unfortunately, she died."

"Oh," Kristen said, genuinely surprised. "I'm sorry. I didn't—"

"It was a long time ago," Morgan interrupted. "In college. We were very young and very happy."

Kristen stared at Morgan in silence, obviously searching for the appropriate reply.

Quickly and cheerfully Morgan cut through the tension. "If you're hungry, we have some hors d'oeuvres," he said, waving a hand toward the bar. "They're very good."

ON DANGEROUS GROUND

"I think I'll just stick with wine for now," Kristen answered, "but you go ahead."

"Well, let me know when you feel hungry. We can have something brought up. My servants never sleep, you know."

"Perhaps later," Kristen said, returning his smile. She sipped her wine and stepped a few paces away toward the attractively screened fireplace that was surrounded by heavy moldings with the rich texture of fine craftsmanship. The mantel was topped by an original oil—an impressionistic rendering of ice skaters on a country pond. Kristen looked at the painting in silence.

"Do you like it?" Morgan asked, easing up behind her.

"Very much," she said without turning. "The Impressionists and Postimpressionists are my favorites."

"I really don't know very much about art," Morgan said softly. "But I appreciate beauty." He slipped one arm around her shoulder and leaned forward, his face brushing across the soft fluff of her hair, his lips tasting the curve of her neck.

Kristen closed her eyes as she reached up and back with one hand. Her fingers spread eagerly through his thick hair as they urged his head forward. She lifted her face up and back, her lips seeking his. Their kiss began with hunger and urgency, their mouths devouring one another in a quick burst of questing, as though the pleasure that exploded through their senses could only be sustained through some deeper melding of their lips and tongues. Then, as the taste and feel of her soared to an even higher pitch of sensual delight, Morgan raised his lips to a more gentle slant, his tongue gliding softly along the surface of her lips, his passion easing into tenderness and obvious appreciation. Gradually, their mouths became less insistent, then finally parted.

Kristen turned to him, a long sigh audible in the stillness. She rested her face against his shoulder as his arm held her even closer. Morgan began to sense the awkwardness of their position, each with one arm outstretched, wine glass still in hand. "Let's get rid of these glasses," he whispered.

Kristen was silent for a moment. She drew her head and arm away and stepped back, smiling demurely as she once again cupped her wine glass with both hands. "Mind if we sit for a bit?" she said.

Morgan felt slightly embarrassed, wondering if he had made a mistake. "I'm sorry," he said. "I didn't mean to rush things. I guess I got carried away."

"Promise me it'll happen again," Kristen laughed, reaching a hand for his.

Morgan's smile made the relief he was feeling obvious. Her hand in his, he led her toward the couch and chairs that formed a conversation area.

Kristen settled gracefully into the large down cushions, her brown legs gleaming warmly as she crossed them. Morgan sat down beside her, a discreet distance away. He could sense her nervousness as he waited patiently for a conversational lead.

"Tell me," Kristen said finally. "Are you as good at tennis as you are at squash?"

Morgan laughed at the inference regarding his athletic prowess. "I get out there, but golf is really my game. What about you? Do you ever tee it up?"

"I was never much good," Kristen admitted. "Despite the lessons I've had. I guess I never really appreciated the subtleties and nuances of the game. I like the one-on-one of racket sports. My opponent must deal with *me*, with balls *I* hit, not some nebulous thing like par."

Morgan laughed, thinking, This is some woman. Where the hell has she been all my life?

"Your point is well taken," Morgan said. "But beating Old Man Par becomes an addiction, like gambling. Your next time out, your next shot, will make you a winner. As we addicts are fond of saying, 'Life is golf—but in miniature.' "

Kristen chuckled warmly at Morgan's gag, her face alive with exuberance. "I did win a golf tournament once," she said. "I mean, in a way I did."

"Tell me," Morgan smiled.

"The fifteenth fairway and green at our club are right alongside the tennis courts. One afternoon—the club's member-guest championship was on—this golf ball comes sailing onto the court. It rolled along the clay right to my feet. I just picked it up and whacked it straight toward the green. Last I saw, it was flying through the oak trees. Later, I heard that the ball's owner found the thing lying on the green and figured it had caromed there off a tree. He sank the putt for a birdie, and his team went on to win the match.''

Morgan laughed expansively. "Definitely not in the strict rules of golf,'' he said.

"Golfers cheat all the time anyway,'' Kristen said, sipping her wine. "Can't happen in tennis.''

Morgan was enjoying himself, really enjoying himself. Gone was the tension he had carried back to the apartment after his day in the office. He felt loose, relaxed—like a different person altogether. Kristen had already brought him a great gift, he realized, just by being there.

During the next hour, Morgan felt himself pulled deeper and deeper into a rare mood of pleasure and tranquillity. Kristen seemed to be enjoying herself as well. They chatted about sports mostly—of matches won and lost, players they admired, of amusing anecdotes and interesting clubs where they both had played. They discussed fine points of the games they loved, as well as training and exercise techniques that seemed to work for them. They opened a second bottle of wine and stood beside the bar for a while, picking at the hors d'oeuvres. Both were more animated now, laughing unabashedly. Without their fully realizing it, the apartment became almost dark as deeper shadows cloaked the building.

Morgan looked out the window at the last golden shafts of sunlight melting behind the distant buildings. Below the apartment, Central Park was indistinct in the haze and shadows. He switched on a lamp and walked back to the sitting area, where Kristen had curled up on the couch, her shoes off, her legs under her. "Why don't you take off your tie?" she asked. "I meant to mention it before.''

"Good idea,'' Morgan said. "And why don't you do the same?'' Laughing, he set his wine glass on the coffee table in front of the couch and started unbuttoning the collar of his shirt. Kristen removed her string tie. When he sat down beside her, she didn't seem surprised.

"I almost didn't come,'' she said, abruptly.

Morgan grimaced, a sinking feeling in his stomach. "Aw no,'' he said in a hurt tone. "Why?''

"I don't know exactly. Just nervous. Afraid.''

ON DANGEROUS GROUND

"You don't have to be afraid of me, Kris. And I'll tell *you* something. *I* was nervous too."

"Was?"

"That changed when you walked in the door. I stopped worrying once you were really here."

"Somehow that doesn't seem to fit. You? Nervous? The walls must be snickering."

Morgan laughed. "I'll admit I haven't lived like a monk. But— You really want to know the truth?"

"Wait a minute. Now I'm not so sure I do."

"The truth is that I haven't had a serious relationship in many years. Nothing that ever felt like this."

"That's nice," Kristen said. "I'd like to believe you, even if you're not telling the truth." She laughed at her own candor.

"That *is* the truth." He smiled at her and she looked away, reflective. Morgan took a sip of wine, wondering, Now what the hell? Am I going to lose her? When she turned back to him, her expression seemed tense, set with resolve.

"You may not believe this," Kristen said, "and I may be frightening you off by telling you, but this is all new for me. I've been a straight arrow."

"Why should that frighten me?"

"I don't know. It's just that . . . I am still married. Technically. We're not exactly meeting on equal terms."

"We don't need *anybody's* approval."

Kristen looked at him timidly as he reached for her and brought his lips toward hers. "What matters now is what we want for each other," Morgan said.

She trembled slightly as he kissed her, so he held her closer, his mouth searching hers, demanding to be welcomed. Her lips were warm, but passive. Her hands fluttered on his upper arms, remained there, wavering. He didn't have her! Disappointed, he started to pull away to regroup. Suddenly she grabbed his shoulders decisively, pulling him closer, demanding that he continue.

Now *her* lips were the insistent ones. She kissed him the way she had on the squash court, and again the sensation took his breath away. Her body was a promise that stirred and burned beneath the irritating sheath of their clothing. He could feel her breasts heaving against his chest. A scalding erection slanted down his trouser leg, aching to be caressed. Then, suddenly, she pulled her lips away, leaning back as she looked at him, breathing hard. Morgan moved toward her again but was quickly blocked by her hands, jerking in a T-sign. "Time-out," she gasped. "Please."

"You used your only time-out on the squash court," Morgan said, trying to lean forward.

This bit of levity failed, and Morgan felt his optimism fading again as she brushed back her hair and regained her composure. "What's wrong, Kris?" he asked, weakly.

"Morg, I'm a little ashamed at the way I've thrown myself at you. Like I'm leaning on you . . . using you."

Morgan shook his head. "You don't understand. I've been attracted to you for a long time. But I never figured to have a chance . . . until that moment on the squash court, when we came on to each other. It's like a dream come true."

Her warm smile returned. Her hand caressed the side of his face. "You barely know me," she said.

"Nor you *me*," he answered. "But unless you don't like what you've seen so far, what difference does it make?"

"I just didn't want you to think . . . well, to think that I was only looking for a quick fix—and you happened to be convenient. The truth is that I made the first move because I'm very attracted to *you*."

"You make me feel very fortunate," Morgan said, his heart pounding.

"Perhaps we both are." Kristen's eyes teared and she stood. When Morgan rose to stand beside her, she reached out to take him into her arms. She laid her head against his chest. "Ever wonder what sex must be like between two terrific athletes?" she asked.

"All the time," Morgan whispered.

Kristen lifted her face. Her eyes were afire. Before Morgan could kiss her, she suddenly moved toward the bedroom, her arm in his, urging him along.

The bedroom was dark. Morgan's hand automatically hit the wall switch, turning on three lamps that created a blinding flood of light. He turned off the main switch, made his way to a smaller lamp by the bathroom door, and created a faint, mellow glow. He turned around to see Kristen standing beside the bed, her back to him. She was unbuttoning her blouse.

Morgan eased up behind her and gently placed his hands on her shoulders. Her hands lingered on the front of the blouse for a moment, then fell to her sides, dangling passively. His lips roamed softly down her cheek, nuzzling through her hair, finding the smooth warmth at the curve of her neck and shoulder. She turned her face back to him, offering her lips. He molded his body to hers as they kissed, the exciting curve of her thigh pressed against his groin. As he moved his lips away slightly, her tongue urged him to continue. His mouth lingered for a while, then pulled back as he lifted the blouse from her shoulders and let it slide down her arms. His fingers found the catch of the bra, and he lifted it up and away without touching her skin. As he let it fall, she sighed deeply, "Oh . . . ohhh . . ."

Morgan's lips muted the murmurs, and now his hands found the unfathomable pleasure of her breasts: the velvet roundness lifting from his palms and fingers, the wide aureoles which his fingertips traced, the exploding hardness of the nipples. He caressed them like precious gems, his fingers circling, always moving, pressing, pulling. He ached to take his lips from hers and taste the treasures his hands now explored, but her generous mouth and tongue claimed his lips for their own pleasure.

After a while, Kristen suddenly reached for the buttons on the side of her skirt. Morgan slid the skirt down over her thighs and let it fall in a pool at her feet. He slipped his fingers into the elastic of her half-slip and slowly revealed her bikini panties. He pulled back and stared at her. The panties were cut high at the legs, the material a taut wisp of translucence over the shadowy slope of the prominent lips. She was breathtakingly beautiful.

Kristen looked at him tenderly. "Come inside me," she said. "Hurry." She sat down on the side of the bed and reached around to pull down the covers.

Morgan wasn't even aware of the few seconds it took him to fling away his clothes. Suddenly he was there on the bed beside her, a breast in his mouth, his tongue exploring hungrily around the aureole and nipple. His hand slid along her thigh to the crotch of her panties. She spread her legs, inviting his touch to the warm dampness beneath the fabric, sighing again.

Morgan knelt beside her and used both hands to pull her panties down, her hips rising to let the fabric slip away, then her legs parting as he eased between them. She raised herself slightly and looked down her body to see his throbbing erection. "Yes . . . yes . . ." She closed her eyes and settled back, her hand gliding silkenly over his rigid penis, urging the head against the warm lips awaiting it. As Morgan bent his mouth to hers, he felt her slick satiny flesh as a tightening circle of warmth through which he slid with mounting elation. She existed for him; there *was* no other world. His body devoured the pleasure of her body. He slipped his hands beneath her backside, urging her into his long slow thrusts. Her tongue darted deeper into his mouth, searching, and at the same time he felt her legs rise slowly and cross over his back.

Locked even tighter by her velvet thighs and long clinching legs, Morgan discovered the notion that it was *he* who was being devoured. He was wanted and needed, and he was *giving*—not just fulfilling his own pleasure, but creating hers as well.

Trembling violently, she pulled her lips away, sighing, "Ohhh . . . yes, yes . . . ohhhhhhh."

Close to the bursting point, his penis signaled an extraordinary new sensation as she tightened deep secret muscles, squeezing him with wantonness, shattering the last vestige of his control.

Morgan sighed aloud, certain that at long last he was loved again.

EIGHTEEN

The silver blades of the spinning lure flashed in the sun as the bait arched across a run of smooth dark water. Towing a gossamer thread of monofilament, the lure slipped beneath the surface with a barely audible *plop,* and the line curved downstream with the pull of the Toubok current.

Derek Hill reeled awkwardly with his tiny left hand. His other hand and gangly arm worked the long graphite rod in a crude imitation of the quick jerks his father always used to impart a feeling of aliveness to the lure. Shadowed by his Stetson cowboy hat, Derek's face was locked in a grimace of determination.

Cody smiled at her son's efforts. He was certainly a persistent little bugger. He had caught nothing in the half hour they had been on the stream, yet he continued to flail at the water with enthusiasm, casting reasonably well for a five-year-old. She was surprised there had been no action. This stretch of the river was one of Jonathan's favorites and always yielded a fish or two.

The current ran strong and deep here, gathering and swirling in a pool beneath the slope of the spruce hillside, then plunging on out of sight through a wide set of rapids that curved away through the alders. On this side of the stream, a rocky beach slanted out from the birch and cottonwood forest and was a good place for easy walking and for working a lure into the pockets where trout would be holding. Out on the gravel and rocks beside the current, the afternoon sun was strong in the clean, shining air. Back by the trees where Cody was unpacking their snack, the shadows made a pool of coolness.

Buck sniffed inquisitively at the open pocket of the pack as Cody dug out the few things she had brought along: granola bars, apples, and a thermos of lemonade made from dry crystals. Looking up at Derek, she felt a sudden return of the rush of terror that had gripped her on the trail. Never had she been so frightened. She doubted now that she would ever be able to recall the experience without shuddering.

The yellow Lab poked his muzzle deeper into the pack. Cody tugged his collar playfully. "Wait for your little buddy, you bum," she chided.

A squeal from Derek sent Cody hurrying across the rock toward the stream. Squinting in the sun's glare, she saw a blurred slab of leaping silver crashing down in a watery detonation. The youngster struggled to keep the bucking rod from being torn from his grasp.

"Hold on!" Cody cried as she came alongside the embattled angler. "Don't try to reel. Just hold him."

"He's too big," Derek yelled, his arms trembling from the pressure of holding the rod aloft. Buck barked furiously as the rainbow went airborne again.

"Let me help you," Cody said. She reached around Derek's shoulders, bracing his arms with her own, and placed one hand on the rod and the other over the tiny fingers that clutched the reel handle. She could feel the trembling, deep-boring power of the fish as the line slanted into the depths downstream. The drag of the reel made a metallic shriek as line melted from the spool.

If he doesn't stop, we'll lose him, Cody thought. We'll never be able to follow him downstream.

Finally, the pressure of the bowed rod began to do its work. The fish turned short of the downstream boulders and sulked in the current.

Slowly, Cody was able to coax Derek's hand through a few turns of the the reel handle. Losing ground now, the fish panicked into an upstream run. The reel handle whirled under Cody's fingers, picking up the slack line. When the line went tight again and the rod bowed double, the fish was only yards away but still pulling strongly.

"Get him!" Derek cried.

"Don't try to reel," Cody said. "Just walk backward and hold on." She stepped back, coaxing Derek, her arms taking the strain of the rod.

Gradually, they edged the fish toward the side of the

stream. The steady pressure of the rod was unrelenting; the line held. The tiring rainbow slid onto the pea-sized gravel at the edge of the water, its gill rakers twitching.

Not very sporting, Cody thought. But we got the job done.

Yelling with pleasure and excitement, Derek dropped the rod and raced toward the fish. Buck was already on top of the trout, sniffing and barking.

"Stay back! Both of you!" Cody cried. "The hooks!" She rushed past Derek and knelt beside the fish.

The cold, hard sleekness of the rainbow was beautiful in the sunlight. The muted stripes along the sides of the fish blended into a silvery background topped by black-spotted olive shoulders. The gills continued to fan spasmodically, the eyes bright in the arrow-shaped head.

Cody squeezed the shank of the barbless hook and slid the point from the corner of the jaw. She reached both hands beneath the belly of the fish and lifted the flopping heavy body toward the water.

"I want him!" Derek shouted. "He's mine!"

Cody eased the fish into the shallows and started rocking the trout's head and gills from side to side. "Your daddy wouldn't want us to keep him," Cody said as she looked up at Derek. "We don't need him to eat, so we'll let him go."

The rainbow slipped from Cody's hands with a quicksilver shimmy. Cody stared after the fish, her gaze held by the lingering vision of the trout streaking through the shafts of sunlight that slanted down like a misty wall out where the shallows dropped off to the dark, heavy current. Trance-like, the spell of the moment hit her hard. She suddenly felt as though she were in two places at once, stretched across time itself.

She was remembering another fish. And she was remembering Jonathan.

The fish was a smallmouth bass, rusty-brown in the afternoon sunlight as Jonathan grasped it by the lower lip and lifted it from the water. He turned in the front seat of the canoe and smiled at Cody, who sat in the stern and sculled a paddle to hold the craft away from the snags along the pine-covered shoreline. Jonathan hefted the chunky, dripping fish with obvious pride and said, "Nice one. About four pounds." He stuck the butt of his fly rod down between his legs and reached his free hand to the pudgy jaw of the bass to remove the popping bug the fish had mistaken for real prey. Cody watched in surprise as Jonathan eased the fish back into the water.

"Hey!" she said. "That's our supper!"

"Too big," Jonathan laughed.

"What do you mean? I thought it was the little ones you let go."

"That's what most people do. But I've been hooked by the theory of some fish biologists who think it's the big ones that should be released. They grow to be big because they're survivors. Perhaps they represent a strain of wildness and genetic strength it's important to pass along."

"I never discuss science on an empty stomach," Cody laughed. "And I was counting on something besides freeze-dry tonight. Pick up that rod, Mr. Darwin, and see if you can bushwhack a couple of that critter's young'uns."

"Yes, ma'am." Jonathan was grinning broadly as he turned toward the shoreline and lifted the rod high over his head. Even with a smile, Jonathan's face looked almost villainous under three days' stubble of whiskers and an unkempt thatch of hair combed with his fingers. He had never started growing a beard before this trip. In the eight weeks since Cody had first met him back in New York, she had never seen him forsake his neat, polished habits of grooming. Until now.

The line swished in the evening stillness, then curved into the shadows. The bug smacked the water beside the rocky shoreline. Jonathan watched the ripples die away, then he twitched the rod. The bogus insect began to wiggle. "Hold on to your hat," Jonathan exclaimed. "He's there! I can feel him coming!"

Cody was not surprised when the bug disappeared in a heavy swirl. The rod bowed over, the taut line sliced the surface as the fish ran for deeper water. Suddenly, Cody knew she would never forget the picture of that moment: the lake stretching away toward the low hills where the sun was about to disappear, the pine-covered shoreline starting to turn gold in the light, Jonathan looking professional and impressive as he held the trembling rod against the runs of the fish. She had been very fond of him since first meeting him at a Craig Publishing party. Now she was in love with him.

The deep feelings she no longer mistrusted or wished to deny had been overwhelming since the very beginning of the trip, four days before. Certainly so by the time they had taken their first portage trail, leading deeper into the heart of the lake-strewn wilderness that comprised the Quetico-Superior forest and the Boundary Waters Canoe Area on the Minnesota-Ontario border.

Plunging steeply downhill through the birches, the last hundred yards of the trail were eel-slick with mud and lined with varicose veins of rock. At the bottom of the ridge, a narrow, brush-choked channel of backwater led toward a treeless horizon. Presumably, the lake was somewhere underneath.

Cody dropped her pack and sat down on a fallen birch that looked as if it had served other wilderness travelers for rest from time to time. The day was fair and without wind, but now in early September the north-country air held a crispness that did not yield to the sunshine. The flushed feeling that lingered from the exertion of hiking the winding two-mile portage dissipated quickly beneath Cody's cotton jersey and khaki trousers. Pack-weary muscles and a trotting pulse rate felt almost normal again when she looked up the hill to see the inverted hull of an aluminum canoe bobbing above the bushes. Moving carefully over the treacherous footing, his hands holding onto the front thwart as he balanced the craft on two lashed paddles whose blades rested on his shoulders, Jonathan reached the bottom of the slope and paused. He raised the front of the canoe and looked around for a few moments.

"Are we tired and lost . . . or just tired?" Cody joked.

Jonathan swung the canoe from his shoulders, balanced it on an extended knee for a moment, then eased it down. He unbuckled the large backpack he carried, shrugged out of the straps, and let the load fall heavily as he slumped onto the log alongside Cody.

"I'm all the way out," Jonathan gasped. "I shouldn't have tried to do that without stopping."

"The corruption and sins of our New York lifestyles show up quickly out here," Cody laughed.

"Speak for yourself, woman," Jonathan said, still breathing

hard. "You happen to be talking to a master woodsman, a scout who should have been with Lewis and Clark."

"All I can say is that the Old Scout looks a lot different right now than he did when he was sitting in '21' day before yesterday. Seems hard to believe it's the same person."

"The guy you were with back there was an impostor. You've got the real Jonathan right here—out of shape, gasping like a beached whale, and altogether happy." His smile was as warm as his words.

"Me too," Cody said. "I'm glad I came." She leaned toward Jonathan and kissed his warm, dry lips, flicking her tongue across them, tasting the perspiration along the edges of his mouth. He pulled her to him, his own lips urging her to continue. When they drew apart after a few moments, she said, "How much farther to camp?"

Jonathan looked at the horizon, reflecting. "Two lakes and one more portage—if you're up to it. We'll be there by dark."

"Lead on, then," Cody said, nodding toward the canoe. "Mustn't keep the bears waiting."

Jonathan laughed. "You won't joke like that when a big old black bear comes wandering into camp, trying to bum a free meal. They can be a hell of a nuisance."

"I've heard all the lectures, thanks. Camping trips with my father and Matt. Never did see one, though. Things that went bump in the night always turned out to be raccoons."

"You're lucky. I'm sure you were in real bear country," Jonathan said. He hefted the canoe to the edge of the slough and slid the craft into the water. "I don't want you to be frightened, though. It's very unlikely we'll see one around here."

"I didn't realize they were so dangerous—the blacks, I mean. Not the grizzlies."

"No," Jonathan said as he settled the larger pack into the canoe. "They're not like the grizzlies, but that doesn't stop them from performing the occasional facial on campers. Six people have been killed in Canada in the last ten years."

Cody shivered. "Sorry I mentioned it. Let's hope they stay clear."

Jonathan took the stern seat and shoved the canoe along the narrow water trail with strong strokes of the paddle. In the bow, Cody watched the twisting channel gradually widen to join the open blueness of a vast lake, bright and sparkling in the sun. Jonathan headed the canoe directly across the expanse toward a notch in the blue hills along the far shore. Cody picked up her own paddle, and the canoe surged ahead as her strokes joined the rhythmic dips of Jonathan's.

Cody squinted at the high puffy balls of cumulus clouds. She found herself speculating on the tremendous view one could have from that height—an awesome scene of vast wilderness country, 3,200 miles square, literally covered with lakes, great and small. Some rivers would be visible, but not the countless thousands of creeks and spring runs hidden by the dense forests. Moose, bear, wolves, wolverine, fox, otter, grouse, ducks, and geese—this vastness was host to all.

Cody could feel the pleasant glow of physical exertion begin to flow through her body. Every stroke of the paddle seemed to loosen the kinks of urban living. Like Jonathan, she managed to exercise regularly in the city with strenuous sessions of jogging and racketball. These workouts always left her feeling she had taken a quick and massive fix of physical activity. Here the hard, pack-laden walk on the portage trail and the steady paddling were different: they were an integral part of living itself, like the feel of the country and the weather.

"Take it a little easier," she heard Jonathan admonish as she leaned into a particularly hard stroke, rocking the canoe. "Smooth and easy gets it done."

"I'm okay. Besides, you're doing all the work."

"Only my share, love," Jonathan laughed.

They were nearing the middle of the lake now. The view of the distant shoreline was beginning to assume form and color: the deep shadowy greens of the pines and spruces, the lighter misty shapes of birches and popple, the splashes of crimson where maples were already beginning to turn. Out on the open water, the light breeze produced an easy chop that slapped at the bow as it lifted and dipped with the passing wavelets.

Jonathan's voice suddenly boomed out in song, startling Cody. The words were some kind of bastardized French. She turned in the seat and looked at Jonathan quizzically. He smiled and continued singing as he paddled.

> *"A la claire fontaine*
> *M'em allant promener,*

ON DANGEROUS GROUND

J'ai trouvé la'eau si belle
Que je m'y suis baigné.
Lui ya longtemps que je t'aime,
Jamais je ne t'oublierai.''

"What's that all about?" Cody asked as Jonathan's voice staggered over the remnants of the song, then trailed away.

"Mademoiselle, your Bourgeois is ashamed to say. Mademoiselle would blush."

Cody let her paddle trail in the water as she reflected on this for a moment. The voyageurs! Of course! Last night, the conversation had been full of stories of the great fur brigades of French voyageurs who explored the Quetico country between 1650 and 1850. They had mapped the routes through the wilderness, the lakes and rivers, the portage trails that linked them together. The leader of each brigade earned the respect and title of *Bourgeois*.

"I assume those so-called lyrics are very bawdy," Cody said as she began paddling again. "Take my advice: it'll never make the charts."

"Mademoiselle does not understand," Jonathan said, playfully. "It is zee song of a lonely man, far from home. He realizes he may never see his true love again, and he is very sad."

"Might make a scene in a movie, at that," Cody said, smiling as she looked ahead. "I can picture it: guy singing soft and low by the campfire, then all these voyageur cats foot-stomping and leaping about. The finale will be a freighter canoe showing up with Brigitte Bardot standing in the bow and Louis Jourdan wielding a paddle."

A dash of cold water sprayed across Cody's back. She looked around in time to see Jonathan's hand reaching into the water to splash her again.

"Hey, no fair!" Cody squealed, shaking her shoulders.

"The Bourgeois cannot permit such insubordination. Mademoiselle must be taught respect."

"I'll get you for that one," Cody laughed, turning back to the paddling.

The second portage turned out to be much shorter than the first. Still Cody felt very tired and grateful when they had paddled across another smaller lake and their ultimate campsite came into view. The sun was offering pure gold through a slot in the distant hills. The ridges alongside the lake threw cold shadows across the water. There was a sense of urgency in Jonathan's paddling now, and the canoe surged toward a point of land dominated by tall pines.

Jonathan eased the canoe alongside a level, wave-splashed slab of rock that jutted from the shoreline. Cody climbed out stiffly and walked to a darkening path that led up a gentle hill. The campsite stretched away, brown-needled and clean, in a park-like setting beneath the pines. In the best north-country tradition, the last party through had thoughtfully left a stack of firewood beside the blackened stones of the fireplace. The site was tidy and pleasant, with a vista up the lake to a point where the water curved out of sight around a shoulder of a hill.

Cody felt shamefully useless in the next half hour as she watched Jonathan turn the campsite into a wilderness home. He moved with practiced efficiency as he started a fire of twigs and small branches, snapped the two-man pup tent together and snugged it down, put down the foam mats and sleeping bags, and laid the cooking utensils and packages from the food pack onto a ground tarp beside the fireplace. As he worked, he paused a couple of times to build up the fire with larger branches. By the time he went down the hillside to turn over the canoe and secure it with a painter line, the blaze was showing cheery-bright against the darkening wall of the forest. Cody stood close to the circle of warmth, her face aglow. Over the sounds of the crackling wood, she could hear loons calling nearby. She recognized the call of a great horned owl, tuning up somewhere back in the hillside darkness.

Jonathan was carrying their five-gallon water bag when he came back up the hill. He filled a cooking pot with water, then hung the polyethylene-lined sack on a snag that jutted from the trunk of a pine. He bled some water into two stainless steel cups, set them on the tarp, and dug into the pack for the plastic bottle he had filled with cognac. Kneeling, he poured two generous slugs, then stood alongside Cody as he handed her a cup.

"I reckon cognac to be the right drink out here," Jonathan said. "Shouldn't admit it, but I'm afraid I speak with the voice of experience."

ON DANGEROUS GROUND

"Just my luck," Cody joked. "I'm in the middle of God-knows-where with a Jeremiah Johnson clone who turns out to be a boozer."

"We'll have to pace ourselves," Jonathan laughed. "That jug is all we've got. Now, how about some supper? How would you like your steak? Tomorrow we go on freeze-dry—and fish, of course."

"I'll take my meat just like yours," Cody said. "And just as large a hunk. I'm starved." She shivered slightly in the firelight. "Hey, it's getting cold. I need a sweater."

"In the tent," Jonathan said. "In the other pack." He handed her a flashlight as he knelt beside the fire to start their supper.

Away from the campfire, the tent and the scattered pines were dark and mysterious in the deepening chill. Cody switched on the flashlight, unzipped the front of the tent, and crawled inside. The interior seemed cozy and nook-like and was pine-scented. Her hands and knees pressed into the cool softness of a down sleeping bag, spread over twin foam ma-tresses. The bag covered virtually the entire floor of the tent. Cody grinned wryly as she opened the pack and dug inside for her sweater. She shrugged into the bulky wool and tried to straighten her hair.

Outside again, Cody found that the savory smells of cook-ing food were already wafting through the pines, aglow in the campfire's circle of light. The logs crackled and popped, an occasional burst of sparks drifting up and disappearing above the shadowy tops of the trees.

"That's an interesting sleeping bag," Cody said as she came back to the fireside. She could not stifle her smile. "I've never seen one like it."

"Tent for two, sleeping bag for two," Jonathan said, grin-ning sheepishly as he looked up in the firelight.

"Very tricky," Cody said.

"Actually, that's the one thing our outfitter didn't supply. It's my regular bag. Really it's two separate bags, made to zip together into one." He paused, watching her smile slowly begin to melt. "Cody, your half has never been used. Never been out of the box."

"That's nice," she said, the smile returning.

"Your Bourgeois thinks of everything," Jonathan laughed. *"N'est-ce pas?"*

Cody felt famished by the time Jonathan heaped their plates with food. With the steak, he had prepared some freeze-dry specialties: onion soup, mashed potatoes, green peas, and a peach cobbler. Devoured beside the campfire, the meal was not only immensely satisfying but was so delicious that Cody's sense of taste seemed to have been awakened from a long sleep. They washed the dishes at the edge of the lake and stowed the food pack and supplies beneath the tarp for the night, along with a generous supply of kindling and birch bark.

"It's best to keep the foodstuff away from the tent," Jonathan said, "even though I don't expect any trouble here. In really serious bear country, we'd have to hoist all that into a tree."

They carried their coffees down to the edge of the lake and out onto a rocky, treeless point to have a look at the stars, startlingly clear in the moonless night. Here, far from light pollution or atmospheric smog, the Milky Way resembled a river of light, arched across the endless vault of the heavens, brilliant enough to seem to be a part of the earth itself.

"I love looking for the Andromeda galaxy," Jonathan said, his arm around Cody. "It's not up high enough yet, but if we get up early one morning, I'll show you how to find it."

"Matt beat you to it," Cody said. "He loves the night skies. Especially Orion and Andromeda. He taught me how to line up the pointer stars of Cassiopeia with the corner of the Pegasus square to find Andromeda. Just seeing that tiny smudge of light is a real high for me. Another galaxy, over two million light-years away. Just one of billons of other galaxies."

"You're unreal," Jonathan said, surprised. "As stargazers, we have something else in common."

"It's awesome to think about," Cody teased, but her head still craned upward. After a few moments she said, "All those suns and worlds. What's out there? Lakes and forests, primordial swamps, civilizations struggling? Or just rocks and swirling gas?"

"I'm happy with the little piece of the universe I've got right here," Jonathan said, holding Cody closer. "Especially with you along and at this time of the year—mild days, cool nights, no bugs."

"I'm surprised there aren't more people here now," Cody said. "We haven't run into a single party."

"After Labor Day, not many come out. Everybody's married, with kids in school. They're stuck at home!"

"You make marriage and kids sound like a frightening thought," Cody said. "That why you're still on the loose, luring strange women into your sleeping bag?"

"I'll confess to enjoying my freedom. But the truth is that I've never met the right person. I've never really thought about getting married."

Cody turned to face Jonathan, her hand on his shoulder, her body pressing into his. Her lips were moving toward his in the darkness as she whispered, "Same here. But if I ever do think about it, you may be the first to know."

They stayed at that campsite for five days—days filled with the fun of small adventures and a magical sense of discovery. Usually, Jonathan was up first, and Cody awoke to the sounds of red squirrels chirring and woodpeckers hammering, the ax biting into the firewood, and the crackle and popping noises of the campfire. Sometimes when she emerged from the tent, a blanket of fog covered the lake until the sun burned through and the breeze pushed the shroud away. Other times the mist rose in smoky wraiths, as though individual fires were burning within the water. Ducks trading between lakes often hurtled out of the mist, saw the campsite, and banked away, their wings whistling in the stillness.

After breakfast they tidied up the campsite, replenished the firewood supply, and paddled out to pluck whatever experiences they could from the laps of the generous weather and country. They carried a day-pack with lunch and emergency gear in case they were stranded by a sudden storm. The portage trails connecting the lakes were taken leisurely, with time to enjoy the bird life and such diversions as berry-picking and photography. One or both usually did some fishing in the late afternoon as they paddled back to camp. They caught small-mouth bass and northern pike for fun, releasing the fish, and worked jigs on the deep ledges for walleye, coveted supper fish. The meaty fillets were very white and cold and seemed almost to quiver when shaken in a sack of cornmeal, salt, and pepper, and fried over the open campfire.

The good weather held until the last hours of their trip, when a wedge of smutty cloud—the leading edge of a front—loomed on the horizon across the lake. The appearance of the floatplane, a distant speck against the darkening sky, deepened the sense of disappointment Cody had been feeling since she and Jonathan had paddled away from their campsite for the last time. Returning to New York and her work did not bother her; what she disliked was the feeling that the week with Jonathan was already resigned to the past. Could the magic of their trip be relived in New York or on some future outing? Only time would tell. She wondered whether Jonathan was feeling the same melancholy. On the flight out of Minneapolis to New York, they both sat quietly, reading some, dozing, brooding—emerging from the euphoria of the adventure like a pair of sleepers tentatively facing the realities of the morning.

As the taxi from JFK crawled through the crowded approaches to the city, Jonathan suggested stopping at her place. Her spirits immediately perked up again, but later, after they had made love and coasted into euphoric sleep, she awoke startled and afraid. The bed beside her was empty. A draft of cool air played across her naked body, and she looked up to see Jonathan closing an open window. Thunder rumbled high overhead, and torrents of rain streamed through lightning flashes that exploded off the wall of the adjacent building. When Jonathan crawled back into bed, he pulled a sheet up over their heads and took her into his arms. She wrapped a leg around his, rested her head on his shoulder. Dreamily, she imagined they were still in their tent, snuggled deep in Jonathan's sleeping bag. The thunder seemed to be marching away; the rain settled into a steady murmur. She wanted to hold the bliss of the moment forever, but she could not. Sleep took her.

Just as her earlier premonition had predicted, her state of happiness was to be short-lived.

Before they could even manage to have dinner together, Jonathan seized a sudden opportunity to join an American Everest expedition as a support photographer. He left New York after a necessarily hurried phone call.

Back into her workaday routine as an associate editor on *Country Lifestyles,* one of Craig's homemaking books, Cody found herself reading everything on Everest she could find at bookstores and the library. Hastily scribbled postcards told of Jonathan's journey to Katmandu, where the real trek to the mountain was to begin. From her books, Cody mentally charted Jonathan's progress day by day as the languid late-summer skies that smothered the city gave way to the tangy freshness of autumn. Wearing sweaters for the first time since the canoe trip, she embraced the changing season with the feeling that the center of her life was being shifted in new directions. By late October, this exciting premise had faded into uncertainty, wilting like the dying leaves.

For a while, Cody found solace in her work. She discouraged the attorney and art dealer, both of whom had been regular dates before she met Jonathan. She avoided new relationships, casual encounters. She realized she was drifting, waiting for the currents to sort things out. Eventually, she thought, Jonathan will get his cute ass back here and then we'll see where we stand.

On a Saturday morning in early December, Cody received the first note from Jonathan in many weeks. The expedition had retreated to Katmandu after failing to reach the summit. He wasn't sure exactly when he would be back in New York.

Languishing over her coffee and the *Times,* Cody spotted a small ad for the Japanese documentary film "The Man Who Skied Down Everest." After her rounds of small Saturday morning chores and shopping, she caught the mid-afternoon show at a small theater behind Bloomingdale's. The film turned out to be exactly what she had hoped to see: a cinematic look at the power and grandeur of the mountain that had been such a formidable challenge for decades of adventurers.

Emerging from the theater, she peered into the gloom of an approaching storm. By the time she exited the subway, small flinty snowflakes were whipping into her face on a knife-edged wind. She tied the hood of her jacket and hurried into the tempest.

When she turned down Seventy-fourth Street toward her apartment, she saw a taxi pulling away from the curb in front of the small brownstone. A figure stood huddled beside the door buzzer, surrounded by boxes and other shapes, indistinct in the dusk. As she approached, squinting against the painful snowflakes, Cody realized that nobody was answering the parka-clad stranger's buzzes to open the door.

She drew abreast of the steps, then stopped. Two large duffel bags sat in the snow. Leaning against them was a silver metal suitcase, crudely labeled with stencil type that had faded into an indistinct streak. One word jumped from the smear. Everest! And in that same instant, as she cried "Jon!" the parka at the top of the steps whirled around. The face she saw beneath the loose shroud of the hood caused her to gasp in surprise. The man's hair was long and his beard heavy and unkempt. Beneath the gaunt, deeply tanned features, a brilliant smile left no doubt as to who this was.

"I took a chance . . . came straight from the airport," he said, pushing back his hood. "But just now, when you didn't answer the buzzer, I felt like an arrogant fool for not calling."

"You lucked out," she answered, opening her arms to him.

The lips she kissed were familiar in their urgent questing, but very different from the soft, voluptuous ones of a few months earlier. Everest had parched and cracked them. She teased her tongue over the soreness, flicking gently, then moved into his mouth, tasting him, feeling his arms strong around her through their bulky coats. He drew his face back. The smile was gone.

"I have to tell you something," he said.

"Let's go inside," Cody said, reaching for her keys.

"Listen a moment," he said. He reached for her hand and held it gently. His hand was warm but hard and callused. "For months, I've thought about one thing so much that you'd think I could find some fresh way of saying it. I'm in love with you, Cody. It's as simple as that. I can't face the idea of living the rest of my life without you."

She pressed her face against his shoulder. "Jon," she whispered, feeling the tears on her cold cheeks. "Always come back to me."

After they were married three months later, Cody found herself recalling again and again the memory of that moment in the snow and the pleasures of their honeymoon in Portugal. But the scene she relived in her thoughts most often was the moment on the lake when Jonathan had released the bass—the moment when commitment and hope had merged in her heart.

NINETEEN

O f all the strokes of editorial flair Marla Ashton displayed in re-vamping *Charm* magazine, one of the most interesting to Matt Richardson was her handling of the word *beautiful*. She had made the word taboo, banned it from all covers and editorial pages. As Marla explained to Richardson and to her staff, *beautiful* was a threatening word, suggesting a level most women found difficult to attain. The word she preferred was *pretty*.

"Pretty works," Marla said. *"Beautiful* is not on."

Matt could not help reflecting on this bit of magazine philosophy as he watched Marla follow the maître d' toward his table in a rear corner of Pen & Pencil, a favorite late-supper spot. If you can't call her beautiful, Matt thought, you might as well take the word out of the language.

Marla walked with the easy grace of a dancer enjoying her body. She was not tall—barely over five feet two, in fact—and most men, when seeing her at a distance, sensed an air of delicate vulnerability. Up close, this illusion was shattered by the heat and self-assertiveness generated by her dark, striking face.

As black as a crow's wing, her hair was a voluptuous, thick mane that begged to be touched. Brushed from the side, with no part, the hair was full and smooth at the crown then erupted into a tangle of curls that just covered her shoulders. Her dark eyelashes set off eyes that blazed with confidence and authority, never lingering as they surveyed the scene. High cheekbones sloped down to a strong but appealing chin and generous lips lightly tinged with color. A Gucci bag, strapped from her shoulder, jostled against a navy blue raw silk suit, cut smartly in front to reveal breasts that were gently concealed by a striped white blouse. An emerald and pearl necklace vied for attention next to her startling smile.

Spotting Matt, Marla gave him a little wave.

Richardson felt all the old passion for her that he had been putting out of his thoughts for so long. He rose to greet her.

"I've got a head start on you," Matt said, indicating a bourbon and water next to his plate as she took her seat.

"That won't last long," Marla said. She turned to the waiter. "A very dry Tanqueray martini, please. Up, with an olive." She smiled at Richardson. "This is a nice surprise. It's been ages."

Matt frowned guiltily as he studied her face. "There should be a law against looking so good after a full day's work."

"It's all an illusion," Marla laughed, obviously pleased. "Witchcraft, taken straight from the pages of *Charm* magazine."

"Then no wonder the book's selling so well," Matt joked.

Marla's martini arrived. She raised the glass in a toast and clinked it against his. "To all good things," she said. He nodded.

"I'm sorry this dinner had to be so late," Matt said, "but that damn newsletter of Korner's . . ." He nervously twisted his glass between his palms. "I've been on the phone for hours. The fallout has already started."

"Korner's just a messenger boy," Marla said. "Who really planted the item? Morgan?"

"Probably, but I'm not sure."

Matt started to hand Marla a menu, but she waved it off. "I know what I want," she said. "Steak and salad and some wine."

"That's the kind of two-fisted supper I come here for," Matt said. He signaled the waiter.

They ordered their steaks, a bottle of excellent Burgundy, and another round of drinks.

"Can you pull it off, Matt?" Marla asked abruptly.

"Which? Save the magazine—or save my ass?"

"That's the rub, isn't it?" Marla said. "Flush that jerk-off magazine down the drain, and your bid for the presidency becomes stronger."

Matt grimaced. "You know I can't do that."

"Don't be silly," Marla said, shrugging. "The idea bombed. The dogs won't eat it."

Marla's joke was an old favorite among Madison Avenue's apocryphal tales. A well-financed company hired the world's leading experts to concoct the most nutritional form of dog food ever sold. The launching of the product was the subject of one of the most extensive and expensive advertising and marketing campaigns in history. Within a few weeks, the company was out of business, the packages of dog food gone from grocery shelves. The dogs wouldn't eat it.

"Call it mid-life crisis, if you want a label," Richardson said. "I've decided to dig in, make my stand."

"But you've done so much. All the books . . ."

"Just magazine messes I was able to clean up for Tony Craig. This book is mine. It's me."

"It's a stiff," Marla said. "Ten million bucks' worth. Our fellow board members want their pound of flesh."

"Believe it or not," Matt said, "I intend to put up one hell of a fight. Once Jonathan takes over the book—"

"That won't feed the lions," Marla interrupted with a sarcastic laugh.

"I have some other moves I'm making," Matt smiled. "I won't bore you with them now."

Marla sipped her martini and studied him without smiling, her eyes dark and serious. "How can I help you, Matt?"

"Obviously, I need your support."

"Is that all? You could have told me that on the phone. For the first time in months, you've asked me out."

"I guess I wanted to turn back the clock," Matt said. "I'm not enjoying the present all that much."

Marla started to speak, then paused as a waiter delivered their salads. She picked up her fork and stared pensively at her plate for a moment. When her eyes came up to meet Richardson's, her expression showed a mood of concern, a touch of sadness.

"What's happened to you, Matt?"

Richardson stirred uneasily. He laid down his salad fork and picked up his drink in its place. "I'm okay," he said casually, then took a sip of bourbon.

Marla leaned forward, her eyes glistening. "I've never heard you talk about the past . . . about ever going back to *anything.*"

"Come on," Matt sighed. "Give me a break."

"The Matt I used to know was always looking ahead."

"He still is. How about going up to my place after dinner?"

As soon as the words were out of his mouth, Matt realized his remark was a lame, weak stab at lightening the mood. Marla's expression revealed she had no intention of letting him off the hook. "I thought you had gone back to Kristen. I thought that's what you wanted."

"We're still separated. It's over."

"That's too bad," Marla said. "I suppose I should feel guilty. But I don't."

"I'm glad. I feel the same way. I wouldn't change a page you and I wrote together—except the ending."

Marla had first attracted Matt's attention four years before, when she had been a rising star at *Redbook*. Previously, she had done successful stints on smaller magazines, working her way up the ladder with creative ideas and the ability to write titles and blurbs that hooked and pulled readers. With the revamping of *Charm* on the horizon, Matt had lured her from *Redbook* and brought her aboard *Charm* as a senior editor. Her quite brilliant career had soared while she was rebounding from a disastrous marriage to a French businessman, a wealthy aristocrat with a drinking problem. He had the nasty habit of belting Marla as casually as he belted down Scotches, beginning in midmorning.

After Marla had been at *Charm* for a year, Matt was convinced she had the stuff to handle the new direction he had been contemplating for the book. He made her editor in chief and formally launched the new concept.

While he and Marla had been engrossed in the turnaround of *Charm*, their meetings on the book's new editorial slant and graphics had brought them together almost every day. As the occasion for showcasing the new concept approached, their planning sessions became more intense, spilled over into the evening hours, then dinner dates. Finally, over a long weekend Matt had been intending to spend alone at his lakeside cabin in the remote forests above Virginia's Shenandoah Valley, things came to a head.

Despite Matt's pleas to have her join him, Kristen was

playing in a squash tournament back in Princeton. Her heavy sports commitments were a constant source of friction between them, one of the major tremors shaking their marriage at that time. Matt liked to get away from the pressures of New York to the peace and solitude of the country. He hated sporting games of all kinds, abhorred country clubs and their inherent atmosphere, and stayed away from cocktail and dinner parties unless they were related to business. He knew he should be living on a farm—or having one as a weekend place, at least—but such an idea seemed too ambitious for his heavy schedule—the commuting, the nights spent in the city, the stuffed briefcase that stayed with him like an appendage.

This aspect of his life, while irritating, was not the bedrock of the problems he and Kristen were having.

She wanted a child—and he could not give her one. Every test, every experiment, and the consultations that followed, made his loins the culprit. Kristen was understanding, sympathetic in every way as they tried every physical and psychological potion they could find. Ultimately his ardor began to suffer at about the same time Kristen began to immerse herself in sports and fitness to the point of professionalism. As she grew more beautiful and desirable, his nerves tightened with frustration, and their sexual compatibility faded to infrequent and inadequate performances in bed. Once the noose of guilt and fear had settled over him, he could feel it tighten with every move he tried to make.

At some point he felt his mind begin to gnaw on the idea that the eleven-year difference in their ages was the real source of their problems. He could feel himself aging, feel the shadow of his own mortality. Even though the gamble on *Charm* seemed to be developing nicely, he felt professionally vulnerable and at risk. The job of turning around the Craig stable of magazines was sapping his energies, demanding his utmost concentration. He lived day by day in a crisis atmosphere, and the stress carried over into his personal life. Instead of being a refuge, his marriage had become one more center of tension.

Alone at the cabin that Saturday, he had walked the woods for hours, noting with pleasure the many winter birds along the trails and the flash of deer and wild turkeys disappearing into the trees ahead. He chopped firewood until he felt the soothing relaxation of honest fatigue and hunger. He had just stoked up the fire, laid out a steak for supper, and poured himself a drink when the sudden crunching of gravel on the lane outside signaled an intrusion that was to change his life.

The final dummy of the revamped magazine in hand, Marla had flown to Dulles airport and rented a car. She arrived at Matt's vacation cabin, unannounced, to show him the result of their labors of the past several months. Matt's show of exhilaration—he knew in his guts that the magazine would become a success—was followed by intense passion and sexual bliss in front of the fireplace, where blazing oak and maple logs cast a glow over their naked bodies.

Then came the underground warfare of their illicit affair: the secret meetings, the lies and excuses, the constant vigilance undermined by their knowing glances when they were together in public. The situation was new to Matt; he had never cheated on his wife. It was inevitable that she would become suspicious and have her suspicions confirmed. When the blowup came, she had not asked for a reconciliation or that he end the affair. She simply wanted Matt out of her life.

As *Charm* became successful, Matt's priorities shifted from Marla's magazine to his longtime dream, the creation of *In Wildness.* Piloting *Charm* on her own, Marla sought his input less and less as she immersed herself in the magazine phenomenon they had created. Her lifestyle soared like the newsstand and advertising numbers the book now enjoyed. After Matt's successful bid to land her a spot on the company's board of directors, the first cracks began to appear in their personal relationship. While she was ready to fly to Cannes or St. Moritz at the drop of a Vuitton bag, he preferred a less frenetic pace and, given the opportunity, would opt for a few days at his Virginia cabin or a good fishing trip. The closer he stood to the heat he and Marla had generated with the *Charm* turnaround, the deeper he felt a conflicting sense of values. On the one hand, he was obsessed with his dream of seeing *In Wildness* duplicate *Charm*'s success; on the other, he felt curiously detached from the event he had created. He sometimes felt he had climbed to the top of the hill only to find no clear view at all, only another hill, far away, murky in the distance. That distant peak was called *In Wildness,* and Matt knew he would have to climb it before he could feel he had accomplished *any-thing.* The spoils of the editorial wars he had won so far were to be enjoyed by others—the company, Tony Craig, Marla. His personal battle still raged, and he discovered with Marla, just as he had with Kristen, that his affection was not limitless. His priorities were shaped not by the nurturing of a relationship but by deeper forces he could not deny. He could *share* only so much with interest and enthusiasm. He could *give* only so much with devotion and commitment. Part of himself remained deeply personal and private, locked away from others but with a voice he, at least, could always hear, a voice strong and demanding.

Affairs generally do not languish like tired marriages. Lived on the keen edge of emotional intensity, they are apt to explode, rather than decay. Matt and Marla's relationship was no exception. A bitter shouting match that followed Matt's refusal to accompany her to Palm Springs over a weekend prompted Marla, a week later, to gracefully suggest that the romance had run its course. Matt argued, rather weakly, on behalf of continuing, with promises of compromise and accommodation, but to no avail. Their lifestyles were too divergent, Marla ruled, their personalities each too strong to accommodate one another. Hurt but not bitter, Matt had resigned himself to his loss. During the many months while work and the crisis over *In Wildness* had kept him occupied, he had suffered his fate in silence and tried to keep her out of his mind.

Until tonight!

Marla studied Matt as she poked at her salad. "If you knew Kristen would take you back, right now, would you go?"

"She won't."

"Did you ever really believe she would? Is that why you let us drift apart?"

Matt's face showed genuine pain. "Can't we try again? Don't I deserve a chance to rewrite that ending?"

"I don't know what you deserve. And I don't understand you, Matt. What is it you want? Bed and breakfast? A shoulder to cry on? You already know you've got my support at the board meeting."

"I *was* counting on that," Matt said, sheepishly. "I can't win without it."

"And beyond that?"

"After I save the magazine—and I still believe I will—I've got to address myself to another problem: becoming president of the magazine division. Beating Morgan Procter isn't going to be a cakewalk."

"No, it isn't. But what do I have to do with that?"

"I need you with me, really with me, all the way. My personal life is shattered. I can't go on like this."

Marla reached across the table for Matt's hand. "Matt, you're like a strong, beautiful bird, caught with a wing down right now. When you're well again, you'll fly on, wandering. You can't help it. I'll be frustrated again, wanting to actually throw something at you this time."

"You're tempted, aren't you? Say it! You still feel something for me."

"Of course I do, Matt. But that doesn't mean things haven't changed. The irony is that we've swapped places. Now I'm the one who's not sure about my feelings. I like the way I'm living my life right now. It's what I've always wanted. I'm not ready for commitment . . . complications."

"Just like that, we write 'The End'?"

"It hasn't been *just like that.* We drifted apart a long time ago, Matt. It's not my fault you didn't notice, or care."

Before Matt could respond, the waiter hovered over the table with their food. Matt and Marla were silent as they watched the captain open the Burgundy and pour a sample. Matt nodded his head casually and waved at the bottle. When their glasses were filled, he picked his up and offered a toast, smiling again.

"Truce," he said, clicking his glass against hers. "I want you to enjoy yourself."

"I shall," Marla said enthusiastically, "as long as you don't turn morbid on me."

Matt laughed and picked up his knife and fork. They both fell to their food and wine with enthusiasm. The conversation shifted to *Charm.* Marla loved talking about her magazine, and Matt was a good listener.

After a while, Matt began to feel as though he were in

some sort of time warp, back at the height of their affair. Marla seemed to be enjoying herself as well, relaxing, becoming more animated and responsive. She even suggested brandy and dessert.

Matt picked up his snifter and swirled the pool of cognac. "I guess this means we're having our nightcap here, instead of . . . elsewhere," Matt said, smiling.

The line did not provoke the lighthearted putdown he'd expected. Marla gave him a knowing look as she said, "It's been rough, hasn't it, Matt? You haven't had a chance to run and play in a long time."

"No, ma'am. I surely haven't."

Marla studied him across the table, staring silently. Her mouth broke into a mischievous little grin.

"Tell me," she said, "why haven't you answered my memo on the book excerpt I want to buy from *Loving and Winning*?"

Matt laughed and leaned forward. He spoke in a whisper, as though the entire room were trying to focus on their conversation. "You mean the advanced guide to condom etiquette?"

" 'Etiquette' is too dull a word," Marla said, chuckling. "I think the text is more exciting, more mischievous, than *that*. I especially like the part about using flavoring during fellatio."

Richardson could not contain his laughter, nor the blush that flooded his face.

"The publishers think the book is going to be a huge seller," Marla continued. "And I agree. I want that excerpt in *Charm.*"

"Marla, it's very explicit."

"It's tasteful and well done," she countered. "And the author knows what she's talking about."

Marla picked up a cream-filled cannoli from her dessert plate.

Fascinated, his loins churning with excitement, Richardson watched as she brought the pastry seductively to her mouth, flicking her tongue around its tip, then slowly caressing it with her lips, her eyes never leaving his. Finally, she took a nibble from the sweet, licking her lips as she swallowed in mock ecstasy.

"Ummm," she moaned. "That's heavenly."

ON DANGEROUS GROUND

Before Matt could respond, she added, "How would you like to discuss the pros and cons of this in more detail?"

Matt signaled for the bill.

Abed at the Plaza Hotel, waiting for sleep that would not come, waiting for the end of the weariness that seemed to have permeated his very bones, Jonathan Hill tried desperately to free his thoughts from the turbulent events surrounding him.

He tried to recall when he had last gotten some decent sleep. It was the night before he had discovered the grizzly tracks, the night before Matt's message had arrived. When had all that happened? A week ago? No, he realized. Only two days ago—two days that had brought him even closer to the truth about his own future and the fate of the magazine.

There was nothing he could accomplish here. The magazine was doomed, and Matt was stupid—a blind fool—to think the company would let him make a fresh start. Even if Craig and the board accepted the new game plan, Matt was backing the wrong horse for the second time; the editorship was something Jonathan knew he could not handle. His visit to the *In Wildness* offices had confirmed his deepest fears about the condition of the magazine and the responsibilities of running it.

Did Matt really want to hear the truth? Did he want to know that the book lacked guts and focus? That the layouts were bland, the pieces long-winded, the titles and blurbs written like something by Cotton Mather? Surely Matt was aware of these things already. Why then had *he* been sent over there? An acknowledged spy whose very presence had spread a pall of fear among the staff.

Jonathan had begun his visit by reviewing layouts in the art department, then going over the tentative editorial lineups Ted Walsh had prepared to go into production for the next two issues. As he roamed through the offices, Jonathan had sensed the staff's growing tension, especially that of the senior editor, Don West, and the art director, Jeff Wheaton. Their faces were tight with fear, their gestures and speech excited and defensive.

Jonathan had decided to relieve the pressure by calling a meeting.

Walsh's office, where they assembled, was barely a cut

above the grubby offices and cubicles that housed the magazine's staff. Every surface seemed to need paint, the carpet was faded and worn, and there was only a small window to offer a smudge of light from the alley outside. Walsh's slovenly ways, which his secretary apparently could not control, contributed to the general dreariness of the room. Piles of manuscripts were scattered about, along with layouts, books, and stacks of galley proofs of articles in production. The stuff was just *there;* no sense of order or priority seemed to exist.

"This place certainly looks lived in," Jonathan said to the group at large.

"Or died in." The immediate quip from the lone female of the group, an associate editor, brought a burst of laughter that cut through the tension.

"Wait a minute," Jonathan said, laughing with the others. "It's not quite time for a wake. And we're not going to throw the baby out with the bath water." He paused, looking at each person individually, then went on.

"Okay. You're asking yourselves: 'Why is this guy here?' You've heard rumors . . . newsstand sales down . . . the ad picture dismal . . . the book losing money, about to fold. Well, I want to tell you a few things unequivocally. One, the book is not folding! Two, I am not here to take Ted's job or to purge the staff." Already there was a general surge of relaxation among the faces that stared at him. "I came in at Matt Richardson's request to see if I might offer some ideas we can all work on together to turn this thing around. Sometimes a fresh viewpoint can be useful, and that's all I've been asked to provide. I'm going to offer my opinion and get back to the Toubok River as quickly as I can. You'll find me there, catching trout, while you guys do the real work here." Again laughter. The tension was broken.

"Did you know that Ted is heading for your cabin on a surprise visit?" Don West asked.

"Why, no." Jonathan was shocked. What the hell was Walsh up to? "I didn't even know he was in Alaska until today."

"Good timing, anyway," Jeff Wheaton said sarcastically.

"You've all been under a lot of pressure," Jonathan said quickly. "I'd like to concentrate on your individual feelings about the book. That's why I would like to suggest now that we break this up, and that I meet individually with each of you for a few minutes before you leave today. I'll start with Don, then call each of you as we move along." The editors started to rise slowly, reluctant to leave this charismatic man. "Remember," Jonathan added as they started for the door. "We're all in this together. We *are* the book!"

When the room had cleared, Don West was ready to talk. "That was a nice piece of bullshit," he said. "I even think one or two of them believed it."

"I happen to have been telling the truth."

"Come on. Do you think I'm a fucking imbecile?"

"Specifically, what do you mean?"

"You expect me to believe that Richardson brought you all the way to New York for an opinion? Ted's out on his ass . . . and I assume you'll want to pick your own number two. Shall I begin to pack?"

"Think what you wish," Jonathan answered. "You're obviously married to the notion."

"I have good instincts when it comes to danger."

"I'm sure Matt wished those instincts had helped Ted make this book fly."

"Oh-ho!" West cried excitedly. "Now we're a team, Walsh and me! Well, you and Richardson don't know that this asshole"—he pointed at Ted's desk—"has totally ignored my input here. The man will not listen!"

"Why didn't he put somebody else in your spot if he thought you were so wrong?"

"Because he has no guts! He chose to work around me, leave me in limbo rather than fight it out in the open."

"If things were so bad, why haven't you resigned?"

"Because I'm not a well-connected hotshot," West said angrily. "I'm fifty-five years old. I've got a kid at Yale. I was with *Look* and it went under. I was on the old *Post* when it went. Do you know what my résumé is worth out there on the street now?"

Jonathan was quiet, watching him. West stood and walked over to the window, looking out at nothing particular. "You know," he said, "I had such great hopes. I loved the whole idea of this book so much. Oh, not that I'm a skilled outdoorsman like you, but I do love wilderness, and I'm a hell of a good editor."

"I don't see what your problem is."

"You've looked at the book. The answer is right there."

"Would you care to enlighten me?"

Contempt was etched on West's face. "I can't help you. This kind of thing has happened to me before. I'm through teaching school without being paid for it! You pick my brains, map out the program to turn the book around. That's the scenario, right?"

"I thought you said you cared about the book."

"I do. And if Richardson wants me to help, he's got to come to me. I won't be ignored anymore."

"I'll tell him that."

"Good. He knows where to reach me." West looked at his watch. "Look," he added. "People are waiting for me for dinner. Talk with me some more tomorrow. Perhaps I'll feel better. This is all quite a shock right now, you swooping in here like this. I resent the hell out of it!"

"I'm just following orders."

"No . . . it's more than that. You're blind! Just like the rest of them! They put a fool in charge of the ship, then they're surprised to see it hit a reef."

"You're not bothered by loyalty to the people you work for, are you?"

Don West paused at the door. "You know, it's funny you say that. Because I was—when we started. I truly was. I guess they took that away from me along with the rest."

The interviews that followed were no better. Every staffer voiced disappointment, recriminations. Morale wasn't merely low; it didn't exist. A couple of people even told Jonathan they were wishing he *had* arrived to take over the book.

Later, after sending out for sandwiches and milk, he turned his attention to the inventory, the actual manuscripts purchased for future use. He did not try to read every piece but searched through each effort quickly to get a feel for what Walsh had been buying and assigning. It was while immersed in this task that he discovered something which still bothered him. More than thirty articles and their accompanying photographs were missing from the inventory. They had been checked out of the office by Don West.

More of the same tomorrow morning, Jonathan thought as he tried once again to shut down the parade of anxieties that was keeping him awake. He would be meeting Matt for lunch. He would try to tell him the truth about the magazine, then sneak out of town as fast as possible.

All right, Jonathan thought, you've decided: tomorrow you tell Matt that you're going home—to stay! You warned him before you came that you weren't going to take the reins.

What reins? The book was going under!

Why can't you relax and get some sleep, then?

The noise was keeping him awake, he decided. The night sounds of the city were oppressive after living in the wilderness for so long. He could hear the groaning machinery of a garbage truck, lifting its load on a nearby street. Occasionally, voices passed in the hallway. Water hissed through the plumbing, and the air conditioner rumbled incessantly. The lateness of the hour had not stilled the traffic.

He tried to think about the Toubok, about Cody and Derek and Buck and the way the cabin would look now in the evening shadows. Perhaps they were out fishing; it was a nice time for that. He could picture a rainbow trout leaping from the stream, imagine Derek's excitement.

Another garbage truck joined the first, triggering an explosion of nerve-grating noise. Were they going to be doing this all night?

A shrill voice echoed past the hall door, jolting him fully awake. He could make out some words as the sound trailed away: "Dave, just relax, for Christ's sake! I've already got my five best people on this!"

Shit!

Jonathan turned to his other side. His face found a cool, fresh spot on the pillow.

He would try going back to the mountains now; perhaps that way he could finally get some rest. He turned his thoughts to Everest, remembering.

The trek to the mountain led over brown, sun-baked hills, climbing steeply through high forests cut by gorges where streams were torrents surging down from the eternal snows. At

Namche Bazar he had his first good look at the black triangular shape of the summit, thrusting over the rim of the Nuptse-Lhotse massif, trailing a wavering flag of snow into the indigo sky, a silent reminder of the winds that rage on the upper reaches of Chomolungma, Goddess Mother of the World. Approaching the Thyanboche lamasery, he pondered a parable of Buddha: *If, every ten thousand years, a feather is brushed against the highest mountain, there will come a day when the mountain will be eroded away. . . .* The monks were spinning their prayer wheels, endlessly chanting *Om mane padme hum* —Hail to the Jewel in the Lotus. Base camp was at the beautiful and dangerous Khumbu Icefall, the groaning, shifting glacier that had almost taken his life. Above the river of ice, the Lhotse face led up to his highest camp, at almost 26,000 feet on the South Col, a bleak, rocky saddle from which the final assault teams launched their two-day bids for the summit. In his mind, Jonathan was there on the Col now, huddled deep in his down sleeping bag, the wind tearing at his small tent, roaring down the southeast ridge like the voices of gods defied.

He slept.

TWENTY

The early morning hours were Cody's favorite time for writing. The cabin beside the Toubok seemed especially peaceful then, with Buck out for his rounds and Derek still in bed. Only the occasional burst of typewriter keys broke the stillness as she worked on her manuscript. Her old portable sat in a pool of light from a lamp using long-lived lithium batteries. The small alcove that served as her office was dark, and behind her the main room of the cabin was dusky with shadows that the light from three windows and the screened front door could not dispel.

Cody had been hunched over the typewriter for an hour. She paused now, stretched her arms, and got up to make herself a cup of tea. She wore khaki shorts and an old plaid shirt, faded and softened by many washings in galvanized tubs and the ancient hand-cranked wringer she used.

The large main room of the cabin was organized into two separate living areas. The kitchen was built around a wood cooking stove and contained a dining table and chairs, numerous cabinets, and a counter with a spacious sink. A huge Franklin stove at the other end of the main room served as both fireplace and heater during the cold months and was the focal point of a sitting area, which contained cushioned hand-crafted chairs and a sofa. Bookshelves and cabinets were built into the paneled walls, but even this abundant storage space and a spare bedroom could not hold the equipment that was constantly arriving for field testing and use in articles. Snowshoes, packs, tents, stoves, gadgets and gizmos—the stuff overflowed into the main room despite the family's constant efforts to maintain neatness. Heavy equipment, including the generator and the gas-operated water pump that pulled water from the river for storage in a 300-gallon tank built into the house, were kept in an outbuilding attached to the rear of the cabin. The toilets were in a primitive outhouse, but a combination shower/sauna in the main house served for baths, and the kitchen sink had running water. Casual cooking was done on a couple of countertop Coleman stoves, sparing the main stove for more elaborate meals and additional heating during the frigid months. Light was provided by kerosene and lithium-battery lamps, except for the rare occasions, mostly during midwinter, when Jonathan felt like turning on the main generator.

When the kettle sang out, Cody poured steaming water over a couple of tea bags and carried the cup to the screen door. Beyond the grassy hillside, past the river and the trees beyond, she could see distant peaks, white in the sun. Mosquitoes pressed against the screen and whined in the drowsy stillness. She sipped her tea as her thoughts slipped away from her writing and settled on Jonathan. She was lonely without him, lonelier knowing he was so far away.

The first strains of Buck's distant barking were not unusual and did not arouse Cody's immediate interest. She was aware of the yellow Lab's discordant voice, but she continued thinking about Jonathan and Matt, about New York itself: the Craig Publishing offices, the streets and shops, the restaurants. For a moment, she wondered if she had made a mistake by not accompanying Jonathan. The trip could have provided an interesting break in her daily work on her book. Was she afraid, diffident about resisting Matt? No, she decided. Her writing was going well; that was the only reason she had not gone with Jonathan.

When she turned to put down her cup and resume her bout with the typewriter, Cody realized that Buck's full cry was still ringing through the stillness. Whatever the dog was hassling was no pushover.

Cody opened the screen door and looked out. The sound was coming from down by the river, upstream a distance. This was not Buck's snowshoe hare bark, his porcupine or skunk outrage. The dog had tangled with something unusual this time.

Without hesitating further, Cody picked up the .375, bolted a cartridge into the chamber, and went outside. She could not see anything unusual as she walked down toward the river, the rifle in her hands.

She turned upstream on a path that led through the birches alongside the chuckling, steady current. Buck's barking seemed to be coming from one spot, not far ahead.

At the edge of the birches, the path emerged onto more open ground—tundra and clusters of spruce. Finally, she could see the dog, but not the source of his agitation. Buck was running up and down along the bank, barking furiously at the stream. Cody began to relax. This couldn't be a bear or anything dangerous. Either the dog or the beast would have fled. But what the hell was it?

"Easy, boy!" she shouted as she moved on.

Buck ran to her, barking and panting, then immediately spun around and raced back to the edge of the water, barking at something on the other side of a tangled mass of driftwood logs that had been stranded by high-water floods during springtime.

Cody stepped around the cluster of sun-bleached branches. She gasped as she saw the yellow keel of a kayak bobbing in the sunlight, trapped in a snarl of dead limbs in a backwater eddy. The main current slid past, out beyond the swirling water that pushed the upside-down craft first one way, then another, always failing to free it from the grasp of the branches.

Cody looked upstream, squinting in the sunlight as she cupped one hand over her eyes. The landscape was empty. Buck's incessant barking had stopped, and the only sound was the rush of the current past the snags of the downed limbs.

There had been an accident! That much was obvious. Somewhere upstream—probably in the rapids five miles away —somebody had dumped while running the river. Where was the person now? Wet and cold on the bank? Beside a fire, joking with friends?

Or drowned?

The thought set her heart racing with even greater anxiety. She had to *do something!*

She decided she would walk upstream for a short distance and see if anybody was there.

She placed the rifle over her shoulder and started up the trail, glancing back at the kayak. One end seemed to be coming free. The craft could be slipping away, she realized. She often kayaked along the river with Jonathan and knew that if the craft broke free of the snags, it could be carried downstream for miles. She turned back to fetch it.

Cody propped the rifle against a snag and waded into the eddy. The water was a cold shock on her bare legs. She got both hands on the keel and started to pull. The craft seemed extraordinarily heavy. An underwater snag could be holding it, she reckoned. She pulled harder.

The opposite end of the kayak tore loose from a snag with a lurch, and the current instantly shoved the craft from her grasp, pushing it broadside against a log she could see just beneath the surface.

The deck caught on the log, and the powerful push of the water flipped the craft upright in one sudden motion.

Cody screamed, turning and staggering toward the bank. She dropped to her knees in the sand, vomiting in one aching gush, then gasping in piteous cries.

The image would be in Cody's mind forever: the arms dangling uselessly to the sides of the slumped body; the bright-red flotation vest zippered neatly up to the collar, ending in a shadowy hole.

The body's neck, its head, were gone.

TWENTY-ONE

Nicholas Bertorelli, the art director of *Charm* magazine, groped through the canvas satchel slung from his shoulder, cursing under his breath. Where the fuck were his keys?

Bertorelli's designer jeans fit so tightly that they would not permit space for a dime, much less his set of keys. The anxiety and anger that surfaced simultaneously in his eyes were hidden behind Cardin sunglasses. He wore a Greek fisherman's hat that had never been any closer to the Aegean than East End Avenue. His denim work shirt was unbuttoned halfway down his chest to reveal a thatch of black hair and a gold chain festooned with a medallion. The shirt had never known the stain of perspiration, for the only time it was in the sun was when Bertorelli was entering or exiting a taxi, as he had just done in front of his townhouse on East Eighty-first Street.

The empty street of attractive brownstones echoed the chirps of sparrows and the footsteps of a passing couple. Small leafy trees, painted by the midday sun, cast pools of shadow on the parked cars and across the sidewalks. Bertorelli's anxiety wiped out any solace he might have felt from owning one of the loveliest homes on one of the most fashionable streets of the area.

The *Charm* staff meeting he had escaped twenty-five minutes before had left him nervous and agitated. First of all, he had tangled with the managing editor, Bob Gainer, over the succession of tardy layouts that had resulted in late copy and missed closings. Then Marla Ashton had blown into the meeting, over an hour late, acting like the Queen of Fucking Sheba, as usual. She had challenged Bertorelli's choice of a model in tennis garb for the cover of her latest brainstorm: an entire issue devoted to health and fitness.

He could hear her voice now, mocking him. "Tennis has been done a lot, Nikki."

"Darling," he had countered. "Remember the rule. If Bertorelli did not do it, then it hasn't been done."

"I'm not convinced," Marla had replied, coolly.

The meeting had broken up without a decision being reached. Then the annoying wait for the elevator and the interminable cab ride had added cumulative points to Bertorelli's soaring irritation.

With his keys in hand, he threw the two dead-bolt locks on the front door. In the dim, cool foyer, he tossed his hat and satchel on a hall table and bounded up the carpeted stairs. Even before he reached the main living area on the second floor, he was aware that the apartment was empty. Had Marcy been there, her presence would have been announced by the sounds of her current rock favorites: Van Halen's wild guitar licks soaring into the ozone, abandoning even the outer limits of control; Bon Jovi's anthems exalting the emotions of multitudes. Nicholas's current live-in love was a model whose interesting face had recently attracted the attention of the dream merchants of advertising and who was enjoying a spate of bookings.

The living room Nicholas entered from the stairs was an explosion of Art Deco color and shape. Stone, glass, and metal —helped by a smidgen of wood—formed the artifacts and furniture. The stark white walls were emblazoned with abstracts, Bertorelli's own, bright in the sun that streamed through windows overlooking the greenery of a courtyard. He crossed the living room to the door of the bedroom and looked in, swit on the light.

Even though the room was an unkempt mess of clothing, bedding, and dishes—the housekeeper would not arrive until the afternoon—it held an obvious satyric ambience. The bed was massive, with convenient controls of a projection television system and nearby stacks of stereo equipment. A walk-in closet and a huge bathroom, both with lights left on by Marcy, completed the setup. Nicholas turned off all the lights and shut the bedroom door.

Between another bathroom and a large, well-equipped kitchen with an adjoining breakfast nook, a small set of wooden stairs curved up toward another level. Taking these, Bertorelli climbed on up to his studio.

ON DANGEROUS GROUND

The skylighted room, almost the playing area of a tennis
court in size, created a sensory fantasy of being on an island
between earth and sky. A verdant burst of tall plants and leafy,
vine-covered planters completed the illusion of the outdoors.
The room was divided into three work areas that accommo-
dated their owner's passion for the visual arts. In one, a draft-
ing board was surrounded by myriad shelves and drawers of
pens and paper and a long wide table now covered with layouts—"boards" as they were called in the magazine business.
In another section of the room, Bertorelli worked in oils, acryl-
ics, and watercolors on his various canvases. In the largest
area of all, the assorted cameras, lights, and prop accoutre-
ments allowed him to plan and shoot everything from micro-
closeups to lavish fashion scenes.

Nicholas paused at the entrance, checking the thermostat.
He switched on the adjacent stereo receiver, and the sounds of
Mozart became a gentle presence in the room. Nicholas walked
over to the table and stood looking down at the three rows of
layouts that completely covered the surface.

The logo and cover had given him the most trouble, and
the board where they were pasted down held his gaze now.
The words *In Wildness* had been difficult enough to work with,
but the problem of tacking on the phrase *Is the Preservation of
the World* had tested his graphic skills. The phrase had to read
quickly, or it would become lost in the clutter of the cover
blurbs. On the other hand, if it appeared too sizable, it would
detract from the power of the larger title. He had found a solu-
tion in one of the newer families of sans serif type, something
completely unlike the traditional faces used by men's magazines. The type was sleek but bold and powerful. It reeked of
Madison Avenue. That was its strength, Bertorelli decided. The
break with traditional outdoor magazine graphics created an
aura of compelling freshness about the book. The sans serif
logo and blurbs were a perfect marriage with the cover photograph, which was another bold departure in itself. The shot
was of a pretty young woman, leaning down to net a trout,
while her male companion tended a frying pan over a campfire
in the background. Beyond their tent, the Grand Teton mountains rose in lofty splendor to complete the wilderness setting.

As Bertorelli walked along the table, his critical gaze

sweeping over the boards that had occupied the greater part of his time for the past four months, he felt more than satisfied. He was elated. The graphic theme begun on the cover carried through to the final page. His secret redesign of *In Wildness,* the creation of this new dummy that would be the showpiece of the book's new direction, had been completed at three o'clock in the morning. Now for the rewards!

Nicholas's optimistic contemplation and the music-sweetened peace of the room were shattered by the startling sound of a harsh door buzzer. He hurried for the stairs, reminding himself for the thousandth time to get that goddamn bell replaced with a gentler chime. Downstairs, he could feel his excitement mounting as he peeped through the security viewhole, then opened the front door.

As always, the tall figure of Morgan Procter looming in his doorway was unnerving to the five-six Bertorelli. Procter removed his sunglasses, smiling. "Are we ready?" he asked.

"The boards are," Bertorelli answered, looking past Morgan into the street. "But where's West?"

"I thought he'd be here," Procter said, starting inside. "I guess he's late."

Nicholas leaned outside the door and saw Don West hurrying up the street. Spotting Bertorelli, he waved and broke into a trot. He was out of breath as the three men climbed the stairs together. As they crossed the living room on the second floor, West exclaimed, "What a setup!"

Bertorelli laughed. "It's trompe l'oeil: an illusion that makes me *look* like a rich man. Anybody want a drink?"

Don West started to reply but was cut off by Procter's quick "No! I want to get on with this. I've an important lunch date."

"Let's go, then," Nicholas said, leading the others up the stairs.

"You've seen most of this in various stages," Bertorelli said when they stood in front of the table of layouts. "Well, here it is —finished. It's more than a revamping. It's a revolution!"

Procter moved slowly down the table, studying the layouts, saying nothing. Bertorelli followed at his shoulder, fighting back his urge to articulate the ways in which each presentation soared to new heights of graphic excellence. For now, Nicholas decided to allow the boards to speak for themselves.

And speak they did. The pages were charged with a power that blocked out any possible sense of lack of interest in the subject matter. The words themselves were a part of the bold-ness of the graphics instead of disjointed islands of uninterest-ing type. Teaser lines led into or out of short titles that were quick blasts of bold type, in exactly the same way the logo had used the boldness of *In Wildness* followed by the phrase *Is the Preservation of the World.* Teaser—title—blurb. On every opening layout, the combination hit the viewer with three rea-sons to be pulled into a piece and start reading. The effort did not lag after the opening spreads. Instead of the usual gray masses of type, the runover pages were replete with sidebar boxes, each with separate headings, pulling sections of the text with useful information and data into prominent display in-stead of allowing them to become lost in the narration of the article itself. Quotes lifted from the pieces—boxed off in attrac-tive type—were graphic invitations to keep reading. Every-where one looked, the magazine seemed to be saying *Read! . . . Look! . . . Use Me!*

One of the boards stopped Procter's review and held him fast. Shaking his head, he smiled at Bertorelli. "That's absolute dynamite! It'll be the talk of the business."

Bertorelli acknowledged the praise with a nod. "I like it too," he said. "If it doesn't win every layout award in town, I will kiss your ass in Macy's window. In fact, if the whole book doesn't win the Best Magazine Design category, I'll give back my fee."

The layout that produced this outburst began with a double-page spread that was almost entirely made of type. The teaser line reading into the main title read *Gentlemen, The King!* Below the block letters of the one-word title, "HAMA-DRYAD," a one-line blurb was presented as a subtle after-thought. It read, *There Is Something Hiding in the Elephant Grass That Can Kill an Elephant.*

The smallish color illustration in the right-hand corner of the spread was in startlingly vivid contrast to the surrounding type. The picture showed the edge of a tawny patch of high elephant grass, typical of East Indian terrain. Down in the grass, the small tip of some sort of animal's black tail ran off the page to the right. The artwork was devastatingly effective. It fairly dared the reader to turn the page and complete the vision.

The second spread carried the tease to its shocking climax. Turning the page, the reader saw the tip of the tail merge into the sinuous massive coils of a king cobra reared to the grass-tops, its fan-like neck spread in attack, its cold eyes of death directly on the reader.

"The thing that makes it work so well," Don West said, "is the surprise. You feel like you're right there, that you blundered into this guy and now you're going to pay for your mistake."

"Remind me to stay out of elephant grass," Morgan Procter said, moving on down the rows of layouts.

Morgan completed his review of the layouts without speaking. He walked back to the head of the table and pointed at the cover. "I still don't know about that shot," he said.

"What? . . . No! . . . No! . . . It's fine!" Bertorelli exclaimed, gesturing wildly. "It's got everything we're trying to do!"

Don West slid into the argument. "You see, Morg, what we've done here is become people-oriented. People and service —personal reader involvement instead of the sermons and celebrations the book is serving up now."

"That girl looks too young to me," Procter said.

"We're going after young people!" Bertorelli cried. "I tell you it's dead right!"

"It sure as hell ain't traditional outdoors. I'll give you that," said Procter.

"Look," said Bertorelli. "The shot's a story in itself. She's landing a trout at the edge of the stream . . . or goddamn lake . . . or whatever it is. He's getting the supper going, watching her . . . a strong, good-looking guy. A today kind of guy. He's got the tent all set up and is doing the work while she fishes. A role reversal—get it? So she's a great looker and her tits aren't small and we show more long brown leg under those shorts than the L. L. Bean catalog ever would! So what? The story is there! They're going to have a drink . . . or smoke a little grass . . . and eat a steak or some fish . . . and end up fucking their brains out! What do you want on the cover? A goddamn moose?"

"Morg, I think Nikki is right," West said. "Young people seeing that shot will want to be there . . . doing that!"

Procter laughed. "All right—you've got me. The rest of the stuff is so great, I'll go along with you on the cover too. But if it gets too much heat, we may have to back off."

"Nobody but Richardson will question it," Bertorelli said. "And he won't matter after tomorrow."

"By the way," Don West quickly interjected. "I didn't have a chance to mention it, but Richardson brought his bearded wonder in from Alaska to poke around and make suggestions. He was over there yesterday. Everybody on the staff thought Ted Walsh had been fired and that we had a new editor. I stayed out this morning, because of him."

Morgan Procter was expressionless as he answered. "That Jonathan guy? Writes for the book and takes pictures?"

"Yes. As a matter of fact, he took a lot of the shots we've used here in this dummy."

"I wouldn't worry about it," Procter said.

"What if he sees his stuff missing and tells Richardson something's up?"

"So what?" Procter answered. "He'll get his pictures back —and a check. It'll all be over at the board meeting at ten-thirty tomorrow. If we continue to publish, you'll be all set. If we don't . . . you'll see a big hunk of money for all your work with Nikki in this"—he waved at the dummy—"the words and the pictures."

West still looked worried. "Frankly, I sure hope we keep going. This new look should make a big difference."

"Stop worrying," Procter smiled. "If the worst comes, I'll find some other editorship for you within the company." He put his arm around a relieved Don West's shoulder. "Now let's just go through these once more with your personal interpretation of why the presentations are so different."

Bertorelli watched them move over to the table. He saw West gesture toward the layout on the cougar. "This is a particularly good one to discuss," Don West said. "When the piece originally ran in the book, it was presented with this same photograph used very small."

The shot showed a mountain lion, coiled to spring from a rock outcropping. Pinyon pines and hard blue sky were in the background.

West went on: "The title was 'Top Cat of the High Wild.' Walsh thought that was clever as hell. No blurb . . . no teaser . . . nothing to really sell the reader."

West pointed to the new layout. "Now consider the way we've done it here."

The photograph had been blown up to full bleed, bringing the cougar twenty feet closer to the reader. The shot was so magnificent that you could practically smell the animal's breath. In big block letters, the main title was "AMERICA'S LION," beneath a lead-in teaser.

"The difference," West said, "is more than boldness in graphics. 'America's Lion' makes the piece personal."

Bertorelli had heard all this so much that it had become tiresome. He wandered away from the others toward his photography area, hearing bits and pieces of West's continuing indoctrination of Morgan Procter. "Take winter camping," West's voice went on. "Ted ran a big piece on 'the joys of winter camping.' Another goddamn celebration . . . but not one word on how to buy a down jacket these days without getting ripped off. There was no reader service at all."

Bertorelli pulled a Hasselblad from the shelf and fidgeted with the lens settings, escaping West's monologue as he became immersed in thought. He was about to make one of the most important moves of his entire career. He had flung every ounce of his creativity and energy into this project, never doubting that the results would be worth the effort. The job had crystallized and focused his ultimate goals. Now, on the very eve of those ambitions being fulfilled, he worried about the possibilities of something going wrong, pushing him back into the obscurity he had fought so hard to escape.

Despite the well-being suggested by his brownstone and lifestyle, Nicholas Bertorelli was an anxious and desperate man. Now thirty-five, he had held the art director's chair at *Charm* for only two years, and his rewards from the position were incomplete. The redesign and turnaround of *Charm* had been created and orchestrated by Matt Richardson and Marla Ashton, working with an outside art director from J. Walter

Thompson, who did the basic design and retained a "design consultant" status. Bertorelli had been brought on board *after* the successful redesign. He had established a good, workmanlike reputation from his stints on lesser magazines.

For Bertorelli, working in the shadow of Marla Ashton was daunting. Her media exposure, her rumored salary, her position on the Craig Board of Directors—all grated on his nerves to the point of pain.

During his frequent lunches at the Society of Illustrators, the main watering hole for art directors, Bertorelli was accepted by the giants of magazine art direction, but he was not one of them. Since he had not engineered the dramatic changes that made *Charm* a smash, he was not on a par with the legendary figures of magazine design: people like Milton Glazer, Will Hopkins, Suren Ermoyan, and Art Weithas. Those of the power elite acknowledged Bertorelli's position and they appreciated his lively social manner and occasional outlandish parties, but they continued to hold him at arm's length—and they still called him "Nikki."

Snatches of conversation between West and Procter told Bertorelli that they were almost finished. He put down the camera and walked back over to the table. West was making a final point about the two travel articles included in the presentation.

"Our destination pieces use a lot of color and good photography on the opening pages to sell the reader on the *place*. Then, when we've got him slobbering at the mouth, ready to get on an airplane and go there, we give him what he needs to make the trip happen. Maps . . . data . . . things to write for . . . phone numbers. It's all there. Now the whole experience becomes possible. It's not just a dream!"

"Terrific stuff," Morgan said. "That about covers it, don't you think?"

West glanced at his watch. "I'd better get over there. Anybody want to share a cab?"

Hurriedly, before Procter could answer, Bertorelli said, "Morg, can you stay a few minutes? There's something I need your advice on."

Procter looked at his own watch. "Okay. We'll talk while I pack this stuff up." He reached for the large portfolio case that stood against the wall. "Go on without me, Don. I'll call you as soon as the smoke clears."

West paused at the head of the stairs, looking back. "We're a good team, Nick. Given the chance, we can make this thing work."

Bertorelli smiled and nodded. "See you later, Don."

Morgan Procter moved along the table, carefully stacking the layouts. Bertorelli approached him, circling cautiously.

"This is like back in the early sixties when Otto Storch and Herb Mayes redesigned *McCall's* and created such a stir." Bertorelli gestured with his hands as he spoke. "Storch did amazing things—like taking a cucumber and blowing it up full-size across a spread. Back then, nobody had ever seen anything like it."

"Before my time," Procter said. "But I've heard about it. He created shock waves throughout the business."

"I studied about it in art school. And the impact of *New York,* the job Milt Glazer did on it."

Morgan Procter slid a batch of layouts into the case and looked at Bertorelli. "Look, this is great stuff, Nikki, but believe me, you're not going to be carried through the streets in a sedan chair because you turned the graphics of *In Wildness* around."

"Why not? Why can't this be a major success?"

"Because the subject matter is too limited. Madison Avenue is only beginning to realize that outdoor people aren't limited to redneck hunters and catfishermen. You're ahead of your time with this."

"Then why did you kick off this project?" Bertorelli shouted, waving his hand toward the layouts. "Why are you, a space-peddler, taking in an *editorial revival* for a book you think should get the ax?"

Procter glared at Bertorelli, redness flushing through his temples. "Because it's just one more way of showing them I can run the whole show up there! This book is a financial nightmare. By breathing some semblance of life into it, we can recover our losses and sell the goddamn thing!"

Procter's words unleashed the fury that had been boiling inside Bertorelli. "Sell it! You mean we're not going through with it?"

Morgan Procter turned back to the layouts. "For a while—

to set up the market. Sam Zeigler has worked out the figures. What are you worried about? You've more than done your job."

His eyes blazing, Bertorelli grabbed Procter's shoulder, turning him around. "Get your fucking hands off my work! That stuff stays right here!"

"Have you lost your mind?" Procter said calmly, shaking himself free.

"I'll never see any real money out of this!" Bertorelli roared. "I'm getting screwed!"

"I told you that I would take care of you." Morgan Procter's eyes narrowed as they focused on Bertorelli's.

"Fuck that! I want a quarter of a million—*up front!*"

Nicholas Bertorelli did not hear the fleshy, sickening *slap* that exploded through the room as Morgan Procter's open palm smacked into the left side of his face. He did not hear it, because when the blow landed it came as a searing wall of pain and impact that made his ear erupt with a hollow ringing. Open-mouthed, numb with shock, he stared straight ahead with empty, unfocused eyes, his mind tearing him away—back, back to the Bronx, back to the vision of his father standing before him in a rage, his hand going back for another blow. Then that image was gone, replaced by the very real glowering mask of Morgan Procter's face. Nicholas could not speak or cry out. His throat was held in an invisible noose.

The twin of the first *slap* burst on the other side of his face, driving him to his knees, gasping for breath, his eyes burning with tears, the ringing in his ears a shriek now. Then he felt the spurt of wetness in his shorts, felt the warm liquid running down his legs. *He was peeing in his pants!* his mind screamed. He rolled onto the floor, covering his face with his hands, and finally tore some sound from his throat.

"Naaa . . . don't . . . naaaa . . . please!" The words were followed by gasps for breath, racking sobs.

Morgan Procter turned back to the layouts.

"You know, Nikki, when you started taking kickbacks on photographers' and artists' fees, I bet you thought you'd just do it once or twice. Perhaps for some financial emergency. But you couldn't stop, could you? It was too easy, the bucks were too good. Not big stuff—just steady. It wasn't enough to buy this place. That's why you started dealing some coke."

Bertorelli sobbed on the floor, hiding his face. Procter zipped up the portfolio case and tested its heft. He was ready to go.

"We know all about it, Nikki," Morgan said. "If we want to, we can put you away for a long time."

His face buried in his hands, Bertorelli heard Procter's footsteps move to the door and pause.

"You know," Morgan Procter said, "being in the slammer might not be so bad for you. Maybe they could give you a drawing board to use. You could lean over it and do layouts while your cellmate gets happy."

More footsteps then, receding on the stairs. The genuis of Mozart became an audible presence in the room once again.

Nicholas Bertorelli laid his face on the coolness of the wooden floor. He could not remember ever feeling such panic. He closed his eyes, longing for peace.

TWENTY-TWO

Flat on his belly in the shadowed heart of a stand of tall white spruce, Horribilis felt a measure of strength begin to flow back into his exhausted, abused body. When he'd crashed into the thicket, still running with all the lurching, desperate speed he could muster after several miles, he was close to collapse. Caution and control had evaporated when the strange-smelling creature attacked him in the center of the river, racing toward him the same way the sky-thing had done. Hurtling from the stream, crashing and scrambling through the brush like a runaway tank, he had fled the river in panic. For a while, his terror obliterated his inner compass and carried him far back downstream. Unbeknownst to him, the overland route he was taking traversed a wide horseshoe bend in the river and eventually led him back near the very currents he was trying to flee.

Now as he lay among the dark spruce needles, he began to hear the river again, flowing somewhere off to his left. The presence of the stream bolstered his revived instincts. He could sense he was on the right side of the river now, with a new route to the mountains lying before him. A little farther downstream, he could reach the lower slopes of the range, then follow the ridges back to the high passes above the upper part of the river, far from the danger that stalked him.

As the great bear rested, his sense of the terrain became more acute. His instincts began to turn him once again from fear to determination. Suddenly he scrambled to his feet and limped heavily through the thick, rasping branches.

When he reached the open tundra, moving slowly but steadily over the muskeg, he could feel the land begin to rise. Islands of spruce were huddled all across the open ground, their long shadows falling across the moss in a web of dark trails. Horribilis followed the shadows from clump to clump, avoiding the strong afternoon sun.

ON DANGEROUS GROUND

The river fell away from him for a while, the ground rising steadily toward the blue, smoky hills ahead. On and on the grizzly plodded, his ragged gait gradually eating up the distance. After a while, the stream curved back into view again, a silvery sheen disappearing straight ahead toward a notch in the ridges. It was toward this cut in the skyline that the great bear made his way.

Horribilis knew it was time to leave the river. The pine-clad hillside rose gently from the edge of the current, then steepened to loom in rising shoulders that formed the beginning of the range. A stand of birches separated the hillside pines from the edge of the stream, and as he was moving through the slim white trunks, the grizzly caught a sudden jolting scent.

Horribilis tensed, the hair on his neck and hump standing erect. *This was extreme peril!*

He could smell a keen, animal-like scent that he instantly sorted from an assault of other strange odors he recognized as belonging to the putrid two-legged creatures he feared: wood smoke and ashes, torn earth and green plants of a garden, cut timbers of a cabin.

As great as the trauma caused by these smells, it was the animal scent that troubled the great bear the most. He knew it came from the small four-legged creatures whose trails he had smelled many times, whose kills he had fed upon after driving away the snarling creatures. Sometimes they circled him warily as he fed, afraid to attack but bold enough to slink nearby.

Horribilis knew the odor he was picking up now was somehow different from the smells he had experienced in the past. What he did not know was that he was accustomed to smelling wolves.

The strange new scents flooded his nostrils with a mixture of the familiar and the curiously different. He could smell the coats of the beasts, their feces on the ground. It was very strange to encounter these scents along with the smells of the two-legged creatures.

Horribilis eased to the edge of the birches, peering through a break in the leafy branches, his nostrils questing for more information.

Now he could see it all, the man-thing itself. The cabin and outbuildings were perched beneath the hillside, across a clearing at the edge of the river. He could make out four Eskimo sled dogs standing at the front of the man-thing.

The dogs began to bark fiercely, jumping in agitation.

Then Horribilis saw the dogs lunge forward as one. Abreast, they looked like a flowing, snarling line, racing straight down the hill toward him.

TWENTY-THREE

he room was a time machine that floated through the years in unchanging defiance of the tumultuous world outside its doors. Jonathan Hill had not been in "21" in two years, but the atmosphere was so familiar—and his arrival here so sudden—that he seemed to be part of some strange dream. Despite the restaurant's well-publicized remodeling, the downstairs dining room still exuded a club-like feeling: the burnished light, the dangling knickknacks, the rich woodiness of the bar and floors, the piquant scents of food, the lilt of exuberant conversation, and the crisp tinkle of well-filled glasses. Even the face and voice of Matt Richardson were the same as they had been during their last meeting here, only yesterday it seemed now. Matt sat alongside him in the banquette, looming over his usual table, gracefully handling the captain and the waiters, chatting with occasional passersby, commanding his little niche of the ultra-saloon like a captain on the bridge.

Despite the ambience, Jonathan felt uneasy, depressed. He was here under a flag of truce; there were negotiations to be conducted, issues to be settled. So far, through three glasses of wine and their lamb chops and salads, Matt had been stalling, reliving happier times, content to languish in the pleasure of their reunion. Jonathan knew this relaxed mood would soon evaporate. He could feel the pressure of the oncoming storm growing by the minute. He was surprised when their coffees arrived, and Matt launched into another anecdote.

"I was on assignment with Buddy Devlin for *Sports Illustrated* to do a piece on backpack fishing for cutthroat trout. Since we were near the ranch, we stayed there when we weren't actually camping. When we were finished, Buddy was loading the station wagon when my father came out to say goodbye. Dad was about seventy then. Anyway, you should have seen all the crap Buddy's putting into the back of the station wagon: cameras, telephoto lenses, strobes, exposure meters, tripods, and about a hundred rolls of exposed film. Looking at all this, Dad says to Buddy: 'You boys worked mighty hard on all those pictures, Mr. Devlin. I sure hope some of them come out.' "

Jonathan laughed with Matt, picturing the scene. It was a good story to remember. He watched Matt take a sip of coffee and look around the room. His smile had vanished.

"All right, buddy," Matt said. "I'll lay it all out for you. At ten-thirty tomorrow I've got to try and keep the board from killing *In Wildness*. From you I need two things. One, a yes answer that you'll take over the book. Two, what the hell got us into this mess? Is the book that bad?"

Jonathan sighed. He could feel Cody's presence. "I think I can help you with the book. But I haven't changed my mind. I'm not taking the editorship."

"Goddammit, Jon," Richardson scowled, "you cannot do this to me! If you turn your back on me, *In Wildness* will be a corpse by this time tomorrow."

"Matt," Jonathan said in irritation. "All this pressure . . . Why are you doing this to Cody and me?"

"Pressure! What's pressure to you? A day when you have to can beans instead of going fishing? An hour or two scribbling on your book?"

"Cody and I hit the typewriter hard. We earn our living."

"Meanwhile, an idea we both originated—a magazine that is now a living, breathing thing—is about to go under because you won't do the work needed to save it!"

People at the adjacent table were staring. Matt made a concerted effort to lower his voice as he continued. "Let's face facts. It's the work, isn't it? You two just aren't going to live here and try to cut the mustard—not as long as you can get somebody else to do it. There'll be no payback, will there? You don't pay back."

"I've worked as hard as anybody to make people appreciate and defend the wild places of this planet!" Jonathan shot back loudly. "Keep this up, Matt, and I'll be on the next plane out of here!"

"I can't reason with you," Matt said disgustedly. "I thought I knew you, but now I see I don't anymore."

"Cody and I had the guts to go after the lifestyle we both wanted. You know our Western roots run deep. We're happy living the way we do. If we were back here, doing what *you* want us to do, we'd both be miserable. No thank you."

"Just a *Mother Jones* version of the idle rich," Matt said, shrugging his shoulders.

Jonathan reddened. "Better that than the kind of serfdom you propose: hanging on a subway strap or sweating out the seven twenty-three from Princeton or Greenwich."

"What serfdom? I'm talking about being editor in chief of an important national magazine. Is Dan Jenkins a serf? He's done books and films and TV shows and still kept his job with *Sports Illustrated* for years. Is Helen Brown a serf? She writes books, edits *Coz*. What about Jimmy Breslin, or Dick Schaap, or William Buckley? They all write books—they all have jobs. You could do the same."

"It's not just the time. It's the quality of life."

"A permanent vacation!"

Jonathan allowed Matt to stare him down. He turned away, facing out into the room, fighting back the urge to bolt from the table. "This line of attack isn't going to work, Matt," he said, without looking at Richardson. "What say we drop it and talk about the magazine instead? I think you'll find that to be a lot more useful."

Matt sighed, slumping noticeably. "How bad is it?"

"I consider the book to be almost beyond repair. Fixing it will take a maximum effort—*if* you get the chance."

Matt shook his head. "Ted Walsh. I hung in there with him too long."

"Do you want to hear it now or later?"

"Let's go to the office. You'll need copies of the book for your critique. After that, we'll look at the film. I can show it to you in the boardroom, scene of tomorrow's dance."

Matt looked up in surprise. The captain was approaching the table with a telephone in hand. "A call for you, Mr. Richardson," he said, as he snapped the plug into a socket beside Matt.

Matt knew this had to be bad news. Unlike many of the power players who frequented "21," he had never indulged in the telephone games played here. He expected Helen Sullivan's voice on the other end of the line and that's what he got.

"I'm dreadfully sorry to disturb you," she said, "but Mr. Craig's office phoned with an urgent message. He's flying back from Washington. He wants a team meeting on *In Wildness* in the boardroom at five o'clock. You, Mr. Procter, Miss Ashton, and Sam Zeigler. He is hoping Jonathan will attend as well."

"What's he got in mind?" Matt asked.

"He didn't elaborate. 'Team meeting' was *his* expression, however."

"Did Solokin's people bring over the film?"

"It's here."

"Good. Please have it set up and ready to go. Jon and I will be back there shortly."

Matt frowned as he put down the phone. "Bad news?" Jonathan asked.

"You won't believe this, my lad, but you're about to take part in a meeting that will probably determine the fate of our magazine and possibly our careers."

"Wait a min—"

Matt's shaking head and voice waved off Jonathan's protest before he could get it started. "The boss wants you there along with the rest of us," Matt said.

"I can't do it! I'm not prepared to discuss the book at any length yet."

"My friend, you do not have enough arrows in your quiver to ignore the commands of a man like Tony Craig. Crossing him could cost you plenty someday."

"Goddammit, Matt, I wouldn't have come here had I known coercion was what you had in mind. You are too much!"

"Hey, I have nothing to do with this. I'm just as surprised as you are."

"Tell him I've left town!"

Matt ignored this. "Please do me one favor," he said, softly. "Don't let them know you're not taking over the book."

"I'm not!"

"Okay, if that's what you want. But for now, just don't announce the fact. Everything's riding on you. You have to do this for me." Jonathan was shaking his head in bewilderment. "I'll handle the fireworks," Matt continued.

"This is ridiculous," Jonathan replied, mumbling under his breath as they got up from the table.

Outside the dusky interior of the restaurant, they squinted through the afternoon shadows at the high brightness over Fifty-second Street. As they walked west, brooding, Matt's silence added new substance to Jonathan's feelings of guilt and frustration.

"Do you ever spend any time with Don West, Walsh's number two?" Jonathan asked, trying to break the tension.

"Walsh is disillusioned with him. They bicker a lot. Why do you ask?"

"He seems very frustrated. Claims Walsh has been ignoring his input. Could be he has some good ideas."

"*I've* never heard any of them."

"There's something else. He's been taking a lot of articles and photographs out of the office."

"Good," Matt replied. "So he works at home a lot."

"With over thirty articles, *and* the accompanying photos?"

They turned up Sixth Avenue. Matt stopped suddenly and stared at Jonathan as the crowd brushed past. "What do you make of it?" he asked.

"I'm not sure. But I was wondering if you had authorized him to work on a new dummy with an outside art director—give the book a new direction."

"No, I haven't done that," Matt said slowly, speculating. "Although I probably should have, the way things've been going." He reflected for another moment. "Do you suppose he could be working on something like that on his own, intending to bring it to me?"

Jonathan shrugged. "It's the only reasonable explanation I can come up with. It's been done on other books."

"Well, see if you can find out what it's all about." Matt's expression revealed no concern, only curiosity.

The old Matt would have been more interested, Jonathan reflected. Was he slipping, after all?

The question would not leave his thoughts as they walked on without speaking.

After he had ordered the wine—a 1978 Puligny-Montrachet —Morgan Procter turned the task of ordering food over to

Marla Ashton, fascinated by her excellent French as she reviewed the day's luncheon specialties with Lutèce's captain. Morgan had no skill with languages and he often felt remiss over his failure to develop at least some facility in some language other than English. He liked to travel and enjoyed being in foreign countries. Seated now in the downstairs garden dining room, he felt relaxed and comfortable with the illusion that he was in France.

Filtered by the high translucent ceiling, the sun bathed the room with a soothing mellow flush. The flowers and plants, the white-trellised walls, all gave the widely spaced tables a feeling of country elegance and charm. Somehow, too, the room remained quiet though filled with diners and the busy, attentive staff.

Marla and the captain agreed on a main course of cold poached lobsters, garnished in decorative splendor by artichoke hearts, tomatoes, eggs, and truffles. Dessert, which both of them generally resisted, was irresistible today: tiny wild strawberries from France with whipped cream.

Throughout the meal, Morgan kept the conversation low-keyed and pleasant. The tensions created by his earlier encounter with Bertorelli gradually faded as he and Marla chatted about France—especially the Paris neighborhood where Marla had lived for a year during her marriage—potential new advertising coups for *Charm,* and even some of Marla's editorial plans. Morgan was actually beginning to enjoy himself, returning, he realized, to the mood of contentment created by the night with Kristen. She was still in town, doing her squash clinic, and tonight she would be in his arms once again. The very thought of another evening together produced such a pleasurable sensation that he had to remind himself that there was work to be done. Despite the friendly atmosphere of the luncheon so far, Morgan knew Marla's nonchalance was as studied as his. She was obviously playing the same kind of waiting game, which kept him from being the first to mention the ongoing corporate intrigue.

Finally, over dessert and coffee, Marla goosed him into action. "You seem more relaxed than you did on the phone yesterday," she said. "Have you talked to the old man about all the gossip?"

ON DANGEROUS GROUND

"I wanted to, but I couldn't reach him. I guess he's not returning from Washington until tonight."

Morgan watched Marla study him from across the table, obviously looking for the right opening.

"What are we celebrating?" she asked. "Lunch at Lutèce is quite a gesture, even coming from a high roller with an expense account like yours."

"I promised you a memorable meal, remember? You were very kind to work me in. I know you're booked."

"I admit I was intrigued by the urgency of your plea."

"You should have been. Things are happening. This board meeting tomorrow is not going to be a company picnic."

"Because of that newsletter? We've seen that kind of thing before. Why should everybody be rattled by it now?"

"Perhaps those are not just rumors. I can't believe you haven't considered that for once in his life Doug Korner and his gossip sheet may be on to something."

"Naturally, the thought had crossed my mind, but I really meant what I told you on the phone yesterday. I hate company politics *and* politicians."

"You wouldn't feel so cozy if you were going into that meeting with a lot at stake." Morgan leaned back in his chair and watched her.

Marla's confident smile said more than words.

Morgan was tiring of this game. She was good. She was very, very good. He decided to move onto the attack.

"Would you mind my being very frank, instead of dancing around the way I do with my usual sales pitches?"

"I've been waiting for *that* since I first sat down."

Morgan smiled sheepishly and went on. "The company needs a leader. One person walking the bridge, running the show. If I'm not mistaken, Tony Craig has come round to that same view."

"And you see yourself as captain?"

"Who else?"

"There's a fellow named Richardson around. He might like the job for himself. Also, how do you know that *I'm* not interested?"

"I don't. Frankly, that's why I wanted to talk to you. To size up your interest and see what your feelings are."

"Don't worry about me," Marla said, unconvincingly. "I think you'll find Matt to be quite a handful by himself."

Morgan shrugged. "Nothing personal, you understand—I appreciate many of the things he's done for the company—but he's not presidential timber. He proved that with the *In Wildness* debacle."

"He may yet come up with the big play. He's done it before."

"Not this time."

Marla reflected on this for a moment. "You seem very confident. There must be a reason."

"Let's just say I have my ducks in a row."

"Perhaps Matt has too. He doesn't look very worried to me."

Morgan's face showed no concern or even interest in Marla's speculative remark. "Allow me a hypothetical question, strictly from left field."

"Fire away. I *might* answer it."

"Suppose, just for a moment, that I *did* get the nod. Is there any reason we couldn't work together?"

"With you as my boss?"

"You'd still run your own show. You know that."

"I've already told you: don't worry about me—now!"

Morgan grinned wryly. "I have to. You could create a lot of mischief."

"I'm going to tell you something, Morgan." Marla leaned forward, her eyes glistening, her features hard. "You *are* nothing but a space-peddler! You always *have been* a space-peddler! You always *will be* a space-peddler!"

The words cut deeply into Morgan's confidence and pride. He tried to hang on to his composure. He wanted to retaliate, to hand her back the pain that shot through his gut, but for the moment he was weaponless. Frustrated as he was, he would have to wait—wait for the opportunity to deal a blow of his own.

"You don't know *what* I am," Morgan said. "Pretty soon, you'll understand me better, discover my hidden talents."

"That'll be the day."

Before Morgan could reply, the captain was beside him,

bending over him with a crisp piece of message paper. "For you, Mr. Procter," he said.

Morgan opened the note and glanced at the handwriting. "Tony Craig wants to see us," he said, handing the paper to Marla.

"I thought he was in Washington," she said, obviously surprised.

Morgan shrugged and signaled for the check. "I just hope the old man doesn't have this table wired," he said, laughing.

TWENTY-FOUR

Cody could not stop pacing. No longer dizzy and nauseous from shock, she moved around the main room of the cabin, occasionally opening the screen door to see if anyone was coming up from the river. The tension and anxiety that still gripped her was, she figured, an acceptable trade-off against the gut-wrenching horror she had experienced earlier. Her eyes were red and swollen and her sinuses throbbed with pain, but she was beyond tears now. In fact, she felt she was in control, despite the rapid hammering of her pulse. Somehow she would cope. Derek was playing in his room, thank God, and Buck was curled up in his favorite spot on a rug beside the stove, snoozing as if nothing had happened.

When she had regained her composure after discovering the body, Cody had raced to the cabin, her breath still coming in ragged gasps. She checked to make sure Derek was still sleeping quietly, then hurried outside to fetch a plastic tarpaulin from the equipment shed built onto the back of the main cabin.

Back at the river, she had walked past the limb-snagged kayak without looking directly at the craft and its horrible occupant. She patrolled upstream for several hundred yards, Buck ranging ahead. Nothing. Then, summoning what was left of her courage and strength, she got the kayak loose from the snags and managed to pull it onto the bank.

After she had gotten the torso covered, weighting down the edges of the tarp with heavy stones, she sat down for a bit to steady herself. Later she got up the nerve to tear the spray curtain free from the kayak cockpit and pull the craft away from the body. She could see there was no wallet in the trouser pockets. She gently pulled the tarp on down over the legs and sneakers, finally, mercifully, hiding the entire body from sight.

As Cody had expected, the interior of the kayak held waterproof plastic bags filled with equipment. In one was stuffed a ditty bag that contained what she was seeking. She carried the pouch to the cabin and laid its contents on the table: a wallet, a camera, some film, and a notebook.

When she opened the wallet and saw that these things belonged to Ted Walsh, Jonathan's editor at *In Wildness,* Cody began to cry again. "Oh no!" she moaned, over and over again.

Walsh—the man who took the spot Jonathan had been groomed to fill. Walsh—who Jonathan and Matt had told her was floundering in the editorship. Walsh—whose book on rivers was a distinguished piece of work and occupied a place of honor on one of the bookshelves of the cabin. Walsh—who had obviously lost his life while paddling down the Toubok for a surprise visit.

It didn't make any sense, but there it was: Walsh had drowned somewhere upstream, probably by turning over and snagging his head in limbs and rocks on the bottom of the stream. That's why the body was mutilated. The current had pulled on the kayak and the torso with an awesome force, tearing them free.

But where the hell were the man's companions? Nobody would kayak this river solo.

Or would they?

Cody looked out the screen door again, in vain. She knew it was time for action. The waiting game she had been playing was based entirely on the premise that Walsh had not been alone on the river.

The idea of the Tolkats and their shortwave radio had been simmering in Cody's thoughts. She turned to the option reluctantly. The trek would be long and strenuous for Derek, and a sense of yesterday's fright would be haunting the trail. They would have to stay overnight, but they often did that with Jonathan along, camping right there on the Tolkat place.

Still pacing, Cody found herself back at the table. She picked up Walsh's notebook. When she had first flipped through the thick sheaf of loose-leaf pages, trying to decipher the scribbling, she felt curiously ashamed of her violation of something so personal and precious. Some of the pages were very old, with notes on the Alaska Pipeline dating back to the mid-seventies. The last pages were crisp and new, but the jottings were undated and could have been made anytime recently. There were no clues here on Walsh's timetable, if indeed he had had one.

Suddenly a fresh idea occurred to Cody. She put down the notebook and walked back over to the door, looking outside again.

A helicopter could have brought Walsh to the river! The realization was as clear to Cody as the disturbing sound that had floated into her hearing for a fleeting moment yesterday when she and Derek were fishing. The intruding noise had been no more than a distant rumble that could barely be heard above the rush of the current. The sound was gone as quickly as it had come, and she had seen nothing in the hard blue sky. The appearances of floatplanes and helicopters were not daily occurrences on the Toubok, but they certainly were not unusual.

Now Cody wondered if that craft could have brought Ted Walsh to the river.

She looked at the river gleaming through the birches, the upstream path empty and silent. She thought of Walsh's body under the tarp in the sunshine. Soon ravens would be attracted to it, maybe a fox, or even a wolf if one were poking around the area. There was nothing she could do but go for help.

She *had* to get to the Tolkats' radio, even though she did not feel up to being alone on the trail with Derek again, so soon after the harrowing experience of the previous day's trek. Another means of transportation was right at hand—the river itself! Often she and Derek had floated down to see their friends with Jonathan manning the oars of their wide, flat-bottomed rubber raft. The craft was the same sort of sturdy casting platform so popular with fly-fishing guides on rivers all over the West. Nearly indestructible on the rocks, the raft was roomy and stable. There were no heavy rapids downstream, and the few stretches of fast water and the occasional rocks were easily negotiated by the raft, which bounced forgivingly away from boulders that would crack up a canoe or spill a kayak.

Quickly now, Cody began to form a mental checklist: rations, foul-weather gear, ax, first-aid kit, water jug, tent, and sleeping bags. She would get the raft from the supply shed, inflate it with the foot pump down by the river, then pack the oars and equipment. That should take a couple of hours. By then, if no one had appeared from upstream, she would assume her waiting was a lost cause and shove off for the Tolkats'.

The plan was logical, safe, and necessary.

She heard footsteps padding across the floor behind her. Barefooted and wearing only his flannel shirt, Derek grabbed her leg, offering the paper he had been coloring.

"I want you to take a nap, partner," Cody said, as she embraced the child. "After that, we're going for a little boat ride."

TWENTY-FIVE

The film was working.

A cautious look at the dimly illuminated faces around the table of the Craig boardroom gave Matt Richardson a fresh surge of confidence. The brilliant images on the rear-projection screen at the end of the room held the small audience transfixed as the film reached the climactic moment when the words *In Wildness Is the Preservation of the World* appeared over a final vista.

At the end of the table, Tony Craig looked immensely pleased, like a man unable to control his features after a first peek at his poker or bridge hand. Flanking Craig loosely, their chairs turned toward the screen, Morgan, Marla, and Jonathan seemed to be in a state of complete rapture. Only Sam Zeigler looked unimpressed. His fingers tapped nervously on the table and his calculator, his quick eyes continually flicking to Morgan Procter and Tony Craig.

Zeigler's apparent lack of enthusiasm was of no consequence to Matt. He had been in too many meetings with Craig's chief financial officer to expect anything different. Many of those meetings had taken place in this room, where the paneled walls, bookcases, plush leather, and rich wood could not smother the underlying tension that invariably made the air feel charged with electricity, as though a thunderstorm were approaching.

The lights came on, followed instantly by spontaneous words of praise tossed at Matt. "Bravo!" "Stunning!" "Brilliant!" Tony Craig was silent, but his smile made words unnecessary.

"What is the fellow's name, Matt—the one who did this?" Craig asked.

"Solokin. Stan Solokin."

"Mr. Solokin is a superb craftsman. He is to be congratulated."

"He's very talented, as is his son, who was involved with a lot of the fieldwork."

"What did *you* think, Sam?" Craig asked Zeigler. "Didn't you like the movie?"

Zeigler's coy smile cut through the expectant silence with a message of its own. "It looked very expensive to me."

"That's right, Sam," Matt smirked. "Be cautious, stick to the bottom line."

"Thanks, I shall do that, with your permission, of course," Zeigler shot back, calmly. "We're looking at red ink, gentlemen and ladies. We're talking about *ten million bucks* down the drain here! Do you realize what that's going to do to our per-share stock issues and warrants when we go public? The board's coming in here tomorrow to protect its interest, and *you* want to face them holding out your hand for another half-million bucks for a TV show!"

"The money's not—" Matt shouted before Craig cut him off.

"Gentlemen!" Craig interrupted. "This is exactly why I called this meeting today. We're not coming in here tomorrow for a free-for-all. And we're certainly not going to have one among ourselves. The magazine division will present its case to the board as a *team.*" Craig stared at Matt sternly. "Now, to do that, we're going to have to look at some hard facts and agree on the right play. It's important that we all state our feelings."

"That's what I'm trying to do," Matt answered.

"Then proceed," Craig smiled, indicating the group with a wave of his hand, as if he were making a gift of everyone's attention. "It's still your turn."

As Matt gathered his notes, Craig turned to Zeigler, patted the financial report for *In Wildness* that he'd distributed before the meeting, and laughed. "Now, Sam, you've already shown us the numbers. Let Dr. Richardson tell us how we're going to get well."

The elation the film had given Matt had been cruelly short-lived. He looked down at his rough notes, hastily scribbled when he first sat down. Tony Craig's cavalier attitude could only mean one thing: the old man had already made up his mind! Craig expected no surprises here today; the meeting was a dress rehearsal to solidify decisions he had already reached and would present to the full board tomorrow.

From the moment Craig had kicked off the meeting, with apologies for the abrupt way he had returned from Washington and pulled the group together, two things had seemed strange and obvious to Matt. First of all, Craig had made no mention whatsoever of the *Inside Korner* newsletter. Perhaps the old man was going to save the subject to cap off the meeting, Matt reasoned. Also, Craig had been uncharacteristically quippy and smart-ass, as though some inner torment was driving him toward comic relief. Matt could sense what that torment might be and, suddenly, it seemed to him that the wearying process of thinking the unthinkable for so many months had finally exhausted his own energy and enthusiasm. There just wasn't that much more he could do to prevent the demise of the magazine, unless he decided to go down with guns blazing.

Matt's gaze swept over the nervous faces staring at him. He felt vulnerable and ill prepared. Not only had he failed to convince Jonathan to take over the editorship, he had been forced by the suddenness of the meeting into hearing Jonathan's criticism of the editorial product in one quick gush of words. There had been no time for debate, for new ideas to be explored. Jonathan himself looked awkward and ill-at-ease at the table, his long hair and beard combining with his frumpy suit to make him appear alien and slightly dangerous. Seated next to Jonathan, Marla met Matt's glances with an alert, interested look that he knew was carefully perfected and controlled and would give no hint of last evening's passion.

Last night. Was it a finale or a new beginning? There had been no promises or hint of commitment. Her lips and tongue—then her body—had created a banquet of sensual pleasure that he had consumed until utterly satiated. When he woke at seven o'clock, he slipped out of bed and left her apartment without disturbing her. He left a note that read, "I'd buy that book excerpt. Thanks."

When she came into his office a few minutes before the meeting began, Marla had seemed uncharacteristically tense. At first, Matt figured their evening together had somehow upset her, but he was wrong. She had something else on her mind.

"I had lunch with Morgan. Something's up. He's acting as though he's already been made president."

"How can that be?" Matt asked in amazement.

"I just don't know. But he has something going for him, something we don't know about."

"Bastard. Maybe he does . . . and then again, maybe not."

"Be careful, Matt."

Now as his eyes traveled down the table, they rested gratefully on Marla, then moved on. He saw the obvious coconspirators, Zeigler and Morgan Procter, cut furtive glances at one another across the table. Matt had often wondered about the strange bond that had brought the two men together. Was it Vietnam? Procter had been wounded there, Matt knew, and Zeigler had been a Marine lieutenant. How had he come to the world of finance and the magazine business? It didn't matter now. The only thing that mattered was what Tony Craig was thinking. Dressed as though he had not changed clothes since the breakfast with Matt two days before, Craig peered down the table with the intensity and authority of an umpire.

Matt picked up his copy of the latest circulation study. "We've all seen numbers like these before," he began. "Newsstand sales terrible, subscriptions renewals running a low 20 percent. New mailings and subscription promotion efforts are going to cost three million to maintain our rate base guarantee to our advertisers. I'll admit that the picture is a bit bleak.

"But, what if we had panicked back when *Charm* was in this same position? What about some of our other books? I tell you, we have a solid idea here—and there are tremendous profits to come." As he looked around the table, Matt could see that Tony Craig was the only one not perusing the circulation report. Craig stared at Matt without emotion.

"I need three things," Matt continued, looking straight at Craig. "Time, a new editor, and that television show."

"By editor, I assume you mean this highly regarded person," Craig said, waving his hand toward Jonathan, who stirred uneasily in his chair. "I'd like to hear his views on what got us into this mess. But before we do, let's go back to the TV issue. Tell me, Matt, why is a *print man* like you suddenly courting television?"

"This show." Matt gestured toward the screen. "Thirty minutes a week over one hundred stations; it'll be seen in an estimated ten million households. Some of that exposure is bound to stick to our ribs."

"We didn't have to gamble on TV to get *Charm* turned around," Craig countered.

"In a different way, we did. Marla got the job done for us. Personal appearances, celebrity tie-ins for pieces in the book. She knows how to get ink—plus more time on the tube than Helen Gurley Brown." Across the table, Marla smiled and nodded. Matt could not tell if she was being supportive or thanking him. *"In Wildness* is obviously different," Matt continued, turning to Craig again. "You can't expect grizzly bears and vanishing wilderness to grab the public's attention like sex, love, marriage, careers, health and fitness."

"I don't expect it! I never did!" Craig shot back. *"You* were the one who pegged the book at five hundred thousand. We can't even maintain that."

"I'm tired of slugging it out without people knowing we're out there. I know how you feel about pouring big bucks into promotion. The TV show is the answer to helping us build a strong national identity—along with certain editorial changes, of course."

As Matt spoke, he saw Procter and Zeigler smile gleefully. What the hell was going on? he wondered.

Craig leaned forward, his face stern with new intensity. "Yes," he said. "The book itself. That's where the real problem lies, doesn't it? Promotion has nothing to do with the fact that 80 percent of the subscribers who were getting the magazine this past year won't renew their subscriptions. Their message is clear: they don't want the damn thing!"

Craig looked down the table, expecting Richardson to challenge him. Matt's silent stare was weak and ineffectual. Craig went on:

"Newsstand sales and subscription renewals are the absolute barometer of how the public feels about a book. I don't give a good goddamn about promotion, reader surveys, market studies, or letters to the editor. Bullshit! All of it! The magazine is out there. People could buy it if they wanted it! Besides that, we flooded the U.S. mail with cheap subscription offers, and the ones we managed to hook for twelve issues are telling us to stop sending them the book!"

"I guess you can't win 'em all," Zeigler said, with a tone of finality.

Depression surged through Matt like poison. He knew he was nearing the end of his tether. His earlier appraisal of Craig's position had been correct. This was all an exercise.

"You're stating the obvious, Tony," Matt said, trying to dig in and hold his ground. "But you're right, of course. I need more time, as I told you."

"Time to do what?" Zeigler asked. "Keep losing money? Plus spend a bundle on this TV show?"

"I'm sticking with the fellow who brought us to the dance." Marla's voice followed Zeigler's outburst with speed and conviction. "If Matt says he can turn this thing around, we ought to give him the time and resources he needs." Matt smiled at her, but the deep sense of gratitude he was feeling was hidden by his overall look of desperation.

"I share your fondness for the man and his judgment," Craig said quickly, trying to soften the mood. "He knows how I feel about him, but that's not the point. Nor is the TV show the main issue here. What we all have to know, Matt, is how you intend to revive the magazine. If you really don't know, then we should pull the plug."

"Knock it in the head," Zeigler said.

"You want specifics . . . at this point in the game?" Matt asked defensively.

"Yes I do!" Craig said. "For instance, this young man . . ." Morgan Procter snickered as Craig waved toward Jonathan. "What does *he* think about the situation?"

"That's not fair," Matt replied. "Jonathan only arrived yesterday. He's barely had time to look around the magazine a bit."

Craig waved off this defense as Jonathan did his best to look invisible. "Then we'll all share his initial thoughts," Craig said. "We're all in the same boat here. Jonathan was involved in the early stages of the magazine and has been a steady contributor ever since. Surely he has some opinions." Craig looked directly at Jonathan. "Come on, son, just tell us something—anything—about our problems here." Craig held up a copy of the magazine. The grizzly in Jonathan's photograph glared down at the boardroom table.

Jonathan looked at Matt, who smiled at him and nodded. "Go ahead, Jon. Don't worry about *me*. Let's have it."

Jonathan gulped and started to speak, but Craig interrupted. "Remember, son," he said, "good writers aren't afraid to be brief."

Everyone laughed, except Jonathan. "I don't know if I'm a good writer or not," he said, softly. "But I can be an expert on brevity. My basic feeling about the book is that Ted Walsh has totally abandoned our original concept of providing useful reader service and information. *In Wildness* has become a shrill, windy polemic."

"Now that's what I've been waiting to hear!" Craig shouted, rising to his feet. "When you talk like that, my boy, I can really believe that you fellows are beginning to see the light!" He looked at Morgan Procter. "Morgan, you take it from here."

Matt watched in astonishment as Morgan Procter walked across the room and picked up a large portfolio case leaning against the wall. He laid the case flat on the table, unzipped it, and started pulling out and stacking paste-ups of the magazine layouts.

His conversation with Jonathan on the way over flashed through Matt's mind. Something about text and photographs being taken from the *In Wildness* offices. Something about the possibility of a dummy.

Before Matt could react, Craig said, condescendingly, "Now don't get angry, Matt, but Morgan's been doing some poaching."

"I have indeed," Morgan Procter said as he straightened the layouts into a neat pile. "But it's like doubles in tennis: sometimes poaching wins the point. And, anyway, we're all on the same team."

Matt felt stunned, unable to move or speak. He knew in that moment that he had not merely failed. He had been defeated.

TWENTY-SIX

Casey Miller, operations chief and part-owner of Nor-Air, wiped his hands on the paper napkin and tossed it into the box full of crumbs that was all that remained of a Kentucky Fried Chicken deluxe dinner. He lit a cigarette, took a puff, and leaned back in his chair, sipping the dregs of a cup of coffee and staring out the window.

Beyond the open bottom half of the grimy patch of glass, the empty, oil-stained ramp of Nor-Air stretched away toward the grass and runways of Fairbanks International Airport. Casey could see the tower and the sprawl of the main terminal buildings, where an Alaska Air 727 was being pushed back from the gate.

Three P.M. to Anchorage, he noted mentally, glancing at his watch. Fifteen minutes late.

Then the roar of jet engines diverted his attention as another 727 began its takeoff roll. Casey watched it thunder past his position. For a moment his mind was in the cockpit with the crew. He could see the concrete of the runway sweeping under the nose of the ship, hear the voice of the copilot: ". . . 125 . . . 135 . . . V-One . . . 145 . . . V-Two . . . Rotate!"

The nose of the plane cocked jauntily into the air, remained suspended until the wings accepted the burden and the ship began to climb.

Casey knocked back the last of the coffee and dug into the pocket of his flannel shirt for the familiar feel of a roll of Tums. The late lunch was over. It was time to end romantic daydreaming and get back to reality. And reality dictated that on this June afternoon Casey Miller would have to come up with some answers before he would be a happy man again.

He rose laboriously, hitched a single crutch under his arm, and moved slowly through the empty, cluttered, three-desk office, swinging his artificial leg in a wide arc. He opened the door to the outer office, passed the cluttered desk of the firm's secretary, and headed through the open door of the radio shack and operations room.

Smiley Jacobs, a sometimes pilot who doubled in every job from radio operator to gofer, saw Casey coming and hurriedly put down the copy of *Playboy* he had been perusing. The bank of radio equipment in front of his chair was aglow with lights, but silent except for the dull static from an open speaker.

"You work Fox River yet?" Casey asked, referring to one of Nor-Air's outstations and refueling points, close to the Alaska Range.

"Just now, and the answer is 'Nope!' They ain't heard word one from Youngblood and those guys since they departed there yesterday."

Casey sat down wearily beside the younger man and looked around the room where so much of his life had been spent during the past thirty years. The charts that lined the walls held the name and numbers, destinations and schedules of the company's three choppers and fifteen fixed-wing aircraft —many of which were working on floats from the nearby Chena River. Each ship represented both the dreams and the living history of the work involved in building the firm from its original two Cessnas, one of which Casey had smashed in a whiteout, a blizzard so thick that it seemed to suck all visibility, all light, from the air. It had left his ruined body and airplane on a slope of Atigun Pass in the Brooks Range.

To Casey, each name and number—those on the line now and those that flew only in his memory—represented something for the people of Alaska: supplies, emergency medical care, rescues, exploration, and even recreation. The pioneers of aviation, as much as the homesteaders, had made Alaska livable. And the mighty land had extracted its price in the final flights of hundreds of bold men.

"Smiley," Casey said, "what do you make of it?"

"Okay. Youngblood was supposed to go up to 3,000 feet and call Fox River at noon. 'Cause you can't send a good signal from the ground. Not in there, right?"

"You know the procedure."

"Right. So he missed the twelve o'clock. That's happened before to some of the boys, due to one thing or another. But now he's missed the backup call-in time. Fox River didn't hear nothing at two o'clock. Which means—"

"Let's just sort out the options," Casey interrupted. "One, the fishing could be so good he just didn't want to quit for a while."

"Very likely with Youngblood."

"I don't think so, tell you why. He knows he's on probation. One more incident, one more time of screwing around with our ships, and he knows it will be his ass. We can't keep flying for Pipeline-subsidized companies with black eyes like he's been giving us. Just today a report came in from T.A.P. about him buzzing caribou on the way down here. I fixed it up, but this shit is getting serious."

"Radio out, maybe?"

"Unlikely. His ship just came off full maintenance."

The two men sat quietly for a moment, their thoughts flirting with the vision they wanted to avoid.

"You know, Smiley," Casey said. "When I crunched in up there at Atigun, I lay there for twelve hours, hurting like hell, but all the time, I never thought I was going to die. I got the tourniquet on my leg, or I'd have bled to death. Course, I kept passing out and couldn't loosen the thing the way you should, so later I got gangrene, and that was it for my leg.

"But all the time I was lying there, I kept saying to myself: 'They won't forget me. The boys will come. They'll be here soon to take me home!' It was a mighty comforting thought, I can tell you."

Smiley looked down shyly. Casey did not often share such intimacies.

Casey stood and made his way to the window. From their low, three-room building, he could see through a grove of birch trees to the muddy swirl of the Chena River, lapping against the supports of the floatplane docks and shops. He looked at the sky and frowned noticeably. The perfect blueness of the last three days had been replaced by a long band of high, wispy clouds formed into arched lines. This was the classic mackerel sky of high cirrus clouds that indicated winds aloft and an approaching front. Casey did not need a weather report to tell him conditions would deteriorate within hours.

He continued to look out the window. "They're down,

Smiley," he said slowly. "I feel it in my gut. We've got to go get 'em!"

Casey turned around. No more indecision now. He was committed to action, come what might, like a final approach to a runway you couldn't see in the fog.

"Smiley, get Fox River. Is Three-Eight-Four Zulu there?"

"Yep."

"I want 'em to get it loaded with first-aid and emergency stuff and follow Youngblood's route over to the Toubok."

"Be pretty rough in Misty Pass after a while, Casey."

"They can make it if they get their asses moving!"

"Do you want to declare an emergency, Casey?"

"No! Keep Search and Rescue out of this until we check it out ourselves."

As Smiley picked up the mike, Casey headed for the other office to phone Trans-Arctic Petroleum.

TWENTY-SEVEN

organ Procter could hold a room.

He no longer needed the new layouts Bertorelli had designed. The boards lay in a neat pile on the conference room table as Morgan stood beside his chair and delivered his summation.

He's asking the jury for an execution, Matt Richardson thought, powerless to interrupt, still licking his wounds over Procter's coup. Matt's protests over Morgan's usurpation of editorial responsibilities, Marla's outrage over the clandestine activities of her art director—both were laughed off by Tony Craig with the wave of a hand and the comment "The responsibility is mine. I authorized Morgan's action after he convinced me he was on to something. I'm the one who pays the bills around here, remember?"

The first run-through of the proposed "new look" had silenced both Matt's and Marla's indignation. The design was brilliantly conceived: each layout combined visual power with intelligent story concepts. Useful information exploded from the pages, along with a careful blend of fun, environmental concern, and even a few tastes of armchair travel. There had been no denying the effectiveness of the presentation. Matt's reluctant words of praise had blended with the accolades expressed all around the table as the group perused the layouts until the subject was exhausted. Matt's own efforts on behalf of *In Wildness*—the television program, his attempts to recruit Jonathan for the editorship—had not merely been upstaged, but had been blown away. Now he was resigned to waiting for the shock waves from the explosion, for the deadly fallout.

"Timely, useful information is our compass," Morgan was saying. "We steer by it on all our books, and it's never let us down." Morgan picked up and waved the June issue of *In Wildness*. "This book has gotten off course. Jonathan's piece on the grizzly is quite good. I enjoyed reading about the big bears, but after that the book is all sermons, a mishmash of ranting and raving." Matt immediately recognized *sermons* and *mishmash* as having been used in the *Inside Korner* report. Morgan went on:

"There's nothing *useful* in here—like how to buy a good down jacket or sort out the maze of backpacks currently on the market. Any nuggets of information that did manage to slip past the editors are surrounded by more words than *The Brothers Karamazov*." Morgan paused here, smiling, noting with pleasure the chuckles he had gotten from everybody in the group except Richardson.

Morgan was ready to close now. "It doesn't matter *how* this happened. With this new look, we can begin a comeback, and I'll really have something to sell for a change. To tell the truth, as much as I've opposed the book in the past, I'm now excited about the prospect of showing this on the street."

"You and your people have done a hell of a job selling the book up to now, Morgan," Tony Craig said. "We all know you haven't had much to work with. But even with this new look, the numbers are against us."

"Not if we take cigarette advertising," Morgan said.

Matt could feel all eyes turn his way. "Goddammit, no!" he shouted.

"It'll save the book," Morgan replied, calmly. "Since when did you become Mother Teresa to the magazine public? We take cigarette advertising in all our other books."

"I'm ashamed that we do!" Matt shot back. "Ashamed, do you hear me? The goddamn things kill people!"

Morgan's expression feigned boredom. "So do Fords and Chevrolets."

"We have a responsibility—"

Richardson was cut off by Morgan's trumpeting shout, *"We have to run a business here!"* He paused, then repeated his charge, softer this time. "We have to run a business here!"

Perhaps it was because Morgan Procter was standing and loomed over the others. Perhaps it was the effectiveness of his words. A decisive moment had arrived: Morgan Procter was taking control of the Craig Publishing Magazine Division. Everybody in the room knew it, including Matt Richardson, who sat silently, doodling some numbers on his note pad.

Zeigler's voice broke the stillness. "If we can generate enough excitement with this new concept, turn the ad picture around and improve newsstand sales, I think we could maybe sell the book at a decent price. I've worked up some figures."

"I thought that's what you were all driving toward," Matt said, still looking at his note pad and scribbling.

"Now, Matt," Tony Craig said. "We haven't reached any decisions. We're only speculating here."

Matt could endure it no longer. So, this was the end. It was strange, he thought. It wasn't at all as he'd expected: something like an explosion or a crash, being slammed into nothingness. No, it must be like this to freeze to death. You just couldn't stop the cold. It came on and on, draining away everything you had, until finally even your feelings were gone. Then, painlessly, you just drifted away.

Matt tried to reach inside himself and find something.

There was only one thing left—one resource he had not lost. It might yet hold back the darkness.

Richardson spoke directly to Craig. "While you're speculating, I think you should mull this over: I am resigning, effective immediately. One final—"

A chorus of protests exploded around the table. Tony Craig's voice was not among them.

"Please!" Matt pleaded. "Listen to me! I have to say something." The voices gradually fell silent as Matt waved his arms.

"One final request I would make of you, Tony, is that I be allowed to purchase the magazine—*my* magazine, really. I have three million dollars, or thereabouts, coming to me from the company's profit-sharing and bonuses. Isn't that right, Sam?"

"Give or take a few thou," Zeigler answered.

"I'll pledge those funds to the deal, plus form an outside syndicate, if necessary, to meet any fair price."

Matt's words hung in the silent air. Tony Craig looked astonished.

"This is ridiculous," Craig said.

"Yes or no?"

"Marla, gentlemen," Craig said. "I must ask that you leave us now. I want to talk to Matt alone."

Zeigler rose from his chair, but Marla and Jonathan remained seated, staring at Matt in shock. He nodded to them and tried to force a smile. "Please wait for me in my office," he said. "I won't be long."

Morgan was stuffing papers into his briefcase. "Should we plan on coming back, sir?"

"No," Craig said. "We'll meet soon enough. Tomorrow, all of us, right here, nine-fifteen. As far as I'm concerned, we've settled nothing here today."

"Tony, you couldn't be more wrong," Matt said. *"Everything's* been settled!"

TWENTY-EIGHT

Cody peered into the misty gloom that hung over the Toubok, trying to make out snags and rocks that jutted above the metallic dullness of the current, her arms pumping on the oars from time to time to straighten the raft. Thick clouds that threatened rain had smudged the afternoon into near-darkness, and the river felt cold and dangerous in the murk. She had not expected this, despite the precautions she had taken in bringing the foul-weather gear which she now donned. Thank God, the Tolkat cabin would be appearing around the next bend.

Buck sat in the front of the raft, staring ahead, guide and sentinel. Derek, stirring restlessly near Cody's feet, looked elf-like in his bright orange flotation vest. Cody, facing downstream from the oar seat, was beginning to get the hang of controlling the sliding bobbing craft by letting the current do the work and using the oars only to check the line of the drift.

Except for the murmur of the current and the occasional squeak of the oars, the stream was hushed in eerie silence, as though no birds, animals, or fish existed here.

As the bend straightened, Cody could make out open ground on the right bank, slanting up a slight incline toward the heavier darkness of a hillside. Her mission was almost complete. The cabin would be nestled in the spruce trees up there. She would get on the radio right away, and soon the proper authorities would know what had happened to Ted Walsh.

The raft slid aground on the sandy beach at the edge of the Tolkats' clearing. Buck leaped out, sniffing the ground expectantly. Cody's cramped legs felt a flush of relief as she stepped from the raft and looked toward the cabin, barely visible through the mist. She started to turn back to help Derek. Suddenly she paused. Something was wrong!

The silence felt like death.

The dogs! Where were the dogs? The sound of their bark-

ing should have been wild and frenzied by now, followed by
John Tolkat's loud shouts to control them.

Were the Tolkats away—to Talkeetna or Anchorage? They
usually left a dog or two behind when they traveled from the
cabin. Where were those dogs?

Everybody's probably asleep, she decided, reaching to
help Derek over the humped side of the raft. Immediately her
fear returned, clutching thickly at the base of her throat as she
started up the slope toward the cabin. A strange shape lay in
the grass ahead. It looked like a dog—sleeping. That could not
be!

Other shapes were nearby, scattered about a patch of
ground that looked as though it had been torn and savaged by
some large vehicle. Cody moved into the center of the great
mess, then stopped, gasping.

The shapes were all that was left of the Tolkat dogs.

Cody wheeled instantly, grabbed Derek's hand, and raced
toward the raft as fast as she could. She grabbed the .375, an
increasingly familiar object in her hands, and admonished
Derek. "Stay right here. Don't you wander off, do you hear me!"

"Where did our friends go?" he asked.

"Just stay here," Cody repeated. She whistled up Buck and
snapped a check cord to his collar. Derek picked up a handful
of stones and began tossing them into the water.

Cody held Buck close as she eased slowly back up the
slope toward the cabin. She was feeling sick again, almost nauseous. Her pulse was a pounding sledgehammer in her temples.
Holding the rifle and the straining dog at the same time was
going to be impossible for very long.

Nothing she had ever known before—not even the horror
she had experienced earlier—could have prepared her for the
devastation she was forced to witness now.

She could remember reading—in Hemingway especially—
how it was possible for an experienced observer to walk over a
battlefield and tell from the position of the corpses, the battered remnants of the equipment, just how the fight had developed.

What Cody saw now was a battlefield.

The paw prints of a huge grizzly littered the scarred,
blood-soaked ground. The bodies of the dogs showed how the

beast had fought its way across the clearing, then turned toward the cabin. There the savage rampage had produced its ultimate tragedy: John and Kichna Tolkat looked like smashed waxen mannequins abandoned in what was left of the front doorway. The grizzly's charge had splintered the door and part of the wall, leaving a gaping hole.

Cody closed her eyes, fighting to hold on. She could feel herself beginning to hyperventilate. She sucked in a slow, deep draft of air, trying to steady her breathing.

She stepped around to the side of the opening, carefully avoiding the pool of darkness that spread from beneath the bodies. Everything she could see in the gloom inside was wrecked. The table where the radio usually sat was crushed against a wall.

Still gasping for air, Cody bit her lip and took a last reluctant look at the bodies. The stock of John Tolkat's .300 magnum Winchester lever-action slanted out from beneath his body. He had obviously been about to make a fight of it. She wondered if he had gotten off a shot. No empty cartridges were to be seen.

Why? Cody's tormented thoughts screamed. Why had this thing happened?

There were no answers—only silence filled with gutwrenching pain.

She wheeled toward the river and began trotting down the slope, Buck running alongside. Her legs felt rubbery and uncertain and she realized she was going too fast, going to fall headlong. She slowed to a walk, her breath a knife in her lungs.

Cody lifted Derek into the raft without speaking.

"Where are our friends?" he asked.

"Gone away," she said, as she slid onto the oar seat. She laid the rifle close to her right hand and waited for Buck to jump aboard. The yellow Lab scrambled to his favorite perch as Cody pulled hard on the oars. The raft spun into the current.

Cody fought back the tears she did not want Derek to see. Her eyes ached and made it even harder to see in the dimness. Rain seemed more likely by the minute.

She began to feel the calmness of resolution bolstering her shattered nerves. She knew exactly what she had to do now, and she was going to see the job through. About three hours downstream, she would make Knife Lake, a favorite spot for fishing parties to fly into. If nobody was on the lake, she would camp therein anyway and wait.

She flicked the oars quickly to slide the raft into the tongue of current that would take it past some rocks that suddenly loomed in the dusk.

Three more hours of this, she thought. Then she would be off the river.

After that, she never wanted to see the Toubok again.

TWENTY-NINE

"It's malignant and it's terminal."

Tony Craig's words rang in Matt Richardson's ears like a deafening blast of gunfire. A stunning, unrelenting silence gripped the Craig Publishing boardroom, purging the air of discord and anger, instantly shrinking the empty room to an uncomfortable closeness from which there was no escape. For the moment, nothing mattered except a single fact so devastating that it could be neither banished nor evaded: the old man was doomed. Matt was speechless as he leaned forward from his chair, his hands gripping the edge of the table. He listened in numb disbelief as Craig explained the progress of the cancer, already well advanced.

"I'll be lucky to see Christmas," Craig said. "Or unlucky, depending on . . . the circumstances." He looked down at his hands, as though expecting to see some visual confirmation of the illness, the pain and debilitation to come. "It's a dirty trick —the way so much comes down to a bunch of stupid invisible cells that can't get their act together."

"I wish I knew what to say, Tony. I wish I had known."

"I understand," Craig sighed. "I've been there myself, seen friends dying right before my eyes. I never knew what to say either."

"I'm deeply sorry," Matt said. "I truly am."

"We all have to cross the river sometime. But when you're the one about to get on the boat, you do wonder: 'Where the hell am I going?' "

"I wish I knew, Tony."

Craig's face was set with melancholy. He seemed distant, almost dreaming, as he said, "You have your faith."

Matt blinked in obvious surprise. Craig knew he was not a particularly religious person.

"The great outdoors, I mean," Craig went on. "The natural

order of the universe, everything linked together, everything changing yet eternal."

"Something like that," Matt said, solemnly.

Craig's eyes sharpened as he stared over the table at Richardson. "We've run out of time, Matt. Both of us."

"There's never enough," Matt said, nodding.

"This little proposal you threw on the table. Was it greasepaint and tinsel—all for dramatic effect?"

"You know me better than that."

"And you don't care that you're upsetting the larger picture."

"There is no larger picture," Matt sighed wearily. "You're handing the company over to Morgan. You set the whole thing up—the newsletter gossip, the crisis over the magazine."

"I was just doing my job. The board needs some answers. I had to sort you fellows out."

"Well, you've got your man now," Matt said. "I imagine that I'm going to end up thanking you."

"I hope so, because you've given me no choice. You know I can't control the board. I sold too much stock back when I had to raise money to get our books over the hump. I can't sell *you* to them, not even with Marla's help. Morgan has clearly demonstrated his ability to lead."

"You've got him, Tony. I'm not standing in your way."

"Well, frankly, it would help if we went in there with a sense of unity on this—you continuing as editorial director."

"This disease has fucked up your brain, Tony," Matt said softly.

"I've never been more lucid."

"All I want is to take my magazine and get out the door. Please, don't fight me on this."

"I can't authorize that without putting it on the table for the board."

"Then please do it. Tomorrow."

"You're throwing away your career, Matt." Craig's eyes narrowed frostily. "The same way you did your marriage."

Richardson winced. "Things happen, people change. I've served the balance sheet well enough. I'd like a little time for myself."

"This will destroy you."

Richardson shook his head. "It will give me a great deal of satisfaction"—he patted his heart—"here."

Craig started gathering together his notes and papers.

"I'm a tired old man," he said. "Let's get some rest and pick this up together in the morning."

Matt started to protest, to demand an answer—but Craig was already rising from his chair.

At the door, he offered Matt his hand. As the warm, stricken flesh pressed against his palm and fingers, Matt fought back a flush of tears trying to surface in his eyes. He stood in the hall and watched Craig as he went into his office and closed the door without looking back.

Morgan Procter lay flat on his back with Kristen's head on his shoulder and one leg entwined with his. He could not remember ever feeling so physically relaxed, so sexually satisfied. Once again, she had driven him to unprecedented heights of ecstasy, not only matching his every move, but orchestrating passionate rhythms of her own—tenderness and fire, giving and receiving. Only one thing disturbed him now: the disquieting sense of guilt he could not help feeling about Kristen's husband.

What was happening to him anyway? Here he was, on the brink of the professional triumph he had worked years to achieve, and he was fretting about the man he had beaten.

Not really, he suddenly realized. What he was really worrying about was Kristen.

Would he be diminished in her eyes when she found out what had happened at the magazine? As much as he dreaded the thought of hurting her in any way, he was sickened by the idea of her rallying back to Richardson's side. What he wanted more than anything right now was to go on just as they were. Was the entire experience an illusion, about to drift away like a short dream? Or was it really a new beginning that could change both their lives? *Tell her what happened,* his thoughts commanded, *before she hears about it from somebody else.* But something deep inside him resisted, made him wary and unable to speak.

"Morgan?"

"Ummm?"

"Would you be interested in taking a trip?"

He smiled broadly. "Only if I'm violating the Mann Act."

"What's that?"

"An old law about transporting young females over a state line for illicit purposes."

Kristen giggled, kissing his neck. "I'm your girl. Anytime, any destination, but I'm probably beyond the age covered by the Mann Act."

"All the better." Morgan's thoughts were already soaring at the prospect of her invitation. "I know a neat little place in the Swiss Alps. It has tennis, great hiking, good food. It's always cool there."

"You've taken somebody else," Kristen chided.

"No. I was there with a friend from college—a guy."

"Can we go?"

"Absolutely. Let's check our calendars and block some time. I'll make the arrangements."

Kristen's hand was roaming aimlessly along his thigh. He felt it pause over a sensitive, familiar patch of flesh.

"What's this puffy little place alongside your cock? It feels like a scar or something."

"A goddamn gook shot me."

"Shot you! A what . . . ?"

"A Viet Cong. In a place called Vietnam, remember? We were in a war there once, not that anybody gave a damn."

"You poor thing. You must have been very brave. Most guys were trying to stay the hell out of there."

"I was just a dumb scared kid. I volunteered for the Army and Nam because there didn't seem to be anything else to do right then."

Kristen was silent as she continued to touch his old wound. "He almost did a Jake Barnes on you, honey," she said.

"A what?"

"Jake Barnes was a character in Hemingway's first successful novel. Got his basic equipment shot up in Big Fracas Number One."

"That ought to have kept him out of trouble," Morgan laughed.

Kristen's hand moved over to his soft penis and began

stroking it. "No, the book is very sad," she said. "He's in love with this interesting lady and can't have her."

Morgan could feel a new erection beginning to form in Kristen's fingers. He hoped she would not stop until he was hard enough to slide into her once again.

He got his wish. A few moments later, as their bodies melted into each other, she whispered in his ear, "I'm afraid I'm falling in love with you."

Matt Richardson was contemplating the prospect of quietly getting drunk.

The first bourbon he had poured for himself at the small bar in his office had gone down without producing any significant change in his jangled nerves. Guiltily, he poured a second helping of Wild Turkey nearly to the brim of his glass. He returned the bottle to its roost in the recesses of the handsome liquor cabinet and carried his drink over to the couch. He settled back on the cushions with a deep sigh, exhausted and emotionally drained. Marla sipped her glass of white wine and watched him anxiously from the end of the couch.

Pleading weariness, Jonathan had just departed for his hotel. Although obviously shaken by the events of the past few hours, he had promised to be on hand early the next morning.

"Well, that's it," Matt said, grimacing with a shrug of helplessness. "You're going to have a new boss."

"Craig didn't actually say . . ."

"You want another replay? He *did say.*"

Marla stood abruptly and walked slowly through the dimly lit office to a corner bookcase. Matt watched her face as she leaned back against the polished wood of the countertop and sipped her wine. Her features were cloaked in shadows, but a shelf lamp back-lighted the luxurious sweep of her hair and curvaceous outline of her figure. She set down her wine and came forward decisively, her eyes shining, her smile so feeble that it seemed pasted on. As she sat down beside him, crossing her legs under her on the couch and reaching for his hand, Matt could sense another crisis beginning.

"We have to sort things out," she said.

Matt nodded and managed a weak, "Yes."

"What do you want me to do?"

"You've done all you can. I'm sorry things went against us today." Matt rubbed the top of her hand tenderly. "I'm sorry I let you down."

"I'm Okay. I figure I'll just hang in there. It's *you* I'm worried about."

"I'll muddle through."

"To what?"

Matt checked himself, searching her expression. Compassion was there, honest compassion. But there was something else: a sense of resolve he had failed to recognize before.

"It'll be a new beginning," he said. "I guess I knew it all along—that I'd have to start over to really be happy."

"Good," Marla said. "Then we'll both be happy. I've already got what *I* want."

"With Morgan Procter driving the wagon?"

"I'm not afraid of him. Perhaps I should be, but I'm not."

Matt swirled his bourbon. It wasn't the same drink as in the good times: the fireside with a friendly book, the campfire out on the trail, the time of sharing quiet moments with someone at the end of a good day's work. He looked up to see Marla staring at him expectantly, awaiting a response.

"I guess we've come to a fork in the trail," Matt said, trying to smile.

Marla nodded. Her eyes glistened as she whispered softly, "I can't go with you, Matt. This is where I have to get off."

Richardson raised a hand to her face, the tips of his fingers soft and burning. She closed her eyes and grasped his hand, pressing it closer.

"Someday you'll understand," Matt said, softly. "I had to try."

"I'm sorry," Marla said, tearfully.

"You've done well," Matt said. "I'm glad I was around long enough to share it with you."

"I owe everything to you," Marla said, grasping his hand in both of hers. "I'll never forget that."

"The debt is mine," Matt said. "Where would I have been if you hadn't come along—turned *Charm* around? I never would have been given a shot at *In Wildness*."

"Your marriage down the drain—now your career. Aren't

you being a little cavalier about the way things have turned out?"

"My career is entering a new phase, that's all. I'm sick of having other people shape *my career.*"

Marla shook her head in confusion. "I can't take any more of this tonight." She reached around to the coffee table for her handbag, stood up suddenly, and bolted toward Matt's private rest room.

Matt took a final sip of bourbon, clunked down the heavy-bottomed glass, and rose slowly. He felt weary beyond words as he shuffled over to the closet and retrieved his suit jacket. As he shrugged into the coat, he regarded the image in the full-length mirror that backed the door.

You look like the kind of day it's been, he thought: dreadful. He ran a comb through his disheveled hair and stared at his eyes: the bloodshot whiteness, the sagging pouches of flesh beneath. The day's whiskers shadowed the curve of his jaw, giving him a vaguely sinister look. Frowning, he closed the closet door and leaned back against it, waiting for Marla. Suddenly, nothing mattered except the image of his apartment and the promise of rest. When it came time to drop Marla off at her place, he knew he was going to say goodbye right there in the cab. He was sick of making speeches, of having to act noble. And he was fed up with having to ask people to do things they didn't want to do.

As he stood looking about the room where he had committed so much of his time and energy, Matt realized his office looked like an empty stage now, set with props, softly lighted, waiting for the right players. His own show was finished here. His run was over, for whatever it had meant. Now he would move on—and try again. Alone.

THIRTY

The steady whisper of the rain on the nylon tent was beginning to make Cody drowsy, calming the anguish that flooded her thoughts. Her down sleeping bag was a cozy cocoon she felt she never wanted to leave. Derek was nestled beside her, bundled in his own bag, and, at her feet, Buck breathed heavily in the sleep of innocence.

Cody had snapped the small tent together and shepherded her mates inside without bothering with a fire and hot meal. Her physical and emotional exhaustion made her feel ill, as if wracked by some disease. Derek was so tired that he fell asleep with a half-eaten granola bar clutched in one hand. Cody had given the tidbit to Buck and crawled into her bag with her clothes on, weary beyond belief.

They were cramped on an open tundra bank, just where the river emptied into the broad expanse of Knife Lake. Her view up the lake was limited by the light rain and mist, but she could see that the reach of shoreline was devoid of human activity. She would have to wait. Eventually a fishing party would come. And if they didn't, she would be ready to signal passing aircraft with an emergency mirror once the weather cleared. Bush pilots in Alaska and Canada were constantly on the alert for the flashing signals of reflected sunlight.

As Cody listened to the rain on the dimly illuminated dome overhead, she found herself wishing Buck were not asleep. She counted on his alertness for protection. The .375 magnum was lying beside her bag, loaded and ready to deal with any intruder. But she would need some warning, especially if a grizzly was poking around.

Grizzly! She shivered. Surely the outlaw bear that had killed the Tolkats couldn't be this far downriver. Surely the danger was behind her.

What had provoked the beast to unleash the savage attack? Was he wounded, hiding in the bush? An injured grizzly was a death trap, waiting for the unwary. The world *had* to know of its existence!

If only a plane would come.

Cody's thoughts lingered on the deadly creature that stalked the river valley. In the Western rural country where she had been raised, grizzlies were a universally hated menace, despite their dwindling numbers. To the ranchers and other landowners on the wilderness fringes, all grizzlies were potential livestock killers and man-eaters, a threat too dangerous to tolerate. The beasts that had once roamed the West in vast numbers without fear of any other living creature had taken a hell of a beating from the one predator too wily and numerous to banish: man. Their populations had been reduced to an estimated one thousand to fifteen hundred in Montana, Wyoming, and Idaho, with Yellowstone and Glacier National Parks containing the most concentrated numbers of survivors. The two hundred or so bears thought to live in Yellowstone were resigned to an ignoble existence as subjects of research and controversy. Radio-collared, drugged, transplanted from area to area, they lived amid a storm of wrangling and outrage over how best to ensure their survival while still allowing man access to their environment.

Alaska's twenty-thousand-bear population was a healthy one, but even in the Great Land—whose vastness would seem to suggest room for all—an old persistent cry could still be heard: "The only good grizzly is a dead grizzly!" It was hard to convince people who lived under threat of a grizzly attack that the bears had rights too. How many people, Cody wondered, who had witnessed what she had, would march for the grizzly's protection?

No. Even here, the bears did not fit into man's world. They would probably go.

Cody felt Buck's body stir, jolting against her feet. She raised herself onto one elbow and clasped a hand over the stock of the rifle. The Lab's head was raised in the dimness, alert, listening. Suddenly his barks exploded in the stillness.

"Easy!" Cody admonished. "Easy, boy!"

Derek turned over, but continued sleeping.

Cody unzipped her bag and crawled over it to the closed

front flap of the tent with the rifle in tow. Buck scrambled to one side, squeezing between the wall and their small packs.

Cody paused, listening, with one hand on the front zipper. The only sound was the swish of the rain.

Buck barked again, looking directly at Cody.

"Hush!" she cried. She looked around for her boots and pulled them on.

Cody flung the flap of the tent open and peered outside. The gloom was oppressive, despite the daylight that had come on since she had pitched the tent. The surface of the lake was leaden beneath smoky veils of mist and rain, the brown tundra a sodden carpet dotted with brooding stands of spruce, huddling indistinctly in the murk.

Buck suddenly rushed past her outstretched arm, nearly knocking her over. He shook himself vigorously as he stood outside the flap.

Cody crawled on out and stood beside the Lab, the rifle in her hands. She ignored the cold, penetrating rain as she looked around expectantly.

The empty landscape belied Buck's alarm. The yellow Lab stared at the horizon, still expecting visitors. A new chorus of barking was swallowed up by the vastness.

Cody glared at the empty horizon, puzzled by Buck's persistent alarm. The cold rain pressed against her face, trickling into her eyes as she strained to detect the source of the Lab's agitation. She cupped one hand over her forehead, warding off the irritating drops.

Still nothing. Goddammit, there was nothing out there— and she was getting wet!

Frustrated, she turned back to the tent and was carefully wiggling into the dry refuge, trying not to wake Derek, when the distinct, booming thud of helicopter rotors popped into her hearing. She grabbed her parka and hurried back outside. The sound was already louder, its location indistinct in the echoes that seemed to reverberate through the mist from all along the horizon.

Cody clenched her fists, hoping desperately to see the craft float out of the mist. Buck whined and jumped about excitedly.

There seemed to be a pattern to the movement of the

noise. The sound would be steady for a while, then waver, then come on strong again.

The river! The chopper was following the river, bending and turning with the flow.

Suddenly she felt a crushing sense of doubt. Was the sound still receding after that last turn? Her fingers were cramped and aching as she clenched them tighter, her breath suspended.

Enough already! her mind screamed angrily. This isn't happening!

Quickly now, her hearing confirmed what she feared most: the sound was definitely retreating upriver. In a moment she and Buck were alone in the murmur of the rain.

Cody turned back to the tent, trying once again to regain her composure. The disappointment was sickening, but one ray of hope shone through. There were aircraft in the area, just as she had surmised there might be. Eventually someone would come to the lake.

What would the chopper be searching for along the river? she wondered, as she crawled back into her sleeping bag.

An agonizing thought crossed her mind. Jonathan could have returned! She had been a fool not to leave a note!

No, she quickly decided. That wasn't possible. He had only been gone two days.

Suddenly, the puzzle clicked together in her thoughts. If a chopper had brought Ted Walsh to the river as she suspected, the craft might have returned to rendezvous with him.

They were searching for Ted Walsh along the river! They would be back!

Cody nestled into the warmth of the bag, relaxing at last, certain now that her ordeal was almost over.

THIRTY-ONE

The beauty of the fair New York morning was lost on Morgan Procter as he stood at his apartment window, sipping coffee, and gazed out over the sunlit greenery of Central Park. He noted that he would not need an umbrella or raincoat and turned away from the view that normally would have fascinated him. Today his mind was on Kristen Richardson, who had just turned off the shower.

Morgan set his coffee cup on the tray room service had provided and glanced at the bedroom door, expecting to see Kristen emerge at any moment.

What he was about to do was absolutely necessary. To go on seeing Kristen, something he desperately wanted, he would have to tell her what had happened at Craig Publishing. He could not bear the thought of office gossip reaching her ears, gossip which no doubt would assassinate his character while elevating Matt Richardson's to the status of martyr.

She walked into the room, smiling with joy, wrapped in one of his blue cashmere robes. His growing affection for her—the sheer sense of physical excitement she aroused in him—surged past the barriers of doubt his thoughts had been building.

"Hi," she said. "Miss me?"

He held out his hands, smiling with the pleasure she made him feel. "Kris, there's something I'd like to talk to you about."

"Oops!" She frowned. "I was afraid of something like this. Can't you just keep it a secret?"

Morgan shook his head. "This won't keep."

"You're married!"

"No."

"You're leaving the country!"

Morgan smiled again. "No."

"I know you like me," Kristen said. "It can't be that." She paused, reflecting. "You're not bi?"

Morgan laughed.

"I've got it!" Kristen exclaimed. "You've got a whole passel of illegitimate Vietnamese children."

The headshake again. "I probably set a soldiering record in that regard. I got shot before I got laid." His smile vanished. "Come on, Kris. This is serious. You're making it more difficult."

She put her arms around him, her wet hair touching his face. "It'll be all right," she said. "Whatever it is won't change the way I feel."

He wanted to thank her for those words. He wanted to believe them. We'll see, he thought.

He led her over to the couch, his arm around her. When they sat down, Kristen buried her face in her hands for a moment, then looked up as he began to speak.

"I know you don't want to talk about the magazines—about your husband—but there's something I have to tell you."

She shook her head. "I don't want to hear about it. I'm not involved."

"We're all involved," Morgan said. "I want you to listen to me very carefully. The way I feel about you makes it very important to me that you hear about this from me, instead of somebody else."

She nodded, obviously moved by the appeal in his voice and face.

"There's been a war going on over who's to be president of the magazine division. Matt wants the job. Naturally, so do I. We've had quite a battle, but right now it looks like I'm going to get the nod."

"Congratulations!" Kris cried, with genuine warmth. "You should be very proud."

Morgan waved this off.

"I've had to sink *In Wildness*. It's what Craig and the board want. Your husband's taking it pretty hard. He blames me personally for doing the book in."

Morgan saw he had touched a nerve here, just as he'd expected. Kristen looked away, obviously collecting her thoughts. "That magazine was his dream," she whispered. "For a very long time."

"I'm sorry," Morgan said.

"It must be very hard for him," Kristen said softly, as though talking to herself. "Seeing your dream die."

"There was nothing I could do," Morgan said. "I have dreams too, you know."

Kristen turned to him, her expression calm but serious. "Was the magazine losing lots of money?"

Morgan nodded.

Kristen's expression seemed to perk up at the thought. "You shouldn't feel guilty. Doing the magazine wasn't your idea."

"Matt feels that the company let him down, didn't give the magazine a fair shot."

"Did you?" Kristen asked, interested.

"Yes. We're not in business to lose money, though. Especially now, when we're about to go public."

Kristen reflected on this thought for a moment. "Matt should see some real money out of that stock thing," she said.

Morgan sighed. "He wants to resign. Buy the magazine from the company with his profit shares and bonuses. He said he would form a syndicate and go into debt if he has to."

"Part of that money is rightfully mine," Kristen said, angrily. "He has no right to touch it."

"I don't know about that," Morgan said. "All I know is what he's planning. You'd better talk to your attorney."

"You're goddamn right I will," Kristen said.

"You mean you don't care what happens to the magazine?" Morgan said, surprised.

"It doesn't matter to me what Matt publishes. I just don't want my money involved."

"He probably won't be able to save the magazine without it."

"Then let it go under! He'll find some new toy to play with. He always does."

Kristen looked away quickly, obviously embarrassed by her outburst. The strain was etched on her face.

"Why are we dwelling on this?" she asked. Her face softened again, warm and appealing as she looked at him intently. "Morg, what you did doesn't change anything about us."

"I was afraid it might. Sometimes a personal crisis pulls people back together."

Kristen smiled broadly and reached for his hands. Morgan felt a quick and ecstatic release of emotion.

"Thanks for telling me," she said. "Now stop worrying about it. The only problem we have is that I can't be here tonight, because of tomorrow's tournament."

"Ask for a bye."

She shook her head. "I can come back in a few days . . . if you want me."

"I've never wanted anything more," Morgan said. He bent his face to hers, and the cool, sweet taste of her lips bolted through his senses, stirring him deeply.

Kristen's fingers traced the *MP* on the pocket of his crisp dress shirt. "You'd better get on down to the factory before you get in trouble. I'll let myself out."

"I'd take the day off if I could. You know that."

"Start to work on Switzerland. Don't waste the whole day on Craig Publishing."

Morgan laughed and stood up, his reflection rising in the gilt-edged mirror on the side wall. He stared at the image he saw there, shocked at the exuberance on his face, the sound of his own laughter still in his ears. It seemed a miracle that two nights had worked such alchemy. His apparent victory on the corporate battlefield had been capped off by this splendid woman's affection, which now seemed like some treasured new possession, one he could not afford to lose. He held out a hand to Kristen, and she rose to stand beside him. They started for the door, arms around one another.

"I'm sure you won't be surprised if I confess that I really love my work," Morgan said. "I always look forward to going to the office."

"Unlike most people," Kristen answered.

"Yes, I'm lucky. But there's more to it than that." Morgan stopped in front of the door and turned to her. "For a long time, there just didn't seem to be anything else I really cared about."

"And now . . . ?"

"I'd like to think I've found something I lost. I'd like to think I can keep it this time."

Kristen's eyes answered Morgan. They were glistening and hugely inviting as her lips moved to his. The morning freshness was in the taste of her, the scent of her flesh, the feel of damp tendrils of hair. The familiar, demanding urgency of her body burned through her robe and his clothing. As her tongue teased through his mouth, Morgan felt himself sliding back into their private world of peace and pleasure, a new surge of confidence telling him it would last forever.

"Well, that tears it!" Matt Richardson slammed down the phone and stared at it as if he wanted to toss it out the window.

Over the years, Jonathan Hill had seen Matt in many moods, from elation to heartbreak, but never had he seen his friend's face so contorted with anger and frustration as it was this morning. The mask Matt wore was further heightened, Jonathan wryly noted, by the puffiness brought on by too much booze and too little sleep.

"What is it?" Jonathan asked, timidly.

"The end."

"Come on, Matt. I'm not a mind reader."

Richardson picked up a copy of *In Wildness* and stared at the grizzly on the cover. He slowly shook his head. "That was Kristen's attorney. They're going to freeze all my assets until the divorce is settled." He looked up at Jonathan. "How the hell did they get wind of my plan?"

"Probably just a coincidence," Jonathan said. "Fate has a hell of a sense of timing."

"Fate my ass!" Matt barked. "Somebody told her. Craig, Zeigler . . . Morgan, somebody."

"She would have found out anyway," Jonathan said.

"That's right. Look on the positive side. What the hell do you care? You're flying back home in a few hours!"

"Matt . . ." Jonathan said, shaking his head.

Richardson slumped back in his chair, closing his eyes. "I'm sorry, kid. I've had more than I can take." He tossed *In Wildness* onto the desk.

Jonathan picked up the magazine and settled back in his

chair, staring at the grizzly. He could remember the instant when he had clicked the shutter, remember the bear's sudden alertness at the sound of the motor-drive. The bear had gazed inquisitively in his direction for only a second, then had bolted away through the brush. Suddenly, Jonathan was thinking of another grizzly, the great bear he had never seen. He looked up at Richardson.

"This new grizzly I found, Matt. If I can relocate him, the shots will be spectacular."

"National Geographic will love them," Matt said, bitterly.

"Wouldn't you like to come with me? It'll be terrific—the two of us up there in the ranges, working on the story together."

"Just what I need," Matt said.

Jonathan could feel his spirits soaring with the prospect of getting Matt to Alaska for a while. He leaned forward enthusiastically, his smile glowing. "And the fishing should be great. We could fly out to some of the salmon rivers on the Peninsula."

"Let's do it," Matt said. "Kodiak Island too. I've always wanted to fish Kodiak."

"That's easy," Jonathan said. "How about a little climbing? Feel up to it? Or a canoe or kayak trip?"

"Perfect," Matt said. "Hell, let's do two or three of the very best." Suddenly, Matt leaped to his feet and began pacing as he continued talking. Jonathan's heart began to sink as he realized what was happening. "After that," Matt went on rapidly, "we ought to swing on back down toward the Yellowstone country. Hit the Madison, the Snake, and the Big Hole."

Jonathan slumped in his chair, too disappointed to protest Matt's bitter outburst, which had now become a monologue delivered in a binge of staccato images.

"Silver Creek fishes late," Matt went on, "so we'll save that for last and just stay right there at Sun Valley until the skiing gets good. Christmas, I figure we'll spend in Vail. After that, I'd like to find some good powder. Where's everybody skiing powder these days, Jon? Let's find out. Taos, Snowmass? The Bugaboos in British Columbia? Anyway, along about March, I figure we'll be just about skiied out, so to speak, but that's the perfect time to push on down to Argentina for some more trout fishing. Down there, March is like our September, and a lot of rivers should be good: the Chimehuin, the—"

"Stop it!" Jonathan shouted.

Matt glared at him furiously, his face livid. He started to say something, when his eyes turned to the door. Helen Sullivan was standing there.

"There's an emergency," she said. "Mr. Craig wants you both in the conference room right away."

When he had closed the boardroom door behind them, the first thing Jonathan noticed was Morgan Procter, sitting alone at the table in the same chair he had occupied the previous evening. He was slumped over the polished surface, his face in his hands, oblivious to Tony Craig and Sam Zeigler, who stood in a far corner, talking in whispers.

"We'll be right with you," Craig called across the room as he saw them enter. He turned back to Zeigler and resumed their conversation.

Matt tapped Procter on the shoulder. "What's up?" he asked the strangely silent and withdrawn figure.

Morgan looked up slowly. His face was pale and strained.

"I killed Ted Walsh," he said softly. He rubbed his hands together, as though trying to relieve physical pain.

"What the hell are you talking about?" Matt asked. He turned to look at Jonathan.

Morgan stared blankly into space as Tony Craig and Zeigler hurried over to the table.

"It's true that Ted Walsh is dead," Craig said. He patted Morgan on the shoulder. The expression on Procter's face made it obvious that he did not feel the old man's gesture. "You've got to get a grip on yourself, son," Craig continued. "It's not your fault."

"Yes it is," Morgan said, looking directly at Richardson. "I sent him up there."

"There's been an accident," Sam Zeigler said. "In Alaska."

To Jonathan, the first wisps of a chill breeze seemed to be blowing into the room. He felt pinpricks spreading over his scalp.

"What happened?" Jonathan asked, angrily. "Be specific, man!"

"We don't have much detail," Craig said. His face gave no
hint of grief or concern over the situation.

Zeigler picked up the slack with a certain smugness, obviously enjoying being the center of attention.

"We got a call from the Trans-Arctic Petroleum PR office.
Walsh and T.A.P.'s field PR man had been poking around the
wilderness is one of the company's helicopters."

"He was on a PR junket to the Pipeline," Morgan interrupted. "I sent him so we could get the T.A.P. business."

"Anyway," Zeigler continued quickly, "the helicopter
turned up missing—so the company sent another out to look for
it. They found it—crashed and totally destroyed. They're still
investigating. The weather is terrible, and only the one chopper
has been able to get in."

"They don't have a positive ID. But they called it 'a non-
survivable accident,'" Craig said.

"Non-survivable," Morgan repeated, shaking his head.

"Where'd it happen?" Jonathan asked, his voice taut with
apprehension.

"A river . . . way the hell and gone up there somewhere."
Zeigler looked at his notes. "It's called 'Tou . . . bok.'"

"That's where I live!" Jonathan shouted. He felt his heart
sinking with anguish.

"What?" said Craig.

"I think he was going to pay you a surprise visit before he
went to the Pipeline," Morgan said. "Anyway, he *said* he was
—after I forced him into going!"

"Morgan, for Christ's sake!" Craig exclaimed. "You're turning this into a Greek tragedy."

"What is it, Tony?" Procter shot back.

"It's not personal. The man was on a business trip. His
aircraft crashed. His survivors will be well taken care of."

"It's not your fault, Morg," Zeigler chimed.

"This is a fucking mess!" Matt shouted. "On top of everything else!"

"On *my* river," Jonathan said. "I just can't believe it." He
spotted the phone on the side table. "I've got to get a message
to Cody," he said, rising.

Suddenly, as if by a signaled interruption, the phone began
to ring. Craig was nearest, and he quickly walked over and

picked up the receiver. "Yeah," he barked. He listened for only a moment, then hurriedly put down the phone and started for the door. Glancing toward Procter, he said, "I have to take a call in my office. I'll be right back."

Zeigler started talking about other occasions when company personnel had lost their lives while doing their jobs. Jonathan only half listened, as his thoughts tried to picture the scene on the river. The anxiety he was feeling had turned into a rising tide of funk. He eyed the phone again, then decided to wait until he could retreat to Matt's office.

"We had two field men from the circulation department on that DC-10 that went down leaving Chicago," Zeigler was relating. "The one where the engine fell off."

Jonathan fidgeted nervously as the minutes dragged by. Finally, Craig came back into the room. He glanced at some notes in his hands for a moment, then said, "There's something new."

The silence was excruciating as Craig nervously studied his notes again. It was obvious to Jonathan that the old man was uncomfortable with the news he was obliged to report.

"That was Dick Kline," Craig began. "Some of you may not know that he's an old and dear friend. Anyway, the agency has been in contact with T.A.P. on a hourly basis. They've finally got people swarming all over the . . . ah, accident . . . site. Just as we feared, Ted Walsh is dead."

"Dammit!" Matt uttered. Morgan Procter winced visibly.

"But Walsh wasn't killed in the chopper," Craig blurted. "His body was found elsewhere—mutilated in some way."

"What the hell is going on?" Matt shouted.

Jonathan started for the phone.

"Wait a moment, son!" Craig called. "Your wife already knows about it. She and your son are on the way into Anchorage in a helicopter right now. I'm sure she'll be calling in a few minutes."

Jonathan stared at Matt, then turned back to Craig. "What happened?" he said calmly, deeply relieved.

"Some people have been killed," Craig said, blinking as he tried to meet Jonathan's gaze. "There's some kind of killer bear loose on the river."

"What?" Jonathan felt stunned, as if he had taken a physical blow.

"That's what they say," Craig continued. "Evidently, it all had nothing to do with the helicopter crash."

"I don't understand," Matt said, sitting down beside Procter, who stared at the others as though the words he had been hearing were in some indecipherable language.

"Nobody understands—yet," Craig said. "But Dick Kline is sending somebody up there on the company jet immediately." Craig looked at his notes. "Mike Williams, the man on the account. You got the business from him, right, Morgan?"

Procter nodded.

"I'd like to get on that plane," Jonathan said.

"I'll call 'em for you," Morgan said, rising from the table.

"Do that, Morgan," Craig said, quickly. " 'Cause I want you to go too."

Incredulous, Procter muttered a weak, "What for?"

"A gesture of goodwill for my friend," Craig answered. "After all, we *are* involved."

"Involved how?" Matt Richardson asked. "In what?"

"Our editor was on a T.A.P.-sponsored trip. That's involvement!"

Jonathan looked at Matt's reaction. Richardson's face was contorted with anger. "You're holding out on us, Tony. What the hell is this really all about?"

"Isn't it obvious, Matt?" Craig barked. "It's about doing business, something you care little about. While Morgan and your editor, Walsh, were working to put some points on the board with T.A.P., you had your head up your ass and your brain in Egypt! Do you even realize how much business we do with Kline-Wolfe on an annual basis?"

"That's beside the point!" Richardson stormed back. "You're not—"

Matt looked away, surprised at the sight of Helen Sullivan standing near the table. She came forward as Matt's eyes met hers. "I'm terribly sorry," she said, "but your sister"—she glanced toward Jonathan—"Mrs. Hill is on the phone from Alaska. She must speak to you both."

"We'll take it in my office," Matt said, glaring at Tony Craig.

The look was not seen by Jonathan. He was already out the door, racing down the hall.

"What I'm asking is more like a personal favor. I can't let Dick Kline down."

Anthony Craig clasped both hands and leaned across the boardroom table toward Morgan Procter, who fidgeted uncomfortably under the steel-cold glare of Craig's eyes. "But, Tony," Morgan protested. "The board meeting . . ."

"There is no meeting," Craig snapped. "I canceled it after I talked with Kline."

Morgan Procter endured a sickening flush of disappointment. Pain shot through his gut, and he sensed the reek of bile in his throat. He fought to steady himself, to regain control of his feelings. "I don't know what I can do," he said. "I'm sure Mike Williams can handle things."

Craig shook his head. "Dick suggested that you go along. Williams says he needs you."

Morgan cursed under his breath. "What the fuck for?" he cried in frustration.

"They've got a real mess up there," Craig sighed.

Morgan blinked in surprise. "Then Matt was right. There is something going on."

"Yes," Craig said softly. "They were hassling the bear with the helicopter. That's why it crashed . . . and that's probably why the bear went on the rampage."

"How the hell do they know that?" Morgan asked.

"Who knows? What difference does it make anyway?"

"I don't understand," Morgan said. "Why would Walsh and those people do a thing like that? The guy loves bears more than he does people!"

Craig shrugged. "They did it. And when the press gets hold of what really happened, it's going to make T.A.P. and Kline-Wolfe look like Godzilla in the Garden of Eden. Us too!"

"What can I do?"

"Stick with this guy Williams. Dick Kline doesn't trust him completely. Smother this thing! If it starts to get out of hand, your fallback will be that Walsh *rented* the chopper. He was on holiday. It had nothing to do with *anything.*"

Morgan emitted a low whistle and slumped back in his chair. "This isn't going to be easy."

"That's why I'm sending *you,*" Craig said. He looked off toward the window, reflecting for a moment. "I'd go myself," he said. "It's just that I'm not feeling on the top of my game lately."

"I'm sorry," Morgan said. "I didn't mean to act uncooperative. It's just that there's so much happening here."

"It'll wait," Craig said. "Matt has muddied the water anyway. I need to think about his idea . . . and yours. I'll keep the board settled while you're away."

"You think a lot of Dick Kline, don't you?"

"Without his support, this company would have gone under in the early days. He not only pushed business our way, but he ran our PR and promotion for gratis. Years later, when we were in trouble again, he spread the word that we were coming back, rallied new money to our cause. Most of our board members came to us because of him."

"I see," Morgan said.

"I thought you would," Craig said. "It begins to get personal, doesn't it? This whole unfortunate affair."

"This town's nothing but a little village," Morgan said, trying a smile.

Craig's expression refused to reflect Procter's stab at humor. "On your horse, Morgan. I don't care what you and Williams do or how you do it. Just clean this up and get on back here."

"What about them?" Morgan asked, gesturing toward the door.

"Looks like you're stuck with 'em for a while. T.A.P. says Matt's sister—Jonathan's wife—doesn't really know what happened. Make sure they don't. It'll just be a nice little family reunion, that's all."

"What if they find out?" Morgan said, unconvinced.

"Then they'll have to play ball!" Craig barked, angrily. "If Matt ever wants to see his magazine again, he'd damn well better listen to you!"

"I'll try," Morgan said, rising.

"I'm not sending you up there to *try!*"

Craig's icy stare warned Morgan to keep his mouth shut

and get on with the job. As much as he wanted to vent his spleen over the anguish *In Wildness* had already caused him, Morgan knew he would have to hold his fire. So this wasn't going to be his great day after all! There was more work to be done, more obstacles to be smashed aside. Only then would the magazine division presidency be his. The prize was within his grasp, yet he could not capture it. Well, he had come too far, endured too much, to be shaken now.

Morgan turned sharply and walked out the door without speaking or looking back.

The Craig limousine bearing Jonathan and Matt toward the Plaza Hotel moved with agonizing slowness through the crowded midtown streets. Jonathan glanced anxiously at his watch every few moments. "We barely have time to pick up our stuff and get out to the airport."

"We'll make it," Matt said. "Or they'll wait for us." His face was pensive as he stared at Jonathan. "I'm sorry, kid. Sorry to put you through this."

"I'm Okay. It's Cody who's been through hell."

"She'll be fine," Matt said. "I could tell over the phone."

"You can't blame her for being upset. What a thing to live through. I feel guilty for not being there."

"She's a strong person, Jon. She'll bounce back."

"And our life on the river?" Jonathan's voice was bitter and accusatory. "Will that bounce back? Will she ever want to go back there?"

Matt looked away, remembering clearly the anguish that had been apparent in Cody's voice, despite the poor quality of the telephone transmission. Now he couldn't wait to see her, to comfort her. "Once we're all together, things will be all right," he said to Jonathan.

"And the bear?"

"Horribilis," Matt said, gazing off into space, almost as if he were dreaming. "Don't you see it? He can help us save the magazine."

"Dead or alive?"

The bitterness in Jonathan's voice jolted Matt. He turned slowly and stared at the stern face that confronted him.

"Does it really make any difference?" Matt asked, pensively. "The story . . . the pictures if we're lucky . . . will put *In Wildness* on the charts. Finally."

Jonathan's lips formed the beginning of a reply, then paused, trembling. He slumped back on the seat, staring straight ahead, content to keep his thoughts private.

The two men rode in silence, as if they were strangers.

THIRTY-TWO

They were coming for him now.

All day, the noise of helicopter rotors had been thudding like gunfire along the course of the Toubok. The great bear Horribilis heard the sky-things approach his mountain again and again, their cries so frequent and numerous they sometimes blended into one continuous pall of thunder that seemed to be rolling up the slopes. Then, suddenly, the noise would disappear for a while. Though he watched and listened for hours, the grizzly could neither smell nor see any trace of the intruders he instinctively knew had come to destroy him.

The place where the bear hid now was high above the river, adjacent to his denning site, hidden in an invisible gully deep in a tangle of birch brush, the last greenery among the talus pitches and snowfields of the high ridges. The immediate terrain he surveyed was only part of the world mapped in his mind: tangles of willow and birch brush; the places where glacial seepage kept the vegetation lush all summer, teeming with the roots, flowers, and herbs he liked best; the slopes where the autumn berry crops would be thickest; the trails of ground squirrels; the dens of wolves; the windless draws where Dall sheep liked to bed down.

Horribilis could move through this world with furtive quickness, always using whatever cover was available, seldom risking being in the open. He could be a clown, desperately trying to dig up a morsel of a ground squirrel. He could be a deadly hunter, sneaking up to kill and eat a recently dropped caribou calf.

Now, crouched over the still-empty slope, the great bear depended upon his nose to tell him when the two-legged creatures entered his domain. All day, the scents his nostrils had pulled from the soft air were all the familiar elements of his nearby range: the ground-hugging tundra grasses and flowers, slides of loose rock, talus pitches rimmed with frost, lichen-covered boulders, rotten melting snowfields, and deeper crevasses of glacier ice. When a half-dozen Dall sheep ewes and lambs fed through a nearby grassy basin, he smelled them pass.

Then the evening shadows began to fall over the slope the grizzly surveyed, and he lost the advantage of scent in the heavy cooling air. When the noise of the sky-things disappeared completely, a strange sense of restlessness began to grip the bear.

He needed to move around, survey the nearby ridges while the dusky shadows of the short evening pressed down.

Horribilis did not know that he was dying, but the pain-danger burning inside him had given him a sense of rage and fury that flamed through the weakness that had been devouring his body. Just as he could prey to eat, he could prey to protect himself—to drive away the danger by stalking it down and destroying it with whatever powers remained in his hunter's body. Then he could rest, become well again.

The great bear slipped from the cover of the birch brush, stalking through the shadows, heading down the ridge.

The campfire had burned down to a bed of glowing embers that seemed to pulsate as Morgan Procter gazed deep into the heart of the coals, his face pensive, his eyes held by the hypnotic dance of the dying fire in each lump of the cinders. He sat with his back against the trunk of a birch and absently ran his hands over his aching feet. They had given him a bitch of a time this day, as evidenced now by patches of dried blood on his thick woolen socks.

When he and Richardson had purchased their field outfits in Anchorage two days before, neither had reckoned on the breaking-in time new boots required. Now they were paying the price of their ignorance in blisters and abrasions too tender even to touch. Walking through the Alaska backcountry had been an incredible ordeal because of the boots. Tomorrow, Morgan knew, remembering his army days, the soreness would be an agony until sheer numbness took over.

The fire was getting too low. Morgan reached to one side for another slab of split birch and tossed the wood onto the coals. The log landed heavily, spewing sparks, then its sides blossomed in reddish orange flame as the paper bark erupted.

Seated on the ground directly across the fire from Morgan, Jonathan Hill looked up from the notebook he had been perusing for the past half hour. "Listen to this," he said, squinting down at the pages in the muted late evening light of their campsite, a hillside of white spruce and birches that rose steeply into the shadows.

"What is it?" Matt Richardson called from off to one side. He was seated on the edge of a piece of plastic tarp, tinkering with an assortment of camera bodies and lenses laid out before him.

"Listen," Jonathan repeated. He began reading aloud: *"After you have exhausted what there is in business, politics, conviviality, love, and so on—have found that none of these finally satisfy, or permanently wear—what remains? Nature remains: to bring out from their torpid recesses the affinities of a man or woman with the open air—the sun by day and the stars of heaven by night."*

Jonathan looked up from the pages.

"Ted Walsh wrote *that?*" Richardson said, incredulous.

"No," Jonathan answered. "Walt Whitman wrote it. But Walsh remembered it. It's the last thing he put in his notebook. Probably just before he died."

"Dangerous words," Matt said. He picked up a long telephoto lens. "Notions like that could lead some dumb bastard to start a magazine." His face was cold and expressionless as he raised the lens to one eye and squinted through the glass.

Morgan Procter listened to this byplay without comment. The subject had been wrung dry—and he was sick of it besides! If these two were going to prattle on and on about what had happened, then he was going to crawl into his tent and sleeping bag and sack out. Eventually, he was going to do that anyway, but right now he was enjoying the look and feel of the fire, cozy against the evening chill that had come on sharply as they climbed into the higher ranges above the Toubok. Just a little higher and they would be above the tree line—into snow. Tomorrow.

What would happen then? Morgan reflected. Would there be more surprises? Would they find that damn bear?

He tossed another piece of birch onto the fire, intrigued by the curious eruption of flame. He was wishing he had brought along some liquor—a flaskful at least—in spite of the weight.

Morgan cut furtive glances toward Matt and Jonathan. Both were still engrossed in their projects.

They had become a strange pair, Morgan thought. The catastrophic events of the last few days had left them reeling, like boxers ready to go down. Not that he was in such great shape himself: still plagued by guilt, missing Kristen, worried sick about what Tony Craig was up to back in New York. But these two guys! Their obsession with their magazine had now been overshadowed by their zeal to find this bear. Fish and Wildlife people were wringing the area dry looking for the beast, already legendary in its rampage of death and destruction. But Jonathan and Matt had taken up the quest as though the creature was their personal responsibility. And both men were using the pursuit to play out their private fantasies.

Richardson was the worst. Clearly, the man had taken leave of his senses. He had designated himself head photographer of the expedition and was talking nonsensically about the way the photographs could ultimately be the salvation of *In Wildness*.

"That grizzly is going to be the most famous wild creature since Elsa the Lioness in *Born Free*," Matt had said. "If we can get him on the cover of the magazine, we'll have a million-copy seller—and the book will be on the way!"

Jonathan's purpose was equally dark. Morgan could see it in his eyes earlier when he'd watched him attach a scope to the .375 Winchester magnum rifle and check the action and loads of the .44 magnum Ruger Redhawk revolver.

Why couldn't the young man leave the killing to the experts? Did he think that when the bear was destroyed, his little valley would be made livable again? That he could persuade his wife to return to the scenes of the hell she had witnessed?

Sitting here in this tranquil scene, Morgan found it hard to believe that the carnage of the past few days had happened at all. He had been hardened to the reality of violent death on the streets of New York by years of headlines in the *Post* and *News*. But the idea of death stalking through these forests and hills seemed remote and unconvincing, especially now that he had just spent two days walking through the same country where the tragedies had occurred. The discomforts of his aching feet and the ubiquitous mosquitoes had given Morgan no realistic hint of the fate that could await the unwary in this wilderness, the fate that had struck down Ted Walsh, wiped out all the others.

By the time the Kline-Wolfe Learjet had landed in Anchorage, the press was already swarming over the story like a pack of feeding wolves. Cody had gone public with her version of the events, triggering a simultaneous burst of activity by the T.A.P. public relations office and the Fish and Wildlife Department.

Despite the activity by the press and the bureaucrats, nobody had penetrated the veil of secrecy that surrounded the seemingly unrelated copter crash and the murderous attacks by the bear. The story Mike Williams of Kline-Wolfe and his cohorts in the T.A.P. public relations office spoon-fed the media had become established fact: Ted Walsh had drowned in a kayaking accident. The helicopter he and Jack Burke of T.A.P. had rented for a fishing holiday, completely unrelated to business, had crashed after dropping Walsh on the river. The outbreak of grizzly bear attacks in the area at the same time was entirely a coincidence.

Nor-Air, the company which owned the Jet-Ranger, had confirmed this version of the tragedy. And Morgan himself, representing Craig Publishing, had deftly provided the frosting on the bogus cake by issuing statements lamenting Walsh's tragic death as the loss of one of North America's greatest conservation leaders.

As he looked up from the campfire, Morgan's gaze swept across the folded hills of the river valley, over the violet bays of shadows, framed by the peaks beyond. In spite of the beauty before him, he bit his lip, grimacing as he remembered Walsh's face across the table at lunch, the lunch that had cost the man his life. Morgan tried to shake away the vision, but he could not. He felt his throat tightening with emotion as he relived the moment when he had stood before the reporters and TV cameras and talked about Walsh with a gush of words so effective they seemed to have come from a prepared script.

"The love Ted Walsh had for the land and its creatures

was apparent on every page of his magazine," Morgan had said. "All I know about what happened is that he was very happy on the day he died. He was happy with what he was doing, he was happy about being in Alaska."

The ease with which he had coolly pulled these thoughts together gave Morgan a shiver of fright now as he gazed back into the fire, rubbing his hands over the glow. How had he come to possess such a dangerous weapon? His gift for talking his way out of trouble was best used sparingly, saved for occasions when maximum effort was called for. The events of the past week had whipsawed his emotions to the breaking point. He wondered which side of his personality and life would prevail. The dark side, which could smash down a man like Bertorelli in anger, which could always go into hiding behind a smile and handshake, the skillfully chosen words, the legitimate excuses? Or would the light shine through, the light he had forgotten he possessed? The light Kristen had brought back to life for two glorious evenings.

"We'll leave the packs and tents here tomorrow," Jonathan said suddenly. Morgan looked up from the campfire to see him lay the notebook aside and stand up, stretching.

"This will be base camp while we work the higher ridges."

"How long do you think this will take?" Morgan asked. "I've got to get back to New York."

"I'm staying until I find him," Jonathan said, his eyes blazing in the light of the campfire as he came closer to the flames, warming his hands. "But Red Mullins—the guy who brought us in—will be back on Hidden Lake in two days. You can go out with him then if you want."

"What do you think our chances are, Jon? Really." Matt was stowing his cameras and lenses into the shoulder pack he had brought along from Jonathan's cabin.

"Pretty good—if we get lucky. These people"—he gestured toward the skies—"are working too low. They'll give that up and move higher eventually. I just hope we can get there first."

"You talk like a professional hunter—not an environmentalist," Morgan said.

"I'm both," Jonathan said. "I kill my own meat when I need to. And I use hunting skills to get close to wildlife with my camera. It's part of my work."

"You're up against another hunter here—bigger, stronger, deadlier!" Matt said. "Are you sure you can handle him?"

"I wouldn't be here if I wasn't," Jonathan said. He looked toward the peaks on the skyline. His thoughts seemed to be far away for a moment. "I have a feeling about this bear," he said finally. "Like I know him."

Morgan could not help wondering if Jonathan really knew what he was talking about. The results of the search so far had been nil, and Morgan was seriously toying with the idea of shoving off for New York, despite Tony Craig's admonishments over the telephone for him to stick with Matt and Jonathan for a while. "If they come up with something, I want to know about it." Despite some feeble protests, Morgan had ended up joining the hunt with a certain amount of curiosity. What was so unusual about a magazine executive spending a few days in the backcountry? Lots of people planned for months for such a vacation. The kind of people who were supposed to be reading In Wildness. The kind of people who would be enraged if they ever knew what had really happened to that grizzly bear.

The only thing the Fish and Wildlife Department knew about the bear was that the beast had turned killer and could strike again at any time. They were also concerned that, as their spokesman had confided off the record, "Every son-of-a-bitch with a magnum rifle is going to be out there trying to find that bear and kill it. They could wipe out the entire grizzly population of the area by mistake!"

F & W had succeeded in having the Toubok Valley declared an emergency area and sealed off to all but authorized officials—a mixed bag of scientists, bureaucrats, pilots, and game wardens (some of whom were former professional hunters). Since the area was adjacent to Denali National Park, a vast wildlife sanctuary, F & W had plenty of clout behind its threats to arrest free-lance "helpers."

Jonathan's exemption from the ongoing restrictions came not only from the fact that he lived on the river, but also because he was friends with most of the F & W officials running the show. He promised that he and his associates—Morgan and Matt—would not "get in the way" and had Red Mullins fly them into Hidden Lake behind the cabin. When they landed, they were immediately challenged and had to use the written authorization they carried. On the way to the Tolkat cabin, they ran into a team of scientists armed with tranquilizing guns as well as rifles. They confirmed what Jonathan already suspected: the main search was being conducted along the river and the lower slopes of the range. The dull thud of helicopter rotors had been a constant noise along the river.

After looking around the scene of the Tolkat tragedy for a while, Jonathan led the small band up the slopes behind the cabin, heading toward the higher peaks upstream. If his hunches were correct, they would find the bear there, not far from the place where he had first discovered the tracks of the grizzly, only days before.

"I can't figure it out," Matt said as he zipped up a flap of the camera pack. "Why a grizzly would turn killer in an area so big. He's not only got this valley, but there's all of nearby Denali National Park to roam around in without ever coming across humans."

"Something went wrong," Jonathan said, his face still moody, reflecting. "I can't get a grip on it. It's like . . . an accident."

Morgan looked away, gazing at the mountains as though he was not listening.

"A head-on collision," Matt chimed in. "Inevitable when man meets grizzly."

"Seems that way," Jonathan said. "As sorry as I am to admit it. As a matter of fact, when the last California Golden Grizzly was killed, the state had more wilderness land left than any in the West. It wasn't enough."

"I hope we get to see this one," Matt said. "It may become part of history."

"Seeing him is one thing," Jonathan said. "Getting a good photograph is something else. I wouldn't count on it, Matt."

"I have to try," Matt said, standing. He started for his tent, then turned and looked back. "One lucky shot, and I may yet save the book. It would be ironic if that bear became the instrument of the magazine's rebirth." He knelt and crawled into the tent without waiting for a comment.

Jonathan shrugged as his eyes locked with Morgan's.

"I'm going to turn in myself," Procter said. "I guess you'll want to hit the trail early." Morgan hobbled toward his tent.

Watching him, Jonathan grimaced. "We'll try some more bandages in the morning," he said.

Morgan stood in front of his tiny tent, staring at the distant peaks.

"Do you like any of this, Morg?" Jonathan called.

"What?" Procter said, looking around, surprised.

"Being out here . . . the wild country."

"I guess I would," Morgan said, pensively. "Except for my feet . . . and the feeling I'm getting."

"What do you mean?" Jonathan asked.

"I told you about Nam," Morgan answered. "In a way this reminds me of that. It's . . . like a mission. The last time I went out on one I nearly got killed."

He knelt and went into his tent.

Jonathan threw another log on the fire and watched the sputtering flames kick into life again. He was feeling too tense for sleep, even though he needed the rest.

A sense of despair tainted his thoughts like a pall. What difference would tomorrow make anyway? Cody wasn't coming back to the river. The life they had been living there was as dead as Ted Walsh and the Tolkats. He could still feel Cody's trembling body, hear the tearful description of her ordeal, the words gushing out in a bursting dam of pent-up emotion, the control that had carried her through the terror finally relaxed. He could still feel the sense of shame and guilt that had welled up inside him as he tried to comfort her—shame and guilt over not having shared the nightmare, of not having prevented it from happening in the first place.

"We'll start somewhere fresh," he had promised her. "A year sooner than we were planning, that's all." He left her and Derek with friends, telling her that he was returning to the cabin to pick up their manuscripts and some clothes and a few other things they would need right away. His ultimate purpose —the hunt itself—was kept hidden behind his confident banter.

All day he had been thinking about what he was going to do if he *could* locate Horribilis, if his theories proved to be correct. The only thing he knew for certain was that, like Matt, he desperately wanted to photograph the beast without provoking a charge. After that, he wasn't sure what he would do:

retreat from the mountains, call in the F & W people—or pull the trigger himself. Whatever happened, this was a destiny that had to be fulfilled. His life had been linked to the grizzly's since the morning he had discovered the tracks.

Jonathan left the campfire's circle of warmth and walked over to the edge of the campsite perimeter, where the ground slanted sharply downhill, past low birch brush and stunted spruces.

Go ahead, he told himself. Admit it. You're going to try to cash in on this. You're hoping there's a book in it—and a fat advance that will keep your lifestyle going in spite of everything that's happened.

That's why you wanted to be in on the execution, isn't it? There's money to be made!

The thought haunted him like a stalking shadow of some unknown danger.

I have to write and take pictures! His mind seemed to hurl the words at the mountains. *It's my work!*

He turned away from the horizon and started back to the fire, angry with himself. He kicked the outside edge of the log into the center of the coals. Smoke billowed into his nostrils for an instant, then melted into the cool mountain air.

As he held his hands over the flames, a sudden inexplicable chill swept over him, leaving his scalp tingling and goose bumps running down his back. He shuddered at the passing of the strange wave, suddenly aware of a sixth sense, a premonition he had felt before when alone in the wilderness.

He was being watched.

He tried to shake off the idea as he looked all around, his keen eyes searching for the slightest anomaly in the now familiar pattern of trees and shadows.

Nothing.

He continued his visual search, turning first one way then another, his ears tuned to the slightest sound. The disquieting feeling would not go away: he was locked in the radar beam of strange fixed eyes, hidden somewhere nearby.

The mountain slopes, the skies, the trees beside the camp —all were quiet and lifeless. Even the wind was hushed, leaving the empty silence to ring in his ears. He was beginning to feel like a dumb cheechako, alone on the trail for the first time. It was time to get some rest.

As he turned toward the tent, a flash of movement suddenly pulled his gaze toward the beginning of the hillside steepness where the spruce timber gave way to birch brush and the tundra on beyond. A ptarmigan hurtled out of the trees and slanted downhill, its stubby white wings a blur against the chestnut summer plumage. A hundred yards or so down the ridge, the bird cupped its wings and sailed over the low bushes, its body rocking from side to side.

Jonathan stared after the bird, wondering if something had spooked it—the same *something* whose presence he had been feeling so strongly. He usually trusted the intuitive side of his feelings, especially out here. What one actually observed was not enough. There were hidden meanings in everything: the way the sun gleamed off a cornice of snow, telling you the slope would not support your weight over some deadly height; the way a grouse, running awkwardly, a wing down and dragging, along a portage trail meant she had young nearby; the way a few high cirrus clouds in the brilliant, cold winter sunshine told you to be ready for a blizzard within twelve hours. The signs were always there, imbedded in your instincts through experience and knowledge. They were as essential to wilderness man as food, shelter, and warmth, even weapons. They were not to be ignored.

Jonathan hefted his .375 from the plastic tarp where he had taken the rifle apart and cleaned it. The bolt closed with a smooth metallic *snick,* chambering a cartridge. He eyed the trees where the ptarmigan had jumped.

He was ready to have a look around before turning in.

Deep in the heart of the spruce thicket, Horribilis still smelled the ptarmigan that had burst into flight moments before. He had been slipping through the shadows, his great body gliding through the thick branches like liquid, every sense he possessed focused on his prey. The stench of the two-legged creatures assaulted his nostrils in a storm of odor. He could smell their flesh, their food, their tents and equipment. The smoke of their fire was particularly strong for a moment, and in that instant he smelled the bird. Too late! The ptarmigan had

vaulted into flight in a feathery explosion that caused the great
bear to freeze rock-still.

Now as he watched and waited, he ignored the flies on the
rotten stinking flesh of his wounded paw. He ignored the odor
of the pain-danger that raged upward through his leg and
shoulder, into the depths of his body.

They had done this to him! *They* had to be driven away so
that he could finally rest and make the pain-danger disappear.

His great nose was picking up something new now. The
scent was changing, growing stronger somehow. In another
moment, he could hear something moving along the edge of the
trees. The scent was massive! One of them was coming!

Horribilis lowered his crouch, his rear legs tensed like
steel springs. Then, dimly through the scattered branches, he
could see the shadowy figure. The intruder was moving slowly,
deliberately, every step measured.

The bear's instincts told him to wait. Only a few more
steps . . .

Jonathan looked for an opening in the spruce trees, a place
where he could slip back into the forest itself for a distance,
hunting outward in a wide circle that would eventually take
him back to camp. He carried the rifle casually, held on his
shoulder by one hand on the stock. Already, he was beginning
to lose faith in his idea. There wasn't anything out here. He
ought to be getting to bed.

This was about the place where the bird had jumped, he
thought, stopping. The forest was less thick along here. The
walking would not be too difficult back in there among the
trees.

He pulled down the rifle, holding it ready with both hands,
and stepped into the trees.

Far behind him, somewhere across the valley, a sudden
booming noise reverberated through the hills.

Jonathan stopped. Helicopter rotors! The sound was unmistakable. He wheeled and pushed back through the spruce
branches to stand in the open once again, gazing into the distance.

The drumming noise grew louder, pulsating angrily
through the empty skies. Suddenly he saw the craft, a tiny dot

against the sweep of the tundra, much lower than he had expected. The chopper was boring straight toward him, as though he were reeling it in with invisible line. The rotors were staccato detonations as the craft slanted up the ridge line toward the camp, climbing steeply from the river valley.

Now, what the hell? Jonathan thought. Was it somebody from Fish and Wildlife? Had they found the bear?

He could see now the helicopter was a Jet-Ranger, and as it neared the camp, he could see the blue-and-white colors and logo of his friend Pat Warden, whose Warden's Flying Service employed Red Mullins.

Jonathan looked up in amazement as the Jet-Ranger circled over the camp, a couple of hundred feet up. He waved heartily at the two indistinct figures he could see in the craft.

"What's up!" shouted a voice behind him, barely noticeable above the din of the chopper. He turned to see Morgan and Matt standing outside the tents, each trying to button his shirt, their faces both anxious and quizzical at the same time. Jonathan shrugged, shaking his head.

Suddenly the Jet-Ranger veered out of the circle it was making and headed back downhill, moving slowly. The three men were speechless as they watched the craft scout down across the ridge, pausing occasionally, obviously looking for a landing spot. When it was about a half-mile away, it settled to the tundra. A figure detached itself from the machine and darted to one side in a crouching run.

"I don't have the slightest idea what this is all about," Jonathan said to his companions.

As the Jet-Ranger lifted skyward, the figure waved and quickly started walking up the hill toward the camp.

The sound of the Jet-Ranger faded over the same route as before. The mysterious visitor was making good progress up the ridge, weaving around the thicker patches of birch brush, climbing steadily without pausing.

Jonathan could see a bright orange backpack, obviously heavy-laden by the way the figure moved. Then he could make out what looked to be gray trousers, and a green sweater, and—

His heart jumped up into his throat. He couldn't believe his eyes.

"I'll be damned!" he said aloud. "I'll just be goddamned!"

"Who is it?" Morgan asked, squinting into the sallow light.

"You're not going to believe this," Jonathan answered. Now he could see the long red hair, held on the forehead by a black headband. Even the stride was familiar, the long, ground-eating legs, one arm swinging vigorously, the other holding a rifle.

"Cody!" Matt Richardson shouted excitedly. "My God, it's Cody!"

She paused some twenty yards from the edge of their campsite, looking up the last part of the slope. She smiled and waved a hand as she called to them. "Hi, guys!"

"You shouldn't have come!" Jonathan's voice was an angry whisper in the snugness of his tent.

"You shouldn't have misled me. I thought you were just returning to the cabin. It was a mean thing to do." Cody sat on her sleeping bag, taking off her boots, glowering back at the brooding figure of her husband. Jonathan lay atop his own bag and stared at the tent top, where the light of the new day was already gathering.

"After what you've been through—what you said about never coming back to the river—I figured you wouldn't understand. I didn't feel like arguing."

"I'm not coming back to the river—to live. I came back to see *him!* While he's still alive."

"Horribilis," Jonathan said to the dome of the tent.

Cody laid aside her boots and socks and reached into a side pocket of her backpack.

"Actually, I've already seen him," she said suddenly.

Jonathan raised himself onto one elbow, his face incredulous. "What?"

"I wanted you to know before the others. There've been some new developments." She handed Jonathan a 4 × 5 manila envelope. "A camera was found at the helicopter crash site—damaged but miraculously whole. These are prints of some of the film."

"Where'd you get these?" Jonathan asked as he started to open the envelope.

ON DANGEROUS GROUND

"I got 'em—the collected photographs of Jack Burke and Sonny Youngblood."

"The T.A.P. PR man—and the Jet-Ranger pilot?"

"Right. It was Burke's camera."

Jonathan flicked through the seven prints hastily, devouring the images. Most were blurred by camera movement, but one—the last he came to—was startlingly sharp. He gasped audibly. "My God!" he exclaimed.

"Now you've seen him too," Cody said. "Now you know why I came."

Jonathan could not take his eyes off the photograph. The sides of the image were blurred in a tunnel-like effect caused by the speed of the Jet-Ranger and the telephoto lens. In the center of the shot, the towering figure of Horribilis stood on two legs at the edge of the Toubok, looking directly into the Jet-Ranger as it bore down upon him.

Jonathan shook his head, speechless as he stared at Cody.

"There's more," Cody said. "They found one skid of the chopper with fur and flesh stuck to it."

"They hit him!" Jonathan said, looking at the picture again. "He's been wounded ever since." He looked back at Cody, his face pensive. "That's why he killed."

"Except for the camper—Larkin. That happened first, when he blundered into the bear's moose kill."

"I can't believe it," Jonathan said. "How did you come up with all this?"

"Burke's widow. She trusts me. T.A.P. doesn't know about the pictures. One of the pilots who found the wreck turned the camera over to her without thinking—before they found out about the skid. They've clamped the lid on *that*, but I found out about it from Red Mullins. You know how pilots talk—the Good Old Boy network."

Jonathan handed the photographs back to Cody.

"What do we do now?" he sighed.

"We keep quiet about it—and we go on," Cody said firmly. "We're journalists—it's our story. There's a book in it—you know that!"

"You're not going," Jonathan said, shaking his head. "You want our son to be an orphan?"

"I *want* to be in on the finish of this business—just like you!"

"It's too dangerous!"

"Then get on back to Anchorage. *You* be the one to play it safe. I'm pressing on!" Cody grabbed the edge of her bag and threw it over her legs, angrily. She lay down and stared at the ceiling.

"Haven't you had enough? What you've been through would have put most people into therapy," Jonathan said.

"It just made me stronger," Cody said softly. "I can stand anything now."

"Cody, this bear has become a killing machine, more dangerous than I thought. He could get the jump on us—if I can find him. Which, by the way, I seriously doubt with a gang like this on the hunt."

"Send the *others* back if you want. I'm going!"

"Shit!" Jonathan said, turning away. He pulled the top of his bag over his head.

Cody snuggled deeper into her own bag. "You and your caballeros are the ones with no right to be here," Cody called, the words muffled under the down covering. "The three of you were out to lunch when everything happened. Now you want to cash in! Give me a break!"

"Shit!" Jonathan called again, scrunching toward the wall of the tent.

THIRTY-THREE

The morning sun had painted the mountainside for hours, burning into the chill that had pressed down from the lilac skies during the two and a half hours of twilight. A tide of warming air had begun to flow up the slopes, so subtle at first that only the great nose of Horribilis could sense the wispy presence. He had been trying to detect its coming ever since he had watched the redness of the new sun flooding through the jagged outline of the distant peaks, pushing an ever-widening wedge of pearl-gray sky up the horizon.

Now, in midmorning, the warming wind finally brought him the message his instincts had told him to expect: his enemies were on the mountain, and they were moving toward him.

He waited for some trace of sound to be borne by the wind, watched for the two-legged creatures to approach. The world was strangely quiet at that moment. The sky-things had not appeared today, leaving the vastness empty of sound, as though all living things had been chased away or destroyed.

When he had fled the sky-thing the night before, he had expected it to follow him right up the mountain. All sense of the prey he was stalking had been temporarily forgotten the instant the noise of the chopper thudded out of the midnight skies, swinging up from the river. He had scrambled back up the slope to his den with all the speed he could manage, stopping occasionally to see if the deadly beast was coming up behind him.

The scent was growing stronger now. The great bear's instincts compelled him to remain crouched and hidden instead of making a stalk. As long as the wind told him the creatures were still coming, he knew he must wait for the moment when they were almost upon him.

They wouldn't be able to run away then. He could kill them with ease.

They came across a gentle slope of tundra meadow bordered on one side by a final persistent stand of dwarfed spruce and on the other by the glaring whiteness of a snowfield that spilled down from the cold harsh heights. Ahead, the colorful, flower-spiked grasses ended at the foot of a glacier-gouged chute of fine scree and chunks of shale running up to the face of the ice flow itself, turquoise in the sun. The ridge line above soared steeply, blocking the view ahead, slicing into the unbending blueness of the midmorning sky.

Jonathan slipped off the light day-pack he was wearing and dropped it at the edge of the tundra mat. He laid the Winchester across the pack and turned to give Cody a hand with her own small pack. She sat down on the spongy cushion of plant life, plucking a delicate yellow arctic poppy from the array of tiny blossoms and regarding it intently.

"I'm glad you called a break," she said to Jonathan. "I didn't want to have to ask."

"Macho woman," he laughed as he dug into his backpack. Below his foul-weather jacket, he felt a hefty canteen among the clutter of emergency gear, which now included a TPX-720 radio that could broadcast distress signals. He handed the water to Cody and looked back down the hill.

Matt and Morgan were still a hundred yards or so behind, trudging wearily, their gazes fixed at their feet. Matt carried the Weatherby magnum Cody had brought to camp as though it had become a log in weight. Behind them, the country the little party had climbed through that morning fell away toward the Toubok Valley, the glint of the stream a distant thread.

"Those guys have had it," Jonathan said. "Especially Matt."

"I feel sorry for Procter," Cody said. "He looks tough and in shape to me. Too bad about his feet."

"It's just as well," Jonathan said. "Maybe I can talk 'em into waiting here." He turned and looked at Cody. "You too, I hope."

She shook her head as she handed back the canteen. "No way," she answered. Then she added, sarcastically, "Partner."

Cody looked up the reach of hillside looming over them.

"Aren't we getting awfully high for a grizzly? What is this guy —half goat?"

"This isn't your average walking-around grizzly. The reason I think he's here is a place I saw up here once, while I was looking for sheep. It looked like a perfect denning site: thick, hidden, and . . ." He paused and shrugged, embarrassed by a loss for words. "Hell, I can't explain it. It's just a feeling I have."

"Much farther?"

"No. But I don't want these guys with us. Two people are too many as it is!"

Matt and Morgan were limping up now. Procter's face was grim, but Matt managed a smile as he said, between hard breaths, "Sorry we're holding up the show. Between my feet and my lungs, I feel like . . ." He slumped down on the tundra. ". . . that damned bear's already worked me over!" He rolled over on his back, staring at the sky.

Morgan sat down and started pulling off his boots. "How high do you figure we are?" he asked. Unlike Matt's, his breath was as normal as Jonathan's and Cody's.

"Over five thou," Jonathan answered. "Maybe even close to seven. Air's getting a little thin, eh, Matt?"

"They'll never ask *me* to go to Everest," Richardson said to the sky. "It's a sin what soft living has done to my body."

"Well, you can take it easy now," Jonathan said. "No need for more of this torture."

"What do you mean?" Morgan asked quickly. The fresh socks he had put on that morning were covered with blood. He carefully began peeling the fabric from the frayed skin and soaked bandages.

"We're getting too high," Jonathan said. "I thought we'd find some sign of him by now."

"You mean we came all this way for nothing?" Morgan said.

"Maybe not. We'll hunt back down by a different route. Maybe we'll get lucky."

"Be easier going downhill," Cody added.

"When you get down, send a chopper back up to fetch me," Matt groaned.

"You'll feel better after some rest," Jonathan said. "While

you're doing that, I just want to check one little spot up ahead a little ways. There used to be a bunch of sheep around there. I still need a picture or two for an article I'm doing."

Morgan was hunched over his feet, unconcerned about the scenario Jonathan had developed. "I think I'll wait here too," he said. "Start cutting my losses."

"I'll tag along with Jon," Cody quickly interjected. She stood up, obviously anxious to get going. "You guys keep the pack. There's water and granola inside. Keep the Weatherby too. I don't feel like totin' it."

Jonathan picked up his own pack. He looked down at the .300 magnum lying beside Procter. "Do you know how to use that thing, Morg?" he asked.

"I told you I was in the army," Procter said in boredom, without looking up.

Jonathan adjusted his pack straps, hitched the .44 magnum revolver higher on his waist, and picked up his rifle.

"We'll be back inside an hour," he called as he and Cody started up the ridge. She carried her single-lens reflex 35 mm lashed to her chest with Kuban straps, which prevented the camera from jiggling and moving.

They both moved easily and gracefully over the talus-covered ridge, their well-worn mountain boots clutching the rock firmly while supporting their ankles and providing a barrier against the jagged edges of the stone. In a few minutes they topped the crest of the immediate slope and gazed upon a new vista that revealed the sweep of the country just ahead.

A couloir of crusted snow sliced steeply through a jumbled mass of glacier-strewn boulders and shale, ending in a bench of thick birch brush that grew across the ridge in a wide band. Toward the center of the band, the brush was heavier, thrusting on up the slope in a tangled pocket of greenery. Beyond this, the gray rocks rose to another snowfield that seemed to soar right into the spires and pinnacles high above.

Jonathan frowned at the summit line, squinting into the glare of the snowfield. A band of dark clouds stretched across the horizon, emerging from behind the peaks.

A front was moving in, a storm brewing. Already the wind had shifted. It blew down from the frozen pitches high above, cold and heavy and smelling of aeons of ice.

"It's going to get a lot colder," Jonathan said to Cody. "Take my jacket out of the pack when you need it."

"I'm still Okay. Long as we're walking."

Jonathan nodded, and they moved on up the ridge, weaving through the rougher sections of rock. As they came to the bottom of the couloir, he stopped in mid-step. He turned to Cody and pointed at the crusted snow in the blue shadows of the rocks.

Horribilis's footprints showed as gaping holes punched in the hard-surfaced whiteness, linked by plowed furrows where his paws and legs had plunged ahead.

Cody gasped, surprised. "My God," she said. "Which way was he going?"

"Shhh," Jonathan admonished, swinging the rifle into the ready position. "Up," he whispered. "I think. I can't tell how old this is." He stared up the slope, his heart pounding with anticipation.

Now he knew he had been right all along. Horribilis was nearby, perhaps just ahead, perhaps watching. The circle had closed.

"Stay right at my shoulder," he whispered to Cody. She had her camera in her hands, adjusting the lens. "Anything can happen."

Jonathan reached down and touched the track, as if expecting to feel some warmth of the beast.

A great squawking noise exploded overhead, shattering the silence.

He looked up to see a pair of magpies circling, still squawking nosily as they flapped this way and that, occasionally diving in mock attack.

The harsh guttural squawks were caught by the wind, flung into the great spaces beyond the couloir.

When he first heard the magpies, Horribilis was already sneaking down the side of the slope. He paused at the edge of the birch brush as the sound of the birds cut through the slanting wind. He could smell nothing, for the wind was wrong now, pushed down the mountain by the approaching storm. After the breeze had begun to freshen, swirling aimlessly at first, then stiffening and plunging down from the peaks, the great bear had experienced increasing difficulty smelling the enemies he knew were approaching. Finally he had lost the scent altogether, and it was then that he had bestirred himself. He slipped through the thick brush with no more than a ripple of movement, lost among the wind-thrashed branches.

Now the familiar cries of the birds told him what the wind could not: the two-legged creatures were still coming—and they were very near.

To strike them down, he would need the wind. Instinctively, he knew he would have to move lower on the ridge, to circle until he had the wind in his face again. The maneuver was as familiar as the terrain.

He eased from the brush and quickly glided into the shadows of some huge rock debris off to the side of the couloir. His good front paw dug into the slope, holding back his great mass as he moved down through the cover with a crouching, almost catlike motion.

When he smelled the intruders again, he would swing back up the ridge.

He would be ready to kill.

"Romantic notions always get me into trouble," Matt Richardson said as he painfully tried to slip his boots back on over fresh socks and bandages. "Thinking about trekking around in these mountains is one thing. Actually doing it is something else."

"The right boots would help," Morgan said. He was perched on a nearby boulder, studying the country through a pair of binoculars he had found in Cody's pack.

"What bugs me is that I only see what I want to see—until it's too late. It's like being half-blind."

Procter lowered the binoculars, looking at Richardson. "What do you mean?" he asked warily.

"Well, take coming to these mountains. I couldn't be bothered with thinking about the hardships: the sweat, the blisters" —Matt slapped a mosquito on the back of his hand—"the bugs." He looked up at the surrounding mountains. "Even the danger of meeting a grizzly has been something I've preferred not to think about."

"We'll never find that bear," Morgan answered, turning back to his viewing.

"It's the principle I'm talking about," Matt said. "The way certain realities have eluded me. Like the magazine I've wrecked . . . the women I've let down."

A wave of tension stabbed through Morgan, set his pulse into a gallop. Did the man *know?* Until now, there had been no indication that he suspected anything about Kristen. Morgan lowered the glasses again and stole a cautious look at Richardson. He was still engrossed with his boots, as though he had been talking to himself.

"You hate to fail," Morgan said sympathetically. "So do I."

"I always thought our work was important," Matt went on dreamily. "Despite what people say about my huckstering—*Charm* in particular. You see, Morgan, we're invited into people's homes. We have an opportunity to talk to them, help them, make them feel something. It's a very special thing—being invited into someone's home. I never took it lightly."

"I never thought about it that way."

"What *do* you think about, Morgan?"

"What do you mean?"

"It's obvious how much you've wanted to sit at the head of the table. Now that you're going to do it, what are you looking forward to?"

The question surprised Morgan. What the fuck was the man talking about? Didn't he realize that being a general was a lot better deal than being an enlisted man? That you kept moving ahead—or you went under? For a moment, words failed Morgan. He felt the breeze sharpening, blowing down the mountain now. He looked up to see a raven beating against the invisible current. Suddenly the bird seemed to give up, and spiraled effortlessly back downhill.

When Morgan looked back at Matt, he saw by Richardson's cool, steady gaze that the man had no intention of abandoning his question.

"I guess I need more than most people," Morgan said, ending the stall. "What is ambition anyway? That's a question for you editors and writers. I know I've always been a space-peddler. But I have dreams too."

"Is it respect you're looking for?" Matt asked. "The mega-bucks? The power and satisfaction of calling the shots?"

"You *are* a nosy bastard!" Morgan said.

"I'm sorry," Matt said. "I'm not trying to take a shot at you. I'm truly interested."

"It's not easy to say," Morgan replied. "I have no family, few close friends. I guess my work is my life. Excelling at it gives me a great deal of satisfaction, but that's not all. It makes me feel . . . well, safe."

"Safe?"

"Safe." Morgan nodded.

"From what?"

"Pain. I've had more than my share," Morgan sighed. "When things are going my way, it's because I make 'em happen. I don't trust luck anymore, and I don't like drifting."

"The way I did?" Matt said, dejectedly.

Morgan shrugged.

Matt gazed at the far peaks for a moment, reflecting. Turning back to Morgan, he said, "I never did have the guts to thank you."

"For what?" Morgan said, incredulous.

"For the new design for the book. The dummy is brilliant. While I was farting around with the film, you were doing my job for me. I hope you'll let me take it with me—if Tony lets me buy the book and by some miracle I can raise the money."

"Be my guest. You'll have to make a deal with Bertorelli."

Matt nodded and stood up. Abruptly, he turned away and walked over toward the edge of the tundra and stared across the distance over the Toubok.

Relieved at the break, Morgan left his perch on the rock and limped in the opposite direction, his feet hurting less now after the fresh socks and bandages. He wandered aimlessly toward the edge of the snowfield. Behind him he saw Richardson had broken out the camera and was taking shots of the distant peaks.

Doubt had crept back into Morgan's thoughts, wrenching his gut with the same anguish he had felt every time he thought about the possibility of Kristen turning back to her husband. Why did everything seem so twisted? His attempts to get some advertising for *In Wildness* had resulted in Walsh's death. His

affection for Kristen was tainted by his professional associa-
tion with Richardson. His efforts to become head of the magazine division through hard honest work would probably result
in the death of a magazine.

Perhaps he *was* a ruthless prick, as Richardson had im-
plied. What the hell was he supposed to do? he wondered. A
man shouldn't have to suffer for doing the things that seemed
clear and right to him.

At the edge of the snowfield, he grimaced as he looked up
the mountain and saw the line of dark clouds sweeping along
the horizon.

He knew it! The weather had been too good to last. Now
they were going to get some rain—or snow! It was time for him
to get the hell out of here and back down to that lake. Tomorrow he would be on his way back to New York.

A hard gust of wind whipped across the snow, flinging a
dusting of minute frozen particles into his face.

A sudden odor assaulted his nostrils—the nauseating
scent of something rotten, something dead.

He used the cover of the dwarfed spruce trees perfectly,
weaving through the branches and shadows as he made his
way across the brow of the hill, closing in on the putrid scent
that flooded his nostrils. He could smell the edge of the tundra
in the distance, the snowfield just ahead.

He crept past the last of the low spruces and paused before a smooth hump at the beginning of the snow.

Something was wrong! His prey had separated. He could
detect two distinct sources of the evil scent, both moving farther away it seemed for one moment, then coming closer the
next.

The wind was swirling, teasing his nostrils with first one
message, then another.

He had to *know*—to sort out his target.

Horribilis stood erect, his mighty body rising above the
curve of the snow slope.

The stench flooding Morgan's nose was overpowering. He
turned to call Richardson, and as he looked around he saw
Matt's sudden look of shock and heard his startled gasp across

the twenty yards that separated them. Instantly he wheeled to follow the track of Matt's eyes, and he was looking at the impossible sight of the monster grizzly standing not twenty feet away. He saw the blackened, swollen mass of an infected paw held dangling opposite the awesome claws of the good foot. The face that loomed above the massive wall of brown was startlingly plaintive: small dark eyes darting, nostrils flaring.

Morgan stepped back, an instinctive reaction he was totally unaware of making. He gasped as he tried to scream, the sounds damming up in his clenched throat, emerging as incoherent noises.

Finally some words tore free. "Shoot!" he screamed. "Shoot!"

Frantically he looked around, and in the next micro-second he knew he was going to die.

Richardson's face was hidden behind the camera. The rifle was lying useless at his feet.

Jonathan paused beside the couloir, frowning with displeasure as he studied the slope ahead. The tracks of Horribilis suddenly veered from the crusted snow and were lost in the moraine alongside the glacier-sculpted gulch. Up ahead, the belt of birch brush was stretched across the face of the heights.

He turned and whispered to Cody. "I don't like it. We're going to have to go down."

"He's right here," Cody said, surprised by this change.

"We can't handle this alone," Jonathan said, shaking his head.

Cody started to protest, but he cut her off with a blazing look of anger. "It's over! We're not going to die here!"

Before she could answer, the sound of a shot echoed through the mountains, rolling up from the slopes below.

When he saw the grizzly rise out of the snow hump, Matt Richardson felt an instant of total shock, followed by a serene sense of calmness as he began to move without conscious thought.

The camera in his hands was suddenly pressed against his eye, and what he was seeing was not real at all—only an apparition, existing for him alone, his destiny fulfilled. So cut off from reality was he in those few seconds that he never heard Morgan Procter's shouts, never thought about the rifle at all.

Then, as he looked up from the viewfinder, he felt himself thrust into a strange new dimension he could not fully comprehend as he emerged from a coma-like trance. Then a blood-curdling scream and massive roar tore him from his private world.

He fell to his knees, grasping for the rifle, babbling "Oh my God!" as he saw the grizzly catch the fleeing figure of Morgan Procter in three great bounds, the momentum of the charge carrying the great bear far past the body he had smashed to the ground.

The grizzly skidded on the snow, turning, as Matt felt the rifle in his hands. He brought the stock toward his face, felt it snag on the camera strap. He tried to brush the leather strand aside, but it was stuck against the bolt, and Morgan was screaming again—"Shoot! Shoot!"—even though the bear was on top of him, biting and clawing. Then his finger must have touched the trigger, because the gun went off, kicking right out of his hands. He scrambled to pick up the Weatherby, the din in his ears like the core of an explosion. He worked the bolt, feeling a strange new sense of calm, then got the stock on his shoulder properly this time. The iron sights hovered over the melee. Bear and man were one swirling image, Morgan trying to roll free, the beast biting and slapping at the screaming victim.

To shoot now could mean murder! But what choice did he have? Procter would be dead within seconds!

"No!" Matt screamed, running forward, the rifle lowered. He plunged into the fray with the barrel outstretched, pulled the trigger as he felt the muzzle slam into the grizzly's side. He felt a lightning flash of pain in his hand as the recoil ripped the rifle from his grasp, and he saw the grizzly's head swing around, a horror of snarling teeth and ultimate rage.

Something exploded on the side of Matt's head then, a massive blow from nowhere that blasted away all conscious thought. Almost instantly, it seemed, he could feel himself spiraling up from the darkness, strange sounds shrieking in his ears, his face pressed against the snow. He tried to stand, rising to his knees, the earth spinning beneath him, the side of his face in flames. Fangs closed on his shoulder, and powerful jaws lifted him bodily and pulled him along the ground, shaking furiously.

He was beyond pain now, even though he was aware his face was dragging in the snow. Then he seemed to be sliding quickly down a snow chute, faster and faster, and he wondered if he had gotten away, and suddenly he was flying off the snow ledge into darkness.

Stumbling, barely able to keep his feet, Jonathan approached the final patch of shale chunks that led into a dip where the ridge line blocked the view ahead. He tried to hurry in a sort of half-jogging gait, skidding on hard patches of talus when he tried to brake his descent. He paused at the sudden bowl-like depression in the terrain, breathing hard, and looked back to see Cody coming down quickly behind him.

Jonathan plunged on up the slope ahead, his boots tearing holes into the fine scree as his legs churned for leverage. He topped the crest, gasping as he looked down the ridge.

A hundred yards away—at the edge of the moraine, where the snowfield curved in from the right to meet the tundra meadow and a belt of dwarf spruces—the bear he had come to find was killing Matt and Morgan.

The scene was one of pandemonium, a strange dance of chaotic images that seemed unreal. Jonathan ran forward a few steps, starting downhill, foolishly shouting, "Hey, stop it!" Then, with sudden clarity, he saw Horribilis holding on to Matt's shoulder, dragging him like a puppet, leaving a bloody swath in the snow.

Jonathan slid to a stop, his mind screaming for him to hurry. He sat down and drew up his legs, his back pressing against the rocky slope as he brought the Winchester forward. He snuggled his arms against his knees, steadying the rifle as he leaned into the stock and got his eye to the scope.

In the next instant he was aware of Cody standing beside him, muttering "Oh my God!," and he could see the cross hairs sweeping over the strange, unreal scene. He breathed deeply, in control now, and when he saw the cross hairs pause on the grizzly's shoulder, he realized with cool detachment that Matt's body was in the same circular picture, dangerously near his point of aim. He swung the rifle toward the rear of the beast, the cross hairs wavering over the brown mass of the thighs, and he touched the trigger.

The report slammed through the mountains as the .375 pounded his shoulder, and almost instantly he heard the solid *thunk* of the bullet striking.

Horribilis whirled like a spinning top, dropping Richardson, biting furiously to find the enemy he thought was grasping his rear thigh.

"You got him!" Cody shouted as he bolted in another round and tried to steady the cross hairs again, knowing he had not dealt a killing blow, only further enraged the beast with the ineffective rear-end shot.

But the bear was standing alone now, confused for a moment. Jonathan saw the strangely calm and benevolent face staring directly into the scope. The cross hairs swung down below the jaw, disappearing into the dark fur of the massive neck. As he touched the trigger, he saw a blur of motion as the bear lurched to the side, and he knew this was going to be a miss.

He looked up from the jarring blast to see Horribilis limping across the snowfield, two legs buckling grotesquely as he plunged toward the side of the cliff.

For Jonathan, nothing existed except the bear. He staggered across the slope as he bolted in a fresh shell, slanting toward the edge of the ridge where the snowfield met the moraine rock and disappeared into emptiness. He ran badly, staggering, breathing in uncontrollable gasps. Frantic, he could see the bear's advantage gaining. He was going to make the edge of the ridge! He was going to get away!

Jonathan tried to hurry, hating his legs' betrayal as they seemed to weaken and grow slower and shakier with every step. One boot smashed against an unforgiving boulder, and he was flying headlong, rolling as he landed, trying to protect the rifle by folding his body over it. He tumbled over the rough ground, felt the hot slash of stone across his forehead. He stood up, reeling, his vision swimming as he tried to raise the rifle. Blood flowed into his eyes, and when he reached to wipe it away his hand felt a deep gash on his forehead. He sat down quickly and shouldered the .375. Blood covered his eyes again, and when he wiped it away he could see the grizzly had stopped at the edge of the snowfield and was staring his way. He got the scope to his eye, the cross hairs invisible in the sudden circle of fur that filled his bloody vision.

As the gun bucked angrily, he felt a stunning blow around his right eye. He fell back against the slope, his face in his hands.

The Winchester clattered onto the rocks.

Cody's eyes were locked on Jonathan as she scrambled over the steep ground. She heard the clap of the rifle and again the distant but distinct *thunk* of the heavy bullet as Jonathan lurched backward, holding his head as he collapsed onto the edge of the snowfield.

"Jon!" Cody cried out, coming up to him now.

Dazed, he tried to look up at her, the blood streaming down his face as he muttered, "The scope . . . it banged my eye! I can't see!"

Cody's immediate instinct was to reach down and try to help Jon. But then she looked across the ridge and saw the grizzly lurching directly toward them, staggering as its huge claws pounded into the snow, propelling the snarling brown hulk with shocking speed.

She dropped to the rocks beside Jonathan and tried to pick up the rifle. One of his legs covered the .375, and as she tried to snatch the gun free she saw Horribilis coming on and on, and suddenly she realized she didn't want the goddamn rifle anyway because she couldn't remember how many shots had been fired—and the .44 magnum was sitting right there where she could get her hands on it.

She sensed rather than saw that the grizzly was about twenty yards away as she tried to slide the revolver from its holster. The gun would not budge, and the grizzly was fifteen yards away as she flipped the holster strap and looked up . . . and then he was ten yards as the gun pulled free of the leather and was coming up smoothly . . . and at five yards she clicked the hammer back and got both hands locked in a combat grip . . . and the brown wave broke over her then, blotting out the sun, as her hands became thunder and fire hurtled into the face of the attacking storm.

Her arms took the shock of the recoil, her hands felt the sudden scraping motion of wet fur—then she was rolling beneath the plunging juggernaut, feeling the massiveness pass overhead in a rush so blurred and breathtakingly swift that she seemed to be dreaming, without pain or shock or any feeling at all. Then she was aware of the sky and sunshine again, and the harshness of the rock slope at the edge of the snow, and Jonathan lying beside her—and she definitely had been dreaming all along, it seemed now, because there was no bear. Suddenly her hand began to throb with the pain of the magnum's recoil, and when she saw the Ruger lying on the rocks she jerked upright in a surge of panic, the dreaming ended now. She wheeled around on her hands and knees, expecting a new attack, but saw instead the empty hump of the rock slope.

She picked up the revolver with her left hand and stood up, her legs weak and uncertain. A strange light-headedness engulfed her as she clambered to the top of the slope and looked over.

Ten yards away, down the steeply pitched snowfield, Horribilis was trying to crawl back up through the bloody swath he had made when he plunged over Cody and tumbled down the hill. His face bobbed sickeningly, spewing flecks of blood, as each heaving motion of his massive body gained a foot or so of the slope. Mesmerized by the startling vision, Cody could see the swollen black mass of the beast's injured paw and the deadly claws of the good foot, flailing at the snow as they fought to find a grip. The dark pinpoints of the eyes burned into her own but had no message for her—neither of fear, nor of hatred, nor of remorse. She felt a confused strange rush of pity that out of all the things the great bear had seen in his years on earth this vision should be the last: a human with a gun.

As she tried to raise the revolver she began to shake, sobbing quietly, and she realized then that her hands were trembling, hurting so much from the previous shot that the heavy gun was difficult to raise.

She never felt her finger touch the trigger. Suddenly, the blast of the magnum slammed against her eardrums, her hands stinging with the ache of the recoil. She saw the great bear's head jolt back and flop limply to the snow. The tiny eyes still seemed to gaze directly at her, and she knew he had seen . . .

had known. And now he was sliding away, his great mass glissading down the snow slope, faster and faster as he approached the sheer edge of the snowfield, and suddenly he was gone.

The smell of rotting flesh lingered over the blood-smeared swath down the empty slope. Cody looked anxiously toward Jonathan. He was sitting up, rocking from side to side, his face pale and bloody, gashed by an angry red half-moon cutting into the eyebrow and another gaping slash across his forehead. She dropped the revolver and quickly knelt beside him.

"Jon! My God!" she cried anxiously as she grasped his shoulder.

He tried to blink away the blood, then wiped some of it off with the back of his hand. "He almost had us," Jonathan gasped as he looked up, dazed. "What you did . . . so brave."

"You're really bleeding," Cody said. "What should I do?"

"Get on the radio," he said, swinging his arms free from the straps of the pack. He dropped the pack onto the rocks and dug inside for the first-aid kit and emergency transmitter. "I've got to see about those guys. You call for help."

"Your head . . ."

"I'll be all right." He handed Cody the TPX-720 and began pulling the antenna. "Go ahead," he urged. "It's got to be done."

He held the plastic-wrapped first-aid supplies in one hand, picked up the revolver, and started down the slope, jogging awkwardly through the snow.

The eerie quiet belied the ample evidence of tragedy: the crimson splotches in the churned-over snow; Matt and Morgan lying facedown, unmoving, their arms and legs akimbo; over here, the Weatherby, half-buried beneath torn-up snow chunks; over there, a pair of smashed binoculars—and the gaping back of a camera. Beside the 35-mm, a long gray strip curled from a split-open cannister, the film twisted and snarled like some worthless piece of ribbon.

Richardson was closest, and when he knelt down beside him Jonathan deliberately chose the side away from the bloody shoulder and neck. He tried not to look at him at all as he raised one arm and felt for a pulse. The wrist was cold and wet as his fingers probed for the life-giving throb, alternately pressing down or barely fluttering over the veins. His own hand was shaking, making the job more difficult, and his breath was still coming in hard gasps. He looked at the sky, thinking, *Please . . . please. . . .*

Nothing.

He scrambled around to the other side of Richardson, grasped his uninjured shoulder with both hands, and pulled him over. Matt's eyes were closed, his face strangely relaxed despite the bloody horror that was the side of his head. Jonathan tore at his shirt, ripping the buttons free. He flung open the fabric and got his ear down to his naked chest, still warm.

There was no arguing with the silence. Jonathan's only hope was that he was wrong, that he didn't know what he was doing. He put his arms around Richardson, trying to lift him, sobbing through the blood in his eyes, "Matt . . . come on . . . for God's sake, Matt!"

His plea went unanswered, except for the cold moan of the rising wind. Suddenly a gut-wrenching scream from Cody rent the air, and he looked up to see her standing a few feet away, gasping, her hand in her mouth as she stared down at her brother and husband. She stepped back, collapsing, falling to the snow. On her knees, she buried her face in her hands, sobbing, "Matt! . . . Matt!"

Jonathan was beside her in an instant, holding her close. "Try to hang on," he urged. "Are they coming?"

She nodded, still sobbing. He tried to make his arms and body a veritable wall, shielding her from the horror surrounding them. "Help them!" she pleaded. "Jon, my God, can't you help them? I'll be all right." She tried to push him away, then to raise herself, but she slipped into the snow again. "Go ahead!" she cried, still sobbing. "I'll be all right."

He left her there and trotted over to Morgan. As he had with Matt, he flinched when he saw all the places where blood showed. He got hold of Procter's limp wrist as delicately and sensitively as he could and tried to focus his will on the pulse.

He watched Richardson's sprawled figure while he tried to convince himself that he had just felt a weak throb in Morgan's wrist. Suddenly, the tiny *bump* was there again, just beneath the skin, it seemed, and he shouted toward Cody, "I got! He's weak but I got it!"

When she looked over and saw Jonathan was talking about Morgan Procter, Cody shouted, "Let the bastard die. He started all this!"

The voice was not Cody's voice. It was the voice of a stranger. Jonathan ignored her and turned back to Procter. Morgan groaned as Jonathan turned him over. The sudden sight of Morgan's face caused Jonathan to turn aside, gasping. The grizzly's paw had raked so hideously across the flesh that Jonathan had no idea where to begin putting the bandages. He dabbed ineffectually at the blood with some cotton, and just then he heard the booming, pulsating miracle of helicopter rotors. Down the mountainside, two choppers were sliding up from the valley.

Jonathan turned his attention to one of Morgan's legs, which was bleeding profusely. He fashioned a tourniquet from Morgan's belt and began wrapping bandages over the injury. By the time the choppers were almost overhead, their engines and rotor blades echoing their approach with ear-shattering noise, he had made Procter as comfortable as he could. He hurried over to Cody and wrapped his jacket around her. One of the copters was settling onto a patch of level ground at the edge of the snowfield.

Jonathan stood up and picked up Cody's camera. "I've done all I can," he said, starting back across the ridge, back toward the edge of the snowfield where the great bear had died.

"Where are you going?" Cody shouted.

"To finish it!" he screamed. "You know it's my fault. . . . I led 'em up here, didn't I? Now I'm going to get what we came for! To sell him—and make some money!"

"Jon . . . please . . . let it go."

"That bear's worth just as much to me dead as alive!" Cody could see he was sobbing now, spitting his words into the maelstrom created by the choppers.

"Jon, please sit down!" Cody screamed.

He started away again, then turned and yelled something she could not hear in the chaos of noise and downdrafts kicking up mists of blowing snow. She tore off the coat Jonathan had given her and ran toward Morgan.

She knelt beside Procter, holding the wind-tossed jacket

over him, and when she looked up into the stinging spray of the snow crystals, Jonathan was gone.

The persistent bleeding that smeared his vision and the nauseating ache of his head wounds forced Jonathan to stop several times before he finally located the fallen grizzly. At first, the snow he pressed against his head and gulped thirstily provided welcome breaks of relief. Then the snowfield ended as he worked his way across a rough slope of talus rock directly below the sheer drop the great bear had pitched over. His footing was uncertain, his vision shimmering with misty images. His mind burned with the fever of his passion and remorse, the haunting sense of guilt he knew would never leave him. When a gigantic slab of sheer ledge loomed ahead, blocking his view over the crest, he crawled up to it cautiously, not trusting his wobbly legs, and peered down over the side.

Far below, he could see an open reach of tundra meadow stretching down to the beginning of the tree line and the river valley beyond, somber and dull under the leaden sky of the approaching storm. A blob of brown, tiny from this height, was an obvious anomaly on the lush tundra carpet.

He headed on down, moving carefully, not able to hurry over the rough ground where one slip could tear him off the rocky face of the hillside. He did not have to use handholds, but balance was essential as he clambered down the ledges alongside gaping seams of jumbled rock, gulches filled with birch brush and willows. When he reached the bottom, he felt so weak and thirsty that he had to make a conscious effort not to stagger.

The great bear was lying facedown, sprawled on the edge of the tundra as though asleep. Jonathan pulled the revolver from its holster and slowly approached. His head seemed to be clearing, his injuries forgotten in the excitement that gripped him. He was conscious of the way his boots felt in the tundra grass and flowers, the way the dampening breeze stirred the frost-colored outer hairs of the bear's pelt. He could hear helicopter rotors way off somewhere, and he wondered for a moment how Procter was doing. He thought of Matt . . . dead . . . the way Horribilis was dead right here in front of him.

At the same time as he could see the bear's dull eyes,

staring into nothingness, he began to smell the stench of the beast's injuries, to hear and see the swarm of heavy-bodied flies stirring over the front paw. He stifled a retching sensation in his throat and stepped back, holstering the revolver.

He heard someone coming up behind him, yelling, but he paid no attention as he quickly got his hands on the camera. He looked down at the controls for a moment, then tried to look up at the bear. His eyes ached from the smoke-like essence of perspiration, blood, and tears.

There wasn't anything to photograph, he realized. The thing that had lived in this body was gone now—the thing that had come to the earth in the secret darkness of a frozen hillside while the northern lights ruled the heavens. The thing that could live on berries or flesh or the roots and tubers of wild plants . . . that knew which hillsides first caught the sun, knew where budding willows would lure browsing moose.

The thing that could smell a shadow passing, hear clouds moving on distant winds. The thing that hunted and rambled over five hundred square miles of wilderness, afraid of no living thing—except man. The thing that had been Horribilis, one of Denali's wild children.

Jonathan slipped the camera from around his neck and held it in one hand. Someone was still yelling at him, and he wanted it to stop. He wanted whoever it was to go away and leave him alone, and he turned and saw the man coming up now. He was a stranger, young, carrying a high-powered rifle.

"Well, you got the son of a bitch!" the bearded face snarled.

Jonathan drew back the camera, as if to hurl it at the intruder.

The young man flinched. "What the hell's the matter with you?" he screamed.

"You stupid bastard!" Jonathan shouted back. "This was *his* world once!"

He threw the camera aside and turned away. He started walking down the gentle slope of the tundra meadow, aware of the profane curses following him but not really hearing the words.

All he had to do was to keep his feet—keep moving on down. Eventually he would reach the river.

Then he could wash away the blood.

PART

4

ALASKA

AND

NEW YORK

JULY 10–
SEPTEMBER 30

THIRTY-FOUR

"This is our VIP suite," the head nurse said to Kristen. She paused with her hand on the door. "Luckily for Mr. Procter it's been vacant since he was released from Intensive Care."

Kristen nodded and glanced away, trying to steady her nerves. The wide, antiseptic-smelling corridor bustled with midmorning activity: nurses and aides going about their chores, a group of doctors completing their rounds, a few patients shuffling wearily for exercise. Kristen wanted to escape the disquieting scene—to hurry through the door and finally see Morgan again—yet she paused, afraid.

The loudspeaker blared a message: "Nurse Holland to fourth-floor conference room, please."

"I'm off," the friendly, attractive nurse smiled. "You can go in." She hurried away, and Kristen, who had not been inside a hospital in many years, wondered if head nurses had always been so young. She opened the handbag that hung from the shoulder of her pale blue suit jacket. She stole a furtive glance at her face and hair in her compact, thinking she probably looked a mess after the sleepless night that had followed the flight to Anchorage. Satisfied that she had done her best to repair the damage, she snapped the bag closed and tentatively pushed on the door.

The room was surprisingly bright with sunlight. Beyond an empty bed, the attractive furnishings of a sitting area were arranged beneath a wide bank of curtained windows. Morgan was seated in an easy chair, his back to the door, staring out the window. As she stepped forward, slowly and quietly, Kristen could see the view that held Morgan's gaze: across a stretch of parking lot and a distant line of trees, a range of peaks loomed on the horizon, steel-gray and white in the sun. The Chugach, Kristen remembered, from her reading.

She wondered what Procter was thinking. Surely he heard

her now, and yet he did not turn around. She was only a few feet away, close enough to see that the left side of his face and head was covered with bandages, as were the left hand that peeked from the sleeve of his robe and his left leg and foot, outstretched and resting on a bed of pillows rigged over a pair of chairs.

Kristen stopped, her heart pounding, her fingers working nervously, aching to reach out—to touch and soothe.

"Morgan," she said, weakly.

The silence was excruciating in the moment that followed. Finally, he spoke to her, softly and without turning his head.

"You shouldn't have come."

"I had to. You wouldn't answer my phone calls . . . or letters."

"I'm sorry. I just haven't been able to cope. Still can't. So why don't you just go?"

These were the words she had been dreading—had even been expecting after his long silence. But they stung, nevertheless, and she could not hold back the tears welling in her eyes. "Go? Just like that . . ." Her voice was trembling. "Then everything you said to me was a lie . . . when we were together."

"That's not true!" Morgan answered angrily. "You *know* that's not true."

"Then we don't have a problem," Kristen replied, stifling her tears.

"Nothing that a new eye, an ear, 530 stitches, and assorted pints of blood can't fix," Morgan smirked.

Kristen smiled in spite of herself, her eyes brightening behind the veil of tears. Everything was going to be all right. Morgan wasn't dead and gone or changed in any bad way. He was terribly injured, that was for sure. But his injuries could be healed.

She pulled a simple straight-back table chair from the corner and sat down beside Morgan. He looked away, uninterested, his unbandaged eye glaring dully at the distance. His face was unshaven, his whiskers a shadowy line that ended just above the far side of his mouth where the bandages began. Kristen laid her handbag on the floor and leaned toward him, the tears gone now, her face set with purpose and concern.

"The worst is over," she said. "You're going to make it."

"Yes, I'll make it—with half a body . . . and half a heart. Walsh and your husband are dead because of me."

"It was an accident. Nobody blames you."

"Then why can't I stop thinking about it, night and day?"

"You need time."

"Why are you worrying about *me?* You're not much of a grieving widow."

She answered this insult with the anger it deserved. "My grief is a closed book to you!"

"I'm sorry," he said, turning to her finally.

"You had nothing to do with what happened to Matt and me. What we had once—what we lost—is not for you to think about."

"I said I'm sorry." The blueness of his eye showed through tears now. He raised his arm toward her.

Kristen accepted his hand, came close beside him, leaning forward from her chair. He started to speak, but her lips stopped him. She tasted the side of his mouth, gently, warmly, giving the promise of love. When their faces parted, she was silently crying again.

"Morgan," she said, drawing in a deep breath, "Matt was cremated. That had been his wish—his ashes scattered over the Missouri River. They haven't even floated out to sea yet, and already I'm sitting here with you in the full sight of God Almighty to tell you that I want a life with you. I say that without shame or guilt whatsoever. The reason I'm trembling . . . the reason I can't help crying . . . is because I can't stand the thought of giving you up."

"Kris . . ." Morgan whispered, touching her hair.

"I'll share your pain if you'll let me. I'll even share your guilt. But don't shut me out. 'Cause if you do, then I'm going to lose the best part of myself—just like you did once. You *know* the kind of hurt I'm looking at. You've been there—where the chance for giving all your love is taken away."

Morgan sighed heavily. "Up there in the mountains . . . just before it happened . . . I was thinking about us—about how happy you made me feel. I wanted to stand tall in your eyes, in spite of being the cause of Walsh's death. Then the bear came. Now I'm all busted up—inside and out. I don't feel like I'll ever be strong again."

"You will. I know you will."

"I don't even feel like working anymore. When your best work results in things like this . . . fuck it!"

"Tony Craig told me," Kristen said, a wry smile creasing her face. "Know what he said?"

"Nothing he said can surprise me."

"He said, 'Some leader Morgan turned out to be. His first real battle and he orders a retreat.'"

"Bastard!" Morgan snapped. "He's just as guilty as I am."

"No," Kristen said, soothingly. "He's on your side. He hasn't given up. Everything's on hold. He's waiting for you. But he asked me to tell you that time is running out. The natives are getting restless. I guess he means the board."

"Tell them all I said to drop dead!"

Kristen gripped his hand tightly. "Did you ever think . . . perhaps it was all meant to be?"

"Don't talk like a fool."

"And how are *you* talking? You think that denying yourself the magazine division is going to change anything? You and Matt both knew what you wanted—and you both were right to go for it. 'Cause it's a good job, an important job."

"It's not worth walking over dead bodies to get to," Morgan said.

"I don't give a damn about you ever running Craig Publishing. But those magazines are important. They need you!"

"What do *you* know about it?"

Kristen paused for a moment, instinctively wanting her words to sink in. "I know about the things you didn't tell me: how you came up with a sensational new graphic approach for *In Wildness*. How you've been selling a lot of advertising despite the odds. Seems to me that *In Wildness* couldn't be in better hands. The other magazines as well."

"*In Wildness* is finished. You know that."

"No. Tony Craig has recanted. Maybe it's because he *does* feel guilty. Maybe it's because he's dying, and this is his last chance to do some good in the world. But he wants you to get in there and fight for the book. Make it your first priority as president of the magazine division."

"I can't think now," Morgan said, wearily. "I'm tired . . . confused."

"You can make it work," Kristen pressed on. "And we'll start building a life together. It won't be all business. There'll be time for us: sports, travel, the things we both want."

"Sports? With one eye!"

Kristen could not help flinching. "You'll play better with one eye than most people do with two," she said convincingly.

"You're some crazy lady," Morgan said, managing a smile.

Kristen placed a hand on his shoulder and leaned closer, her face tender with compassion.

"We can have a good life," she said softly but firmly. "A chance to live without regret, or guilt or fear. *In Wildness*, all your work, is the price of that life."

Morgan nodded slowly, his cheek glistening with tears.

In his face, Kristen saw strength beyond measure, appeal that stirred her feelings to the ultimate.

She leaned forward to kiss him, knowing as their lips met that their life's journey had begun.

THIRTY-FIVE

When the *In Wildness* television film ended, the lights came on and applause and chatter filled the room. Sam Zeigler walked over to the bank of windows and pulled the curtains. As the afternoon sunlight hit Morgan Procter's face, he blinked painfully and turned to study the reactions of the ten people seated around the table of the Craig boardroom. They were Morgan's and Zeigler's fellow members of the company's board of directors. This day they would become more than Morgan's peers, his associates. They were to be his judge and jury.

As the group's banter about the film continued, Zeigler pulled up a chair next to Morgan, who was seated off to one side of the room, almost as if he were an interloper.

"Some free advice, Morg?" Craig's financial ace whispered, leaning close. Morgan looked at him expectantly. "Don't blow this!" Zeigler continued. "You can't see the knives, but they're there. That magazine is history! You will be too if you tell them you're committed to it."

Morgan stood up and patted Zeigler on the shoulder, almost playfully. "Stay with the numbers, Sam. They're what you understand best."

The group grew silent as Morgan approached the head of the table. Tony Craig sat in one adjacent chair, Marla in another. The other faces strung along the table were not as familiar to Morgan, but he knew full well the power the key players represented: Ben McGraw of the TV-radio division, looking absurdly young and casual in dress; Jim Vance of the newspapers, who looked as if he could be a Savile Row model; Sam Zeigler resuming his seat, his Wall Street image perfectly projected; and big, always smiling Clint Sanders, who had built a fortune as big as his native Texas and liked to describe himself as a "publishing groupie." "Hell, I never made much money at it,"

Sanders liked to say, "but it's more fun than running nursing homes and construction companies."

Morgan tried to imagine the thoughts that might be behind the faces that stared his way. He could not help expecting to see shy, averted glances, for he knew he presented a physical image that would have to be shocking to all who had known him. He himself had not gotten used to the black patch he now wore over his left eye, the strap cutting across his blond hair like a shadowy chasm, and he could tell that many people tended to be frightened by his new countenance. What was left of his reddened, puffy left ear still needed some plastic surgery, but his other injuries were healing nicely, the scars invisible beneath his clothing. Let them gawk, he had decided some time before. He was lucky to be alive, and the damage done to his body was nothing when compared to what had happened to the others: Richardson, Walsh, and all the faceless victims whose names he could scarcely remember. Emotionally, he was on the mend as well. All he had to do was get through the next few minutes.

"I'm not going to ask for much more of your time," Morgan said, smiling. "I've already exhausted my views—and probably you along with them—on every subject concerning the magazine division." The group chuckled politely. "You know my philosophy, my vision, my style. Now you must decide: am I the one to lead the magazine division? Before I go outside, I must tell you how I stand on the fate of *In Wildness.* I am sure you are wondering why I bothered showing you the film, especially in view of the dreadful numbers we are all too familiar with."

The mere mention of the magazine's name produced the frowns Morgan was expecting. He looked toward the window, thinking about an Alaska hillside, seeing Matt's face.

"I feel that we must press on with both the film and the continued publication of the magazine," Morgan said, quickly and decisively.

There was a moment of shocked silence as the board members looked at one another. "Aw, hell, Matt!" Ben McGraw groaned. "The cat's in the bag. All we want you to do now is take the bag to the river!"

"I can't do it, Ben," Morgan calmly replied. "And I'm not going to let you do it either."

"Gentlemen!" Craig said, rising, waving his hands. "Calm down." He glared at McGraw, then turned to Morgan. "Please continue."

"As the person who led the fight to knock this book in the head, I know I may look ridiculous in what I'm about to say. But the truth is that I've done a 180 on *In Wildness*. Not only do I think we must continue—at least for a year—but my feelings are now so strong on the subject that I must tell you frankly and in complete honesty that I cannot accept the magazine presidency if killing *In Wildness* will be required at this time."

Jim Vance whistled aloud and slumped back in his chair.

"Morg," Sam Zeigler said. "You know we're all very fond of you. You're putting us in a very difficult position. Hasn't enough damage already been done?"

"You mean *money lost!*" Morgan replied. "That's the damage, you think. But that's not the true damage. What we could lose is the opportunity to do our work, which is to publish something that's needed. Needed in the world! Magazines don't find audiences because smart publishers figure out ways to make money. They find audiences—and make money—when somebody has a vision that touches other people." Morgan stared down the table. He could see that he had their attention, that he was not about to be challenged now.

"Just before he died, Matt told me something that I can't get out of my mind. He told me that our work is very special because it allows people to invite us into their homes. And with that privilege comes the commitment to be as good at our craft, as honest and clear in our vision, as we can. Only then will audiences listen to what we have to say. Only then will they give us their time.

"The new editorial format we have for *In Wildness* deserves a shot. Give me a year with it—and the TV show. That's all I ask."

"Do you have an editor, Morgan?" Marla asked. "What about Matt's sister and her husband?"

"They're out of the picture," Morgan said. "They're back in Wyoming, on that ranch they own. Like me, they've taken a hell of a beating from all this."

"Then how can you make it work?" Marla pressed on.

"Don West is temporary editor. He's been getting out the book. I'll find the right editor—if I get the chance."

"You're asking a lot, Morgan," Zeigler said. "This affects the public stock offering. Our future."

"If this company cannot sustain projects of vision—if overnight profits are to be the measure of everything we touch—then you won't have to worry about the future. There won't be any."

In the silence that followed, Morgan realized that his bid was on the table. There was nothing further to say. He had run his race—and Matt's. "I'll await your decision," he said, as he picked up his portfolio of papers. "Thank you very much." He saw no smiles as he turned to leave.

Kristen was waiting for him in the main reception room. She smiled broadly as he approached, and when she took his arm the exhilaration she always made him feel was there again, lifting him from himself, from the doubt created by the haunting reality of the moment: that his career could be finished. She looked incredibly sexy in a long wool skirt, cotton turtleneck, and smartly cut blazer.

As they sat down on a couch, she said, "Buy a hungry lady a dinner? Somewhere nice?"

"I suppose so," Morgan said. "The condemned are supposed to have a hearty meal."

"That bad?" Kristen asked. "No chance, no shot at all?"

"Maybe," Morgan said, wearily. "I can't tell." His face pleaded with her to understand. "Kris, I went for it—all or nothing. I put a gun to their heads."

She brought her face to his, her arms around his shoulders as their cheeks pressed together. "Thanks," she whispered. "You're free now. You'll always have peace—no matter what happens."

Morgan could feel her tears on his face. He knew she meant every word.

Suddenly, over Kristen's shoulder, he could see Marla and Tony Craig coming down the hall, walking quickly. Morgan nudged Kristen, and they stood up. As Craig approached, his face broke into a huge smile, and he reached for Morgan's hand.

After an hour of celebratory drinks in Craig's office, Morgan and Kristen exited the elevator in the Craig lobby just as the rush hour was beginning. They followed the crush of staffers through the swinging doors, and Morgan began looking around for a cab. Suddenly Kristen grabbed his arm and pulled him toward a limo, waiting at the curb just up the street.

"What's this?" Morgan said. "That's Tony's car."

"We're borrowing it. Part of a little surprise I've cooked up."

Morgan frowned in mock disgust. "You know how I hate surprises."

"You'll like this one," Kristen said, gesturing toward the car.

Suddenly Morgan saw the rear door of the car swing open. He watched in amazement as Jonathan Hill climbed out and walked toward him. Cody and Derek waved from the shadows of the rear seat as Jonathan shook Morgan's hand.

"Congratulations," Jonathan said. "I tried to get here in time to help. I hear you made out okay without me."

Morgan looked at Kristen. She shrugged, feigning ignorance. He turned back to Jonathan. "Today was easy," Morgan laughed. "Now I'm really in trouble. I've got to put out a magazine I know nothing about."

"That's why I'm here," Jonathan said softly. Bewildered by the statement, Morgan stared into the young man's eyes, waiting for an explanation. Car horns blared impatiently, a crosstown subway rumbled under the street.

At last, Jonathan began to speak. "I thought I had everything I wanted out there, Morg. But living wild and free wasn't enough. I lost my voice. I want that back. There are some things I have to say."

"You mean . . ." Morgan's face was beaming.

"Matt was right all along," Jonathan said, solemnly. "You have to pay back." He paused, staring at Morgan. Gradually, a smile creased his face. "You run the business, Morg. I'll get the words and pictures together . . . put the commas in the right places."

Morgan felt numb with joy, released from the threatening shadows of failure. He had everything he needed now: a team that could win. Kristen looked away shyly as he glanced at her.

He turned to offer Jonathan his hand again, smiling so strongly the effort actually hurt the old stitch marks on the side of his face and head. "I'll never forget this moment," he said as his hand pressed Jonathan's.

Jonathan nodded, his own smile warm and sincere. "Let's have a nice dinner," he said. "Tomorrow we begin."

Morgan took Kristen's arm and started for the car. "Hi," he called to Cody. "And welcome." He let Kristen and Jonathan climb into the car before he sat down himself, taking the seat directly across from Cody and Derek.

Derek wore a New York Yankee baseball cap. He stared at Morgan, obviously fascinated by the eye patch. "Are you a pirate?" he asked.

Everybody laughed at once, including Morgan. "To tell the truth, son," Morgan said, "there are a lot of people around this town who probably think so."

When the new wave of laughter subsided, Morgan said to Cody, "Thanks for your help. The road ahead looks a lot smoother now."

"We have some good wheels," Cody replied warmly. "It's going to be a fun trip."

Morgan nodded and reached over to close the door. Suddenly he paused, his eyes on a nearby newsstand kiosk.

"Hang on a second," he said and climbed out.

The bored newsstand attendant watched as Morgan looked over the stacks of magazines. Procter's gaze lingered on the titles he had devoted his career to selling. Finally, he spotted a few copies of *In Wildness,* stuck away behind *Sports Afield* and *Field & Stream.*

The October issue of *In Wildness* had been edited by Don West, and its cover was a close-up of a bighorn ram in a high-country setting. The photograph was distinguished by its beauty and superb detail, but it was not spectacular or gripping in any way. Seeing it now, Morgan was reminded that the magazine had a long way to go.

He placed the copies of *In Wildness* on the front row, covering up *Sports Illustrated.*

"What the hell ya think ya doing?" the attendant barked.

"Give it a chance," Morgan said sternly. He turned back to the car.

ON DANGEROUS GROUND

When he reached the limo, Morgan Procter looked back at the newsstand, smiling at what he saw.

In Wildness was still sitting in its prominent front-row position, its cover beckoning in the sun, its pages closed, its voices waiting.

Lamar Underwood has spent his professional life in magazine publishing and his leisure time in the wildest country he could find. At the age of thirty-three he became the youngest editor of a major national magazine when he assumed the editorship of *Sports Afield*, a Hearst publication. Eventually he assumed the editorship of *Outdoor Life*. He is currently the editorial director of the Outdoor Magazine Group of Harris Publications.

Lamar Underwood is the author of numerous short stories and articles on all aspects of the out-of-doors and the environment. He edited the very successful book *Lamar Underwood's Bass Almanac*, and has appeared on ABC TV's "The American Sportsman."

In this novel, his first, Lamar utilizes his intimate knowledge of Alaska and the Manhattan publishing world. Born in Georgia to a career Army officer and his wife, Lamar traveled extensively before settling temporarily in Alaska, where he edited the Fairbanks High School newspaper and worked as a reporter for one of the local newspapers. Although his life has taken him far from Alaska, he has returned often to enjoy his favorite pursuits: fly-fishing, skiing, backpacking, and running wild rivers.

Lamar Underwood lives in New Jersey with his wife, Debbie, and their daughters, Brett and Tracey. Two other daughters, Donna and Marla, live in South Carolina.